PRAISE FOR ALI

*DREAMF*

'Curious and magical... a refreshingly playful love of language, endlessly inventive. Articulate, entertaining, a more than promising young novelist'
*The Times*

'Habens' linguistic fireworks never lose their sparkle'
*Scotland on Sunday*

'A truly astonishing feat of the imagination, supported by a dazzling display of wit and wordplay... surely one of the best first novels of the year'
*Sunday Times*

'Habens' prose is taut with wit and wordplay and she maintains a happily hallucinogenic light touch'
*Publishers Weekly*

'It is refreshing to find a first-time novelist who tastes and savours the meaning of words. She can write sensuously, too.'
*Independent on Sunday*

'Both cruel and amusing … it reads like Lewis Carroll on acid'
*Cosmopolitan*

'Marvellous first novel that crackles with wit, wordplay and subversive underlying truths … Surely one of the finest, most inventive fiction debuts of the year'
*Entertainment USA*

'Wth her first novel, Alison Habens takes on the challenge of out-wondering Wonderland … this novel is tartest at its tautest, its exuberance creditable'
*New York Times Book Review*

## FAMILY OUTING

'Habens vividly presents both comedy and tragedy... Dazzlingly inventive
and not for the fainthearted'
*Elle*

'Habens' prose is lyrical, beautiful and cleverly witty ... deft, sensitive and
very funny'
*Independent on Sunday*

'The perversity of Habens' scenario might seem contrived were it not for
the deadpan humour of her narrative'
*The Times*

# Lifestory

*Alison Habens*

*Lifestory*

ALISON HABENS

First published in Great Britain in 2003 by
Allison & Busby Limited
Bon Marche Centre
241-251 Ferndale Road
Brixton, London SW9 8BJ
*http://www.allisonandbusby.com*

A catalogue record for this book is available from the British Library

ISBN 0 7490 0651 X

Printed and bound in Ebbw Vale,
by Creative Print & Design

ALISON HABENS is the acclaimed author of two previous novels, *Dreamhouse* and *Family Outing*. A lecturer in Creative Writing at the University of Portsmouth, she lives in Southsea with her husband and two young children.

You've read those family sagas that go on for several generations.

Well, this is the story of one soul that goes on for several incarnations.

From a monk to a Gypsy, a rebel soldier to a single mother, the character keeps coming back. And every time, he meets his match.

In every place, from cloister to campfire, battleground to playground, she finds her soul mate. They are born to be together, but they always end up killing each other.

From the 10$^{th}$ Century to the year 2000, the reincarnating couple keep trying to reach a happy ending.

This is a story that lasts for lifetimes, and a love that never dies.

# *Rafe*

It took him two weeks to write one page, the words winding slowly as ivy grows around the trellis border. Two weeks to write one page; not even making it up, just copying it down, word for word, letter by letter, every day until it was done.

Rafe was a monk. He sat with the others, his brothers, in the silent *scriptorium*; never speaking, singing sometimes, for music could make the words perfect; and meditating on his mistakes.

His hand rose from the parchment to his rough shaved head. Rafe had made many mistakes. As a young monk, who still missed his mother, they were mere blots and letters missing.

He dipped his goose-feather pen in the ink again, and grew another line of minuscule Latin on the paper. This was the best book ever written, and Rafe had vowed to spend his lifetime saving it from fading.

Next to him on the stone bench in a black habit sat another monk, and although they never spoke, the silence between them was more companionable than most. Rafe thought of his Brother Jacques as a friend.

They had one Bible between them, but as they both transcribed it chapter by chapter, verse by verse, one Bible became two.

Jacques had a different style. He used to be a jeweler, and had seen the Orient winking in trinkets. When he cast off worldly things, he did not forget their exotic motifs.

Though the scribes were making two different versions of the original, there was only one author. They met Him at the crossroads of writing and painting, the place where words and pictures meet and share their meanings in a blissful union. Like a marriage produces children, Rafe and Jacques were reproducing the Gospels for another generation.


Then out of the quiet writing came an almighty commotion.

The Abbot strode from the cloisters one day, and stood between Jacques and Rafe. His face was red, his robe was red, and there was red wine on his breath.

The next chapter of the book was open on the monks' desk, and their quills were poised to copy it.

The Abbot held up his hand to stop them and Rafe stopped; watching in disbelief as the hand came down on the Bible, covering John 9 verses 1 and 2.

"*Erratum in loco citato,*" he said.

Rafe looked at the knotty message of veins over the words on the page. What did it mean? With his hand on the passage, the Abbot spoke again.

"*Corrigenda,*" he said in Latin, but Rafe understood: cut it out.

The spiritual leader loomed over them till they were all three in the shadow of his unmistakable hat.

"It's heresy," he said, then hurried away.


Rafe had a headache. He'd made a clumsy cut in the verses of John, and now the numbers were all wrong.

His calling was to copy what was already there. That was why he'd become a monk; simply to illuminate the manuscript. He was not supposed to change the story.

At the Abbot's hand, though, phrases were altered, whole paragraphs edited. Rafe was sure a man should not censor the word of God. But orders were orders, and he had taken his. Working on the book every day was a religious experience, like praying, or doing penance.

When he put his pen down and stood up stiffly to go to vespers, Rafe saw the page Jacques was writing; exactly the same as his, or at least it should have been. The other monk's was longer.

Brother Rafe rubbed his tonsured head and read the bit that he had cut, but Jacques had kept:

*As he went along he saw a man blind from birth. His disciples asked him, "Master, who sinned, this man or his parents, that he was born blind?"*

That night, Rafe couldn't sleep for worrying about what Jacques had done. It was a relief to get up for matins, to pray again and chant the familiar psalms. Then he didn't have to think any more; just follow the voice of the *cantor* to a sure refuge in pure song.

Jacques had broken the law of St Benedict by which the monks swore;

absolute obedience to the Abbot. When they all went down on their knees before him, in the chapter meeting next morning, Jacques had to confess. It was a whisper of words he'd been told to repress.

"'Who sinned, this man or his parents, that he was born blind?' I can't see it," said Jacques. "Where is the heresy in that?"

This was the Year 997. Four centuries had passed since the Christian church ruled out the possibility of reincarnation. Yet still they were finding pages in the Bible that had to be deleted: and still they were punishing by death anyone who dared to suggest that ordinary people could live again. Only Christ had the power to come a second time.

"How can the blind man be reborn?" the Abbot spluttered. "A beggar has not lived before, and will never be able to rise from the gutter."

"We are all beggars," said Jacques. "We will all rise."


Jacques left the monastery soon after that, but Rafe stayed at his desk. A tenth-century monk could not believe in reincarnation. He would only live once, would only get one chance to write his name in the book.

The monks who came before him and built the Abbey tried to raise the kingdom of Heaven out of rocks hewn from Earth. Rafe's art was set against this grey background, against its slow-eroding stone he set his life; pouring words of liquid gold onto vellum to preserve the glory of creation.

An age for a page, it did take him. Sentence after sentence of tiny *half-uncial* for the rest of his days. But even as he lay on his deathbed in the monk's *hospitarium* many years later, Rafe remembered the outspoken scribe; whose words in the air were more colourful than calligraphy.

Jacques left the monastery with his John Chapter Nine intact. Rafe took his last breath before the Revelations. Both men had dedicated their lives to the book.

They started it in the same place, and they would end in the same place; but Jacques must have had a more dangerous passage. Rafe took the safer path: reading, writing and not asking questions.

# Rosa

Rosa never learnt to read and write but she was always asking questions.

"What you do?" she said. "Why you do it?"

She was never one to sit on a log and look *kushti*, with the sunbeams tumbling down her berry-brown shoulders and bramble-tangled hair.

Never one to "What you do?" sit on a log and "Why you do it?" look *kushti*; as she watched her father winding a turban round his greasy black hair.

A long string of old silk, green and gold and redder than Rosa, was wound around Dad's Romany head, and she could not find the end of it, ever. The colours were twisted, in spiralling designs that seemed too sublime to be guided by *Dadus'* Gypsy fingers.

Her mother had died giving birth to Rosa. That was why Rosa asked so many questions.

"What did Mama look like?"

"She looked like you."

"What did Mama sing like?"

"She sang like you."

"What did Mama dance like?"

"She danced like you."

"What did Mama cook like?"

"Just shut up and stir the stew."

Rosa did ask but her father, for all his grace with the Gypsy arts of horse trading and basket-making, was very clumsy with his answers.

"*Putcha, putcha,*" he spat. "Asking is not the Romany way."

Anyway, no Rom ever spoke much about those who'd gone before. Travelling folk, they had to move on and leave their forerunners behind.

So Dad didn't tell Rosa a thing about her *Daia*, and he'd thrown away all her belongings. Bad luck, it was, to keep them.

Perhaps the poor girl could have used a skirt that had been worn by her mother; flame-coloured *chaffa*, licking at her ankles as she danced around the campfire.

Mama's trodden-down shoes could have taught Rosa the steps of the dance, the foot stamping flamenco she'd learnt in a hotter place than this; and her frayed gloves could have taught Rosa how to click her fingers.

But it was tradition to burn a dead person's clothes. The Roma were so afraid of ghosts. Her cups and plates were smashed, and her copper pots were sold.

None of the Gypsy band even told Rosa her Mama's name, for fear that she would cry it out and call her back again. And there was another magic word that the waif never knew.

When a Romany baby is born, its mother whispers a secret name; to keep the child's true identity safe from the evil eye.

All the Gypsies knew her as Rosa Long; all the land knew her as Russ Long's daughter. But the girl never knew what her mother called her.


Rosa made do with one of the ample matriarchs of her tribe, and learned the womanly skills of herbs and hand-reading.

There was none better at *dukkering*. Cate Koptic was the best. Anybody could tell fortunes for silver, but she did it for gold.

She had held the hands of noblemen, read the palms of lords. She had even done a couple of monks, on the run when the old king dissolved their monastery.

"You can *dukker* the likes of them," she said to Rosa, "but don't ever *dukker* yourself."

Cate never looked at her own lifeline. She had made too real a journey, too long a line in the sand, over land and sea, to see anything in her hand.

The old lady could still remember where the Gypsies had come from, but the lines on her face were starting to lead her off the track.

"We were musicians to a Persian Shah," she said sometimes. And other times, "We stole off with Jesu's nails. We were prisoners of an Indian war. We were piteous exiles, we were nimble refugees."

"They tried to pin us down, but now we are free," Cate Koptic always concluded. "So long as we travel endlessly."

While her father went *mushgaying* with the men, Rosa stayed at camp with the old woman. And though they kept moving from place to place, there was always a place for the little girl under Cate's blanket cloak with its broad stripes.

15

Her childhood smelled of *shok* and *purum*; cabbage and onion. It was not pretty, but powerful.


Rosa waxed slowly into a woman. One summer she unwound her layers of winter shawls and found a bodice full of bosom. She was changed, but not so changed as the Gypsy men, who had rarely seen maidenhead so well-apparalled.

The boys she'd grown up with no longer threw rotten apples at her, not when they could put a ripe one in her hand, and touch her skin. Nor would they rudely push her into the water, but bring her jugs from the stream so she could wash her hair, and they could watch her bending over.

The boys were her brothers, not blood related, but even Gypsy water was thicker than the red stuff: and she was not tempted by any of them.

The smell of the horses still drew her stronger than the sweat of men. Hay and mane and supple leather tack, seasonally greased and rubbed incessantly; that was the only ride Rosa wanted. Whipping past the clover, not rolling in it, though she let the horses do that afterwards.

One day when Rosa was riding her horse she met a man. He wasn't one of her Gypsy band; he wasn't any sort of Gypsy.

He was a rich man who lived in a big house and his horse was white. Up it galloped like a sickly shadow, and gave the girl a fright. Turning she saw the frenzied countenance that chased her across the lawn; the face of the great estate.

His ruff was longer than his hair, and behind him flew a cloak of blue velvet that only a nobleman could wear. Rosa didn't know, as she blazed on ahead in her fiery raiment, that only the new king could wear purple.

Still, most gallant was the man in hot pursuit; a handsome young heir to the manor; and these other properties he had too. Well-versed in poesy, he could play a chorus on the pipes of Pan, and dance a stately galliard; but the arts befitting such a man were all forgotten as he tried to hound the Gypsy off his land.

Along the avenues of his ancestral cedars, they chased; skirting the grotto and stumbling through the grove, they cantered to where the cultivated wilderness became real wood.

Now there were trees instead of topiaries; and the bushes clipped into mythical characters were dying out. The last one was Ceres, Queen of the Harvest; her daughter, Goddess of Spring, had become overgrown.

The girl slowed to a trot. It was betwixt day and eventide, and the mist was rising to effect the transformation. Birds about to roost flew back out of the trees as the couple clip-clopped beneath.

A hedge of woven willow showed the boundary, up a rise. As they approached Rosa let her steed go slower and slower, until it did but dawdle. 'Twas an insolent enough gait for a horse, but the girl glanced back with a look of sheer defiance.

"Go," said the man. "Get thee hence. This is my father's land."

"So?" said Rosa. "I would not kick up a fuss if you rode your horse on my father's land."

The young man laughed.

"Your father has not got any land."

Rosa laughed too.

"Look, *dinlo*," she said, sweeping out her hand and brushing the tops of the hills that were her backdrop. "See this? All his."

The rich young man had not looked properly at Rosa. He only saw her mane of black hair and a plain brown horse that her father couldn't sell.

But when she spoke from her heart, he looked into her eyes. And he saw there a startling thing: belief. He saw her bond with truth, like to the trees bond with the woods.

Master Fortescue had never seen anyone believe so deep in their own words. Not his father, who argued in the House of Lords; nor his servants, who agreed with him at home.

For all the vowing and bowing, declaring and swearing, that he'd heard; this handsome heir to a country seat had never believed in speech till now.

"What is your name?" he stammered.

"Rosa."

"Oh. Rosamund?"

"Don't call me mud," the Gypsy held her chin high, "just because I'm made of the earth."

"No, Mund. Rosamund means rose of the world." Young Fortescue was blushing. "It's Latin."

Rosa looked at him for the first time. She'd not taken her eyes off his horse, so far; it being the best-looking courser that ever stood and snorted before her.

"My Dad calls me Rosa di Sposa," she said. She couldn't wait to tell him about this stallion.

"Calls you what?"

The young man could not follow her Gypsy tongue; though his wit was his folly, as he fatally asked her to repeat it.

"Rosa?"

"Di Sposa."

"And what does that mean?"

"I killed my mother."

The Viscount took a step backwards, on a skittish horse. Rosa eyed his legs, in their spotless white stockings.

How did he get them so clean? When she washed her small garments they seemed to come out worse than before. The river and the rocks were dirty. Even the rain left stains.

"Murder?"

Rosa held out her hands to the man.

"Can not you see the bloody spots?" she said. "I was covered in blood and slime. Sometimes I still feel it."

He believed her; for believing once was new-born in the feeling, and took all following statements to be true. He believed she had told him a memory; and didn't see she meant an original sin, her birth.

Fortescue tried to meet ill-beseeming fortune with a smile; but the four legs of his horse were backing away.

"Mama's ghost feet dance on mine," said Rosa, hands still raised in gilt. She wasn't holding the reigns, but her horse didn't move an inch.

The Viscount had to admire her leg's control. Nay, by the rood, he paid it more due than her woeful visage; and he noticed not that she wore no shoes. But he'd never known such a horsewoman, never been shown that the words horse and woman could fit together so perfectly.

"What's that?" asked the Gypsy girl.

She'd backed him so far up the path that the bushy tribute to a mythical figure was there again. Fortescue dismounted, and held his own ground.

"Say rather who is that," he corrected; "for this tree breathes. It is a living statue to a Goddess. The heroine of an ancient tale."

"What you call she?"

He laughed at the language; and was surprised as if some animal, a red deer, had come out of the trees, out of curiosity, to look at the sculpture.

"How now," he said. "Dost sniff at the lady of leaves? 'Tis Proserpina, Queen of the dead."

"I know her," said Rosa.

"You do not," Fortescue snorted, "for she dwells in the underworld, where Hades is her husband; and in the schoolroom, where enlightenment is her master."

He would stake his life that she had never seen a book. It was for learning, though, that the Gypsy got off her horse, and looked closer at the figures in the shrubbery.

"They are tree spirits," said she.

Next to them, Viscount Fortescue was as polish to wood. He shone in a cloak of black velvet, lined with ermine, studded with gold buttons. Beneath the coat a doublet and puffed trunk hose, pale blue with slashes of blood red silk, and still more glinting buttons.

Not for him the ragged outline of foliage, his silhouette would be sharp in the gloom. As the light left the sky he took in the shape of Rosa, in rapt appraisal of the boxwood Goddess.

"I do abase myself," he said, "but if you tarry a while I'll tell you her story."

How charming was the noble Lord, as he moved the earth with his opening scene, and had a team of black horses pull Hades from the underworld. How convincingly he portrayed the King of the dead; finding Persephone on the mead, and falling so far in love with her beauty, that he abducted it completely from the face of the countryside.

How sensitively Viscount Fortescue showed the grief of Autumn, who followed her daughter the Goddess of Spring around the earth forever, pleading for life's return.

And Zeus-like, he did decree that if she had taken one mouthful of food from the dead, there would be no return for Persephone; who with a poignant sigh said she had eaten six pomegranate seeds.

"Therefore, six months of every year the Spring must spend 'neath the earth; and while it is gone the Autumn mourns," the Lord concluded, and gave Rosa a bow.

So prettily did the man recount the ancient myth that the pretty young woman shed countless tears.

"Tis very sad," she began, and would fain say more, but for her want of proper words.

"Tis a very sad and vain superstition," Fortescue filled the silences between her sobs, "such as would make a modern man of science laugh."

"No," said Rosa. "Tis very sad that all talk is not stories, for then all stories is true."

Loud was her lament, in woods that were settling down to slumber. Through the trees came the sound of dogs barking.

It brought the Viscount from his mazed contemplation of the girl, who knew not how to speak his natural tongue but as a native to difference; who lived in a mixture of languages, seeded like the patchwork fields of his land; yet still could come to a point.

Fortescue pulled himself back into his saddle.

"I pray thee hence," he said. "If the hounds catch you they won't tell you a tale, they'll tear you to shreds."

Mounted, he did disdain to look so low; but looking lowly saw more than just her Gypsy weeds in tatters. He tore his eyes from her skin, then turned and hied him to the hunt.

Rosa watched him galloping away, broad shoulders and blond hair merging with the hindquarters of his steed; leaving her with the favourable impression that the man she had met was half-human and half-horse.


When she got back to the Gypsy camp, Rosa was a changed girl. Her father found her rummaging in their bender tent, up to her elbows in their *togs*.

"Ain't we got nothing nice?"

"What?" he said.

"Nice," Rosa shouted. "Ain't we got nothing nice?"

Her father was suspicious.

"What you want something nice for?"

Chastised by his tone, Rosa let a handful of rags fall to the floor.

"Nothing," she said. "I just want something nice." She ended in a miserable whisper. "Everything we got is *chikly*." A tear rolled down her grubby cheek.

*Dadus* looked at her in surprise.

"Oh, I see," he said. "It's time you got a husband."

He turned and hurried clumsily out of the tent.

"You'll have something nice, *chey*," he said gruffly, as he went. "On your wedding day."

All the eligible Gypsy bachelors from miles around wanted to marry Rosa. When word got out that she was in full bloom, tribes of brightly coloured travellers started arriving, and didn't stop until the camp had grown to twice its usual size.

The horse field was a mass of nag and dobbin, all dapple and dun in the autumn sun; knee-deep in shit for any poor squelch who had to step in.

And there were noisy children up every tree, fighting a war for territory with acorns and conkers.

Russ Long strode amongst it, a *Rom Baro*, ruling the sod he stood on. The big man had one object; to find his future son.

He gathered his guests round the campfire to *chaunt* and *kel the bosh*; and they carried on singing and playing the fiddle all night long. When the fire died down the uproar went on by the light of the *dood*.

The festival folk cared naught for those who lived in the neighbouring villages. It was their own community spirit that was roused; by the barrels full of *gadda*, which did not run dry until the sun was rising.

When the Lord of the Manor and his son came slithering down the mud track in the morning, Russ Long met them with two half tankards of the Gypsy beer.

"Greetings, gents," he slurred.

Right virtuous was the Earl Fortescue. With feather in cap he was esteemed both in camps and courts; but he gave the cup in the hand of his host a parlous knock.

"Damn you, man. I've been lenient for long enough," he swore.

The beer splashed his doublet, and soaked into odorous green silk. It turned his hose amber and his face red.

Lord Fortescue had indeed been patient. This disreputable band had been pushing the boundaries of his land for many months now. He'd put up with them infringing on his hedges, but having to listen to them singing all night had pushed him beyond his limit.

He pulled it like a weapon from under his cloak, a big parchment scroll with a wax seal; and waved it under Long's nose.

"Do you know what this be?" he asked, aggressively.

Silence came straight, when the call for silence came; the nobleman unrolled it, and started to read aloud.

"*An injunction from the Privy Council,*" he said, "*to the Diverse and many outlandish People callynge themselfes Egyptians.*

"*From hencesforth no such Persone be suffered to come within this the Kynge's realm.*

"*In the year of Our Lord, fifteen hundred and forty-seven…*"

Rosa's dad burped. He was completely *motto*. But if the wretched fellow were as sober as the Lord, he yet had little grasp of months and years.

He knew the seasons like a man may know his wife; could see the summer coming from the first breath of its pregnant morn; could feel the winter's harsh repeal of favour in a single icy yawn.

He knew a year was what it took to sail to former lands, and seven years was what it took to grow into a man. A decade was the time it took for memories to turn into history; and a minute was the time taken to tell it.

This was not a man of dull wits, nor was he without charm; but Lord Fortescue seemed to be talking to a barbarous and simple Indian.

"Three days," quoth he, "to get off my land."

Russ Long shook a gold-tasselled head, and the Lord raised his fingers at him; one two three.

"Or what?" asked the Gypsy King.

"I'll ship you back from whence you came, or sell you for slaves," Fortescue claimed. "Or I'll watch you wither, Sirrah, with all your kin in gaol."

The Romany's future seemed as vague as old Cate Koptic's telling of their past.

"Put it this way," the Lord of the Manor finished, "your women won't look so pretty with their heads shaved. I bid you good morrow." He bowed and marched away.

The mud slowed him down a bit. He'd had the writ since spring, without doing anything about it. Watching the Gypsies, from a distance, had been a time-beguiling sport.

The women were indeed beautiful, and they were all colourful characters. It was clear they had several exotic talents. And though the Earl had not quite had his hand read by one of them, he knew a Marquis who had.

He spluttered up the cart-rutted track; and young Fortescue followed him thither with a sigh, his stockings still as white as paper.

They did bestow but a wordy visit; and the handsome youth had not impressed one girl with the art that had turned her into a tree, an awe-struck Goddess sculpted in leaf, when she stood at the edge of his woodland.

He'd only come to deliver the writ, because he wanted to see Rosa again; but he'd only seen her laughing. Laughing as if the tree had come alive.

The Roma didn't even have a word for reading and writing. To her eyes, his oversized scroll just looked absurd.

The son climbed slowly to the brow of the hill, where the Earl his father waited against a streaky sky, surveying the undulations of his land.

From the avenues of pointed cypresses to the columbines that lined the brook, things were standing codpiece proud. The Lord looked on them all.

His puffed trunk hose were so wide he had to stand with legs astride; black velvet stuffed with yellow silk to fit a man of such an ilk.

Young Fortescue was required to accompany him until noon, exacting tythes from tenant farmers. But the afternoon he spent at leisure, sitting at his reading desk, in a most privileged position.

His study windows showed a garden stretching from deer park to lake; but the Viscount, whose study stretched from the earthly to the astronomical, and would never have to give it up, never looked up.

He pondered the circling planets of Copernicus for the hundredth time; and penned a ballad to the lady on his mind.

The inconstant lady; though she who wears nature's finest weeds must have her head turned by seasonal fashions. The fickle lady, passing fair. First wan, then wanton; what a change was there.

When Rosa Long looked at him in the trees, her eyes had coveted his knowledge, desired enlightenment. But when she laughed at him, in the meadow, there was no such need. He was as much use as a key to a Gypsy.

Two meetings; and each time the Viscount felt a thousandfold increase of feeling. No chance encounter with a peasant had ever caused him such shame.

"Killed her mother?" Old Fortescue had spluttered, on the way back through the shrubbery to lunch.

The young man could not pass the boxwood Proserpina without mentioning to his father that he'd met the Gypsy Queen there. But he spoke of such matters in facts; and that was how his father answered back.

"Pish, boy. Russ Long's wife died in childbirth. I have heard it from several sources, judicial and less official. Wretched woman was barely more than a baby herself, by all accounts."

The power of the landed gent! He knew the history of the travellers like a book in his library, this lonely man who'd lost his own wife in the same way.

And the Viscount, who'd also lost his mother at birth, had volumes that he wanted to share with Rosa; if she'd talk to him straight this time, and not in Gypsy riddles.

So he shifted the revolutionary planets on his desk and scratched a verse or two of a poem that gave vent to his feelings. Then he rolled the paper into a smaller scroll than the writ issued that morning, stuck it tightly in his sheath, and went back to the camp at twilight.

Hiding behind an oak-tree, he saw Rosa in her natural habitat, dancing round the fire. He saw skirts that flickered like the flames, feet that trod on glowing embers and didn't feel the pain.

All around her, the Romany men watched, and whittled and spat and whistled and chewed, and picked their teeth and clicked their shoes; circling Rosa like she circled the fire.

"How could a maid behave with such abandon?" Young Fortescue asked himself, watching from the edge of a copse.

How could he know how abandoned Rosa felt. The more the men crowded in on her, the more she was alone.

She danced to the demands of the fiddle, the insistence of the drums; dreaming to the music that her dead mother or her shining knight might come.

When she saw him standing behind a tree, the music stopped. She squinted through the dusk that seemed to be getting solid.

"Where," she wondered, "was his white horse?"

With a gesture most would say was brazen, but which was only meant to be bold, she beckoned the Viscount closer in the gloom.

He stood away from the tree trunk, but didn't leave its dark ring of leaf cover. Waiting at the edge of the wood's shadow, he saw Rosa come to the edge of the light. She stood at the end of the campfire's influence, with its halo of smoke.

Fortescue couldn't go any further; he, whose inherited wealth gave him access to any club, any castle in the land, whose standing could get him anywhere; he could not move from under the branches of his security tree.

So it fell to Rosa, who had nothing except the earth under her feet and the sky for shelter, to break her circle of friends and fire and run with bare feet across the marshy grass towards him.

When he saw her coming the swain stepped forward, and they met on middle ground; though all the land was legally his, this was a higher, dryer patch of green, a fairy ring.

What happened there seemed magical; a spell of familiarity. Three meetings, and each time Rosa felt its thousandfold increase.

She started asking the questions.

"Where's your stallion?"

"I came on foot. I thought it would be stolen."

Rosa snorted.

"Who could steal a horse?" she said. "They belong to themselves."

"And you, Rosa," said young Fortescue. "Who do you belong to?"

"My father," she replied. "Until I get a husband."

"Have you chosen yet?" The Viscount looked over her shoulder as the fiddlers and drummers resumed their tune; though now it sounded more like a battle than a betrothal. "How will you know which one to choose?"

She seemed to have met her match; the noble Englishman was an equally questioning soul. "They all look the same to me," he said.

"They like my father," Rosa shrugged. "I mean, they are like my father."

She was struggling to master the language, he noticed; and it made his heart race to be in time with the musicians by the fire.

Fortescue pulled the smaller, less imposing scroll from his studded sheath.

"Madame, I humbly recommend me to your good grace," he said, and tried to give it to her. "Thou who knowest fortune-telling and tarantella, pray accept this poor gift of art in good part."

She looked at him as if he had picked up a leaf and offered it to her. Even when he unrolled it and showed her the words, she looked as if they were just a pattern of veins, not knowing that they had meaning.

"It's a poem," he said, more pointedly.

Aspen, she would understand, or beech or silver birch. The tree's the thing that is itself, not standing in for something else.

"Shall I read it?" Viscount Fortescue asked, and started without an answer:

"Persephone lives among the dead
Beneath the grieving Earth
Winding sheets her marriage bed
A bootless hope of birth
Six seeds she eateth cheerly
Six months she must stay yearly."

The Gypsy girl was moving to his rhythm and rhyme; clapping her hands at a
story she could almost dance to.

"Do it again," she said.

"Pomegranate, round as rock
Circling the sun
Each pip a new life, under lock
And key till Kingdom come
Hades doth love her dearly
His kiss, her last breath nearly."

"His kiss, her last breath," Rosa breathed.

"Yes, look," Fortescue pointed a finger at the words on the page. "His kiss."

"That is not it," the Gypsy girl grabbed his piece of paper. "That is not the
kiss. See!" She spat. "It's gone."

"Hey, ungrateful lady," he grabbed it back and dabbed it dry. "Many a
muse would brag to be the inspiration behind these lines."

"I don't know what they mean," said Rosa. "But I only need to see one
word to know that I want a more permanent kiss."

She took the scroll from him again, and tore it in twain.

"You could spend a lifetime scratching this with an inky stick, and never
say truer than I do now." She spoke in the raw space between two sides of a
ripping sound. Her voice made his eyes water; the torn paper in her hands
made his tears fall.

"How can a rock circle the sun?" she asked scornfully.

Then the Viscount's tears were diamonds for his illiterate beauty. He was
smiling through them, answering in delight.

"How can a rock circle the sun? You ask aright, and so say I! But Copernicus
promises us, the very Earth goes in humble orbit around that fiery sphere."

"I liked your story better," said Rosa. "Sad Autumn following her daughter Spring forever round the world."

"Round the world," he said, "but not under it. There is no hell."

"And no heaven?"

Fortescue's pale outline wavered in the darkness.

"Put a bridle on the steed of your thoughts, for if you give them their head, they will fast become deeds," he said. "I knew a man at Cambridge; nay, more than a man, he was a perfect Knight. Henry Howard had the edge on me at fencing, an advantage at tennis, and was a braver huntsman whether the kill be stag or lady. But when it came to poetry, he won the tournament outright. For my cheap ballad, he wrote a classy epic poem."

As he said this, Rosa shook her head, and Fortecue added passionately; "You stop your ears, as if my words are merely drops of water; but hear this. For high treason, Henry Howard, Earl of Surrey, was lately beheaded."

"Deaded?"

"For writing words. So do not underestimate the potency of pen and ink."

"We have been in Surrey," she said, "but don't worry, we'll never go back."

In sooth, the literary matter had no sticking. The pages simply fell away from Rosa, dropping like leaves from the topiary characters.

"Will you keep moving too," he asked her, "like chilly Autumn, chasing the Spring? When you are a married woman, where will you live?"

"Where I've always lived," she smiled. "Nowhere."

With a sort of drunken lurch, she gestured forwards; to the path through the woods that led away from Fortescue's estate.

"Everywhere," she said. "That's where I'll live."

Behind her, he could see the roofs of his mansion, above the trees. There were tiny lights in the attic windows where the servants were going to bed. Even they had a more comfortable life than Rosa, thought the Viscount.

She may have been the Gypsy, but he could predict her future. There would be another winter of wet feet and warming liquor before her first labour. He didn't think she'd die in childbirth, though; he'd seen her dancing, seen those muscled thighs and mobile hips.

The music was quickening; the swarthy musicians were coming closer. The Viscount picked up their pace, sensed their presence; and started to dance too.

At first it didn't seem quite the place for a pavanne. Rosa gave a shout of laughter, echoed by the band of singing Gypsies, marching across the grass.

But Fortescue danced a faster measure. Having slipped into the title of gentleman scientist, he was not most known for what he most was; genius protege of his dancing master.

His feet spoke to the clay with a manly elegance that didn't cloy. His footsteps spun the planet. This foreign music was another new challenge.

"I can offer you the world. No, not the world, you have that already," he shouted at Rosa, over the Romany song. "You might live everywhere, but I live somewhere!"

She clapped, and all the fiddle-sticks and drumsticks kept time with her rapture.

Then Russ Long burst through the troop of musicians with a roar that was by no means tuneful. He'd been summoned from his tent, where he'd been entertaining Roma's most important men; and was furious to find his daughter liaising with a *gadjo*.

Young Fortescue drew his sword and the music stopped. In silence he waited for Rosa's father to bring out some baton with which they could conduct a fight.

But the Gypsy king had no weapon. His power was personal, his strength was a possession.

The Viscount heard Long's voice in his own head. Where all had been ordered like the drawers of his desk, with Latin conjunctions and lawful conjectures; there came a tone that sent the neatly stacked papers fluttering, and threatened to turn the desk itself back into the tree that had died for it.

The young man turned and ran into the wood. He didn't even stop to sheath his blade, and it cut into bark, making it bleed, all the way home.

Rosa seemed to feel the pain. "Ah me!" said the girl who danced bare-foot in the fire and lived without a mother's tender care. She fell against her father, but he shook her off in anger.

"What you doing, *chey*? Why you doing it? You'll make yourself dirty talking to him."

He pushed her back to the campfire, to the fragrant wood smoke and the wild dancing.

"Which one of these fine fellows will marry you if you are unclean? Come," he gave a general shout, "drown my daughter in beer. Play music. Louder! Play, play, before she pollutes us all."

*

For a second night, the party went on till dawn.

Only the Romany children slept, undisturbed by the noise. Bundled up in rags and rugs, under the wheel arches of wooden carts, they were used to this way of life.

But the landowner and his son came back again in the morning, looking weary and worn. One had been pushed too far, the other was forlorn.

"You have kept us awake all night, Long," Lord Fortescue said. "And now you have only two days left."

His tone was abrupt, but his terms were kind; the whole camp could disappear in the time it takes to come before the court assizes.

The leader offered him a cup of Gypsy liquor. This time the Earl could not say no. He would have taken a drink from the devil, if it were alcoholic. He gave the *Rom Baro* a long level look; then tipped the cup and opened his lips.

In the moment of surrender, he lost his son in the crowd. The Viscount found Rosa at the same moment.

This time she got the first question in.

"What's your name?"

He told her.

"I know Viscount Fortescue," she said. "Heir to the Earldom, I've heard others call you. But when your mother calls you, what she say?"

"My riches are many," he said. "For playthings alone I have a chess set made of alabaster, and draughts of silver and gold; but for all I am blessed with beauteous comforts, I cannot number among them a mother."

Tears bedewed Rosa's eyes, to greet this dawning news.

"'Tis burdensome to have no heart," the young man continued. "But the heaviness can be borne. It is the light coming into my dark space that hurts; the feeling of love in that void."

He put his hand in the place where his heart would be.

"It is only now I have fallen in love, that I know how deep the hole is." He stretched out his arm to Rosa. "Will you marry me?"

She stared at him in silence.

"Settle down," he said. "I can give you foundations, four walls, and a roof over your head. I can give you a stable bed, with clean white sheets."

She grabbed him by the wrist and rushed into the trees. No one seemed to notice them go. The Earl was putting on a fine show of sunrise drinking, quickly becoming pissed enough, on a trickle of amber fire, to stop tomorrow ever coming.

The son and daughter of the rival hosts stole into the covert of the wood. Under the shade of the elms, it would stay dark longer.

"I still don't know your name," Rosa whispered.

"John," he said, "John Fortescue." He spoke louder, now that he was not cowering among the members of her family.

"So," Rosa smiled, "you are not the same man as your father."

"He's called John too, actually."

Rosa laughed, but he stopped her.

"Listen," he said, "we haven't got much time. Will you marry me?"

"White sheets?" Rosa replied. If she was starving and he had a loaf of bread, it could not be a better match.

"Yes," said John, "and servants to wash them. Servants to wash you too, if you like, and dress you in garments jewelled, so heavy you'd never have to move again."

"But I'm a Gypsy," said Rosa. "I am on a journey with no beginning and no end. I can't stop moving."

"Then let my servants carry you," he insisted. "I'll even carry you myself."

"Could I ride your horse?" asked Rosa.

"Tallyho, boy!"

Young Fortescue was summoned with a shout. It was not the Earl's usual tone, but he was drunk. It sounded like he was preparing for a right old *chingary*.

"Quick. Give me an answer," John said, though Rosa had asked the last question.

"No," said Rosa. It was unthinkable, marriage between Gypsies and *gadje*. She shook her head.

"No?" said John. "Then the God of the Underworld take you!" He took off his hat and dashed it against his breast, before adding: "It grieveth me that if you were to say that no again, it would not have become maybe."

"It will never be maybe," Rosa said. She had never heard of marriage between a Romany and somebody who wasn't one. It would be like trying to marry a horse.

Again from the clearing came the Earl's equestrian call, and young

Fortescue had to respond. He galloped off and left her by the beeches with a beseeching look, and a last plea on half-bent knee:

"The world needs yet its greatest love story."

"'Tis not us," said Rosa. "Our differences are too great."

John returned to his father, who was so infused with Gypsy spirit he didn't notice that his son had been spurned by it. As the Englishmen walked off up the mud track, side-by-side but not in step; the Roma stood together and watched them go.

"Are we going too?" Cate Koptic asked Rosa's father.

"What, just because the *bistering mush* waved a rolled-up scroll at me?" Russ Long replied. "No!"

The old lady spoke again.

"If you ask me," she said, though questions had never been their way of getting answers; "it's not because of the noble lord we ought to leave, but his son; the one what's waggling his scroll at your daughter."

Her eyes were still sharp, but her wit was not, or else aged Cate would never have said what she'd seen through the trees.

For twice cavorting with the nice white lord, Rosa was made *mahrime*. None of the Gypsy folk would go near her now, because she was unclean.

If tears could have washed her, Rosa cried enough, and tried to cling to her father; but his proclamation was indelible:

"I should have gained a son today, but instead I have lost my daughter."

"It was not what you thinking," she sobbed as *Dadus* walked away from her.

His face was grey, but his mind was black and white. Only the Romany way was pure; any other was polluted. His girl was gone forever to the touch of a *gadjo* man.

"It was only talking!" Rosa cried.

But Russ Long kept walking, and the others followed him. All the eligible bachelors turned their backs on her, no longer available. The women who had been her sisters, her cousins and her aunts, wailed; then shut their mouths on the sound. They would never speak to her again.

The heat went out of Rosa as their circle closed around the fire. Her blood seemed to stop when her family cut her off. This was tradition; a Romany who put a foot too far out of camp could never step back inside.

It would be as if she had died. They would not see her, except as a ghostly outline, mostly denied. Only Cate Koptic, with second sight, let her eyes pause on the flickering form.

Rosa stood frozen as the men stamped the fire out and their wives started packing up the feast. As fast as that, people were ready to move on. Gypsies never stayed in one place for very long, and it wasn't often a whole season revolved around them while they squatted on one piece of earth.

As the cartwheels started to turn, patches of yellow grass that hadn't seen the sun since spring were revealed; and wooden posts, sunk into the ground to tether horses and children and hang up washing, had got so settled there they only came out with a struggle.

Rootless was the Gypsy way of life; but while they collected their belongings from the four corners of the field, and tried to fill the holes left with crude rakes and wild grass seed, Rosa was turning into a tree.

She was growing roots like a *rukker* on the edge of the woods; slowly saying goodbye to her secure way of life where nothing was fixed. None of her family would have a farewell for her.

The tree that she was going to be stood by the fairy ring where Fortescue had proposed. And sure as autumn follows spring she would stand there till she'd grown as bushy as his Proserpine.

If leaves were thoughts, Rosa soon grew thick. Every detail of the young man's question, from the words he used to the intricate design embroidered on his doublet; the vein of every detail, she was dwelling on. She had nowhere else to go.

The Rosa tree had always thought her Gypsy blood was sap, rising up within her from a deep source. Now her main sustenance seemed to be rain; from out of nowhere love was falling on her, a shower of affection.

The Lord of the manor had asked her to marry him. Was it too late to say yes?

She spun the question like a coin tossed to decide her fate, all night long. While the gypsy fiddlers played their final gig, and dancers took a last turn around the fire. While the folk brew flowed, thistle wine and blackberry beer; and spirits distilled from anything found in a hedgerow. While the camp drank to the little piece of earth that had temporarily been their home, till the whole world spun around it.

While the Roma slept under raggle-taggle patchwork quilts, she stood still and thought about white sheets; and then, as the first light of dawn lifted a corner of the sky, Rosa started to run.

She didn't take anything with her. She didn't have anything to take. Only the flame-coloured frock that was falling off her bones, and yesterday's fiery spirit dying in her blood.

Galloping across open fields, the soles of her bare feet hard as hooves on the wet grass, Rosa wasn't exactly a thoroughbred woman, but she would make a good mount for the Viscount.

She had turned down his proposal. Would he be prepared to take her up again; just as she was? Nearly *nongo*; half naked.

"Please, oh please." Her breath came in gasps, and went in gossamer streamers; wreathing around her like a wedding veil, as she ran up the aisle of his drive, under the dark arches of trees.


Rosa had never been this close to the big house. She had only seen it from a distance: an ornate chimney smoking straight into the sky; a windowpane winking through the leaves. She'd glimpsed its brickwork blush in the setting sun, and heard its rude bugle call announcing the hunt.

How brave she was to approach the manor; this fox-red Gypsy wench the Lord would sooner have hounded off his land than welcomed in.

But she was starting to feel the cold now, having fled so far from her old hearth and still the dawn only a strip of the sky, too thin for a blanket. So she threw herself up a flight of stone steps to the front door, to beg to be let in.

Rosa raised her hand to knock, and used such force as would have made a hole clean in the side of a bender tent; but on this hundred-year-old oak, this locked and bolted *jigger*, she made only the slightest impression.

To a Gypsy the place looked like a gaol, but she tried to get in again. She knocked with one hand, with both hands, with fists and elbows; and was just about to use her head when she saw a giant doorknocker with the face of a bulldog almost out of her reach.

Swinging on it with all her weight, Rosa made the tiny sound of metal that slowly brought the whole house to life.

The first light came from below stairs, a guttering candle in the hands of a shuffling manservant, who didn't speak when he opened the door and saw

Rosa; merely started to shut it again as if she were a dirty wood sprite that had to be kept out.

"Excuse me," she shivered, "is Viscount Fortescue at home?"

That should show the smelly hand who was proper and who was not. Rosa could talk properly enough when occasion demanded it; but the man just carried on closing the door.

"Hey!" Rosa imposed her waif-like figure in the gap. "I asked to see the master."

The servant shook his head.

"Thou durst not wake him," he said, in a voice thick with snot.

Rosa took another step toward the relative warmth of the hallway, where dried blood colour rugs and dead animal heads were hung on the walls.

"I do," she said.

At which the man's hand shot out and with a shove sent Rosa staggering backwards. He slammed the elaborate portal in her face. Rosa screamed.

That was the joy of Gypsy living, see; no door had ever shut her out before, no servant had ever been rude to her; not while she had stayed close to her own people. Standing on the doorstep, the girl was cold but her blood was boiling.

"*Atchava!*" she shouted. "*Jass!*" I stay. You run away. And she followed it with the worst of all Romany curses, till the Steward himself came running down the hallway, desperate that the Earl be not awakened early.

"Madam?" the head of the servants said, as the front door swung open again. He saw, at least, raw beauty in Rosa, if not breeding. "How may I help you?"

Rosa relaxed a bit, and her teeth started to chatter.

"Viscount Fortescue," she said, "has asked me to marry him."

The Steward's well-behaved eyebrows raised.

"Viscount Fortescue has asked you to marry him?"

"Yes," Rosa stuttered, "yesterday. Now can I come in?"

The head servant looked at her carefully. His young lord had never proposed to anyone before. It wasn't as if there had been pretty village girls and gypsy bitches arriving on the doorstep every day of the month.

"Come into the kitchen, and wait while I make inquiries," he replied, "but pray make no noise."

"God a-mercy, she's blue with cold," the cook shrieked when she saw Rosa. "Why is she running around in her petticoat?"

Cook herself was layered fat with garments of flannel and calico, bristling about her chilly morning kitchen where the fire had not long been lit.

"Here," she said, unwrapping her topmost shawl, "take this and sit there."

Rosa sat by the hearth with her numb feet beneath her, watching as the large woman scrubbed the long wooden table with a brush of twigs. The soap she was using made Rosa's heart beat nervously; it smelled as new to her as the whiff of semen on a young bride's wedding night; but it made her feel closer to John, and the new life he'd promised her.

The Gypsy girl had been up all night, standing in a field, and now she fell asleep on the three-legged stool, a tree cut down. She slumbered uncomfortably till a copper kettle screamed on the fire beside her and she came to with a start.

The Steward was back below stairs, and his man the meat cook, and a kitchen maid in a dirty leather apron. The cook was pouring beer for them all into mugs with lids that flicked up with the thumb.

"I'll wait until they've had breakfast before I announce this visitor," the Steward was saying. "My lord is like a bear with a sore head this morning."

"More like a bull with a sore bottom," the manservant mumbled. "Gore! You should have smelled the gas off him."

"Jeremiah," the Steward said, "hold your tongue."

"You can't talk," the maid agreed.

Cook shushed her.

"Stir that pottage, Hepzebah," she said. "I smell it sticking."

The maid leaned over the stove and made a show with a wooden spoon, though Rosa could see she was checking her reflection in the shiny pans that hung above it. She had greasy blonde hair tucked into a white cap, with one or two strands teased out strategically. All of a suddenly, the girl whirled round.

"Oooh, the Gypsy's looking," she said, having caught sight of Rosa's dark eyes in a silver saucepan lid.

"Woken up, have we? By my troth," said the Cook to Rosa, "you'll make yourself ill; running round the countryside in your underwear. Winter sets in early, this part of the world, and its grip is strong. Better keep that shawl on, when you go."

"I'm not going," said Rosa. "Unlike the season, I'm here to stay."

The Cook and the Steward shared an anxious look.

"Please tell John I've come," Rosa went on. "I need to get into his warm bed, because this fire is not hot enough."

"Foolish girl," the Cook said. "You've given yourself a fever, coming all this way in your petticoat, on a young man's whim."

"I don't know what's got into him," the Steward shook his head. "Our Viscount has never done anything like this before. We were starting to think he just wasn't one for a-hunting the ladies."

"Well, it's hard for a man without a mother, not used to softness," Cook sighed. "Come on, Hepzebah, they'll be wanting their eggs. Wash that henshit off."

"I haven't come in my petticoat," Rosa said, "I haven't got a petticoat. It's my…what you say…my nuptial gown."

"Put them on the silver tray," Cook went on, "and that pat of butter. Now go and churn some more; there be guests for dinner. By my heel, Bickerstaff," she said, turning to the Steward, "we'd better get the raggedy lady out of here by noon. I'll wager two weeks pay they leave it to us to get rid."

The head servant took the tray.

"I'll tell him now," he said. "Can't swear too bloody much with a mouth full of eggshells!"

A silence descended on the kitchen after the Steward had gone, as everyone tried to follow the sound of his footsteps up stairs and down corridors of ringing stone. And then they heard it, through walls muffled thick with tapestry; the devil of all shouting.

"This means they'll want peacock royal for dinner," said the Cook. "Jeremy, you'd better go and catch one."

When Mr Bickerstaff returned to the kitchen, the screeching could still be heard in the distance. The Lord of the Manor was in high dudgeon, and the very rafters were raised with his questions: A Gypsy girl? Marry you? Are you completely mad?

His son's reply, if any, was inaudible; and the Steward was reduced to a whisper as well.

"My Lord says he'll have the peacock for dinner," he said shakily to Cook.

"I know," she replied, in a soothing tone. "Your man is already slaughtering."

The Steward made for his cup and chair but before he got there, an upstairs maid came running down to summon him back again. She was prettier than the kitchen girl; her apron was not so leathery and her cap was trimmed with lace. At the sight of her, Hepzebah started banging the butter churner angrily.

"He wants more beer," the maid said to the head servant, "and he wants you to bring it up." She stopped and stared at Rosa dozing on a stool. "Is that the Gypsy?"

"No, it's the cat's mother," said the kitchen girl.

The upstairs maid took no notice of this, and continued to stare at Rosa.

"Did he really ask you to marry him?" she said.

Rosa nodded, and nearly fell off her seat.

"That is the loveliest thing I ever heard," said the other girl. Behind her, the meat man appeared, rubbing his hands.

"Marry," he said, "and the loveliest thing I ever saw."

Cook looked up red faced from the bread oven.

"Jeremiah," she coughed. "Didst thou get the bird?"

He was smiling at the serving maid, with spit on his lips.

"Morning, Lizzie," he said. "Fancy a beer?"

The Steward had poured another one for his Lordship and was on his way upstairs again; but he stopped to ask where the peacock was.

"In the flesh larder, dripping blood into a bucket," said the meat cook.

"Well, get thyself back in there and bring salt pork for the pot and some rabbits for a pie. Make haste, man," snapped Bickerstaff, "we've got guests for dinner."

"It's only the Earl of Arundel and his pizzle-face wife," Jeremiah said.

Both maids burst into laughter and the Cook had a lengthy coughing fit. Rosa saw blood in the stuff that she spat on the floor, into the corner where rats scuttled.

"A plague on the lot of you," the Steward tutted, and left with his tray of beer.

When he had gone, Lizzie took a step towards the shivering Gypsy by the fire.

"Do you tell fortunes?" she asked.

"She doth, to be sure," said Hepzebah. "They all do. But you've got no silver to pay her."

"She doesn't want silver," said the Cook, "she wants a drink of wine and something to eat. She'll tell all our fortunes for a piece of this fresh baked bread."

She bent to get a loaf from the oven, and was seized by another bout of coughing.

"Oh prithee," said Lizzie, turning to the manservant with her hands clasped, "fetch the Gypsy some wine, that she might read my palm."

With a gleeful wink he went to the buttery, where butts of beer and wine were; straight past Hepzebah, still churning. Jez had no eyes for her.

"Oh prithee," the kitchen maid echoed bitterly as he went.

Rosa was *panish* now. It was more than a day since she'd eaten and the smell of the hot white bread that Cook was breaking made her stomach rumble like the wheels of Gypsy wagons that were starting to roll.

But though the Romanies had rejected her for her impure actions, her heart was as clean as it had ever been; and the thought of touching these white people's hands was repulsive to Rosa.

The Cook's were charcoal-coloured, Jeremiah's were covered with peacock blood; and the two maids' were ingrained with the dirt of a thousand menial chores.

All of them were so blistered and callused that the lifelines could not be seen; the lines that defined their hearts and souls were distorted by their manual labour too.

But she didn't need to read their palms; the future of Lord Fortescue's staff was obvious. She only had to look at their faces.

"Tell us our fortunes," said Jez, giving her a goblet of red wine that he'd already drunk from.

"Say what you see," Cook added, and she handed over a morsel of new-torn bread.

Rosa ate first, and tasted the unfamiliar drink that had none of the fire of a Gypsy ferment, but a very mellow warmth. The three younger servants drew closer to her, but Cook went back to her pastry table and coughed over the shortcrust.

The Romany girl addressed Hepzebah, Jez and Lizzie in turn.

"You love a man who doesn't love you, you love a woman who doesn't love you, you only love yourself," she said, pointing a finger at each. She still had a mouthful of bread and wasn't trying to make an impression, but they stared at her as if she had performed a miracle.

"Nothing you can do will make him love you," she said to the kitchen maid. "Something you can do will make her love you," she told the meat man.

"You will see what love is when you have an ugly child," she said to Lizzie.

"And what about me?" asked the Cook, her rolling pin held motionless in mid air.

Rosa took another bite of bread, another sip of red wine, before she replied. Twas an ungodly sort of communion, but everyone there was full of awe.

"You'll be dead before winter comes twice more," Rosa said.

She spoke so starkly; black and white like gravestones chiselled against a snowy sky. Her pronouncement was harsh, but the Cook merely coughed and shrugged her shoulders.

The maid Hepzebah, however, stamped her foot crossly.

"For shame," she shouted at Rosa, "you will not witch her away. You rag, you baggage, begone!"

The servant could yell as loud as her master; but still, Rosa had to stay.

"It's my Dad I miss," she sighed. "When he got angry he spoke softer, and when it was really fierce you could hardly hear him."

"Did that keep you in your place?" asked the meat cook, who was now skinning a rabbit for the pie.

"No," she said, "I lived with him is what kept me in my place."

"Why don't you just get up and go home?" Jez suggested, stripping the forelegs. He spoke to her kindly, because she said that the woman he wanted was within his reach: but he didn't know you should never say 'home' to a gypsy.

Rosa burst into tears. Home was a person, not a place.

"I can't," she sobbed. "I swapped my old man for young Fortescue. I couldn't have them both."

Jez cracked the rabbit's bones.

"You should have told your own fortune," he said, "or you'll end up with neither of 'em."

The sound of the Steward coming down the back stairs made everyone jump, as if they had all been dreaming. The kitchen was warm now, and they were drunk on beer and wine because it was too dangerous to drink the water.

A rat rushed out of the way as Bickerstaff arrived at the kitchen door. He beckoned to Rosa.

"My Lord will see you in the library," he said, and held out his arm to escort her.

"And where's the poxy cat?" he added.

"Don't know sir. I'll call her," Jeremiah said.

The Steward looked at him in surprise.

"Have you skinned that bird yet?" he asked.

"Not quite sir. I'll do it now," Jez replied, picking up his knife and brandishing it keenly.

Peacock royal was as unpopular with the servants as it was popular with their master, being the trickiest of all dishes to prepare. When the bird was ready to carve it had to be put back inside its shimmering green and purple plumage to look like it were still alive, from beak to tail feathers.

Then the centrepiece perched on the table as if it could stretch its wings and fly away; but underneath it was stuffed and roasted meat.

Bickerstaff expected the cooks to moan as they performed this fiddley task. They usually did. But today the meat man himself seemed changed, from inside out, by some Gypsy magic.

With a worried look Bickerstaff took the girl up the back stairs, facing the cold stone climb for the hundredth time that morning. The lot of a Tudor Steward was not an easy one.

Halfway up the stairs, Rosa stopped dead. She saw something hanging on the wall; something she'd seen before. The pattern stood out against the peeling plaster, and seemed to lead her past it.

"What's that?" she asked Bickerstaff.

He looked at the embroidered vestments, and said with a yawn:

"Gold. We got it when the old king sacked the monastery. There's one hung in the banqueting hall and decorated with rubies. Used to belong to the Abbot."

"I seen that stitch another time," she said.

The steward kept climbing.

"Rich?" he called back. "He'd never have passed through the eye of a needle."

Bickerstaff was far ahead, but Rosa's eyes were following the path of the sacred braid and her feet didn't move.

"I've seen it before," the Gypsy insisted.

Then the young lord must have taken her up the back way; for Bickerstaff would stake his life that she had never been in an Abbey. He passed a bend in the stairs with a smile.

"The sly pup," he sighed. "Didst no one tell him a fox is to be chaste."

Far behind him, the girl lost her footing and fell backwards; but the pattern of narrative thread pulled her back up the same steps again.


When Rosa walked into the library, where the Earl was waiting, she didn't notice that the walls were lined with books, because she didn't know what books were.

The Romany word for book was *lil*, but she didn't even know that. Still, as she stood between the shelves, Rosa was aware that she had come here to learn.

"Ho, threadbare daughter of a rogue," Fortescue greeted her with a shout. "You have bewitched my son!"

"Bewitched?" she said.

"And you're dirty," he added, when his gaze had focused on the rags that were tattered and torn so becomingly. "Beautiful but dirty. How did you do it?"

Rosa was shivering.

"I didn't," she said.

"Nonsense," Fortescue blustered. "You must have charmed him with some eastern trick. Why else would he propose marriage to a bloody Gypsy? I suppose your whole band of smiling pick-thanks are camped on the doorstep."

"No," said Rosa, "They leaving. Moving on this morning."

"But your father brought you?"

"I came on my own," she said.

Lord Fortescue took a swig of his beer.

"Russ Long sent you to wed the Earl's son, and didn't come too?" he sneered. "'Tis strange indeed. Don't mistake me, I rather like the rascal. But I would number among his traits a rampant opportunism, and what is this if not a rampant opportunity?"

"I didn't tell him," Rosa replied.

"Why not?"

"Because he had cast me off. They caught me talking to John in the woods, and now I am unclean."

For a moment the Earl was lost for words. Surrounded by books, as he was.

"You? Unclean? For talking to him?" he spat at last. Even his beer was agitated. It sloshed over the sides of his tankard.

"Gypsies aren't allowed to marry *gadje*," Rosa explained.

"Aren't allowed to…Why, you patched queen!" Beer splashed the carpet as Fortescue stood up. "You acorn strumpet!"

Rosa turned and fled. She was going to run right out of the library, down the flight of stairs, and away into the woods where she belonged; back into the trees from whence had come all the paper too, every imprisoned page of his Lordship's books.

But the doorknob stopped her. She wasn't used to such a thing, didn't know if it was for twisting or turning. She could only rattle it helplessly, while Fortescue spoke on.

"Indeed, there cannot possibly be a marriage. It would be ill-advised and, I suspect, illegal," he said. "But the refusal is all on our side. You must not imagine otherwise. The situation is unacceptable for us, not you. It would have been a most advantageous match, for you."

He was laughing now.

"What on earth was your father thinking of, to cast you off at your most useful. Still all is not lost. Of course, a wedding is out of the question, but I would not be averse to you working for me. I would be willing to offer you a job."

Rosa turned and looked at him, as he drank from his tankard.

"Work for you?" she said. "How could I? We can only work for ourselves."

"I'd pay you," he pointed out, after a pause.

"I'd never swap your gold for my bones," she said.

And with that she worked out how to open the door, and stepped out into the hall.

Confounded by her Gypsy logic, he shook his fist after her.


John grabbed her hand. As soon as she was out of his father's sight, in the wood-panelled gallery that led to the stairs, he took her hand, and held it to his breast.

Lace, she felt first; the stiffened frill of precious metal that guarded his heart. Then velvet, soft as a mother's part.

The Viscount took her hand, and with it reached inside himself.

"I am broken, Rosa," he muttered, "for I meant to be like the old king and marry for love; but I am only a pot of gold, and money must marry for money."

His hand fell limply to his side, and hers went with it, stroking the sheath wherein lay his power, his poetry. It gave him new strength.

"I swear I will be with you, though your kiss is my last breath," he said. "I will marry you, when I'm free."

"While you have money, that will never be," Rosa gasped. "Kiss me now, for I am breathing my last."

In the wood-beamed corridor, where perspective seemed to lead into the past, he came closer. The space closed between them with a rustle of leaves, as if two sculptured trees were pledging their allegiance.

Then the Earl came out of the library with a shout.

"Be off with you, go on, shoo," he waved his arms at Rosa. "And take the smells of earth and fire with you. Take your wet feet and your windswept hair; I feel cold just looking at you."

On the landing at the top of the stairs, peering through the bars of a great balustrade as though he were a prisoner in his own home, the Viscount watched Rosa leave.

She was running down the staircase with nothing; and nothing was what she'd got from him. She stopped in the hallway, turned round, looked up. Looked like he'd got everything.

"I've given all I had for you," she said.

"No, Rosamund, you still have the world," he whispered loudly.

The Steward was there to open the front door for Rosa, with a sympathetic sniff. 'Twas hard to say which part of the story was saddest, the staying or the going; or the separation of two souls who could have stayed or gone together. Before she disappeared the Gypsy girl turned for a final look at her young Lord. Their eyes met between his ancestral banisters.

"Rosa," he cried in a cracked voice, high as the painted ceiling, "I'll find you again, wait and see."

"You will not know me," she said, and walked out of his stately home.

If he thought she could live between walls mounted with the skins of dead animals and the clothes of dead monks, he did not know her now. And he had never known her, if he thought she could die in the same place, not to move on, not to finish her journey.

The girl he'd asked to marry was just a shadow cast by the branches, the sun through the leaves, of the real Rosa.

But she couldn't be a dancing Gypsy without a Gypsy band. As soon as the door slammed shut behind her, Rosa started to run; down the drive, through the gates, off the road and across the fields. Though the sky was grey she knew from the rumbling in her stomach it must be midday.

A carriage drew up to the manor house as she left; without looking she knew it was the Earl of Arundel and his pizzle-faced wife. That was why the Romanies had to have her back; she was a natural clairvoyant.

"Dadus," Rosa panted, as she ran through the copse at the top of their field, the field that used to be theirs, "Dad!"

She should have dukkered herself. He had gone.

The field was empty, wagons and horses, adults and children, the bright colours of the Gypsy camp had gone; and all that was left was green and brown, scarred earth making a fresh start under the dismal sky, which was just starting to rain.

She walked to where their tent had stood; and found on the bare ground a corresponding shape in her, which ached. She sat down, between the painful places where pegs had been pulled out, but she didn't cry. The sky was crying for her.

Rosa had two men, she could have had any one of a hundred men, but now she had none. She'd swapped a living for a loving.

From the dead heart of her old home, she saw her father leaving. Hunched up in the driving seat of a cart, face clenched knuckle-white as he held the horse's reins. He would no more have wept than the trees could have said goodbye, as he passed under their arches for the final time, and up the mud track.

Up the mud track Rosa went too, watching where the wheels had gone, and the horse's hooves; finding the footprints of a rare Gypsy with a pair of shoes, and following them. Following them across the downs, until she could join up with her family again; because no one, woman or man, it matters not how rough and tumble, would survive alone.

It was easy to follow their trail through the woods; the bracken and branches pointed in the direction of travel. In places she could even smell horses and human sweat on timber and leather, an old familiar perfume of paint and spice.

She found *patrin*, too; arrangements of leaves and twigs the Roma left to show the path they had taken. She didn't know if the waymarkers were meant for her. Maybe Cate Koptic had taken pity on the lost soul. Out of the woods and on the roads she would sometimes see a *pookering-kosh*; but she never knew what they meant either.

The white people's sign posts led her through villages, where the trail was harder to follow; busy streets could take the sudden traffic of travelling folk without a rut or a ripple. The gut-wrenching smells of food sent her off the track, too; but she only had to ask: "Which way the Gypsies go?"

They would always point and stare.

She could have stopped there. There were many ways to sell herself, as a servant or a whore. Wearing only what an Earl would call her petticoat, and a wet woollen shawl given to her by his cook; Rosa was naked enough to start a new life.

But it was impossible for an endless traveller to stop. The girl followed the trail for three days. As the third night approached she went slower, because she knew it would last a long time.

The horse-dung she found was getting older. She would never be able to catch up, unless the Gypsies made camp. With her eyes peeled for the sapling signs of bender tents, Rosa followed the road into the woods.

The night flapped down around her suddenly, cutting the twilight short. Somewhere under the dark trees an owl hooted; *weshimulo*, a very ill omen.

Now the girl was finding her way with the soles of her feet. She was a true Romany; even with her dark eyes lost to the darker night, and her fire-coloured frock burnt out; she looked like one. But she wasn't looking where she was going.

Wishing for her lover's bed, Rosa Long fell into a bush. If the bush had been white sheets, it could not have felt softer. If it had been John's arms, it could not have held her more gently.

Her skin barely noticed the scratches, so grateful were her bones as she lay down. There was only one word, in Rosa's language, for hedge and friend: *bor*.

Funny that, the same word. Funny too, that Romany graves always had thorn bushes planted around them, to stop the ghosts from getting out. So Rosa had a proper burial, even though nobody saw it. Nobody ever knew that she was dead.

Young Fortescue thought she'd gone back to the Gypsies. Dadus thought she'd married a Lord. Neither of them ever stopped thinking about her, but they never knew she'd died in a thorn bush three days after they last saw her.

And if Romanies weren't supposed to live on their own, they were certainly never left alone to die. With no one in the leaf-mold grave to talk to, Rosa's last words were a Gypsy curse.

"I'll find you too, John Fortescue; as I am now you'll be so vexed, either in this world or the next."

She waited for his kiss till her last breath; and Rosa died angry.

Slowly the undergrowth wound around her neck like an ivy noose. Her rage seeped into the root system, to rise as sap. Eventually the branches made way for her restless bones.

# Raji

Raji was born angry.

Everybody saw it. He was born into a family of warriors, but even they were surprised at his rage.

His mother felt it; at every stage, from conception to the quickening, through all the Hindu rites of passage; she knew there was something wrong with this child.

There was trouble at each *samskara*; when they carried him out to see the moon, he screamed. When they gave him food, he spat. At the ceremony of tonsure, he bit the barber-surgeon.

She couldn't bear to remember what had happened at the investiture with sacred thread. It was all written down, though; the major developments and minor incidents, in a family history lettered with corpses.

They were *Kshatriya*, high-caste warriors. Raji's people had fought themselves a small kingdom in the past, won it with the strength of their arms, the courage of their hearts. They claimed their territory and built a fort the colour of bloodshed, red stone.

Now the country was colonised, its dark heart held in a chalk white grasp, but the fortress stood; and everything it stood for was still beating inside.

The Indian prince was raised like a quiet battle cry. It was an ancient way, along which his father led him; first by a tiny fist, then by a strong wrist. At every turn on the path, a new weapon appeared in his hand.

The warrior training lasted until he could fight with anything from scimitar to snicker-snee; and had committed the *vedas* to memory. But this is where Raji fell down.

"You don't understand what the scriptures are telling you," his *Brahmin* teacher said, when the boy had been detained again for making his sisters or servants cry. "Seek and find a way to fight without hurting anybody."

And again, he would explain:

"Learn from Arjuna, in the *Bhagavad Gita*. What does he find? Peace on the battlefield!"

The teacher knew that Raji wasn't ready to find peace yet, though when the prince reached eighteen he had to let him go. He hadn't taught his student everything there was to know, but the physical training was finished. Raji's body was an arrow that never missed its mark.

His mother was worried when she heard he was going. She begged him on her knees not to leave home.

"You will lose your head," she said. But she stayed on her knees to pray to Lord Ganesh for her son's new start. And when she had finished praying, she stayed on her knees to weep; "You will lose your heart." If the boy found himself a wife, the loss would be his mother's.

His sisters were so glad that Raji was going to take his anger out on someone else that they made a garland of a hundred paper flowers, and wound it around his neck.

His father gave him a sword that had killed a hundred men; a sword mightier than the pen that wrote their noble family history. Then he opened the doors of their citadel and set Raji free.

Walking into the red desert, he was sharp as a chip off the stone of their fort. His footsteps were clearly marked in the red dust. Raji didn't have to wonder which way to go. He was only the arrow, not the bow. The archer decides the direction.

Raji flew; across the sweltering distance of the desert. Before long he stopped to take off the garland of flowers. It was wound too tightly around his throat.

He was still within view of the fortress, and his sisters were watching from the roof; close enough to see him shrug off their colourful wreath and stamp on it in the sand, too far away to see that he kept a single paper bloom in his hand.


Raji walked on. As the fort disappeared behind him, a battlement-shaped city grew on the horizon in front. He aimed for this garrison, home of the army. It seemed like a good place to find the fight he'd been looking for.

He slipped between buttress walls, went right to the centre, and found himself in a bazaar.

The prince stood and looked at the scene in such detail that it broke down into colourful particles like the bowls of spices on the stalls. Like coriander seeds and saffron strands, cardamons and hot chillies, the picture before him seemed to be made up of tiny atoms, all moving.

Had he seen it before? As a painting on the palace wall, or in a dream? Colour by colour and shape by shape; with vision sharpened by his *vedic* training, Raji could see how the whole picture was made.

A disturbance in the corner of the bazaar drew the attention of his pencilled insight. Raji moved closer to watch.

An ugly old prostitute, drunk on gin, was shouting at some younger prettier ones. She was a white woman, come from England on what they called the Fishing Fleet, to catch herself a husband.

Any old *nabob* would have done the job nicely, but her year of free board and lodging had expired without a single proposal. So Mistress Leaze was faced with the choice of 'returning empty' in the bowels of a ship to England, or staying to take her chances in the colony.

She stayed, and took to the bottle, and took to the bed of anyone prepared to pay her. But the competition from graceful native ladies, with their midnight eyes and moonlight smiles was strong. Even tatty saris were more seductive than Mistress Leaze's flannel sheets; though her very survival depended on their spread.

"Stand further off, you whores," she was slurring at her rivals, and a crowd had gathered to watch the fight unfold.

Raji stood at the back, tall enough to see over the heads in turbans and hats with feathers that bobbed excitedly.

The slanging match between the prostitutes, half Hindustani, half drunken English that everyone could understand, was getting out of hand. Some men at the front of the crowd were shuffling backward; more afraid of the angry women than they were of other men.

Some men were surging forwards; they who enjoyed seeing women brawl more than other men.

Raji didn't feel like either kind of man. Then he saw three soldiers running through the bazaar towards the fracas. Their uniforms were red with yellow facings and silver lace.

The officer was an Englishman, pale skin, pointed moustache, piercing blue eyes; but his men were Indian. *Sepoys*, swords raised, dark and dangerous.

Raji could see that these infantrymen were no ordinary men; they were high caste Brahmins. The white man, if he'd stayed at home, might have been any old tinker or tailor. But in the East India Company's Army, he ranked above the purest men of all.

Raji moved closer to watch as the soldiers thrust their way through the crowd. When they saw that it was only women fighting the officer laughed and told the *sepoys* to put their swords away.

They were laughing too but disappointed, and made up for it by flirting with the whores for free. The women stopped shouting, but the crowd still listened; and didn't disperse until they were sure nothing more was happening than a half-hearted fling.

Raji carried on watching though, partially concealed by the fragrant drapes of a spice stall, until the soldiers remembered themselves and shouldered their weapons; and the women slumped as they watched the men march away.

Raji didn't know what he wanted to do first; join the army or sleep with a whore.

He waited for a while, ate a mango from a stall, and chose which of the topless women in pantaloons and bangles he would go boldly up to.

But first he had to get past Mistress Leaze; 'Mistress Leaze, what you gets is what you sees'; who was drunkenly selling her wares again.

"God save us, it's a young prince," she said, blinking watery eyes and breathing gin at Raji.

"God save the Queen," he replied.

But he wouldn't touch her with a stick. It would break his caste. He couldn't touch any white woman; and if her shadow passed across his plate, he'd have to throw his last meal away.

So he went and stood in front of one of the nice native ladies, the one who looked least like any of his sisters.

She took him behind the *Lol-Bibbees* bazaar to a row of mud huts, where piles of human shit lay by the entranceways like shoes waiting for their owners.

It was a dark room she took him into, and a darker thing they did there. When he left again, his pockets were a bag of coins lighter, though his sword was still as heavy.

The lady didn't charge as much as he gave her; but he didn't ask how much she charged. He knew he wouldn't need any money, in the army.

When he came out into the alley, the old whore was standing there, looking patchy in the shadow and the light. Most of the English had Indian servants, but some still knew to be servile.

"How do you do," said she, and bobbed a curtsey. "I hope the girl said thank you, sir."

"For the rape or the rupees?" asked the prince. He didn't look at her, but down at the dust instead. Her shawl had fallen off and was lying on the ground.

Raji got out his sword and picked up the woollen wrap. He held it out to her, on the point of his blade.

"I return your shawl," he said.

She took it slowly, as if she thought he was going to cut her hand off. The grubby garment was so long, and had so many folds, that they were both touching it for ages, though they never touched each other.

Raji's caste was intact. He hadn't lost his place in the circle of birth and rebirth. But he spat on his sword to clean it, anyway.

The whore clutched the shawl and curtsied again.

Raji watched till she reached the lowest point, then walked away. Now he needed to fight more than ever before. He followed the soldiers he'd seen and went to join their army.


They were very pleased to meet him, this army which had unseated many a Hindu King during its oh-so-polite invasion and jolly occupation. Many a *Rajah* and a *Rana*, a *Nawab* and a *Nizam* had been rudely defeated; but they welcomed a warrior prince who wanted to fight on their side.

The Sergeant-Major gasped when Raji showed what he could do with a sword.

"But have you ever fired a gun, boy?" he asked.

They gave him a musket, and Raji felt like a mother who'd just been handed her first baby. Brand new, but it seemed that he'd been holding it for ever; the weight and the length were made for his arms, and the smell was heavenly. He was filled with a sense of its potential.

The British officers of the First Native Infantry watched Raji bond instantly with the weapon, and smiled. In time he might even become an officer himself; a *subahdar*, they said. Then they sent him to live in a hut in the native lines.

The warrior prince felt at home among fortifications, and these stretched for six miles along the bank of the Ganges. Along the holy river the English had built their little villages too; indistinguishable from the ones they'd left in their own country, but for the *punkah-wallahs* on the verandas, fanning in a vain war with the heat.

51

The English had servants to bend down for them and servants to pick up; one to shave, one to bathe, two or three to dress them.

If they wore fewer clothes, thought Raji, they wouldn't be so uncool; but the wives of the higher ranks insisted on wearing the high fashions from home, though it floored them in the soaring temperatures.

Rumour had it that one young lady, a captain's daughter returning from boarding school in England, had her waist so tightly laced in stays that she passed out on the Bombay quayside, among all the spice dust and fish bits and rope.

They gathered to see her arrival in the *cantonments*; black and white soldiers alike could appreciate the shape of a woman, but something deformed stepped out of the *dak* carriage.

Most of the men quickly turned away, a bit embarrassed; but Raji stood and stared until the entourage disappeared into the heat haze behind the artillery lines. Somehow, seeing the lady suffer made him feel better.

He thought about her a lot after that, as he lay on his *charpoy* at night and in the heat of the day; while he was stamping his feet on parade, or smoking a pipe under the *pepil* tree.

Why was the woman shaped like an object, with her waist no bigger than a man's hand? It made him want to grab her like he grabbed his gun, the hookah, or his ridiculous pith helmet. He could not touch her; and yet, he could actually feel himself picking her up.

Sometimes the other *sepoys* talked about women too; but more important ideas were starting to spread, round their evening fire.

They whispered about new guns the army was introducing to replace their old muskets; fast muzzle-loading rifles, bullet and powder rammed down the barrel together in little paper cartridges, torn open with the teeth.

They said the cartridges were greased with tallow of beef or pork, fat which should never touch the lips of Hindoos and Musselmen, taboo to both faiths.

"We must refuse to use these tainted bullets," the native soldiers said, "even if they kill us. The army will not make us break caste."

Despite the sullen mutterings, life went on as usual in the gay garrison city. The native soldiers were befriended by the officers, and fawned over by their wives. The bored ladies were always having tea parties and throwing balls, and Raji, whose exotic beauty was made all the more mysterious by his being completely unaware of it, was often invited.

On more than one occasion, he was introduced to the Captain's daughter, whose tiny waist had other women swooning as well as herself, and left the men in stammers.

Raji himself would only stare at Victoria Newcombe and never spoke, though he had opportunity enough to engage her in conversation. He kept his lips clenched on a hatred so great his mastery of her language could not convey it. He would wait until there were no mispronounced words to make her mistake his contempt.

He didn't know why he felt so strongly about this woman, only having known his mother and sisters, some servants and an old whore before. He didn't know how he was supposed to feel about women, but the feelings filled his uniform by day, and his bed every night.

Then the other men on the mats around him would rise up in the darkness, and whisper louder that the army were endangering their spiritual lives.

At nearby Military camp Meerut the *sepoys* had protested about the new bullets. All who refused to use them had been stripped of their uniforms on parade, chained together and taken to gaol.

"We're not trying to convert you," the English officers said, "honestly!" The Corporal and the Colonel swore they respected Indian traditions more than ever. They could not have shown it less.

Rumour was that Meerut's native battalion was planning to overthrow their command. They would murder them, and not stop at the men; English women and children would die too.

With Raji, two hundred miles down the river Ganges, lived the largest population of Europeans in the land. They called it the Manchester of the East. It did a roaring trade in silk and leather, silver and gold. There was diamond entertainment too, from racecourse to racquets court to reading room. The ladies were fond of their amateur theatricals, and native soldiers had to sit through interminable melodramas just to be polite.

It was halfway through one such evening of orphaned heroines and evil uncles that Raji could stand the closeness of the crowd, with its smell of perfume mixed with sweat and the swell of over-emotional bosoms, no longer. He got up from his seat in the middle of the performance and struggled to the back of the hall. He might have managed to stay put till the final, agonising curtain call, if he'd seen that the woman of his dreams was standing in the doorway, fanning herself with a programme, and he would have to pass her to leave.

She gave a demure curtsey, but on rising, looked him in the eye and said;
"Why are you so angry?"

Her directness caught the soldier prince off guard.

"What do you know of anger, white woman?" he replied.

"I may not feel it, but I can see it," she whispered, "in others." She looked
quickly over her shoulder to make sure no one else was listening. "Even when
you stand at ease, you are fighting a battle."

Raji glared.

"I am *Kshatriya*," he said, "warrior caste. Born to fight."

"But not to go on all your life?" the girl inquired.

"Goodness gracious me," he replied. "You are telling me how to be? You,
whose woman's body has been reduced to a man's hand span."

He made a furious gesture at her, demonstrating the width of his grasp, and
making her gasp. Then he pushed her out of the room and onto the veranda,
where punkah-wallahs were fanning a losing battle with the heat being raised
inside.

"The question is rather, why are you not angry?" he hissed. "If only I cared
to hear the answer."

Victoria Newcombe seemed about to cry, but stiffened her lips.

"If you hate me so much," she said, "and my father, your captain, then why
did you join our army?"

"I am a warrior," Raji repeated. "I fight."

"For any cause?" she asked him. "How ignoble!"

"On the contrary," Raji replied, "it is the most noble course. Like *Arjuna*, I
fight without questioning whether I am on the right side or the wrong side,
for God alone sees the entire battlefield. I am only doing my *dharma*."

The officer's daughter shook her head.

"I don't understand," she said, "but it doesn't matter what you say. I've seen
your eyes flash like a sword, and Daddy says that you are a man at war with
yourself."

"God alone sees the entire battlefield," said Raji again. "I am perfectly at
peace."

"But your funny Hindoo gods are not the same as ours," said the girl. "And
you are fighting for our God now. He's not blue, with four arms. He's white."

"You will see, *feringhee* lady," was Raji's dark reply. "You will see who we are
fighting for."

Victoria's two blue eyes searched his face.

"You mean the mutiny?" she said. "We've heard what has happened at Meerut. But my father says it won't happen here. He says our *sepoys* are loyal friends. Besides, he says, it's too hot!"

And with a wave of her programme and a toss of her curls, she went back inside the sweltering hall to watch the rest of the play-acting.

Victoria may have flounced back to her drama, but Raji strode across the parade ground with more conviction. The word in the *sepoy* lines was that Delhi had fallen too, and hundreds of English women and children were held in the fort, baked in hot stone, while the rebels raged outside.

It made him smile – yes, if the bitch insisted, flash his teeth like a sword – to think of her white skin, white ringlets, white petticoats burning. Too hot to mutiny, her father said? The officers didn't know how hot their Indians could get.

In the barracks that night, cooking *dhal* round the fire, someone reported that the General was digging trenches, stockpiling ammunition and emptying the treasury. So whatever stories they were telling their daughters, the truth was that all the Company's men were preparing for a siege; and however they seemed to trust the native soldiers not to rise against them, they were building a wall and expecting to fall.

The recommended ratio of Europeans to *sepoys* was one to three. At Meerut it had been one to six. Here, it was one to fourteen; the General's force was made up of sixty-seven English officers and three thousand, five hundred native troops; plus a hundred of Her Majesty's 84th Foot Brigade, most of whom were in hospital with heat stroke.

And hundreds and hundreds of women and children had made themselves at home in the Manchester of the mud and monsoon.

Next morning, the first bodies were found in the sacred river; white people who'd been massacred upstream and floated down the Ganges faster than a warning could have come by the Grand Trunk Road. And though the telegraph wires were still buzzing, they would soon be cut like the colonial throat.

The town went about its business as usual, and the English officers went to parade their battalions; still walking in the ranks and talking with the native soldiers.

But that night, they started to move their families into an entrenchment.

"See," said Raji, watching from his barracks at dusk, as a flurry of carriages full of hysterical *memsahibs* in nightgowns, and babes in the arms of worried *Ayahs*, disappeared behind the shallow trenches to spend the night.

"They are afraid of us, after all." He was looking for the Captain's daughter, longing to see her flee from his black power, but most of the pale faces passing were a blur.

He watched half the night, standing by his regiment's cooking fire, smoking *bhang*, an explosive hemp.

"How will we know when to start?" he asked.

And he asked it again in the light of day, when a sort of normality returned to the place. The ruffled matrons were conveyed back to their bungalows, and the men strolled back to the parade ground as if nothing had happened.

Raji's wasn't the only muted war-cry in the lines. At lunchtime he saw a *sepoy* grab a bugle and, raising it to his lips, start to signal the cavalry to rise. But after only one note, the bugle was snatched away by a *subahdar* and thrown onto the fire.

Raji spat with disappointment.

"When will the killing begin?" he said.

"Hurry up," hissed Mrs Newcombe, as her servants heaved the large dining table into the entrenchment. Four more followed with the chairs.

There were two huts on the plain, one with a thatched roof kindling in the sun. A half-finished trench had been dug around the buildings, by soldiers whose spades got too hot to handle.

The Captain's wife stepped over the wall of sand. She had already brought a bed from her bungalow, and a screen for privacy. The small barracks-room she was moving into would be packed; but then, the wives of the lower ranks had to make do with a place on the veranda.

Her husband was parading his men again this afternoon. She'd seen him march off, on as firm a footing as ever; but actually he was treading on eggshells. It was Queen Victoria's birthday, but there would not be the usual gun salute, for fear the natives might start firing back.

The dauntless Mrs Newcombe went on arranging table and chairs in the spirit of her Queen. She would bring servants for cooking and cleaning, though she'd heard that water was limited. One well for a thousand people, it was said. But there was a rumbling like thunder as barrel after barrel of brandy was rolled behind the trenches.

General Wheeler was in charge of supplies. His own wife and daughters were going into the exposed retreat too; and Mrs Newcombe had dined with them often, so he must know how much ladies needed to eat and drink.

Once both the weaker sex and the strong stuff were lodged within the entrenchment, the mutiny seemed certain. But the English officers still slept in the lines with their men, as though unconscious of any danger.

Every night some fired up *sepoy* would say; "Now! Come on! Let's do him in, then get the others! Let's go to Delhi and claim our own king!"

Then another soldier would pour on whispered water, "No, they trust us not to turn against them. They treat us better than our own rulers ever did."

"But they are trying to break our castes, and make us lose the faith," another voice would blow like smoke from the opium pipe into the dark sky.

Raji had chewed the end off his pipe with the frustration of not being able to fight. But it was always the quietest voice, the voice that came from the earth, which won the night. Some laid-back *sepoy* on a mat would say; "Let it be."

By dawn, the whole regiment would be lying with their weapons by the remains of the fire.

"Attack them before they attack us," somebody would mutter in his sleep. "They've summoned reinforcements."

Poor *baba-logues,* they couldn't remember what it was like before the yellow faces came and eclipsed their sun; but they knew that the first few settlers had shown them respect, and learned to speak their language properly.

Now the English looked arrogant and sounded ignorant; but were still, just about, human.

For a week, nobody moved in the garrison city. The pendulum that swung for colonial power was hanging in the balance; and for seven days on the scorching, dusty plain nothing happened but deep and secret thought.

Then the British made a stupid move. It was pay day and they changed the rules. Native soldiers must come, one by one, into the new compound, unarmed and out of uniform, to get their money.

The insult! They might as well have given an order to start looting and burning. The native soldiers gathered around their cooking fires to smoke bhang and fuel their unrest as they waited for nightfall.

But Prince Raji, along with a handful of others, changed into his native clothing and went into the entrenchment to collect his wages; not, like the others, because he wanted the money, but because he wanted to see his woman. He needed to say goodbye.

Arrayed in his finest, purple and gold, with a jewelled turban, necklaces and rings, the warrior walked into the makeshift office to collect his pay. The clerk was half English and half Indian, sitting uncomfortably behind the desk. Raji didn't even look at the coins he was given, just fixed the awkward fellow with the sword of his stare.

"Where is the Captain's daughter?" he asked. With so many white women behind the barricades he was unlikely to bump into her by chance.

"Who?" asked the clerk.

"Victoria Newcombe," said Raji, and it sounded like a curse in his heavy accent.

The clerk shrugged.

"Could be anywhere," he said.

Raji walked slowly out of the squat building, peering into overcrowded rooms where women who had recently luxuriated in their own bungalows were living with four or five other families. Still the frilly gowns and elaborate bonnets were taking up more space than they should.

He only had eyes for one woman's shape, though; the hourglass figure whose time was running out; but he couldn't hope to find her so quickly, and couldn't wait any longer with so many English soldiers around, looking for him to leave.

But where the facts seem to rule the day, fate is sometimes reigning. As Raji left the building, he heard her voice; an unmistakable tone, but flat where it had been sharp before.

He turned to look over his shoulder, and there she was on the veranda, bending stiffly in her stays to restrain two small children, her little brother and sister, who wanted to run and play.

"Darlings, you mustn't," she said gently, but held them as firmly as wild animals wanting to be free. "It's not safe now."

Then something made her look up, through the bars of the veranda as if it were a cage, straight at Raji who was standing in the sun looking back at her.

She fell silent, and he didn't say a word. There was no need to; the situation spoke for itself. He was going to walk away and she had to stay; a prisoner in the country her people had captured.

In her eyes there was something deeper than the drama he'd seen there before; she was learning the truth, both the facts and her fate.

Victoria Newcombe would have to contain her hysteria, like she had to confine the children who'd always been allowed to play in the garden. Her sister was crying, and her brother was cross.

Raji smiled and turned to go. He was glad to see the karma working. It strengthened his faith.


And 'For the Faith' was what the Indian soldiers cried, as they burned down the English bungalows at dusk. 'For the Faith' as they broke into the church and killed the Christians hiding there. 'For the Faith' as they looted the bazaar, raided the armoury, and massed with flaming torches on the road to Delhi, ready to march on the capital and claim allegiance to their king.

The army officers and their wives stood in the shallow trenches watching as their houses and all their possessions went up in smoke; watching as their rebel children disappeared on stolen elephants down the Grand Trunk Road.

Then the *cantonments* were empty but for the corpses of a few native soldiers who hadn't turned against their white-skinned parents, and were killed by their brothers of colour.

Raji was not among this bloodless number. He was riding an elephant at the head of the procession; with triumphant cheering, and flourishing of riches got back from the British; but inside he was silent, and his heart was empty.

With every lumbering step the jewelled beast took, he was further away from Victoria; but he hadn't seen her die. Her life wasn't finished yet; he wasn't ready to leave.

So when the parade stopped for the night, and the men round the campfire found their feet away from the Queen's army; and a new king rose like a rather shabby phoenix from the ashes and suggested they go back to kill the English in their entrenchment; Raji was the first to agree.

He headed the procession back the next morning, riding the elephant with altogether more enthusiasm, as the old General's untenable position came into view.

Nobody was looking out of the trenches to see the rebel soldiers returning in a haze of morning heat; the look-out had fallen asleep in the shade of the three foot high sandcastle.

The low wall seemed no match for the natives ready to reclaim the earth from which it was formed, the substance of their country. But perhaps the British rule had touched the natives more deeply than they knew. A messenger was sent with a polite note, informing the General that the shooting would start at ten-thirty sharp.

Then the *sepoys* fired everything they could find, from grape shot to cannon balls into the compound.


From the moment the bombardment began, some of Britannia's matrons and maidens started screaming, and didn't stop until they were personally silenced by bullets, or by parts of the building collapsing on them.

In the heart of the barracks, in a room with no light or air, but many feet of brick between its walls and a war, Victoria Newcombe was learning to control herself.

She was in a privileged position; and sharing it were her mother, brother and sister, and several other high ranking officer's families. If they were of a lower order the veranda would be their home; the long day spent dodging the lethal trajectory of the sun.

She rarely saw her father. He would stagger into the dim room, kiss his wife and children and fall onto a mattress for an hour's sleep before being called back to the frontline.

The trenches were manned by a makeshift army of officers, and gentlemen firing their first cannons. There were a couple of railway engineers from Surrey and a silk and ivory merchant turned into instant soldiers.

The Indian attack was strengthened by *badmashes* from the bazaar; also trying out their first firearms. They made drug-crazed runs at the barracks; but the drunken European defence caused just enough casualties to keep them from charging outright on the two shaky buildings.

Captain Newcombe would come into the room, and collapse groaning on his *charpoy*. Unharmed, his distraught wife and daughter noticed; but each time he appeared his skin was burnt darker by the sun, and his uniform was dirtier.

There was no water to wash with. They were rationed to a jug a day which the *ayahs* would fetch from the well at dusk when the firing stopped briefly; but the servants running to the exposed water hole were easy targets for snipers.

Many a stone jug gave up its precious contents to the dust even as the soul who had carried it lay bleeding into the earth.

"But Victoria, dear," her mother whispered one night as everyone tried to sleep in the clay oven of their room. "There is no need to worry. The 78th Highlanders are coming to rescue us. I had it from Mrs White, who heard it from the General's wife; so rest assured. They will be here within the week, we will not wait longer."

Victoria peered at her mother in the darkness. She could barely see the beloved features; but she had heard a rare trace of the Scottish ancestry in the otherwise impeccable English accent.

"That is good news, Mother," the girl replied dutifully, though she wondered how reliable were the words of the General's wife in a world where all rank and status had suddenly collapsed.

Mrs White was a stable enough character, though, asleep on the other side of a thin screen, where they could hear her snoring. She was proving a great support to her heavily pregnant daughter-in-law, who lay restlessly beside her. Both the husband and son were on night watch, with strict instructions from Mrs White to scale the barrack buildings every hour to look for the approaching 78th Highlanders; but as one was a Colonel and the other a Corporal they probably didn't act entirely on her orders.

It was Colonel White who came the next morning to tell Mrs Newcombe her husband had been shot. When they had left the room without the two younger children, he told them Captain Newcombe was dead.

He took them to a spot behind the barracks where a pile of oozing entrails, bones and hair were wearing Captain Newcombe's uniform. It was a sight no nineteenth century English woman was prepared to see, and it changed both mother and daughter forever.

Mrs Newcombe never spoke again, except to utter in increasingly Scottish tones that the 78th Highlanders were coming, they were on their way, and they would be nae longer than a week.

So it was up to Victoria to listen sensibly as Colonel White explained that graves could not be dug in the hard earth; but there was an old dry well where they were burying bodies quickly, because of typhoid breaking out.

She could hardly hear what he was saying for the buzzing of flies around her father's corpse.

"We go every evening at dusk. It is no way to bury Christians, but you may come if you wish to perform what little ceremony you can."

"Thank you, I will," said Victoria, then went back inside to tell her young brother and sister that their Papa was dead.

"You are the man of the family now, Henry," she informed him.

"Then let me outside to play with the guns," he replied.

"No dear, it's too dangerous," she said, and the day continued much like any other, in a constant battle to keep the lively four-year-old safe inside.

That evening, though, she saw how fragile the barracks buildings were. The funeral procession that made its way through the dusk included not only dead soldiers but the bodies of women and children who had been sitting in their rooms. Cannon balls smashed through the walls and ceilings, turning the very bricks and tiles into weapons too.

Heartbreaking outlines of wives and babies were wrapped up in men's arms; and Colonel White carried Victoria's father, no longer shaped like a man, in a sack on his back. Victoria followed, watering each footstep with the drops of blood that fell; and couldn't think of a prayer to say as Captain Newcombe was lowered into the well.

The vicar himself had gone mad from despair and was wandering naked around the barracks; and the sentries used pages of his Bible for gun-wadding.

When she got back to their room Henry and little Eliza were crying, and her mother was too stiff with shock to comfort them. The evening bombardment was starting and Victoria put both children on her lap, held her hands over their ears and hummed a wordless song. She still could not remember any of the prayers that had been drummed into her since she was as small as her sister.

There were other siblings in between the oldest and youngest; Albert, Clarence and Mabel were still at school in England.

"We must write a letter," Victoria said to her mother, "and let them know what has happened to Father."

"Say the 78th Highlanders are coming," replied Mrs Newcombe, "and they're bringing my mother with them."

The image of a tiny Scottish widow on the march with burly men in kilts almost made Victoria laugh. She hadn't done that since the day before the siege began. But the bubble that rose in her throat stuck there, and became a lump that felt as if she might cry; though she hadn't done that yet either.

When they arrived in the entrenchment the family had a trunk of things they called essential. It hadn't been needed at all.

Now Victoria opened the trunk, looked into its depths, and saw how shallow she had been. The fine clothes she would swap at once for the feeling of clean skin. All the money she would give for her father's life; the jewels she'd exchange to see the children smile.

And the piece of paper she took out to write to her other brothers and sister on, she would trade for a moment of peace.

*I know not if this letter will reach you*, Victoria wrote, *or if we will ever meet again. I only hope that you will have long and happy lives, and never suffer the agonies of discomfort and grief that we have known.*

*I send our very deepest love, and remain your devoted sister.*

Then she waited for news of anyone leaving the entrenchment, and as soon as she heard that Mrs White's *Ayah* was making a bid for escape, she gave the missive to her.

The native lady didn't want to leave the children she'd looked after for so long, especially with another one due any day, but food was running out. This way her rations would go straight into the mouths of her babes.

The tearful *Ayah* left quite bulging with folded paper, and bullet-proofed, hopefully, by all the best wishes written thereon; though whether any of the letters would reach their mark, none of the senders could ever say.


Of all the rebel soldiers who saw her leave, it was Raji who fired the first shot.

There were not many watching, that hour of the night, and not many stars; so he thought she got away in the dark.

Apart from him, the native army was finding that the siege was losing its novelty. Some nights the attack was made up entirely of peasants, come from rebel villages to take pot shots with a brass blunderbuss.

Raji swore by his flintlock pistol, usually, and the only reason he missed the woman was because he was looking too hard, to see if she was Victoria Newcombe.

He saw enough to know that the escaping shape was not hers, not his. The native lady melted back into the darkness of her homeland. When the sun came up next morning the soldier saw that the mud wall protecting the English was still on the horizon; and no man's land went on forever.

As the days passed the rebels' only hope was that the figures they saw behind the trenches were getting thinner. And the thinner they got, the hungrier Raji was for hand-to-hand combat.

The English may have been running out of food, but they still seemed to have plenty of ammo. The depleted rebel army, its ranks made up now of a ragged attachment of men whose only real uniform was the fire in their eyes, tried a big push. It was early one morning, before the sun got so hot they couldn't touch their guns.

Raji led the way. It had been over a week since he'd seen Victoria and he was desperate. She couldn't possibly still be alive in there, behind the baking clay walls of a tandoori oven with no bread and no meat except for the bodies of those who were incarcerated too.

Dying to see her, he was first in the queue to cross the open space between them. So far out in front, in fact, that when the first cannon balls flew from the entrenchment they went right over his head and landed in the main body of men behind. So did the bursts of grape shot that followed.

The desert was littered with bits of soldiers, and there were not enough men left in one piece to make it over the low mud walls. A handful of survivors picked their way back through the crowds of screaming wounded and silent dead; nameless characters, whose blood-stained uniforms had darker patches where they'd torn the army insignia off.

Bitterly disappointed Raji crawled back to his tent. But big plans were afoot in the *Mahratta's* sumptuous marquee, pitched nearby. The mutiny had put him back in power; and his turbans had grown so huge that every thought he now had was shady.


Every day the cannon balls that fell came closer to Victoria's room, carving a rubble path to the heart of the building.

Every day England's gentle womenfolk had their heads knocked from their bodies, and their children torn from their arms; they were deafened by the relentless firing, deprived of sleep, and even rudely disembowelled as they went from the barracks to the inadequate privies outside.

The Newcombe's room was besieged within the siege by families who had lost their spaces on the verandas or in the outer rooms now exposed to the cloudless skies and the hail of grapeshot.

Mrs White was a formidable deterrent, though, refusing access to the most desperate petitioners and the most distressing pleas. Her daughter-in-law had gone into labour, and the sound of this struggle drowned out all others.

Victoria paced the corridor outside their room with Henry and Eliza, finding the screams for new life almost harder to hear than the screams of death. It must be worse, she thought, to come into this world than to leave it; and she watched the birth helplessly from the shell-rocked doorway.

Victoria's own mother was no help either. She was rocking in a corner, only raising her head to exclaim "Hark! Can ye no hear the bagpipes?" as she waited for the arrival of the 78th Highlanders.

The baby that came was a girl called Liberty. The cleanest thing in the refuge; she glistened like a river-washed stone in moonlight. Still with the womb-sheen on her she was put to the new mother's breast, and as she started to suck a little stretch of calm descended on the room.

That night everybody slept; but in the morning Mrs Newcombe didn't wake. Victoria shook her, and shook herself with grief but she still didn't cry.

Henry and Eliza wept for their Mama, but it was with the same abstract tone as the baby, when the milk that should have started to flow from young Mrs White's breasts never came.

Colonel White stepped in to say he would take Mrs Newcombe's body the way her husband's had gone, less than a week before. But later that day his beloved son and the brand new father, Corporal White, died too; killed in action as he manned a cannon that came off its wheels.

The Colonel staggered to the sepulchral well under the weight of his own dead flesh and blood; and Victoria had to pay a servant to hump her mother's corpse there.

She didn't attend the funeral this time. She wanted to remember Mama alive, so she could still have her bosom for a pillow whenever she needed to rest. When she thought of her father now, he was no comfort.

"There are just three of us left," Victoria said to Henry and Eliza, "which means we must be very careful and stay together for the 78th Highlanders who are coming to save us."

Then a cannon ball came into their room and it seemed to be too late. It was the end of the old Victoria, as she tore up her dress to dress the wounds of her little sister, her best yellow silk she had been saving in the trunk for when things got better; and used strips of the skirt to bandage Mrs White's bleeding head.

With the building bombed to its very bones the safest place was the trenches; and under a shelter made of her petticoat, Victoria and the children now lived in a hundred and twenty degrees of heat, and the thunder of gunfire.

Two weeks after the siege had begun the food supplies were down to nothing but a little *gram* which had never been meant to feed the humans, and soup made of the horses. The growing children were beside themselves with hunger, but Victoria had lost her appetite.

She lay quite still, not even jumping when shells or whole bodies fell into the ditch beside her. She saved her energy for holding onto Henry, who still hadn't given up the struggle to go out and play.

For all his filthy skin and bones he was the same four-year-old boy, with the same plans to rule the world. He had just forgotten that the world was once a quiet bedroom, a cool garden and friendly servants to chase him.

"Let me go, let me go," was his constant cry, as he twisted in his big sister's grip.

Barely conscious, Victoria simply grabbed the seat of his breeches and no matter how limp the rest of her body was, her right hand maintained its hold night and day.

And night and day the baby, Liberty White, was crying with hunger, for her starving mother could not give any milk. Night and day, the elder Mrs White cried from the pain of her head, which was turning the yellow silk bandages black.

One morning a mother on the other side of them, a lady who had sometimes sung when Victoria played the piano, snapped. She climbed out of the trench and started to walk across no man's land, holding her two remaining children by the hands.

No one could make out what she was screaming, though the flying bullets were not English and would have found a point. But Colonel White, his red coat bleached by the blazing sun, ran out and brought her back into the entrenchment; cursing her all the while in no uncertain terms.

That afternoon Victoria woke to find Henry wriggling out of his trousers. He'd finally grasped the nature of her grasp.

"No!" Victoria shouted, rising out of the shallow trench to reach for him as he ran away. She watched as he crossed the tract of parched earth, pockmarked with shot that fell like a cruel parody of rain.

"Henry! No!" she shouted again.

He turned and waved to her with a stick-thin arm, full of excitement at the first freedom he'd had for weeks. Raji's bullet, greased with the fat of a lamb, finished it. The boy was still waving when he fell.

Victoria didn't see it. She was looking desperately for the life-saving Colonel White, but he'd gone further along the line.

Henry's death was witnessed by the women, by all the other sisters and mothers living alongside Victoria in the trenches; and none of them said a word. So many loved ones had been lost that there was nothing loving left to say.

Some of them were thinking Hooray! Henry is dead; but they couldn't say that to his sister. Henry is dead; thank God he is safe.

The next day the siege ended. The cannonade stopped, after three weeks solid. They had forgotten what silence sounded like. It made their English ears ring, and they still couldn't hear what anyone was saying.

In the silence a message came from the new *Mahratta*. He'd grown even fatter; holed-up in what used to be a luxury hotel, hardly a mile away from the hole where the Empire's hostages were starving.

*'All those who are willing to lay down their arms shall receive a safe passage to Allahabad.'*

That's what it said, and what it meant was everybody who surrendered would be saved.

General Wheeler and his remaining officers took a while to reply. There were only a few of them and they were still willing to fight to the death; but the pleading of what wives and children they had left persuaded them to accept.

Victoria didn't do any persuading. She'd lost all but one of her family, and had no one to wheedle. Their shady new *Raja's* offer of a boat ride on the river Ganges was neither upstream nor downstream to her.

But everyone else got excited, and that night there was a bit of merriment made for the children. A half-hearted party indeed, with Colonel White playing a pair of battered spoons, and some of his men whistling between their blacked-out teeth; but Eliza and the other children actually got up and danced.

Early next morning an exhausted bugle call signalled the assembly of the survivors. Some had packed their belongings; Victoria decided to leave the trunk. In the ruins where their barrack-room had been she saw Mrs White bury their family jewels.

And suddenly the bullet-scarred yard was full of sepoys. Half-soldiers in red jackets and *dhotis*, native officers and *badmashes* stood there. The army that had tried to kill them were crossing the trenches; not with guns blazing, as they had envisaged, but with curiosity burning to see how the English had survived the siege for so long.

They had been eating horses and dogs. There were piles of bones, ribs picked clean, licked skulls and scraps of chewed fur on the ground.

And they were stripped down to skeletons too, the people who had been so plump in their petticoats, so starched in their shirts. The white cotton and lace was tied in tattered bandages around battered skin, and even the blood was grey.

Men with puffed out pigeon chests, women with stuffed bustles and padded breasts were now straight up and down. They stood in silent groups as the soldiers came over the wall; thin as sticks, still as stones. Could sticks and stones hurt them now?

Pushing to the front of the gun-powder-black mass was Raji. He had been pushing himself forwards the whole campaign, making a name for himself with his new leader. All the rebel soldiers were focused, but Raji seemed to have an extra vision; it wasn't no man's land, it was his.

Now he was looking for Victoria Newcombe in the row of white faces behind the English soldiers. Every bullet he'd discharged into the compound over the past three weeks had her name on it, but when he saw she was still alive his joy soared like a twenty-four pound cannon-ball.

What misery she must have suffered! How it was etched on her countenance!

Never had he seen a woman so changed. She had been repulsive before, and she was repulsive now, but everything else about her was different.

Never had he seen a woman so cursed. The excessive dresses had become a disease. Her greedy beauty had eaten itself.

As he stared at her, she saw him looking and looked back, but there was no recognition in her huge eyes.

"She's forgotten me," Raji thought, and moved closer to re-impress himself upon her in the crush.

Four elephants had been brought to take the British party down to their boats on the river, but their owners wouldn't make them kneel for the memsahibs to mount.

The Mrs Whites; both malnourished, one with a head wound, one with a screaming baby; had to mount the beast by climbing up its tail. Victoria held hands with Eliza and didn't even try.

Most of the garrison were walking the mile from their flattened barracks to the banks of the Ganges in bare feet. Victoria got into step and walked with her little sister.

Raji appeared beside her with his sword drawn. She still did not seem to remember him, but there were so many people come to see the English go. The dirt road was lined with black faces, looking at the state of the ladies and gents who had lorded it over them.

"Your father is dead?" Raji asked Victoria.

"Yes," she replied, looking straight ahead.

The procession was shuffling slowly as a funeral; the bodies of those who'd used their clothes for bandages were burning in the sun.

"And your mother?"

"They are together," she said.

He wanted to make her look at him.

"Your ugly little brother?" he asked.

Victoria turned to Raji then, and he saw that she had every remembrance of their earlier meetings.

"Your weapons didn't hurt me," she whispered. "Do you think your words will?" Her coolness so aroused Raji's fury that his sword jerked in his hand.

"The battle isn't over yet," he hissed back.

"But the war is won." Victoria marched on bleeding soles. "I have conquered myself," she said, "while you are still as angry with everyone as you were before."

"Not everyone," he said. "Only you."

A commotion in front of them stopped him going any further. One of the British officers, stumbling along with his wife, had been tormented the whole journey by native soldiers lately of his regiment. They were taunting him with his favourite sayings from the old days on parade.

"All ship-shape and Bristol fashion now, boy?" the *sepoys* cried with glee. "All Bristol fashion and ship-shape now?"

Until finally, unarmed as he was, the officer turned on them, and was run through by their several swords.

"Give us your money and we'll spare your life," the rebels said to his wife.

She fumbled for the gold ring she'd knotted into the shreds of her clothes and handed it over, only to have the hand cut off and, before she could protest, the head.

Even Raji, with all his warrior training, reeled slightly as the lady was killed; but Victoria didn't flinch. He looked away, and realised that she didn't.

She has seen more dead women than me, Raji thought, and took a step back from the aura swarming around her like flies. Victoria stepped onward, through a pool of blood, making footprints of it along the path the officer and his wife would not walk.

Their bodies, almost skeletons already, were left for the crowds to pick over. Everyone from beggars to bazaar traders were looking for hidden riches the soldiers might have missed; just as the entrenchment was now being dug up for watches and money boxes the English had buried.

Such was their interest, the locals slowed down the leaving procession till they could see it all, in single file. The old, the lame, and the raving mad were yet in sight of the trenches, when the lead elephant containing the General and his family arrived at the docks.

They'd been promised forty boats, but there were only fourteen. They'd been promised cargoes of grain and goats, but no food and drink was to be seen; though the crews had lit cooking fires in the ships' clay ovens.

To the feverish refugees the Indian boats looked like little English cottages with their thatched roofs, moored in the shallows; and there was a great rush to board them.

"Victoria! Eliza! Over here!" called the young Mrs White, and she helped the sisters up the side of one precarious craft. The new mother smiled for the first time. "I met a lady on our elephant who has milk. She lost her own baby but, look, she is feeding mine!"

And there was the little darling, silent for once, swallowing the milk tears of a bereaved mother's breast.

More women and children waded knee deep in the water and struggled up the sides of the boat to claim a space in the shade, though the vessel quickly became overcrowded and most had to sit on the deck, blistering in the sun.

The men on board began to voice their misgivings about whether the boat would actually float.

"I say, old chaps, are you going to get this thing off the sand?" Colonel White asked the crew, who looked edgy and glanced sideways at the bank where the stream of people kept flowing.

*Sati Chowra* was a picturesque fishing village, a favourite place for officers and ladies on their morning rides in happier times. The temple had steps that ran down to the river in the rainy season, but sitting there now, high, dry and mighty, was the *Mahratta*. It was to the new king that the boatmen were looking.

And on his signal, instead of setting sail, the crew set fire to the boat's thatched awnings with coals from the cooking fires, threw their oars overboard and leapt into the water.

On his signal, before all the boatmen had reached the shore, the Indian Army opened fire. Again. Or had there not been a ceasefire, at all?

Had the promise of safe passage to Allahabad been a false one? The last four hundred survivors of the siege looked at each other in disbelief. Had the enemy they'd trusted, the enemy who'd been on their side ever since they crossed the boundaries of India, lied?

Colonel White used a very unEnglish word; a word with Viking horns, Saxon attitude, and Roman conjunctions.

"The fuckers have tricked us," he said.

The last four hundred women and children and wounded soldiers were getting shot at from both sides of the river, and their boats were ablaze.


Crouching in the reeds with his musket in spasms like a lover in his arms, Raji looked into the smoke for the silhouette of Victoria Newcombe on one of the burning decks.

He'd lost her in the rush at the water's edge, but later thought he saw her hauling her little sister up the side of a boat. Raji strained to see her outline amongst the shapes that dithered in the flames. Mothers were throwing their children into the river then jumping in after them, only to drown them under waterlogged skirts.

He shot at anyone who obviously wasn't her, men mostly, swimming strongly after the one boat that managed to get away, though it was only wallowing from sandbank to sandbank, overloaded and under heavy fire.

When the first wave of shooting was finished, Raji splashed into the shallow water; the spare shot between his teeth made it look as if he was smiling. The water was already turning into a soup of skinny corpses but none of them were Victoria.

He swam a couple of strokes to get his clothes wet, then boarded the first of the smouldering boats to find her, killing anyone else that wasn't dead yet. He jumped off the deck on the other side, straight into a group of screaming females.

They were sheltered by the burning hulk from the rebel army's attack and just out of reach of the cannons firing from the far side; but a fearsome Hindoo warrior splashed into the water between them.

"Victoria Newcombe?" he said.

They stared at him stupidly, as if he wasn't speaking English.

"Victoria Newcombe?" he asked again.

Then one of them got it, eyes widening in surprise as she understood him.

"Where is she?" Raji snarled through his teeth-full of bullets.

Before the woman could speak, she was stabbed with a short blade from behind. Fountaining blood she sunk below the surface, leaving the child she was holding to flounder, and follow; and Raji was left face to face with one of his own kind.

The First Native Infantry had got behind the British boats; and were breaking down the boundaries between flesh and fire, metal and bone, blood and water. For nearly an hour the unnatural mingling continued. Only when there were no more women screaming, no more men swimming, did the Indian soldiers stop fighting; and the powerful currents of the mother Ganges separated the forces of nature again. Fires were extinguished and flesh was afloat. The bullets had sunk to the bottom.

Raji was still splashing frantically, searching the shallows and the reed beds near the bank. He had killed many people but none of them were Victoria, and he hadn't seen anyone else kill her either, though he'd been looking in all directions with a hundred eyes in his desperation to find her.

Then a cry went up from the steps of the temple.

"The *Mahratta* wants the survivors," was the command. "No men, just women and children. Round up the prisoners and lead them back to the city."

Raji redoubled his efforts on the river bank, rolling over bodies which lay face down in the mud; some of which, despite gunshot wounds, gashes and guts-full of water, were still alive; though none of them said thank you as he dragged them up to dry in the midday sun.

He ran through the dunes, scything the long grass with his sword. Other soldiers were finding drowned rat-faced fugitives. She had to be here somewhere.

When he found her, squatting in a damp depression that smelled of some animal's shit, with her little sister and a couple of other silly girls, he raised his sword with a triumphant cry that had nothing to do with the actual battle. It was beyond race or gender, outside of history.

He quickly changed it to '*Deen*! For the Faith!' but Victoria wasn't convinced. She saw his sword flash in the sun, and his eyes reflect the anger at its edge.

"I knew you couldn't die without saying goodbye," Raji added, but he said it in a language she wouldn't understand.

Proudly the soldier led his women and children up from the river; but they were the clever ones. They'd survived the siege, the burning ships, the mother of all rivers and the men with swords. Now they joined with the hundred other prisoners of fate, who had stayed alive without really trying.

All the rest were dead; three hundred mothers, brothers, fathers and sons; and the strangers they'd been sharing rooms with in conditions of hitherto unthinkable intimacy.

Their bodies were now lying in the water, waiting to be stripped of identification and shoved out into the current to flow downstream to the anonymous grave of the sea.

"Where is she?" someone was crying. It was Mrs White's daughter-in-law, though there was no more Mrs White. "I can't find my baby. Oh Victoria, help me!"

Liberty was with the wet nurse whose face her mother had barely looked at, so glad was she to see breasts full of milk. But they'd been separated in the fire. Now in the crowd of women who were left she couldn't recognise the generous features of the lady who might have saved her tiny baby.

"I need her," the young Mrs White cried weakly. "Victoria, help me."

But Victoria stopped her friend stepping out of the line that was now being marched back to the city.

"We're prisoners," she whispered. "If your baby is not with us, she is free."

Arm in arm they walked, with armed men on either side; and Victoria

73

didn't have to look round to know that the one behind her was Raji. His look was touching her skin.

Gone was her crinoline. It dressed the wounds of somebody who'd died. Gone was her petticoat. She was wearing nothing but a bodice and bloomers; ripped, wet, burnt and bloody. She was wearing trousers like a man of war.

Beside her, Eliza was completely naked, though she had somehow managed to keep on a dripping sun hat. And young Mrs White wore her dead husband's dress shirt, and tore at her hair in despair.

"I want my baby," she cried.

Victoria held her arm tighter and whispered again;

"Remember what you called her. Let her go."

He couldn't hear what she said, but Raji heard the control in her voice; and thought, just for a moment, that she might be a warrior too.

Then he shoved her with the butt of his gun to make himself stop thinking that.


The Victorian ladies were taken to the *Bibighar*; a dingy bungalow that had once belonged to an English officer's dusky mistress. Now the new Indian king held more than a hundred white women captive there.

The rooms were so small they could not all sleep at once. Some of the ladies who still had their wits about them organised a rota, though there were no mattresses or pillows on which to lie down. Those who still wore their stays took them off and strung them up to make hammocks for the babies.

That first night, the rains came; rains that would have washed their entrenchment clean away if they'd come one day sooner. The timing of the monsoon seemed to say that someone was looking down on the bedraggled ladies of the house.

The *Bibighar* was built around a courtyard, and it was there that the armed guard sat under a *mulsuri* tree, smoking hookahs and drinking tea. Raji was the first to volunteer for the post. The view of the prisoners through the glass doors of the veranda was unsurpassed. He could watch Victoria's every move.

Inside the building the women were cutting off each other's long hair with nail scissors. They were combing out the lice; and taking turns to read from the Bibles they'd saved from the fire and the water. A sort of religious fervour was spreading through the overcrowded rooms, along with the cholera.

When Victoria's time came to read aloud she refused to take the book.

"I'd rather pray to the 78th Highlanders for deliverance," she said.

But with gasps and giggles the others said she should read from the good book; it would be better. They all seemed to know which bits to choose; prophets to bring retribution on the savages that held Christian ladies captive.

Victoria just started reading where the flimsy pages fell open on her lap, as she sat on the dirt floor of an old whore house.

It was Isaiah. It said:

*Go down, sit in the dust, O virgin daughter of Babylon, sit on the ground without a throne. No more will you be called tender and delicate. Take millstones and grind meal; take off your veil. Lift up your skirts, bare your legs, and wade through the river. Thy nakedness shall be uncovered, and thy shame shall be seen.*

*Sit in silence, go into darkness, O daughter of the Babylonians: no more will you be called Queen of the kingdoms.*

When Victoria finished reading there was a stunned silence. All that could be heard was the rain. Then young Mrs White noticed that Raji and another guard had come from the courtyard and were sheltering on the veranda with their faces pressed right up against the windows to the women's room.

She snatched the Bible from Victoria's hands and flipping quickly through the pages found what she wanted to shout at them:

*The lord trieth the righteous, but the wicked and him that loveth violence his soul hateth. Upon the wicked he shall rain snares, fire and brimstone, and a horrible tempest.*

The Indians couldn't hear what she was saying through the thick glass and the horrible tempest; and the righteous souls inside in the room weren't listening. Victoria's last sentence was still resonating; no more will you be called Queen of the kingdoms.

This was a prophesy that had come true. They were almost naked, and they did have to grind their own flour.

Every day a woman called the Begum came to supervise them in cooking *chupatties* and washing soiled clothes. She led small groups out into the courtyard where they learned to squat like natives on the bare earth as they pounded the last of their lawns and linens with stones.

The *Begum* was nobility; the *Mahratta's* sister, they thought. She was tall and haughty, but she always looked down.

"As if she feels worse than we do," said her hungry prisoners, who sat and ate the open air.

Though the atmosphere in the walled courtyard was not exactly fresh, it made Victoria's head spin each time she was allowed out of their close quarters.

After a week of captivity half the women and children inside were dying of cholera, and the main symptom was diarrhoea. There was one privy in the building, but most victims were in no position to stand and queue, making do with a pot or bucket where they lay.

So Victoria leant against a marble pillar at the edge of the courtyard and breathed in air that tasted pure, even with its taint of smoke from the ever-burning hookahs under the *mulsuri* tree. Raji was there as usual too. He stood up rather unsteadily when he saw her, and his lips moved as if he would speak but couldn't think of anything to say.

"Good afternoon," Victoria said, with a nod.

Now Raji was simply open-mouthed. Of all things he had not expected her to be polite. Ever since they'd met she had only interrogated him or ignored him, till he thought their encounters would never be anything but games for her, no matter which of their peoples were in power.

"The more you are treated like an animal, the more you become human," he said.

Victoria went and crouched next to the young Mrs White, who had once been among the finest society ladies in London, and started milling the flour for their bread.

"My dear, how did you keep your temper with him?" said Mrs White.

"I just thought of what the 78th Highlanders will do when they get here," Victoria replied.

Over her shoulder, Raji stabbed his sword into the trunk of the tree. Once again he couldn't hear what the woman was whispering, and he didn't like not knowing the words. It made him feel impotent.

He sat down again and drew angrily on the hookah. At least the smoke kept the mosquitoes at bay. The back of Victoria's neck was studded with red bites. How did she keep so quiet? The girl next to her was about to have another attack of the vapours.

"…too late, too late!" the young Mrs White's voice was rising. "My husband, his Mama and Papa, and our precious baby: everyone I loved in the world has gone before. Ah, why must I still endure?"

Suddenly Victoria's little sister called her from the veranda. Though frail, Eliza had been happy in their unhealthy new home, even managing to play checkers with bits of broken pottery on the few spare inches of floor space; but now she was looking pale.

"I don't feel well," she shouted. "A stomach ache."

Victoria rose to her feet, but the *Begum* rapped her down with a sharp voice. Prisoners of war did not come and go as they pleased.

"Victoria, come," Eliza moaned again.

"Go inside, please," Victoria called calmly, "I'm making the bread, but I'll be back soon."

She did not sound unduly worried, but an unleaven feeling settled in her stomach and stayed there till the shift was over. Then, instead of lingering with the others in the evening air she ran back into the building to find her sister, sick. The symptoms of cholera, the smell, the stains, were unmistakable.

That night, although Victoria did not believe in God any more, she prayed for him to send the 78th Highlanders.

It took them another week to arrive. The legendary Scots battalion was making its way slowly along the Grand Trunk Road from Allahabad, stopping to vent its wrath at every village the soldiers came to. Burnt houses, and black men hanging in the mango groves, marked the path they'd trod.

The rebel-held city was quaking at their approach. Its native army blew up all the bridges they would cross and lay in ambush behind every tree they would pass; but no cunning and no *karma* could beat the sheer brute force of the 78th Highlanders.

The women in the stronghold heard them coming, as did the new king on his shaky throne. The same sound made the women feel stronger, and the *Mahratta* weaker. The Scottish gunfire was getting closer.

Raji and the other soldiers who had guarded the *Bibighar* prisoners were summoned before the king. The order was to take the women out and shoot them.

"You must kill them all," he decreed, "or else they will incriminate you. They are the evidence."

So the soldiers rushed back to the bungalow but the women refused to be budged. With new guts the English ladies linked their skinny arms together and formed a glorious mass.

Half of them were sick, and they were all half-starved, but the soldiers couldn't shift them.

"Three cheers for our pluck!" cried the ladies as the soldiers left. "Hoorah! Hoorah!"

"And hoorah for the 78th Highlanders," said Victoria, cradling the body of her mother's youngest daughter, who was still clinging to life.

But their Scottish saviours were a day away, doing battle at the city walls. The women started writing their names on the walls of their room. And the Indian soldiers were lining up outside the *Bibighar* with new orders from their officer.

"Fire through the windows," the *Subahdar* said. "If they won't come out, we'll shoot them in there."

Raji's heart started to beat faster and he stepped up to the window with a rush of blood in his head. He was going to kill her. Victoria Newcombe, Captain's daughter, would die by his hand.

His whole life had been training for this moment; and this is why his aim had to be true. No boyhood, no girlfriends; he'd given it all to be sure that when the *sepoys* fired their guns into the crowd of women, his would be the bullet-hole in Victoria's heart.

Raji could hardly contain his joy. But the other men were muttering glumly, shaking their heads and shuffling their feet in the dirt.

"We're soldiers," said one, "not assassins. We fight with men, we don't kill defenceless women."

"We won't do it," they all started to say.

Except Prince Raji.

"I will," he said.

But he couldn't do it all on his own, so the *Begum* asked her bodyguard boyfriend to get some help. He ran off into the fallen city and came back with two *Musselmen* butchers wielding swords.

As the sun was setting, the four men went into the house of women. Standing in the doorway, Raji unsheathed his sword and stared into the gloom. White ladies all looked the same in their grey undergarments and shaved heads. Which one was she?

White ladies all look the same when they're standing protectively in front of their children, or falling at the feet of the men who've come to kill them, lifting up their hands to save their heads.

Losing their hands, losing their heads; white ladies, so refined, who haven't had a bath in months. Now there was going to be a bloodbath.

It happened so quickly, the butchers had no time to prepare. Their swords were not sharp, and their blows were not clean. They wouldn't kill animals so slowly.

But then, the beasts didn't speak to them in a language they could understand: for pity! Spare our children, they're as innocent as your own.

The butchers were bachelors, and the *Begum*'s boyfriend had no offspring either, they had no innocence of their own. Raji would never have children; neither would Victoria.

He was determined to find her. No other man must get to her first, for he had to be the one to hear her final word, catch her last breath, swallow it and be the rib cage of her soul for ever.

Raji stilled a raised sword; prolonging another woman's life, though only for a second, to make sure it wasn't Victoria's. He got under the butchers' feet, as they went about their kill.

Never had sheep huddled so panic stricken in the corners of a slaughterhouse, or horses made such frantic bolts for the door. Never had cows bellowed their outrage so loudly; and only if the squealing creatures had been pigs would the Muslim butchers have let them go.

But they were just women and children who used to be pink-cheeked, and who once had pigtails.

"I presume you are looking for me," said Victoria, raising her voice over the screams.

She appeared suddenly at Raji's right hand, and he almost dropped his sword in surprise. Close up, the curves he always told her by were not so evident. She stood straight, and thin as an elephant's tail.

He lifted his sword, and said;

"Are you ready to die?"

"Not until you say why you're so angry with me," Victoria replied.

He raised his sword.

"Please!" She was begging him. The other women were too; but she knew that Raji wasn't killing indiscriminately like the other men.

"Why is it only me?" she shouted.

She was a fighter accepting her fate; exactly the sort of woman a warrior would want for a wife, Raji thought.

If only she wasn't white, though she didn't even look so white, anymore; in the bloody gloaming everything was the colour of his family fortress.

If only she wasn't a Christian, though she wasn't clutching a Bible like some of them were, or speaking its verses in a quivering tongue.

The books were getting torn in the struggle, pages flying around them like stained doves, ink printed and painted with blood.

Everything was fluttering, slashing, staggering; everything was moving, except the people who were dead already.

And Raji and Victoria, who were in the still centre of the chaos, as if they didn't belong to it; as if they were not black and white, not man and woman, not embodied at all.

"Tell me why," she said.

"I can't." His sword was reaching its highest point. "My head doesn't know why. And my heart cannot answer in words. Only in actions."

"Your heart is angry with me?" Victoria said. "What nonsense. Why, because I came to live in your land?"

"You have to die," Raji was bracing himself, "because of what you did in your own land." He wasn't looking at her face.

He had to summon up the strength to act, whether as Victoria's slayer or her saviour it didn't matter, for only God knew the whole story. He raised his voice in a *sanskrit* prayer, and raised his *Kshatriya* sword.

The butchers had blunted their swords on women's bones, and the *Begum*'s boyfriend had broken his completely; but Raji's was still sharp.

One cut severed Victoria's head. It flew across the room and landed in a pile of corpses with the young Mrs White and Eliza; stirring them with a whispered goodbye and a kiss.

Her body toppled in a moment's death, more kindly than any other woman's or child's in *kismat* house.

As he watched the blood gush from her neck, Raji felt an uprush of emotions, an equal fountain that could blow his own head off.

Surging across the room he lashed out now at any woman still standing; not to kill her, though this was the effect; just to relieve the feelings that overpowered the sword in his hand. And the anger that had no words in his language was let like blood from the foreigner's bodies.


When there was no more sound but dripping on the floor of the old whore house, the four men went back outside.

Not two hours had passed since they entered, and the sun hadn't quite set in the sky; so everyone who had gathered to witness the spectacle, from king's men on elephants to bazaar boys who'd climbed the high walls, could clearly see the blood which covered the exhausted slaughterers.

But those who kept watch as night set in heard groans from within, groans which said the massacre was not finished; women and children were still alive in the *bibighar*, unless it was their ghosts complaining.

They waited till dawn, then sent in the cleaners; low-caste men who didn't have the sensitivity, or didn't have the choice, to be disturbed by the sight that greeted them. Then the bodies were dragged out for everyone else to see; barely recognisable as Brittania's gentle housewives abroad.

Everyone saw them except Raji. He was hiding from the *Musselmen*, who'd sworn to finish him off with the butcher's swords he'd kept getting in the way of.

English women smell like meat cooking, if they're left out in the sun for too long. The cleaners were ordered to bury the corpses quickly in a well in the garden. They went in on top of each other, but the deep hole was filling up fast, and half of them had to be bisected to fit.

One fat lady and two small children were still alive. The children were crying at the mouth of the well, where they'd seen their mothers go. The fat lady had lost her legs, and was propped up against the rim, begging for her body to follow.

The burial party threw her in. They threw the children in too, and the last few corpses on top; then everybody ran away.

Everybody ran away, and left the well to a fly-buzzing silence, and flesh-settling stillness; but only for a little while.

For it was only a little while later that the 78th Highlanders turned up, too late to save the day.

When they kicked down the doors of the *bibighar* and walked in, they were ankle deep in blood; it came to the top of their boots. Half submerged in the gory morass they saw tiny shoes and torn lace collars, pages of the Bible and scraps of paper with the names mothers had pinned to their children's clothes. What the women had written on the walls had already been washed off.

The tartan fighting machines, fuelled almost entirely by rum, wept tears they could ill afford. Dehydrated and in despair they sat under the mulsuri tree and swore to avenge the mass murder.

Their General didn't let them rest there. He got them to work right away, rounding up everyone who had anything to do with the massacre and making them pay.

And of course, the first Indian soldier they caught was Raji. The Hindoo prince looked like any other shady native to the 78th Highlanders. He was still loitering on the *bibighar* premises, watching the well; feeling like the children who'd seen their mother's bodies thrown into its foetid hole.

He'd lost Victoria, who'd been growing in his mind ever since she'd arrived at the garrison with her tiny waist. He had never touched her, never laid a finger on her, even when he was killing her; but now he couldn't let her go.

He should have just walked away from the well and gone home; but nothing, his own mother, their firm stone fort, or the regime of his *vedic* master had the pull of a dead English girl.

He was sick. That's what the 78th Highlanders thought of the *sepoy* they caught at the sucking well; sick, and they may well have been right. But sicker still was the punishment their General dreamed up for him, and all the other soldiers found in the vicinity that day.

Before they were hung the Indian men were forced to clean the floor of the *bibighar*, with their tongues. Each one of them had to lick a square foot of bloody matting until it was spotless.

Many were Brahmins, who'd refused to shoot the women through the windows of the house. The blood would break their caste. Raji already had women's blood on his hands; but down on his knees he experienced the greatest degradation a man can know.

The stains they removed from the floor would stay on their souls. White soldiers watched with satisfaction as the rebels gagged on their last meal. But when it was time to hang, they were surprised how easily the men went.

"They're nae afraid of dying," the 78th Highlanders said. "They face it like an old friend!"

And though they hung a thousand of the enemy, for each of their women and children was avenged ten times over, not a single one struggled or showed any fear. As they strung the native bodies from the trees, the Scotsmen were sure that they had won; but the way the other side met with defeat made them wonder. Could they see the whole war?

Buried in a bush, swinging from a *pepil* tree; Raji was dead and the green leaves covered him.

They settled on his shoulders, now that he had settled his anger. They fell on his head, now that he felt ashamed.

# Renee

Renee was born of war. A soldier's daughter; she wasn't fighting for one side or the other, but for what was left when the battle had been lost and won.

A shell-shock baby, she took a long time to come.

Renee's mother and father got married just before the war broke out; but they didn't have Renee until seven years after it was over.

There was a photograph of their wedding day on the mantelpiece. They were both looking past the photographer as if the first bomb were about to drop behind him.

Mum had a small bunch of flowers and one bridesmaid. They were wearing frocks with no frills, not really wedding dresses at all.

"Things were already rather tight," she explained to Renee.

Daddy went straight off to fight. Mummy worked in a tank factory and wore trousers, so they didn't have Renee then. The war lasted for six years, but when Daddy came back again they still didn't have Renee.

"Couldn't sleep in a double bed. He wasn't half the man he was," Mum told the lady who lived next door, when she didn't know Renee was listening.

She always said hello to Mrs Ramsey as they hung out their washing, and one of them usually ended up in tears.

"Which half of Daddy was missing?" Renee asked Mummy, as she helped to fold the sheets and towels. "Was it shot off?"

Mother said that it was a part of speech not a part of his body.

"You shouldn't have been listening, Renee," she said. "We were having an adult conversation."

She always had adult conversations with Mrs Ramsey. They stood one on each side of the garden wall, both sipping from their teacups, but Mummy didn't have tea in hers. She had sherry.

The grass on their side grew so long that in the summer it reached the washing hung on the line. The hem of Mummy's nightdress, and the cuffs of Daddy's trousers touched the grass heads and got covered in seed.

"My husband won't do it," Mum said, over the wall. "Says the lawn mower sounds like death throes of a soldier with his throat cut."

She didn't realise Renee heard it too. Renee was quiet when the washing was on the line, watching it hanging like bodies in a row. It always reminded her of something she could never remember; no matter how long she strung herself out in the grass.

But she wasn't so quiet indoors. It was dark inside their house, because Daddy kept the curtains shut, and sat by the wireless, very close so he could hear its whisper. Renee liked to hear it too, especially *Listen With Mother*, though she knew Mummy wasn't actually listening.

Renee liked to sing along to the music; but Dad tried to turn her voice down.

"Shut up!" he would shout. "The Hun will hear you!"

Mummy sat at the other end of the settee, drinking sherry from a teacup and knitting. She was always knitting jumpers for Renee, and they were always too tight round the neck.

At first the new jumpers just gave Renee a sore throat, but when she grew a bit bigger they made her choke. Mummy said she could never see the knitting pattern in the dark because Daddy had the curtains closed, but Mrs Ramsey said it was due to the tension.

"How did you and him ever beget that child?" she asked Mummy over the garden wall.

"It was a bloody miracle," Mum replied. It was late afternoon and she'd been drinking tea all day. The shadow of the overgrown white lilac at the bottom of the garden had nearly reached the house, and Renee was up to her neck in flowers.

"You see, I keep sherry indoors, for medicinal purposes," Mum said, "and the silly twit got hold of it. He did feel better for a bit; I could almost see my old man winking at me again. But while we were about it, he decided that I was the enemy and he stabbed me to death."

"No!" gasped Mrs Ramsey, on her side of the fence.

"Yes," said Mummy, "but I didn't care, because it started a new life in me, the child I'd longed for ever since we were married."

"And that was the only time?" asked Mrs Ramsey.

"The only time," said Mum. "War took all the love out of him, save the seed that made my daughter."

Renee saw the next door neighbour nod her head, along with the nodding heads of the lilacs. The sun setting on the pollen-heavy air made everything look precious.

But when they went indoors it was dark and Daddy was hiding behind his armchair because there had been something with bombs and bullets on the radio.

"Get down!" he motioned frantically, when he saw them. With another gesture, Mummy sent Renee up to bed.

The next day it was Renee's fourth birthday, and the whole family went on an outing, a bus trip to the seaside.

Daddy looked old-fashioned next to the other fathers, in his war coat and hat, and he smelled like a ghost. Mummy sat next to him on the bus, so Renee had to sit with the other children.

One of the boys gave her a jammy dodger like they never had at home; but one of the girls said Renee's parents were jerry-atrics.

When they got to the beach everyone piled out of the bus and went to lay on the sand or play in the sea. It was a hot day and the beach was crowded. Renee's mother found a space for the picnic basket and her flask of tea; then they all sat down and Renee took off her shoes and socks. She was allowed to paddle.

When she ran back from the water's edge, with salty feet and seaweed between her toes, Mummy said it was time to go.

Daddy was shouting at the top of his voice, and all the people who had been on the bus with them were staring as he took Renee's bucket and spade that were meant for building castles with, and started to dig trenches in the sand.

Sand was flying into people's lunches, as Daddy shouted that the planes were overhead.

"It's time to go," Mum said again, and steered him through the crowds of holidaymakers on the beach, back to where the bus was parked.

Renee trailed behind, watching the other children putting on their swim-suits ready for a dip. One of their mothers hurried up to Renee's to find out what the matter was.

"Dunkirk, that's what," said Mummy tightly, and holding Daddy by the hand, led him and Renee onto the empty bus.

They sat there all afternoon, looking out of the windows at the crowded beach.

"The boats must be coming," Daddy kept saying. "The boats must be coming soon."

Renee was hot in her new birthday jumper, with a neck so tight she got a sore throat. She watched the children running around in their bathing costumes, dripping wet on the yellow sand, until it was time for tea.

Mummy unpacked the meat paste sandwiches and slices of Battenburg cake she'd wrapped in paper doilies. Renee swallowed them quickly in big lumps; but it took ages for the rest of the party to finish their hard-boiled eggs and ginger beer on the beach.

The sun was setting by the time they all climbed on board the bus, chattering loudly. They stopped when they saw the war-torn family sitting there. No one spoke to her mother and father, and no one sat in the empty seat next to Renee.

She fell asleep on the way home; and the next day, and the day after that, even when she wasn't wearing the new jumper, Renee's throat was sore. After three days she started to feel hot all the time; as if she were still on the bus in a woolly pullover, watching through the windows as other children swam in the sea.

Then Renee started swimming too. Everything was underwater. *Listen With Mother* sounded like the wireless had sunk. She badly needed a snorkel. Mummy put her to bed and called a doctor.

"What's the matter with her?" Mummy asked the doctor.

"Diphtheria, that's what," the doctor replied.

Renee didn't know what diphtheria was, but then she didn't know what Dunkirk was either, or which part of her Daddy was missing.

It seemed that she would die asking questions.

"Where did I come from, Mummy? Where will I go to? Will you hang me on the washing line with your nightdress? Will you hide me under the white lilac?"

"Ssshh," said Mummy.

"What will you and Daddy do without me? Will the world still be?"

Mummy, who had been swigging sherry by the bedside all day and all night, burst into tears.

"No, dear," she said. "If you die, the world will end. If you die, I'll want to be buried too. And Daddy... Daddy can go to blazes."

Later, when her mother had fallen asleep in her chair, and Renee was slowly breathing her finite supply of air, her father came into the bedroom.

A new dawn was showing round the edges of the always closed curtains, and although he didn't like the light, Daddy went and opened them. His wince turned into a smile as he turned back to Renee.

"Look at that, old girl," he said. "The sun's coming up." Then he left her room and returned to the darkness of his own.

Renee followed the sun's path across the sky with her eyes, but when it reached its highest peak they stuck. Her eyes were heaven bound. Mummy woke to find Renee paralysed, just as the doctor had said, and was so upset that she didn't know whether it was dark or light, day or night.

She called the doctor again, and even, in desperation, the next door neighbour.

Mrs Ramsey had never set foot in the house in all the years they'd known her. They'd barely ever seen her legs, behind the garden wall; but now she walked into the room with a bunch of the flowers that grew equally on both sides of their fence so no one knew whose side the roots were on.

White lilac: Renee's last gasps of air smelled of that, but sounded like this;

"No! She can't go! One chance in my whole life to make a child, and she came. It was a miracle, but she came. Surely she can't be taken from me now."

"I think you'd better prepare yourself for the worst," whispered Mrs Ramsey, taking off her shawl and placing it over Renee.

"No," cried Mummy. "She can't die. She's only four years old. I waited for her three times as long as that!"

Renee tried to ask who they were talking about. It couldn't be her. She was fast becoming someone who didn't need to breathe in and out like the seconds, the days or the years they were talking about.

She was more like the fragrance of the flowers; something to be breathed.

But her mother was suffocating.

"Don't go, don't die," she cried.

Renee tried not to. It must be a bad thing, a very unhappy ending; but her throat was closing, and there was no more air to spare.

One last question was left on her lips. The sadness of Mummy's last kiss gave her the answer. There is no life after death.

# Beck

Rebecca was colouring in the quiet room. She was sitting uncomfortably on a child-sized chair, but she had been there all morning, keeping the strokes of crayon between the black lines.

Beck was colouring a Christmas tree, in the middle of summer. She was a grown woman, with a part-time job at her son's nursery school.

Alf wasn't one of the quiet children sitting at the little table with her. He was one of the handful of sounds they could hear from the playground; the screech of tricycle wheels and grazed knees, the shush of thrown sand and over-watered sunflowers.

Alfie rarely sat still long enough to colour anything in, which is why most of the art stuck on their fridge door was his mum's. It was voluntary work, Tuesday and Thursday mornings; but these sessions at the nursery school were the most relaxing times of Beck's week.

It wasn't just chunky crayons. There were slim coloured pencils, and sensuous felt-tip pens. There was even glitter glue that gave relief from the grim reality of every day.

The colouring table was a place where red and blue were the characters, purple and gold the personalities. Beck's best friend there was a deaf boy called Jack. There was complete silence between them. The pictures did the talking, and Beck always left feeling peaceful.

She was proud of the Christmas tree she'd done this morning. She had used every shade of green on the table, with finger-pricking detail to the needles. Beck folded the picture up carefully and put it in her handbag. She didn't want any of the teachers to see what she'd done, but she would show Alfie when he came home at tea-time.

Her son wouldn't wonder why she'd drawn a Christmas tree in June. He'd just make a great display with sellotape and scissors; sticking the picture up on the side of the fridge, with his tongue sticking out of the side of his mouth.

Beck made the sign that meant 'lunchtime' to Jack. He put his picture in a tiny rucksack and took his lunchbox out. Through the opaque sides of Jack's container Beck could see carrot sticks and an apple, the crisp colours and clear outlines of a still life.

She could never guess the subject of Jack's art, and didn't have sophisticated enough sign language to ask; but she could tell from a glance at Jack's lunch-box that his mother had a healthier relationship with him than she had with Alfie, who demanded jam sandwiches every day and always got what he wanted.

She led the quiet children to the dining room, and found Alfie standing on his chair with a giant smile.

"Mummy! Mum!" he shouted, "I'm Superman! And he's Spider-man and he's Batman," Alf pointed out his sidekicks with a crisp, "and we're going to have a big fight!"

"Well, just make sure you don't hurt each other," said Beck, sitting him down.

"Okay, we won't," said Alfie, "but everyone has to die except me!"

"I'll see you at tea-time, then," said Beck, smoothing her son's wild hair.

"Okay, bye," said Alf.

Jack had found himself a seat at the lunch table and Beck patted his neat head too, then waved goodbye to the staff on duty who raised their mugs in a salute of thanks across the noisy dining room.

As she left school the smell of the art class was still in her nostrils; the wax of the crayons had a relaxing effect. But the short walk home through the summer suburbs brought Beck's usual state of panic rushing back.

The gardens were in bloom, and over every fence was sprawling lilac, white as you like, with a smell so subtle it could be the air itself. She was never sure if she was breathing it in or out; but with each gasp Beck felt the return of a guilt she lived with, and a shame she couldn't name except to call it normal.

The calm time spent colouring evergreen was forgotten in the pollen cloud, and the first thing she did when she got home was telephone her doctor. Beck didn't need to look up the number in a book.

"It's an emergency," she panted into the phone. There was a pause as the receptionist asked her why.

"I can't breathe," she replied.

Dr Lacey sat at her desk between a plastic skeleton and a computer. She looked up from the screen as Beck entered the surgery and raised an eyebrow but not a smile.

"How can I help you?" she said.

"It's my throat," said Beck, clutching it.

The doctor consulted her VDU.

"Slightly sore again, is it?" she asked.

Beck nodded.

"Open wide," said Doctor Lacey, reaching for a torch. "I'll have a look inside. Say Aaah."

Beck said it.

"No," said the doctor, clicking off the torch abruptly, "I still can't see anything."

You haven't looked hard enough, Beck shouted silently. There's a lump, and it's growing.

"Are you sure?" she whispered aloud.

"Quite sure," said the doctor, tapping notes on her keyboard. "Looks perfectly normal."

Are you blind? Beck's mind was screaming. It's a tumor. Highly malignant!

"Anything else?" asked the doctor.

"Er, yes," muttered Beck, "if it was, you know, something serious…"

Doctor Lacey's expression remained unconcerned. Did Beck have to spell it out for her?

"…If it was, you know, the C-Word," she continued, "how would I tell?"

"You'd have a lump in your throat." The doctor's delivery was deadpan.

"Okay, thank you," Beck whispered, getting off her chair and backing out of the room. "Thanks," she said again quietly, but the voice in her head roared, I HAVE GOT A LUMP IN MY THROAT!

As she went through the door, the pressure changed; somehow the outside and the inside shifted, and Beck found herself saying what she was thinking.

"No," she burst back into the doctor's surgery, "I'm sorry, but I'm not satisfied with your diagnosis. I demand a second opinion."

Doctor Lacey sighed. She should have known that, for a chronic hypochondriac, the woman was got rid of too quickly.

Her case history, glowing on the screen, said there'd already been extensive counselling, or the doctor would have recommended that. All she could do instead, after a few terse words over the intercom, was to say to Beck:

"Doctor Comfort can see you quickly. He's a locum, standing in for my colleague next door."

"Thank you, oh thank you!" Beck was bright red now, with gratitude and embarrassment. She could tell Doctor Lacey was angry with her. She probably wouldn't be able to come here ever again; but then, Doctor Comfort would probably take one look at her and call an ambulance.

Beck knocked on the next door. A voice said 'Come in'. One hand moved involuntarily to her throat as she opened the door, clutching it tightly as she saw the man sitting there, so tightly she couldn't reply to his friendly 'Hello', so tightly she started to cry.

Beck stood in the doorway, looking at Doctor Comfort with streaming eyes and a snotty nose.

He looked back.

"Mrs Salmon?" he said.

She let out a drowning sound.

"Would you like to sit down?"

Beck collapsed on the floor.

The doctor didn't gasp or phone for an ambulance. He didn't even get up; just watched as she sobbed on the carpet. And when she'd stopped sobbing, he quietly indicated the chair again and offered her a tissue.

"Now," he said, "I've had a quick look at your notes. You've seen Doctor Lacey every few weeks for the last six months, but despite your own grave concerns for your health, all she can find wrong with you is a slightly sore throat. Is that correct?"

Beck nodded, one hand still round her neck.

"The problem then," Doctor Comfort continued, "is not so much that you are actually ill, as the fact that you think you are."

He paused, waiting for her to reply; but Beck's only response was with her eyes, which filled with tears again.

"I see you've had a lot of counselling," said the doctor. "Did it help?"

Beck nodded, which made the fresh tears overflow.

"Come on, speak to me," the doctor said. "I can't read your mind. What do you think is going on?"

Struck dumb or no, this deserved an answer; never had a member of the medical profession asked Rebecca for her own diagnosis before. She released the grip on her windpipe and gulped air.

"I just feel so close to death," Beck said.

"Well, we are, you see," Doctor Comfort leaned forward in his seat, enthusiastically. "Every one of us. In the midst of life we are in death."

This wasn't quite what Beck had meant.

"But it's not a bad thing!" the doctor went on. "For every patient like you, who thinks she's dying for no apparent reason; there's some bloke who turns up with a lump the size of a cricket ball, because he's been in denial about a very real disease. You wouldn't believe the number of people that think they're immortal."

Beck blew her nose on the Doctor's tissue. There was no way he was going to send her to hospital, so she might as well go home.

"One last thing," said Doctor Comfort, as Beck stood up. "Do you smoke?"

"A bit," Beck said.

"Give it up," said the Doctor, "and eat more fruit and vegetables. If you really want to stay alive."


Give it up. Ah, now that was the one thing that Beck couldn't do. But she didn't smoke at the bus-stop, outside the Doctor's surgery; and she didn't smoke as she walked home from the supermarket with carrier bags full of fruit and veg. She didn't smoke while she hung out the washing, and she didn't smoke while she hoovered.

She didn't smoke on the way to pick Alfie up from nursery, and she never smoked when they got home together: not while he watched violent cartoons and she made his tea; not when he refused to eat the cauliflower cheese and insisted on something with more 'E's; and not when the battle of bath and bed lasted longer than an hour.

But oh, when it was over, when Alf was sleeping like a baby under his Action Man quilt, and she was feeling bad about the fight it took to get him there; then it was time for Beck to smoke.

Then she would go and sit in her smoking chair. In the corner of her kitchen, by the radiator she would sit and smoke. With the door closed and the window open she would smoke and smoke again. It made her feel better and worse.

Now was the time Beck let each day catch up with her, before she gave it the slip, and disappeared under her own bedclothes. First she would become aware of the buzzing of the fridge; and then of the voices in her head, a whole family of them in heated debate.

Today, the question on all their lips was; how comforting was Doctor Comfort?

How charming he'd been, said one, the way he'd given her the tissue without otherwise acknowledging her tears; nice and old-fashioned.

The Doctor's suit was certainly old-fashioned, cut in another voice. Did Beck not see the width of his collar, the narrowness of his pinstripe?

What about the size of his head, shouted a third. The arrogance of the man! He didn't even look at her throat, just assumed she was hysterical!

But listen, sister, a less militant tone spoke to the feminist within, listen to his message; in the midst of life we are in death.

When Beck extinguished her last cigarette, it seemed to get a lot darker in the kitchen. And when the voices had all shouted each other down, she couldn't stand the silence. It was time to go to sleep.


First, you've never met someone in your life. Then, you start to see them everywhere you go. This is how it was with Beck and Doctor Comfort. One day he was a complete stranger, and the next thing, she was bumping into him several times a week.

Shortly after that first appointment, when he gave her a second opinion, she saw him in the supermarket.

Beck had a basketful of fruit and vegetables; at least, you couldn't see the bags of crisps and sweets that Alfie had put in for the layer of leafy greens on top.

"Hello!" she said brightly, joining the queue at the next checkout.

Doctor Comfort looked up at her from a handful of cash. The face didn't register; he wasn't sure who she was.

Beck held up a bag of apples for him to see, before putting them on the conveyor belt.

"Plenty of fruit and veg," she said cheerfully.

He smiled politely, and she looked back at her shopping, feeling slightly stupid. The poor man must have hundreds of patients, and he probably recommends fruit and vegetables to every one of them. Why should Rebecca Salmon stand out from the crowd, like the only fish swimming upstream?

For once, her queue was moving faster and Beck didn't look at the doctor again till she was just about to leave the store. His eyes were following her with a pleased but puzzled expression. She carried her bags through the sliding door, not knowing whether to feel like a lemon or a melon.

That was Saturday, and on the following Wednesday Beck was in the bank; standing in a queue she didn't have time to stand in, with a bill she didn't have the money to pay.

The stillness of the line was broken only by Alfie's running commentary:

"What are we doing? Why have we stopped? Who are we waiting for? Mummy? MUM!"

"Ssh!" said Beck.

"It's not fair, Mummy. We're not going anywhere," wailed her son.

"Don't worry," Beck whispered, "we'll do what you want to do when we've finished doing this."

Alfie was placated.

"Alright then," he said, "you have your fun first, then I'll have mine."

Beck was silent, but her chequebook screamed and her purse shook in her hands. She could have cried.

"I'm not exactly at an all-night party, Alf," she said quietly as they shuffled forward a pace with the queue.

Now she was one step nearer the cashier, and her son was right next to an artificial rubber plant, which was positioned to make the bank staff seem more human. She could tell that he was thinking about watering it.

"So," she said to distract him, "what would you like to do, dear?"

Alfie struck a fearsome pose, and replied loudly,

"I want to have a war in space."

"Then we'd better go to the common," said Beck. "There's lots of space there."

She was first in the queue now, feeling the eyes of the customers behind her as she stepped up to the desk to pay; her face red as the gas bill and Alf beside her, bouncing like the cheque was probably going to.

Life was so tight, no wonder Beck couldn't breathe. It was one long final demand, constantly threatening to cut her off.

Beck choked thanks to the cashier who took her money for air, and turned to leave the bank, one hand tugging at her collar.

And there he was again, Doctor Comfort, in the queue behind her. Twice, in twice as many days, they came face to face in a public place; both times standing in lines, as if they weren't real people, but pawns getting processed through a series of coincidences.

Beck was not going to draw attention to her already overdrawn self by saying hello to him again, but the Doctor said 'Hi!' this time.

Tugging the tiny space warrior, Beck was moving too fast to stop and reply; and with her eyes averted, all she saw was the wad of money in his hands.

"Come on, Mummy, you promised I could kill you on the common," Alf said at the top of his voice as they left the bank.

"You're killing me already," Beck replied.


They lived in a seaside town, where vast expanses of water, sky and shingle met in a single line. This was a horizon you could walk on, a promenade bustling in summer and bleak in winter. Half a mile of marshy grass lay between it and the shopping centre.

The one thing that stood out in the flatness of this reclaimed land was a war memorial, a fine finger-salute on the skyline. Dead sailors were raised to the vertical, still cocking a snook overseas.

It was one of Beck and Alfie's favourite places and they often played in its shadow, which lay across the common and covered the grounds of war and peace.

But Alf's games were all aggressive; and Beck, who was a sort of pacifist, had never taught him that sport. No matter how much she kept him out in the fresh air, his main influence still seemed to be the TV.

"Why do you want to fight?" she asked him often.

"What else can I do?" he'd reply without stopping to think.

"There are lots of other games to play," she would say, but no matter how many frisbees, or balls, or dice she threw for him, they were never a good enough catch.

The only time Beck ever felt that she was a match for her son was when he was still inside her tummy, and they were still one. From the moment he was born he outnumbered her, easily.

As soon as she saw the tiny boy in a baby-gro she knew the man who would one day tower above her. He had the energy of an acorn, to become a great oak tree. As soon as he gripped her finger she knew his grasp was stronger than hers.

She could have predicted that Alf would be able to outrun her by the age of three, but it still came as a terrible shock, especially as it happened on a busy main road in the rush hour.

This was the third time Beck and Doctor Comfort's paths crossed in the course of a week, but Beck didn't know it yet.

He saw her as he drove home from work in his battered BMW. She was running in the opposite direction, and the look of suppressed panic that he was becoming so familiar with had turned into real fear. She was shouting, something like "Stop! STOP!"

Doctor Comfort peered in his rear-view mirror. There was her little boy, heading for a major intersection, and showing no sign of stopping or even slowing down.

As his car drew level with Beck she was dropping her shopping bags on the pavement, leaving the school satchel and pile of library books and renewing her sprint.

Doctor Comfort had already lost sight of the speeding boy, and the last thing he saw of the mother before he had to take a left turn, was her long hair falling down as she ran, slipping from its tied-back style.

He didn't see whether she reached her son before he ran into the road. Still, the way things are going, the doctor thought, he'd bump into her again in a couple of days, and then he'd find out.

As it happened, Beck saw him next, but the doctor didn't notice her. It was exactly a week later, and she and Alfie were walking by the sea, after tea.

The little boy had forgotten about his big adventure, or maybe he just thought that Mummy didn't remember it. But Beck could still taste her heart in her mouth, like blood and tarmac, when she thought how close he'd come to a road accident; and she could still feel her hand stinging from the slap she'd given him in relief, when his skin was saved.

There was a man coming the other way, a well-seasoned grandfatherly man, who saw at a glance what was happening and caught Alf like a bullet in his experienced hands.

"They all do it," he said to Beck, when she caught up crying. "They test you. One day, when you say stop, they say why should I?"

He put his arm round her shoulder, an old hand at comforting. With children in their thirties and forties, and twenty grandchildren, it was all the same to him if a complete stranger sniffed into his salt-and-pepper hair.

"Would he really have run into the road?" Beck sobbed.

"He didn't get the choice," the man said. "So you don't get the choice of worrying about whether he would or wouldn't have done, either."

With Alfie safe, Beck's concern returned to the library books she'd dropped on the pavement, and she didn't heed the old man's words of wisdom. A week later she was still agonising over what might have happened, though life for her and her son was going on as normal.

They were walking by the sea, in the early evening sunshine, looking at the boats.

"Is that a battle-ship?" asked Alf.

"No, it's a cross-channel ferry," Beck replied.

"What about that one," Alf pointed. "Is it an enemy submarine?"

"No," said Beck, "that's a hovercraft. It's going to the Isle of Wight."

"Has it got guns?" Alf asked. "Mummy? Mum?"

Beck didn't answer. She had just seen Doctor Comfort. He was jogging in the opposite direction along the prom. He was wearing shorts.

"Mum!" Alf shouted. "Has it got guns?"

Beck had turned to watch the doctor go. It wasn't rude to stare after him; he hadn't seen her at all as he passed. He was focused on his inner rhythm. She was focused on his pounding thighs.

"Mummy?" Alf said.

She couldn't take her eyes off.

"MUM!" Alf stamped his feet.

"No, the hovercraft does not have guns," Beck shouted back. "It doesn't need guns, there is no war. Alfred, we are a nation at peace!" She strode ahead in frustration.

Alf ran after her.

"But what about the Isle of Wight?" he said.


It was like Avalon, a mythical island; some days they couldn't see it for the sea mist, some days it could be mistaken for thunder clouds forming on the horizon. Some days it looked so close they could almost see the other people walking on its shores, across the imperfect mirror of the Solent.

In the sunshine each tree and chimney on the island, each church spire was a strand of colour separated from the woven vision by the hand of a great artist.

That Sunday it had the look that locals knew meant rain, even though June had turned into July, and Beck and Alfie were going out to play in shorts and t-shirts.

White-sailed yachts raced with the racing clouds, as they set off along the prom to the park. It was a week since Doctor Comfort had jogged past them, and Beck was still waiting for him to come back the other way. She watched, constantly, while Alf constantly talked.

"I think I'll go on the swings first, Mummy. No, the slide first, then the swings. No, the roundabout first, then the slide, then the swings. No, the climbing-frame, then the slide, then the roundabout, then the slide again because it's short, and then the swings. No, the see-saw first, but who will go on the see-saw with me? Will you go on the see-saw with me, Mummy?"

"If need be," said Beck, "but we usually bump into one of your friends at the park, like Jack or Sam from nursery school."

It was a small seaside town. They always met someone they knew on the see-saw. She spotted the familiar face the minute they walked through the park gate.

Doctor Comfort: and a girl with his hair and his eyes, a girl about Alf's size. Doctor Comfort's daughter. He was pushing her on the swings.

Alfie had settled on the climbing-frame first, and he crawled up it like a spider after a fly. Beck stood at the bottom, in case Alf fell off, and watched the doctor's back through the bars. He had a kid. That must mean he was married.

After the climbing frame, Alf went on the roundabout. Doctor Comfort's daughter went on the slide. After the roundabout, Alf went on the see-saw and Doctor Comfort's daughter went on the climbing frame. Beck had to go on the see-saw with Alf.

She saw the doctor seeing her; as she went up and down, he was watching through the bars of the climbing frame. Beck's legs were so long they barely left the ground, though at the other end of the see-saw Alf was flying; and her breasts, once full of his milk, bounced with him.

Then Alf went on the slide, and Doctor Comfort's daughter went on the see-saw; and their parents still discreetly looked each other up and down, between the metal bars and moving parts of the playground apparatus.

Even their shadow selves were watching each other ripple across the warm wood-chip on the ground, until they disappeared.

The fleet of small white clouds overhead had towed a flotilla of big ones in battleship grey across the sky, completely covering the sun. The park was emptying as people went for picnics in cars or seafront cafes. Suddenly all the swings were free and Alfie and Doctor Comfort's daughter were both heading for them at the same time.

After the hide and seek as they followed their children's separate paths around the playground, Beck and the doctor were going to converge at the swings, stand side by side, and push.

But at that moment it started to rain. Not the sort of rain that is romantic, clinging to t-shirts and making eyelashes moist. Not rain they could have stood under, rain they had to run from, as the battleship grey clouds launched an uncompromising attack.

In the hail of bullets, the bullets of hail, Beck didn't even see which way the doctor and his daughter ran. She just grabbed Alfie's hand and headed for home.

That evening she smoked and smoked, hoping the clouds that reached the kitchen ceiling would lift her heavy heart with them. All the voices in her head sighed in tragic chorus.

"Damn, he's got a daughter. Drat, he must be married."


It rained, on and off, for four days and four nights.

The beach was deserted, and the sea was coming up through the common; seeping through the sparse grass so gulls could paddle. At the park, the round-about shook like a wet dog.

Alf went mad from being kept inside and Beck was barking. When her throat was so sore she couldn't shout any more they had to go out for walkies. They had to go out to play at any cost, even if it meant paying. They had to go to the indoor swimming pool.

It was a place called Paradise. Under a glass dome blue as a sunny sky was a beach with no stones, and a sea with no weed. The waves were regulated by a wave-machine, and though they caught glimpses of the real sea through the tinted glass, it seemed as grey and far away as if they'd come on an airplane.

Alf was almost too excited to get into his swimming trunks, and Beck had to stop him running out of the changing room with them still around his knees.

All the families who should have been spread along three miles of beach were squeezed into the swimming pool. The water was thick as soup with children; it boiled at a hundred degrees of screaming and scolding. Alf jumped straight in.

Around the edges of the pool were chairs and tables, with parasols, though there was no sun; the temperature was equatorial, and grown-ups sat in the artificial shade sipping tea and coffee from plastic cups.

Beck sat down in her bikini. She'd had it longer than she'd had Alf – though it hadn't worn her as thin.

She was watching the water where her son had jumped in, when a little girl jumped out at her. She recognised the curly hair and the crinkly eyes instantly, even though she'd only seen her once before: Doctor Comfort's daughter.

As Beck looked, the little girl's legs seemed to disappear from under her, and an unmistakable bottom in camouflage trunks bobbed to the surface.

"Alf!" Beck leapt into the water, grabbed both children and dragged them to their feet. Her son was spluttering something about being an enemy submarine.

"If you must be a submarine, could you please be Royal Navy," she spluttered back in exasperation.

There was a laugh. Doctor Comfort was suddenly standing right beside her, with naked thighs in the knee-deep water, gently reclaiming his daughter.

"I'm sorry," Beck said, giving her back. "Alfie knocked her over."

Doctor Comfort just chuckled. Beck looked at his chest hair. It had started to go quite grey. He was slightly older than she'd thought.

"You must be more careful," she said to Alf, blushing.

When Beck climbed out of the pool Doctor Comfort climbed out with her and sat down at the same small table. Both of them were naked but for swimming costumes, and dry so quickly in the tropical heat it was as if they'd never been wet; all part of the virtual Paradise.

"How old is your son?" the doctor said.

"He's three, nearly four," Beck replied. "How old is your little girl?"

"She's five."

"She looks so delicate next to my Alf," said Beck.

"Well, she is rather fragile," the doctor said. "My wife and I got divorced last year, and Jade took it very hard."

"Divorced," Beck echoed, nodding sympathetically.

"We never should have got married in the first place. It was what used to be called a bad match. My family advised me against it; they said Sharon was beneath me."

"I see," Beck said, leaning back in her poolside chair. The doctor was talking to her so easily it was as if they knew each other already.

"Of course, I didn't listen to them," he went on. "I hated their snobbery. I married Sharon and cut myself off from my family instead."

"But it didn't work out?" Beck asked.

The doctor shook his head.

"It wasn't anything to do with her social class, though," he said. "It's because she was an unfaithful... hello darling, would you like a drink?"

Jade had appeared at his elbow, and the next thing Beck knew, Doctor Comfort had gone off to buy them all drinks; his daughter and Beck and Alfie too. Everyone was having Slush, ice crystals swimming in luminous syrup. Like the whole Paradise experience, it was virtually refreshing without really quenching the thirst, and the customers kept going back for more.

Later, as the grown-ups walked by a waterfall, each with an eye on their children who were now playing together quite nicely, Doctor Comfort resumed the conversation.

"I don't think infidelity is a class thing," he said, "is it?"

"Not as far as I know," Beck replied.

"It was just her," the doctor sighed.

"Did it happen often?"

"Oh no, just the once," he insisted. "She said she'd found her soul mate."

There was silence, except for the sound of the waterfall, and hundreds of children screaming.

"I don't know what that makes me," the doctor shrugged. "He was a scaffolder."

"Quite high up, then," Beck said. "So it definitely wasn't a class thing."

Doctor Comfort laughed again. A short burst, at first, as if he was a bit rusty; then a longer gusty one that drowned out the sound of the water.

When they left Paradise at tea-time, Doctor Comfort said to Beck how good it had been to talk; but afterwards she remembered the non-verbal communication, like the smile of his swimming trunks and the twinkle in his eyes.

He was such a good doctor; he made Beck feel so much better. The whole afternoon she'd been with him her throat hadn't troubled her at all.

She made one pack of cigarettes last a week, and with the money she'd saved took Alfie swimming again; same time, same place, exactly seven days later. As soon as they were in the pool, she started looking for Doctor Comfort.

He was nowhere to be seen, but snippets of the conversation they'd had were still there, sitting in the plastic chairs where Beck had forgotten them, and whispering to her from the waterfall.

"Don't you think it's a coincidence that we keep meeting like this?" she had asked him.

"Not really," he had replied. "We've been here every day since it started raining. There isn't anywhere else to go."

That's right; and then he had told her that he only looked after Jade for one week in three. He said how she missed her mother when she stayed with him, and missed him when she lived with Sharon.

"So it must be his week off," thought Beck now.

No one would come to this inferno of screaming children if they didn't have one of their own, to dilute in the boiling water.

Alf had found a friend from nursery, Sam; and Beck sat and chatted to Sam's mother Maisie, though her throat was starting to feel sore again.

Maisie wanted to hear all the plans for Alf's birthday party, which was in a fortnight's time. She wanted to know about sandwiches and crisps, pass the parcel and postman's knock.

"I think it's great that you're keeping the old-fashioned sort of party alive," she said. "So many kids seem to have them in those high-tech pleasure zones these days."

"Mmm," said Beck, who couldn't have afforded that.

"Or McDonald's," said Maisie. "Mind you, it's not such hard work for the parents. You just sit back and watch the children being stimulated."

And she continued to probe Beck on the jelly and ice-cream, though Beck's throat was fast closing up with fear at the prospect of Alfie's birthday.

Four years old. He was going to be four. The very word made her feel wobbly and cold, never mind the jelly and ice-cream.

For the next two weeks Beck counted the minutes. She counted everything, in fact, as the party came closer; popping into every shop in town to find the cheapest balloons, and bumper packs of streamers to save a few pennies.

Her throat felt so tight she could hardly speak, but luckily the party was meant to be a secret.

"Mum," said Alfie, "what's in that big bag on top of your wardrobe?"

"Oh, nothing," she replied.

But the bag on top made her wardrobe into something, late at night; the head and shoulders of a tall person, leaning over Beck as she lay in bed. It loomed at her like an unfathomable adult, in the dark, while Beck hid under her covers and held her breath. She was feeling as small as a child, and worried about Alfie being four.

Four. It sounded so final.

The last two nights before his party she didn't sleep at all, but stayed up baking cakes and making sausage rolls and hiding them at the back of the freezer so that he wouldn't see them till the big day. The all-night cooking and smoking sessions in her kitchen were to take their toll, though the morning of the 26th July dawned fresh enough; the sun in glorious Leo to herald the birth of her son.

Though Beck disagreed violently with Alfie's violent interests, like most mums she wanted to give him what he wanted for his birthday; so the little pile of presents on the breakfast table included an enemy submarine for the bath, a pair of Action Man pyjamas, and a plastic helmet with a spike on top.

He went off happily wearing it to nursery school. Maisie, Sam's mum, took him in her camper van; and Maisie was going to bring him, Sam and four other little boys back again for the surprise party at tea-time.

Beck had the whole day to shift furniture, inflate balloons and impale things on sticks.

But first, just as Alfie's school teacher was putting a cork on the end of his helmet spike for safety, Beck uncorked the bottle of wine that she was saving for the grown-ups at his birthday do.

She had to let it breathe. She had to breathe.

The panic was tangled like blue streamers around her throat, rising like a yellow balloon blown up inside. Beck needed to calm down; but after four sips of red wine she fell asleep in the armchair and didn't wake up again until it was too late for the orange jelly to set in time.

"Oh my God," cried Beck, making egg and cress with one hand, cheese and pickle with the other, and kicking the chairs into their positions round the table.

Never was a party prepared in such a bad atmosphere, so lacking in the spirit of the occasion. Beck just went through the motions, hollow as 'vol-au-vents', because that's what a birthday tea meant to her.

The menu was set in bygone times, its ingredients obsolete. Jammy Dodgers? Little boys these days got away with murder. They'd draw the line at meat paste, Beck was sure. They didn't even know what meat paste was, if not a burger that hadn't been fried yet; and she didn't want to remind the kids of MacDonald's when she was offering them an old-fashioned spread. Sandwiches that really had sand in them; now that was a birthday tea.

The table she laid was like an old map, but where it led to, Beck had no idea. The clarity of its vision and her confusion as to why she followed it clashed like the silver cutlery, when the kids were just going to eat with their fingers.

But the two hours sleep she'd had in the armchair had given her renewed purpose, as if she'd been playing hunt the thimble in her dreams, and had found it.

So she sliced up a Battenburg cake, and put doilies on the plates, delicate paper doilies for boys who only wanted to tear away and play. This was going to be the epitome of a party, in case Alf had reached his peak, at four years old.

And, when the appointed time came, and the house was suddenly full of children who wanted to eat chips and watch videos, Beck stood her ground. She made them play musical statues first, and they didn't mind too much because she was using the popular music of the day, the Spice Girls and the Pillar of Salt Boys; and they could get fixed in grotesque poses.

Musical chairs and musical bumps went down equally well, and while everyone was sitting on the floor they played pass the parcel. Then Alfie's friends gave him the presents they'd brought, and the whole party was up to its eyeballs in wrapping paper and unbelievably brilliant toys; no one knows what a four-year-old boy likes like another four-year-old-boy.

Beck offered Sam's mum Maisie and Jude, another mum who'd come to help, some wine.

"It's been breathing all day," she gasped.

"Becky, are you alright?" said Maisie.

"Yes, why?" gasped Beck.

"You seem a bit… breathless," said Maisie.

"Oh, that," Beck giggled hysterically. "I'm on the edge of a panic attack. But don't worry, I won't go over it."

"Let's get the boys to the table," said Maisie, "then I'll make you a nice cup of tea. These do's always stress me out too."

"Urgh, what's that?" the boys said, when they faced the party spread.

"Lovely egg and cress sandwiches, look," Jude showed them, "and cheese and pineapple on sticks."

"Yuk," the boys replied.

"It's so nostalgic," Maisie said to Beck. "Exactly like the parties when we were kids."

"Come off it," said Jude, "this looks more like something from the 1950s. You might be that old, but I'm not and I didn't think Beck was either."

"I was born in '67," Rebecca said.

"Exactly," said Jude. "We're the *Magic Roundabout* generation. My parties were all psychedelic sugar cubes, and Florence and Dougal on a revolving cake."

"That's what we want," said the boys.

But Beck was able to fob them off with ginger beer. They thought it was the real thing and pretended to get drunk; then started using the vol-au-vent lids as frisbees.

Most of the food was dealt with by Jude who was six months pregnant and ready to eat anything.

"Lovely sandwiches, Becky," she said. "Boys, you'd better eat some of those cakes, quick before I get them."

When the little cakes were all gone Beck brought out the big one, the birthday cake she'd made and iced in the middle of the night. Now she turned the lights out and lit the four candles on top.

Although it was a sunny afternoon outside, the candles flickered brightly in Beck's kitchen, reflected in the eyes of all six boys but mostly in Alfie's as he leaned in close to blow them out.

The children sung Happy Birthday to him as a monotonous chant, a plain song, leaving it up to the mums to carry the tune; but Beck was gripping the back of Alfie's chair in silence, and Maisie was watching her worriedly.

As the singing faded away Alf took a deep breath and blew; once, twice, three times; it was going to take a puff for each candle on the cake. His friends were spitting supportively, all over the icing; his mother was collapsing, over the back of his chair.

As Alf extinguished the fourth and final candle, Beck gave way completely. As if his last gasp of air had been her own, she expired on the floor behind him; not dead, just desperate.

The other mums managed, as only mums can, to carry on for the sake of the children. Jude cut the cake, while Maisie dragged Beck out of the kitchen, and none of the children noticed anything but the rich seam of jam and cream concealed within the sponge.

Beck had put her heart in to the cake, and was now lost without it. She lay on the sofa, hyperventilating; not helped by the smell of Maisie's perfume as she leant over her. It was white lilac.

"Becky, what's the matter?" Maisie said anxiously.

"I'm so afraid," gasped Beck, "I'm going to lose him."

"Lose him? Alfie? Why?" asked Maisie.

"I'm so afraid he's going to die."

Maisie frowned in confusion.

"He won't die," she said. "He's only four."

Beck let out a sort of airless roar.

"Children do die when they're only four, you know!"

She didn't know what she was saying, why she was saying it; only that it had to be said because it was stopping her breathing.

"Right, I'm phoning your doctor," Maisie replied, and started flicking through the address book by the phone.

Beck had forgotten how the last time she'd seen Doctor Lacey she had left in disgrace. She heard Maisie talk to the receptionist, but didn't hear the other end of it; Doctor Lacey was on holiday and they would send a locum in her place.

Jude came in from the garden, to collect the donkey with a tail to pin on.

"She needs a brown paper bag," Jude said, with one look at Beck on the sofa, but all they could find was brightly patterned wrapping paper.

"You need a blindfold," Beck panted, as Jude went back out again, to pin the donkey's tail on.

She was still breathing heavily when the bell went ding-dong and Maisie opened the front door. Beck had now remembered that she could never see Doctor Lacey again, but it was Doctor Comfort who appeared.

"Doctor Comfort," Maisie murmured appreciatively. "It was good of you to get here so quickly. She's having a panic attack."

"I see," said the doctor, looking at Beck. "And what are the symptoms of that?"

"Panic," said Maisie.

"More specifically?" The doctor's gaze penetrated Beck deeper.

"She can't breathe and she thinks her son's going to die," blurted Maisie, sounding like the pressure was getting to her too now.

"Oh, look, I'm sorry, I didn't mean to put you on the spot," the doctor smiled at Beck's helper. "Why don't you go and make her a cup of tea?"

"A cup of tea, yes of course," Maisie echoed, rather entranced by his manner. She'd make a cup for him too, but before she reached the kitchen she added one more helpful thing: "It's her son's birthday. They're all in the back garden. I think the stress would get to anyone, hostessing a big party alone."

When she'd gone Doctor Comfort turned back to Beck.

"You're on your own?" he asked. "A single parent too?"

She nodded.

"I didn't realise," he said.

"Well, I don't wear the badge," she panted, looking at the mantelpiece where the row of Alfie's birthday cards all said 'I AM FOUR. FOUR TODAY'. Hers would say 'SOLE CARER'.

He followed her gaze, and howled with laughter.

"I want one that says 'Lone Parent'; that's the wildest expression of the lot."

"Makes you sound like a wolf," Beck agreed, between gasps.

Doctor Comfort took out his prescription pad.

"Look, you've got a choice," he said. "I can either give you some pills, or I can take you out to dinner, but I can't do both. If you choose the date, I must have nothing more to do with you as a doctor, it's not allowed; but then, anyone can give you valium."

His pen was poised above his pad, waiting for her response.

"I'll take the date," said Beck.

"Good," said the doctor, and scribbled something on the top sheet, which he tore off with a flourish.

"It's illegible to most people," he said, as she took it, "but it says I'll pick you up on Friday at eight. Is that okay?"

"Yes, fine," she gasped.

"Now, I'm going," he said and sped away. "No more Doctor Comfort."

"Oh, is he off already?" Maisie appeared with a tray of tea, sighing with disappointment.

"Yes," said Beck.

"Becky, you're better!" It was Maisie's turn to gasp. "That was quick!"

"I'm fine," Beck said. "Thanks ever so much for your help."

"God, he must be a brilliant doctor," said Maisie, watching at the window as he drove away. "I want him too."

While Maisie's back was turned, Beck put the prescription in her bra.

"Shall we take the tea into the garden," she said cheerfully, "and relieve Jude of the fun."

She thought she'd better wait till the party was over, before asking one of the other mums to babysit Alfie on Friday night.


He pulled up in his BMW at five past eight, not long after Alf had gone off with a wobbly bottom lip in his friend Sam's camper van.

Beck wouldn't be able to enjoy her evening if she thought Alfie wasn't enjoying his, but she knew he'd be swinging from the bunk beds soon. So she dug out some dangly earrings, and was waiting by the door when Doctor Comfort arrived.

He'd said she couldn't call him that any more, but she didn't know what his real name was. She was starting to think of him as Alex; the man who'd written *The Joy of Sex*. Not that she'd read it for a long time, but its spine still tingled at her from the bookshelf in the bedroom – Alex Comfort M.B. Ph.D., all beard and pencil drawing.

Her doctor wasn't so academic.

"Blimey," he said, as she opened her front door. "You're shining."

She put her hand to her cheek. It came away glittery.

"Is it too much?" she asked. "I haven't been on a date since the nineteen eighties."

"People might be surprised," he said, "but who cares. Let's go and make the town sparkle."

They certainly did that, though more by the drinking of fermented substances than by their fizzy behaviour. Sitting in the corner of a crowded pub, they just talked and talked. Then they went to another pub and talked some more. It was when they came out of the third pub that Southsea had started to look unusually opalescent.

"I'm hungry," said Doctor Comfort. All that talking and she still hadn't asked him for his first name. "Let's have a meal."

"What do you fancy?" Beck asked.

"Anything," he said, "except curry."

"Don't you like curry?" Beck said. It was her favourite.

"Can't stand it," Doctor Comfort replied. "I like Chinese though."

"That'll do nicely," said Beck.

He had paid for all the drinks so far and she hoped he was going to pay for the food too; or else she wouldn't be able to order much more than a bowl of rice. When the menus came, she blushed.

"I'm a bit skint," she said.

"It's on me," he replied.

She looked down at the tablecloth. That was pink too. So were the serviettes, and the menu's shiny cover.

"I'm embarrassed to let you pay for everything," she said.

"Don't be," he replied.

"But it's politically incorrect!"

"Depends whose politics," said Doctor Comfort. "Take Marx: from each according to his ability, to each according to her need."

"In that case," said Beck, "I really need a crispy duck."

He bought a bottle of wine too, and by the end of the meal she was squinting at his upside-down cheque book to make out what his name was. She'd managed so far by calling him 'you' and 'hey', and if this was going to be a long-term relationship it might well finish up that way too; but there ought to be an inbetween time when she had a proper noun to call him.

She saw the letter J: Doctor J Comfort. Didn't write *The Joy Of Sex* then. Still, he'd probably read it, or at least looked at the pictures. Studying anatomy would have been part of his training.

The doctor left a generous tip, and they both left a hint of something money can't buy, at the table where they'd been sitting. Then they staggered outside, and stood on the pavement laughing for no apparent reason.

"Would you like to go dancing?" J asked.

Beck shrugged helplessly.

"The last time I did that," she said, "my shoulder pads were the biggest things on the dance floor."

J pointed across the road to where a queue of young people in platform heels and flares were waiting outside a nightclub.

"Look," he said, "Seventies Nite! We won't feel too out of place there."

"I'm going to feel like the furniture," said Beck, as they stood in line behind girls who were a third of her width; "well upholstered."

"Then I'll be like the walls," said the good Doctor. "Plastered!"

Beck thought he was so funny that it didn't matter how old he was, how rusty on the dance floor.

"How old are you?" the doctor shouted as they danced.

"Thirty-one," she shouted back.

"That's nothing!" he shouted. "I'm forty-five!"

"I could tell by your chest hair," she said.

"What?"

"I could tell by your chest hair that you were much older than me," she shouted, "in the swimming pool. It's that grey."

"No, it's the way the light reflects off the water," he shouted. "Anyway, if you're only thirty-one, I bet you never went to a real seventies disco."

"We had them at school," shouted Beck.

"So I'll get you another lemon squash!" J bellowed, and headed back to the bar.

Beck probably should have stuck to squash at that point. The room was spinning around her. The only fixed points in space were Doctor Comfort's eyes, locked on hers as they danced in the flashing lights. As long as he didn't look away, she wouldn't fall down.

Their mutual gaze was a black hole between their bodies. Beck danced into it over and over again with a hundred feet; some in schoolgirl's new shoes, some cold and bare, as if they'd never owned a pair in their life. Beck stomped in old army boots, and skipped in sandals across the nightclub floor; and came back to her senses in the ladies loos, wiping sick off her sensible lace-ups with a tissue.

There would be some memorable stains on them tomorrow, but the night was over now and Beck was undone. She found the doctor in the crowded club, and said that she wasn't feeling well and wanted to go home.

They walked back across the empty common.

"There's my favourite place in the whole town," said Beck, pointing at the big dark point on the skyline.

"What, the war memorial?"

"Yes, well, it's Alfie's really, but that's the same thing," said Beck. "We both live in its shadow."

"I've never seen it close up," said Doctor Comfort.

"No?" said Beck, taking hold of his hand. "Come on, let's go!"

They got a second wind then and ran, revived by the sea breeze across the black expanse of grass. By night, the monolith was lit from beneath, casting vast guardian shadows around its pale column. At its base was a sunken stone garden of names, chiselled row upon row of ranks and numbers, with statues of brave men raised on plinths to stand for any one carved in the silent white stone.

"Sshhh," said Beck to Doctor Comfort; turning up blind drunk, to pay their respects. "We have to go down there."

She lead him down a flight of steps to the shrine, whose floor was still littered with faded red paper petals and weathered green plastic stems from the last Poppy Day. Even artificial flowers wither, but never completely biodegrade.

As they entered the sunken garden, the endless obelisque leaned over them; and in its shadows the stone book of the dead opened out before them.

Plaques like pages of the phone directory lined the monument walls. Row after row of names and numbers; little signs of lives all ended on the same big day.

Categorised, they were. Leading Seaman, Able Seaman, Ordinary Seaman, Boy. All the different things a seaman could be; whether he was Chief Stoker or Stoker 2nd Class.

Among the ranks of midshipmen a few warriors stood out; Writer, Photographer, Bandmaster, noticeble only because there were only one or two of each. A long list of Musicians followed; all in the same doomed band.

In front of the line up, on a ledge, were a number of small urns. None had flowers in them any more but they still felt special. They said things like F.W. Britnor HMS GLADIOLUS 16.10.1941 and In Loving Memory Of J.E. Moon.

The rest of the men were alphabetical. Adams, Broadshaw, Coleman, Furlong. Hiscock, Musselwhite, Rathbone and Salmon.

Rebecca murmured the rollcall, seemingly off by heart. She saw J's raised eyebrows in the uplighting.

"Alfie is learning to read in here!" she laughed. "Toogood and Turner, Walker and Waters. Yeats."

Above the memorial pages of stone the monument stood like a pen. If only it had used the sea for ink, the sorrows would soon have washed away. But the naval losses were written in something thicker.

Doctor Comfort whispered.

"So many," he said, "so many names."

"What's yours?" asked Beck suddenly, in a louder voice.

"My what?"

"Your name," she said, "what's your name?" The courage kept in this frigid stone, this cold storage, was making her bold.

"Don't you know?"

"Not your first name, no."

"How have you got so far through the evening without finding out a simple thing like that?" asked Doctor Comfort in confusion.

"At least if you tell me now I'll know it in the morning," Beck laughed.

"Shhh," he said.

"Sorry," she whispered. "I know it begins with J. I saw it in your cheque book."

J shook his head, and looked back at the walls of names; half flood-lit, half moon-lit, all stars.

"James, John, Jack," he said quietly, "Jumping Jehosaphat, what does it matter?"

"What do you mean?" asked Beck.

"Joseph, Jeffery, Jeremiah. There are hundreds of men here with a handful of names. It means nothing."

"But look," said Beck. She stopped to pick up a disintegrating wreath with a card still attached; some old lady's handwriting, the words blurred by tears or rain. "They're real. People remember them."

The paper flowers fell out of her hands. J saved them, just before they landed.

"A poppy by any other name would be as sad," he said.

At that moment, Beck knew she would love this man forever. She'd started already, she wasn't sure when; but now she was convinced it would never stop. This thing was more solid than time. It was carved in stone.

"My name is Jonathon," he said.

They woke up the next morning side by side on her bed fully clothed. Beck, who'd been up at six ever since Alfie was born, was surprised to find it had gone nine o'clock.

"Urgh," she said to Jonathon.

"Mm," he replied.

She saw him try to open one eye, and lift his head off the pillow.

"Did we have sex?" he said.

She lifted her head higher, to see shoes still on feet, trouser belts still buckled and jackets buttoned.

"No," she said.

"Are you sure?"

"Yes," she said. "Even if we could have got our clothes off, we couldn't have put them on again."

"Good," he replied, "I wouldn't have wanted to miss it."

They were spitting feather pillow words and sandpaper sentences out of their mouths; but after that monumental first date, Jonathon Comfort and Rebecca Salmon understood each other completely.

"Urgh, pissed," she groaned.

"Mm, hangover," he muttered.

One of them managed to make two cups of tea, because it seemed to be a matter of life and death.

"Ah, lovely," Beck said with the first sip.

"Yes, listen," said Jon, with the second, "I've got to go and get Jade now, but can we come round later, to play?"

"No, sorry, not today," said Beck. "I've got to lie on the sofa, with my headache pounding in time to Alfie's violent videos. I'm going to be nasty all day long; but if you bring her tomorrow, I'll be nice again."

"Okay," said Jonathon.

They said goodbye on the doorstep with a rasping kiss, the dry kind old married couples give; but Beck was awash with a flood of love as fresh as the cup after cupful of fruit juice she drunk.


For two such different children, Alfred and Jade played well together; but then, children's games are all about binary opposition.

Doctors and nurses, Mummys and Daddys; whenever Jade wanted to be one thing, Alf could be the other; and every time Alf wanted to fight a dragon, there was now a real princess to rescue.

Their parents were getting on well too. Beck and Jon found they had much in common. He was a doctor; she had an unhealthy interest in things medical.

"I haven't seen so many textbooks since I was at college," he said, browsing the shelves in her bedroom, and narrowly missing *The Joy of Sex*.

He was a Daddy, she was a Mummy.

Beck loved looking after Jade, who had easily enough Barbie dolls for two to play with and more clothes than could be put on and taken off them in a single day. They walked the blonde bombshells through several accelerated lifetimes of marriages and career moves on Beck's kitchen floor, while Jonathon and Alfie blew up Action Men in the room next door.

Jade was a fragile child who shared Beck's colds and coughs. They were always tucking each other up in bed, and bringing drinks of hot lemon and honey. But Beck was starting to feel stronger for having a man around to help her manage Alf's iron will and fiery temper, and run after him when he travelled at the speed of light.

Altogether, there was a better balance of sugar and spice with slugs and snails in Beck's house. It got the yin and yang back together, which made everyone feel happier that summer. They could walk by the sea without Alf constantly watching the surface for enemy submarines.

"I feel like a tourist here, this year," said Beck to Jon, as they joined the throng of holidaymakers on the prom. "I've always rather resented their invasion before."

"I've never understood what they came here for," said Jonathon, "but now I see there are loads of things to do."

In a matter of a fortnight, they had become a family, and went on outings together. The first was to Portsmouth's historic dockyard, where they all went aboard Nelson's flagship, the *Victory*; and the *Warrior*, whose splendid rigging had long been on Beck and Alfie's skyline, but which they'd never visited.

It was mainly because Beck didn't have the money, and mostly because she didn't have the heart; but Doctor Comfort said he didn't mind paying, and the wallet in his top pocket was the healthiest of organs.

They saw the spot where Nelson had fallen, the plaque recording his final words, *Kismet Hardy*.

"What does that mean, Mummy?"

"Fate," Beck said, "he thought it was fate."

"What does that mean, Mummy?"

"He didn't fight death like he fought the French," she said.

"Why?" Alf said.

"He was prepared to surrender," Beck answered.

"How do you know?" said Jonathon. The sides of the orlop deck had him stooping in the very tonsils of *Victory*.

"Every great warrior faces his own death before going into battle," Rebecca replied hotly. "Never during it, and not much afterwards."

Jon fanned his face, and Beck coughed, though she was quite comfortable discussing the subject; but when they climbed on deck again and the talk turned to things like topsails and gunwales she went off with Jade to get some ice-cream. It cooled her throat.

The boys caught them up on the ancient dock, still talking the rigging off the mizzenmast. To quieten them down a bit Beck suggested they see the *Mary Rose*, the pride of Henry VIII's fleet, which sank off Spithead, five minutes after setting sail for the first time with the significant improvements he'd just had made.

"The king was watching from Southsea Castle," Jonathon informed them, looking up from his guidebook, "and saw it go down. I bet he was gutted."

"I 'spect he cried," said Alfie with feeling.

Beck gazed in silence at the ship shaped scar tissue which had formed on the seabed over hundreds of years, and been brought to the surface. Behind a glass screen it had to be sprayed constantly, still a watery grave.

The wood was rotten; pulp and pompey salt. But many of the crew's possessions had been preserved: shoes, combs and pocket-sundials. Beck's eyes grew wide at the death-mask detail imprinted on the ocean floor; the map of lives lost and the souvenirs of their souls.

Jon came up behind her in the museum and made her jump.

"Alright, Miss Moribund," he said. "The kids want their lunch."

Beck sighed at his reflection in the glass cabinet.

"I 'spect," he said, "that inhabiting a grey area between life and death you don't feel very hungry."

Beck smiled.

"Come on, let's go," she said. "I always thought boats were boring, but I've had a brilliant time."

They plundered the city for other places of interest. One day they visited the house where Charles Dickens was born; and dragged the kids along what

Becky said was a Literary Leyline. In a single street in Southsea, at one time or other in the 19th Century, all the famous authors lived: Dickens, H.G. Wells, Sir Arthur Conan-Doyle and Rudyard Kipling.

This cultural activity brought the children out in an irritable rash, but they submitted quietly enough to the video of *Jungle Book*, after tea.

The next day was a parade of heavy horses on the common. They came every year, a touring show of drays and their drivers. Huge beasts you wouldn't want to mess with, and diminutive men in aprons that so emulated the beer deliverer of old, that it would have made the Victorian writers salivate to see them.

Beck and Alf had seen them last time, stopping on the prom as the hairy hooves plodded and the painted cartwheels rolled past the summer crowds. But this year, with Jonathon and Jade, they followed the parade back to its temporary stables, and hung around the door.

Beck had never been this close to a horse before; and didn't know how nice they smelled. Leaning against a bale of hay, she shut her eyes to take in the lather and the leather; and the manure that turned it into a perfume.

She could have stood there smelling it forever; but some rattling tack sent a tingle down her spine and she reached out to grab the nearest thing to hand. It was Dr Comfort's hind quarters.

That evening, like every other, Jon had to take Jade home to bed, and Beck had to stay behind with Alfie. Their children still slept in separate houses, and so the parents had yet to share a bed.

They eyed each other hungrily in the kitchen, while the children watched the end of a video in the living room.

"Jade is back with her mum on Sunday," Jonathon said. "Can I come and spend the night with you?"

Beck nodded, but it wasn't soon enough.

"Oh Rebecca," said Jon, "we need a babysitter now!" He pulled her towards him in a passionate embrace, then thrust her back to arms' length again. "Where does your ex-husband live?" he demanded.

If he hadn't been holding her so firmly by the shoulders, Beck might have fallen over in surprise.

"Live?" she said.

"Where does he live?" Jon repeated.

Beck shook her head.

"He doesn't live anywhere," she said. "He's dead."

Jon let her go.

"No!" he gasped.

"Alright, he lives in Heaven," Beck said.

"Dead?" asked Jon, aghast. "I didn't know!"

"How have you got so far into a relationship without finding out a simple thing like that?"

"You never told me!"

"Well, it's in my medical records," she said. "I thought you read them."

Doctor Comfort sat down at the kitchen table. Beck was still leaning against the stove. He put his head in the hands that had been holding her heatedly.

"I obviously didn't read them carefully enough," he said. "I just assumed you were divorced like me."

"Nope, it definitely says widow." Beck was trying to make light of the matter.

"I suppose it didn't matter to me one way or another at first," Jonathon said. "You were just another hypochondriac in need of imaginary medication. But, oh my darling, it explains everything now!"

He stood up and started to approach her, but her face had darkened.

"What does it explain?" she said.

"Your constant preoccupation with death, of course. When did it happen?" He was coming more cautiously across the kitchen floor.

"When Alfred was a baby. Six months old."

"How?"

"R.T.A. D.O.A." said Beck.

"What?"

"Road traffic accident. He was dead on arrival at hospital," Beck said impatiently. "You're supposed to know that stuff."

"Yes, well," Jonathon stuttered, "even doctors aren't usually so abrupt. Please, tell me more. It's such a shock."

"No, it happened three and a half years ago," said Beck. "I'm over it. I'll tell you the whole story, but not now. *Jungle Book* has nearly finished."

A burst of music and bouncing children from the next room bore her out. The kids came in swinging, with slightly longer arms than when the film started; and when Jonathon left to take Jade home, the arms he wrapped round Beck seemed longer too. They went around her twice.

"I'll see you soon," he whispered. "Goodnight."

Alfie fell asleep before his head hit the cartoon leafy floor; and Beck took up her nightly kitchen vigil, in an armchair by the open window, to smoke a potent jungle herb, and brood upon the visions curling up in that green smoke.

It was a long, long time ago, and it was only yesterday, that the police had woken Beck up by banging on her front door in the middle of the night, and seen to it that she wouldn't sleep again for several years without waking up crying.

They asked her if she had a husband called Fred and then they said that she didn't anymore, because he was dead.

At first Beck felt sorry for Frederick; asking if his death had been quick, if he had suffered at all. With the force of a lorry she felt his sadness at leaving their brand new baby.

But by the time the funeral came, Beck was so angry with him for leaving her in the lurch, it was all she could do not to scream abuse at the coffin.

She laid flowers on the grave, and she laid sandwiches on at the house, but only on the understanding that he would walk in when everyone had gone home and take the flak.

"How slack!" she shouted at him inwardly. "How careless to lose your life in a car." She went over every detail of the accident, asking why he hadn't left five minutes earlier or later, driven five mph faster or slower, even if he'd needed to make the stupid trip at all.

All by herself, she argued an argument that would never be won, one way or another. After six months, when the voices in her head had worn out like screeching tyres, she realised it was pointless to carry on. She was a wife without a husband, and Alf was a son without a father.

Once she'd got this straight, Beck's mind slowed down till there was a tail-back of traffic as long as the motorway. Her thoughts never got where they were going. Simple decisions, like what to cook for tea, were still stuck in the jam at breakfast time the next morning.

She managed to sing nursery rhymes to Alfie, and read him stories from books, but in conversation with grown-ups she couldn't complete a single sentence; they were all punctuated by traffic cones, and subject to delays.

It was a long time before things got moving again: the first anniversary of Fred's death came and went in slow motion. But by the second spring, when daffodils started coming out at the roadsides, and Alf said, "Look, Mummy, flowers," Beck was aware of her pulse quickening, her blood pumping and her brain working at something approaching normal speed.

It never rushed, never fluttered, never did anything silly like leaping for joy, but her heart was beating again. She had separated from her dead husband, untangled herself from his corpse in the motionless vehicle, and set off to walk towards the rest of her life; toddler Alfie held her hand and led the way.

As the crash wreckage disappeared behind them, she could tell Alf the truth about his father.

"He was a careful driver," she would say. "It wasn't his fault." And then she remembered all the other nice things about him; how tenderly he'd cuddled his newborn son, how tenaciously he'd insisted the boy would play cricket for England.

As the dead car faded she could show Alfie how his father looked alive, an image of photographic clarity. It was the picture that Alf had on his bedroom wall, and the picture that Beck saw in the smoke she smoked while Alf was asleep.

Now she would have to show it to Jonathon.


Once Dr. Comfort had ascertained that Rebecca was over her husband, had seen that she'd completed the grieving process of denial, anger and acceptance; he seemed to develop his own obsession with the man. He wanted to know what Fred looked like, what he'd done for a living, even what car he'd driven.

Beck thought this was in very poor taste.

"I'm sorry," Jon said, "but I have to be sure. You are the love of my life, and I need to know if I'm yours."

"Listen," murmured Beck. "Love is an elephant and life is a mouse."

"How do you work that out?" he asked.

"Size," Beck replied. "My love for you is as big as an elephant, and my life is as small as a mouse."

"Oh," said Jonathon, looking pleased. He'd always thought size counted.

"And speed," Beck continued. "Did you know, a minute to an elephant is like an hour to a mouse. By that reckoning, I've loved you longer than I've lived."

Jonathon smiled with relief. It seemed that the feeling was mutual.

They were together at last on Beck's sofa with the lights low. Alf was in bed upstairs and Jade was at her mum's. Their children were older than their embryonic relationship.

This was their chance to start it from the beginning, to do teenage stuff like snogging; instead of the married with kids routine they'd been forced into straight away.

This would be it, finally, their first night of love; but Beck should never have started talking about elephants and mice. When the time came to consummate the moment, it seemed that their two bodies didn't fit together.

It wasn't simply that one of them was enormous, and one was tiny; neither of them could point a finger and say 'you're too big' or 'you're too small'. The problem was not physical, it was just an imbalance of power that meant Jon and Beck didn't get connected.

Not that night, though they tried for hours, and not the next night or the one after, though their enthusiasm remained strong, and the longing energy that pulsed between their private parts seemed more determined than ever to short itself out in a sexual explosion.

Every night Jonathon fell asleep in Beck's bed, completely spent; and she sneaked off to the kitchen to smoke. Staring into the grey clouds, she saw the elephant of their love standing still, while the mouse of their lust rushed around in a furry hurry; and she knew not to worry.

But on the third night Jonathon woke up and found her gone, and went downstairs to look for her. He stumbled into the kitchen, rumpling his hair sleepily, then stopped short.

"Bloody hell, Becky," he coughed.

She stubbed it out quickly and waved her hand to clear the fumes.

"Hi," she breezed.

"What are you doing?"

"Oh, just having a smoke…"

"That's not just a smoke," he said. "I recognise that smell from my medical school days; it was all the young doctors' favourite remedy. You're smoking dope!"

"So?" said Beck defensively.

"Well, no wonder you've always got a sore throat." He looked at the paraphernalia on the table; cigarettes with their filters pulled off, torn Rizla packets and the cellophane-wrapped lump itself.

"Give it up, girl, and come back to bed with me. I'll get you higher than that, eventually."

The next day, though, Jade was back in the care of Doctor Comfort for the last week of the summer holidays before she started school in September.

Beck and Jon had to put their nights of passion on hold, and throw themselves into day-trips with the children. They drove out to the country where there was an amusement park in the grounds of an old manor house.

Alf and Jade spent the morning upside down and spinning around, had burgers and milkshakes for lunch, then shook it about again. Beck watched them on a ride called Crazy River.

"What is the attraction?" she said to Jonathon.

But he was looking the other way, past the fairground, through the trees, to where the old manor house was standing sedately.

"I want to go in there," he replied. He'd said it as soon as they'd arrived, muttered it all morning, and regurgitated it at lunch. "I want to go in the big house."

"Boring!" said the children, and Beck agreed with them, although she found the rollercoaster alternative unbearably exciting.

"Why do people put themselves through it?" she said to Jon, over the sound of screaming which came from the scaffold high above them. "Aren't they stressed enough already?"

His wistful gaze returned to her slowly, from the solid brick of the old house.

"Perhaps it reminds them of before they were born," he said.

"What?"

"You know, in the womb," said the doctor. "The motion is comforting."

She shook her head, and smiled as the children dribbled off another ride.

"Please, Becky, can we go inside?" Jonathon asked again. "I fancy myself as the Lord of the Manor, and I want to stride around."

There was no choice, but Beck hung back rebelliously with the kids as they climbed the stone steps to the great portal. They'd left it to the end of the day, and the setting sun was making long shadowy faces in the ornate carvings around the door. Beck started to shiver as soon as they were inside.

A short guided tour took them through rooms of state and the servants' quarters. Jon strode ahead, asking knowledgeable questions about Queen Anne legs and family coats of arms; Beck walked behind, holding hands with the children who were tired and dragged their feet. They were pulling her down, and in the kitchens she had to sit for a minute on a wooden bench to get her strength back.

"Please don't sit there," said the tour guide.

Beck felt red heat race to her face. It was only an old stool.

"It's sixteenth century," said the tour guide.

Beck clenched her teeth and clasped the children's hands.

"Are you alright, Mummy?" said Alf.

She had no voice to answer him, and thought it must be flu; that combination of hot flush and shivers was so familiar. As they left the kitchens and climbed the back stairs, the feeling lifted slightly, but not for long.

Jon was looking at portraits and striking poses in the entrance hall.

"Oh, I do feel at home here," he declared, and set off grandly up the sweeping staircase to a balcony above.

Beck gripped the children's hands to stop them following him up. At the top, Jon gripped the balustrade and leaned over to speak to them loftily.

"Hey, you plebs," he said, "get back where you belong."

Standing by the front door, Beck felt a great opening inside her as if some ancient oak of her own had swung open to let her anger out. She screamed the rusty hinges off her eternal sore throat.

"Fuck off!" she shouted at Jonathon.

The stately hallway gasped. The tour guide, who had been quietly discussing the wood panelling with a couple on the tour, went pale. An old lady who had been looking at the head of a stuffed red deer mounted on the wall fainted as if it had spoken to her.

Jade and Alfie giggled; not really understanding Beck's language, only how loudly it had rung in the repressed manor.

The tour guide came towards Beck, to ask her to leave at once, but Beck didn't wait to be told again. She stormed through the door, and Jon rushed out after her.

Down the stone steps, along the tree-lined drive and across the car park she went, with the children running alongside. She had to go fast, or the tears would catch up with her; and she didn't want to cry in front of the kids.

She turned on Jonathon as she reached the car.

"Who do you think you are, my Lord?" she looked at him defiantly across the roof of his BMW. "You're no better than me!"

"I know," he said. "I was only pretending. But can you please not swear in front of the kids?"

It was their first argument, and, like any storm, it cleared the air. That night the doctor let Jade fall asleep on Beck's sofa so he wouldn't have to go home; and they made love in Beck's bed.

No more elephants and mice, that night they were two lions. The fight had fixed their fluctuating power levels and now they were perfectly matched.


Their relationship went from strength to strength. As the new school term started they got into an autumn routine that burnished the gold of their summer to make it last longer. They walked in beech woods where fallen leaves crunched underfoot like the shingle in August, and sat in front of log fires blazing like the July sun.

And when the days got undeniably greyer, they made plans for a holiday; just the two of them, no children.

"Name a place you've always wanted to go," said Jonathon.

"Easy," Beck replied. "India."

"No," Jon said. "Name another."

"What's wrong with India?"

"We're not going there."

"Why not?" said Beck. "Too expensive?"

"No, it's very cheap actually," said Jonathon, "but we're not going there, so think of somewhere else."

That was the only place she'd always wanted to go: anywhere else would be nice, but only India had that inexplicable pull that places get for people.

Beck put her foot down.

"You decide," she said.

"Hmm," said Jonathon, who could no more explain why they'd go to India over his dead body, than Beck could account for her grim determination to get there before she died.

And so the holiday situation was in stalemate until it was nearly Christmas.

It was nearly Christmas. Beck and Alfie were decorating their tree. They had to be quick: Jonathon and Jade were coming for a pre-Christmas dinner, because Jade was going to her mum's for the actual day; but the substandard tinsel was slowing them down.

Beck couldn't afford any new baubles. Everything in the battered 'Xmas' box was tatty, and most of the decorations were home-made.

"It's not fair, Mummy," said Alf. "I bet Jade's tree is brilliant." He sulkily hung a broken Santa from a low branch. "I bet hers has got flashing lights."

"We've got lights," said Beck, trying to untangle them.

"Yes, but they don't flash," said Alfie. "It's not fair."

It was rather a sorry sight, Beck had to agree; the tree was spindly, and the trinkets were sparse.

"But remember what Christmas is all about," she told her son, as they stood back to look at it. "Remember what…"

"I can see sellotape holding the angel up," he interrupted rudely.

"Well, don't look at it," Beck sighed. "I'm going to turn the lights on."

She squatted under the tree with pine needles sticking into her head, and shoved the plug into the socket.

"How's that?" she asked.

"I wish they flashed," whined Alfie.

Beck wished he would just be silent with awe and wonder, for once.

"Shut up," she said, shifting on her haunches, "and watch this."

She pulled the plug out, and pushed it in again quickly, wobbling the pins in the electric socket. Behind her, Alfie laughed.

"Nice one, Mum!"

Becky made the lights flash on and off some more. Her son sounded so happy. It was little things like this that made…

… the biggest bang! She was turning to look at his face when her finger slipped between the pins of the plug, just a finger but it felt like a giant hand grabbed her, and took her right off that page of the story. The lights went out on the tree and in her eyes.

"Stop it, Mummy," said Alf, in shock. He'd never seen her smoking.

It smelled like she'd burnt the Christmas dinner; but Doctor Comfort arrived early for the meal, and not too late to save Rebecca's life.

He kissed her like he'd never kissed her before, and prayed like he'd never prayed for anyone. Between breaths, he got Jade to dial 999, and Alf to run upstairs for a blanket. Then they came back to ask him what they could do next.

"Kneel down," he said, "and ask God not to take her away."

Jonathon didn't know he was a religious man until that Christmas.


Beck woke up on Boxing Day. There was a piece of silver tinsel on the machine going beep.

She was in Intensive Care. There was a long white tube between her and the machine going ping.

"Your husband's outside," a nurse said. "I'll fetch him in."

It wasn't Fred, it was Doctor Comfort; so Beck wasn't dead, she was in hospital.

"It's alright. Alf's here too," said Jonathon, leaning over the bed.

Beck looked at him, and narrowed her eyes against his backdrop of sterile white and silver; then closed them again and went back to where it was colourful, dirty and smelly.

It was alright. He was there too.


Next time she woke, from noise into silence, from movement into stillness, it was New Year's Eve.

"Oh good," said a quiet voice from the shadow of the machine that had been keeping her alive. "You're just in time for a party."

It seemed rather dull. The little boy was lying asleep in his lap. Where Beck had come from, there was a riot.

"Try and stay with us now," Jonathon whispered, but it wasn't persuasive enough.

Beck closed her eyes and slipped back into the fray. Next time she woke, it was New Year's Day.

Jon smiled at her, and she gave a huge sob. He reached for her hands, but she clutched at her throat.

"Sore," she croaked.

Doctor Comfort laughed.

"That's my Beck," he said over his shoulder to the nurse behind him. "Looks like she's back on line. I'll go and get Alf."

The boy launched himself onto the bed, into Beck's arms.

"Mummy," he cried.

Beck held him tightly, crying too. Jonathon stood back, watching with the nurse.

"They often wake up in a highly emotional state," she said. "Rebecca will settle down later."

Beck fell asleep cuddling her son, and he slept too after the worst Christmas and the longest wait for Santa to come, ever.

Jonathon tucked them in together. It wasn't hospital policy to allow two in a bed, especially not in Intensive Care; but he stood at the door in case a more important doctor than him came along.

In the morning Beck was still really upset. She cried and made mucous noises, but she didn't say anything.

"Not to worry," Jon said to Alfie. "We'll come back at tea-time. She'll feel better then."

The hospital was as bad for Alf as it was good for his mum. Jonathon was keen to get him out into the frosty air, and off to school. That was why Beck's next words were heard by the nurse on duty, and not by her close family or friends.

It was around lunchtime, though Beck wasn't having anything to eat. She was just having the tube that fed her adjusted.

"I died," Beck croaked.

The nurse nodded sympathetically.

"Yes, dear," she said, more or less.

Beck wasn't deterred. She said the same thing again to Jonathon and Alf when they came after work and school and sat by her bed eating sandwiches.

"I died," she said, with a dry mouth.

Jonathon coughed up sandwich.

"What?" he spluttered.

"I died," Rebecca replied.

He looked at her incredulously. "You're not supposed to know about that!"

"Oh, they all say it," the nurse on duty muttered.

"They do?" asked Jonathon.

"A lot of them, yes," said the nurse, examining the machine that went beep.

"Amazing," said Jonathon, returning to his tea. "Amazing, eh Alfie?"

Alf nodded with his mouth full, and Beck smiled at him fondly. She smiled at him until he fell asleep in Jon's lap, then she looked up at Jon's face and burst into tears again.

"Oh dear," said Jonathon.

"I died," Beck sobbed.

"I know," he replied. "It was awful. But you got better," he added brightly. "You came back to life again."

"No, not that me," Beck shook her head till the tubes came out. "I don't mean that me."

Jonathon put the tubes back in. Being a doctor he knew how to do that, but he didn't understand what Beck had just said. He sat down again, and tried to make some sense of his own.

"What happened," he said, "was that you had an electric shock. It was from the Christmas tree lights. Alf said you were trying to make them flash, which was very silly but we won't go into that just now. Your heart stopped beating, but only for a few minutes, because I arrived and resuscitated you. I gave you the kiss of life. So you see," he finished kindly, "you didn't really die properly."

Beck sat up in bed, her tubes wrapping themselves tightly around her neck.

"I was hung," she said.

"What?" Jonathon's patience nearly snapped.

"I did die properly," she said, but there was no pride in her tone, only shame. "You should know. You died too."

Jonathon stood up abruptly, shaking his head.

"I've got to get Alfie home to bed," he said. "I'm living in your house."

He emphasised the word living; underlined it heavily, feeling suddenly cross with Beck. Okay, so she had just come out of a coma; but she could have taken this opportunity to thank him for looking after her son. Instead she was calling him dead.

Jonathon didn't kiss her goodbye, for once. He didn't want to acknowledge the fact that what Beck said had brought his whole body out in goose bumps, which only subsided when he carried Alf outside, into the freezing night air.


Becky had to have a brain scan the next day to make sure there was no permanent damage. She lay in a machine that made her look as if she had no head.

Closing her eyes in the dark tunnel, all Beck could see was the moment she raised her sword and cut Jonathon's head off with a single sweep. As she'd tried to explain to him yesterday, it was not this her, not that him; but it was definitely them. She saw it happening over and over again.

Beck lay in the CAT scan machine for longer than people normally do. The doctor operating it was frowning at the screen.

"There's no damage to the brain," he said. "But there's something strange going on in there."

He pointed it out to the nurse beside him. The electric shock had somehow got Beck's brain working better. It was firing on all hemispheres, and sparks were flying between them.

"Strange," the nurse agreed.

It wasn't something they'd seen too much before. But they decided that if Mrs Salmon could keep down a hospital meal, it would be safe to send her home.

Doctor Comfort was there too when they gave Beck her food. Alf had gone to tea with his friend Sam.

"I've got to pick him up at seven," Jonathon said, sitting by Beck's bed, as the nurse propped her up with pillows and plonked a tray on her lap. "It would be great if I could tell him you're coming home tomorrow."

Her first meal since she arrived there was soup. Tomato soup. Beck took one mouthful and spat it out.

"I had to lick your blood from the floor," she said.

Jonathon blanched.

"What?" he said.

"When your army came," Beck choked, "they made me lick your blood from the floor."

Jonathon tried to ignore her.

"Just eat the soup," he said. "It'll make you feel better."

"Because I cut your head off," Beck went on. "You sort of wanted me to, but I still felt bad about it. I can't eat that." She pushed the soup away.

It splashed Jonathon's white coat.

"Well, it doesn't matter if you eat it or not," he said angrily. "They'll never send you home while you're talking like a nutter."

Again he left her without a goodnight kiss, but he was back at breakfast time. This was eggs, scrambled an hour ago in a kitchen half a mile away, but Beck was trying to eat them all up.

"Come on," Jon encouraged her, "I want to get you out of here."

Beck finished the plateful and shed a single tear.

"I'll go and tell the nurse," Jonathon bounded out, then stuck his head back round the ward door. "If you want to go?"

Beck nodded, without a word.

She was quiet as they dressed her, quiet as they packed the little bag of stuff she'd accumulated during her stay. A couple of nurses walked her to the lift and said goodbye. She didn't reply.

She was quiet as Jonathon drove her home in his car, and quiet when she found he'd moved into her house.

"I've made a bed for Jade in the spare room," he said, "it seemed the best idea. I wanted to be here for Alfie. I hope that's okay."

"Yes, thanks," said Beck, sitting down on the sofa gratefully.

Jonathon sat down next to her.

"I love that little boy," he said, sounding a bit surprised about it.

But Beck wasn't surprised. And she wasn't quiet either as she let out a gleeful shout:

"He was your brother once!"

Then she leaned back on green cushions and fell asleep, leaving Jon mouthing his frustrations to the empty air.

Rebecca wasn't ready to resume the role of mother yet. When Alfred came home from nursery the next day, she sat on the sofa with him and watched violent cartoons. Jonathon had to cook the tea.

She did manage to give her son a bath, but they had such a game of battleships that the floor was an inch deep in water, and Jon had to mop it up. And then in the night she woke up crying so many times that he might as well have been looking after a baby.

Dr Comfort had to work the next day, and Alfred went to nursery. As soon as the house was empty, Beck started looking.

First she went through the drawers in her bedroom, piles of underwear and other personal things; all her own, for Jonathon had discreetly kept himself to a suitcase on the floor. She looked at the clothes hanging in the wardrobe, and read the labels sewn into their soft folds; then she read the spines of all the books on her bookshelf.

In the bathroom, she emptied out the mirrored cabinet, shook medicine bottles and rattled pills. She studied the brand names of soaps and shampoos, and squeezed the toilet roll.

In the spare room, the bed was made up pinkly, with a couple of Jade's Barbie dolls sitting perkily on the counterpane. But all around the walls, Beck's belongings slumped in old cardboard boxes. Dating from school days, there were stacks of Fred's stuff mingled with her own, dusty as ashes.

She'd kept it all, from lecture notes to love letters, birthday cards to wedding invitations. There were appointments for driving lessons, stubs of plane tickets, and certificates for skills as diverse as tap-dancing and lap-dancing. Beck was an accomplished woman, and she looked at all her achievements.

She saw many photographs of people wearing hats, from mortar board to matrimonial, and back into black for the funeral. She flicked through magazine cuttings about counselling and cake-making, articles on pregnancy ailments, teething problems and how to make a Superman outfit. It was all here, all up to date, but she hadn't found what she was looking for.

She went downstairs and made herself a cup of tea, the first since Christmas Eve. It was nice, it was normal, but then Beck blew it by emptying every drawer in the kitchen and looking at the knives.

She opened the cupboards, took out all the food. It was probably lunchtime, but all she fancied eating was rice.

In the afternoon, Beck listened to music. She started with her small collection of CDs, and ended up playing old tapes and even records from the back of a dark cupboard. She sat by the speakers as every melody, every lyric she'd ever seen fit to buy passed her ears. It was all here, note for note, but she hadn't heard what she was listening for.

Beck was in the hallway, trying on her coats and shoes, when the doorbell rang. It was Sam and his mother Maisie, bringing Alfie back from nursery school.

"Becky!" chimed Maisie. "You're back! I was so sorry about your accident. How are you feeling now?"

"A bit strange still," said Beck, standing there in stilettos, an anorak and a pom-pom hat. "I've just lost a whole day, trying to find myself."

"Rattling around in there, are you?" asked Maisie, looking over Beck's shoulder at the empty house she'd have liked to be invited into for tea and biscuits.

But Beck wasn't ready to entertain yet. She bobbed apologetically in her high-heels, and her pom-pom wobbled.

"Still a bit shaky," she said.

"Sure," Maisie nodded, "but as soon as you want to come back on the volunteers rota at nursery, well, we really need you."

Maybe getting back to work was just what Beck needed too, though it was doubtful how much help she'd be at the moment.

"Mum! Look at the mess you've made!" said Alfie, as he entered the house.

They didn't clean it up though. They sat on the sofa and watched swashbuckling children's stories in period costume, until Doctor Jonathon came home in his white coat and did the dirty work for them.

"How are you feeling?" he asked Beck, as he carefully put away the array of knives she'd lined up on the kitchen table.

"I don't think I'm going to get any better just hanging around at home," she said. "Maisie suggested that I go back to work at the nursery school."

"Well, if you're sure you're up to it," he replied, scooping rice back into the packet.

Beck was thinking about the art and craft they did there. About the quiet room with the little chairs, the stack of clean paper and the boxes of chalks, crayons, coloured pencils and felt-tip pens; about the legitimate mess she could make on lovely white sheets.

She was staring at Jon's back as he put things back in the cupboards.

"I've never seen you in a white coat before," she said.

"I did tell you," he turned and smiled. "I've got a proper job, a permanent one at the hospital. More reliable than a locum, if I'm going to be a family man again…" His smile turned shy.

"Congratulations," said Beck.


Things settled down a bit after that, though Beck was still prone to poking around her house, doing archeology in the dark corners best left alone. She went back to work at the nursery school, two mornings a week, and was happy to be in charge of the colouring table again.

It really seemed to bring Beck out of herself; though the first thing she drew was a knife.

It had a curved blade, and a jewelled handle that she coloured in loving detail. She took three hours to do it, and mastered a technique for making crayon reflect the light like emeralds, sapphires and rubies. Then she stuffed it in her bag and took it home.

She didn't show anyone this picture, but everyone noticed her shining face.

Beck couldn't wait for the next session. This time she drew herself holding the knife, a full-length fearsome warrior prince, with a sword too.

In the background, in dusky red chalk, was the outline of his fortress home. The foreground detail, a feathered turban, diamond-studded belt and flamboyant pointed shoes couldn't be completed in a single morning. She hid the character-study at the back of the teacher's cupboard, and finished it the following week.

Saffron, paprika and aubergine; Beck blunted the hot coloured pencils on the picture of a bazaar she did next. Bowls of spices under silken awnings, plump sacks of rice and dribbling jars of oil; the impressions of a market stall were so strong she could hear the chappatis sizzling.

On the way home from nursery school that day, Beck braved the supermarket for the first time since her accident. She brought a trolley-load of frozen curry.

"I know you don't like it," she told Jonathon cheerfully, as she crammed their freezer full of little boxes, "so I just got enough for one."

"But even the smell of it defrosting makes me feel sick," Jon moaned, though he was secretly pleased to see Beck had got her appetite back.

"So I'll only eat it when you're out," she said, slamming the freezer door shut as if the matter was closed. "Here, try a mango."

The bazaar was just a colourful blur in the background of Beck's next picture; the main body of it was whores and soldiers. The class were using finger paints that week, and Beck did a lot of red and yellow dots for the dashing army uniforms. She did the saris in bright colours too, and made them clash with the clothes of the saggy old prostitute who stood apart from the rest.

The whole scene was framed by the feather which curled from her Indian prince's turban, as he stood and watched it unfold.

But no one else saw Beck's art work, except for the deaf and dumb boy Jack, who always sat next to her at the little table, swapping colours and quiet smiles. He watched what she was doing, sometimes, as she watched him; but she felt no more need to explain the world she depicted than Jack did his.

Hers was represented literally, his was in the abstract; but they always left the room together at the end of each session having seen their separate worlds more clearly.

*

Beck was slowly getting her strength back after the accident, growing stronger than she'd been before.

One day, while Jonathon was cooking tea, he heard a commotion in the next room and rushed in. Alf and Beck had been sitting on the sofa watching *Star Wars*, but had leapt up to join in the fight with light sabres. Alfie was Luke Skywalker, and Beck was Hans Solo; but the performance with her arms had sent a stack of things from the top of a cupboard crashing to the floor.

As Jonathon stood there, a sheaf of papers floated to his feet. He picked them up to shuffle back together.

"Oh my God," he said.

Mother and son looked up at him with identical expressions of guilt as they crouched on the carpet gathering Cludo and Ludo pieces, Monopoly money and a scattered pack of cards. Beck gasped when she saw what Jonathon was holding.

"Did you do these?" he asked her.

"Yes," she nodded slowly. "At nursery school."

"Well, what are you hiding them up there for?" he said. "They're very good."

He put them back on a lower shelf, at eye-level, where he caught sight of them again later, after Alfie had gone to bed.

"Rebecca, these pictures are brilliant," he said.

"Do you really think so?" she asked. Her heart was beating like a drum coming closer.

Nodding, he sat down next to her on the sofa, spreading them out to get a better look.

"Brilliant," he said again. "But where did you get the ideas from?"

She laughed.

"Oh, they're just... well," she pointed at the first one, the fearsome Hindu prince, "that's me. And that's a close up of my knife." She showed him the jew-elled sheath, and gleaming blade.

"But..." Jon didn't get it. "Did you copy them from a book?"

"No," said Beck patiently.

It wasn't Jonathon's fault he was slow; all doctors did it by the book, they had to follow diagrams. How else would they know what was inside people, under the skin where they couldn't see.

134

"I did it from memory," she said.

He was staring at the picture of the bazaar, with a frown.

"That's, like, the shopping centre," she said, "in the city where I used to live."

He shook his head, turned to another picture.

"There it is again," Beck said, "with some soldiers," she touched the red and gold uniforms done in textured finger-paint, "and prostitutes. Just looking…"

The doctor looked like he was being forced to see holiday photos of a place too foreign to comprehend. He didn't even pretend to enjoy the colourful scene, but turned to the next picture quickly.

It was a woman, white and quite pretty, with blonde ringlets and a long pink dress; a woman with an unbelievably small waist.

Now it was Jonathon's turn to laugh.

"It's Barbie of the Raj!" he said.

Beck looked at him sideways. He was looking straight; straight at the lady she'd defined so clearly you could see the whale bones of her corset and her own ribs groaning as she struggled to keep in shape.

"That's you," said Beck.

"Pardon?" Jonathon was still engrossed in the picture.

"That's you," Beck repeated. "At least, it's what you looked like the first time I saw you. You looked a bit different by the end."

Now Jon heard her; heard the same sinister voice which said, 'you died too,' when they were still in the hospital.

"Shut up," he squeaked, and jumped off the sofa.

Most of the pictures went with him, but the one of the woman clung to his leg and took ages to fall. When the static wore off it landed on the floor, side by side with Beck's handsome prince but top-to-toe, like a yin and yang thing.

Jonathon's eyes were beseeching her, but she couldn't give him a better answer than that sixty-nine.

"It must have been a dream," he said.

"I wasn't asleep," she replied. "It was a coma. And I woke up remembering where I'd been. It was a life as true as this one. You were there as real as you are now."

"Shut up," he repeated.

"Well, you talk then, if you think you can make more sense."

"I don't know how to speak to you…"

"As a doctor?"

"As a doctor, I say you're sick."

"As a man, then."

"As a man, I say it's the worst thing you could do; to paint me as a woman, especially in a pink silk dress." Jonathon had got into his stride now, all around the room, though he never actually stepped on any of Beck's artwork. "Why picture me like that?" he said. "Do you think I'm a poof?"

"Of course not. You wouldn't be my partner if..."

"And speaking as your partner, I think you've been very selfish. You knew I don't like anything to do with India, yet you went out of your way to portray it in intimate detail."

"All the more reason to believe that I'm not making this up!" said Beck. "Why would I want to hurt you? We're friends..."

"So speaking as a friend, the pictures are great but your story is crap. I can't believe you believe this stuff. Tell me you're not serious."

He flopped on the sofa, fury spent, and looked at her expectantly. After a pause, she replied.

"It wasn't a dream. You know it's true: nobody dreams in a coma."

"Yes, but you sleep on the way out of it," Jonathon slapped a cushion wearily. "You don't just snap awake!"

"It's a memory," said Beck. "It has the same feeling as a memory. The same taste and smell and..." she shuddered "...texture."

"It was a dream," Jon said, dismissively. He reached for the TV remote control.

Beck went and stood in front of the screen.

"I believe that it was a real life. And," she said as he turned the television on, "you were living there too. It was a real place. And," she said as the theme tune to the evening news blurted out urgently behind her, "I'm going to prove it to you."


At first Beck rose to the self-imposed challenge in the way she knew best. She painted another picture; the warrior prince in army uniform, standing on a sun-scorched parade ground flanked by the trees of a strange climate and a familiarly English clock tower.

Then she depicted a whole series of musical soirées, with Jonathon prominent among the white ladies playing the piano, and herself sitting darkly in the audience; a black note in the harmonious setting.

With hazy chalk and harsh pencil she captured the heat and the hardship of their lifestyle; with glossy crayon and treasured felt-tip she showed the opulence at India's seam.

At the end of every art session, she took a picture home to Jonathon. No longer filed away they filled every surface, as Beck tried to bring the story back to life by sheer overkill. The images were wall to wall.

"Please, no more," said Jonathon one night, when he found a picture of the nineteenth century Barbie doll dressed for a ball, on the back of their bedroom door.

But Jade, who'd come to stay for the weekend, loved it.

"Can you do one for me?" she pleaded.

Working to a commission, Beck's illustrations took on a new charm. In the story's sub-tropical garden, a beguiling younger brother and sister appeared. They were Jonathon's other family, the boy about five and the girl four; and though their ages were reversed it was clearly Alfred and Jade, playing with hoops and spinning tops.

"What's her name?" Jade asked, entranced by the girl with her own face and a Victorian pastime.

"I don't know," said Beck simply, "I can't remember." She couldn't remember any of the names, not the children's, not hers, not Jonathon's; not the city where they lived. "I don't know," she said. "Why don't you make it up."

Jon chose that moment to walk into the room.

"Make it up," he said. "Huh!"

"Only the name," Rebecca protested. "Everything else is true."

But fact or fantasy, it was all the same to Jade who, like all the best little girls, lived by her imagination. Soon she wanted more than the pictures; she asked for stories too, and not just at bedtime.

"Did we drive in cars in the olden days?" she said one day when they were driving in the car.

"Your family had a horse and carriage," said Beck. "But I rode on an elephant."

"No, you didn't," giggled Jade.

"I did," said Beck. "It had a really posh seat on top; silk brocade, like a sofa, so you could relax as the elephant walked along. There were straps to hold onto, sort of gold plaits, but it always felt like you were going to roll off as the elephant went from side to side. It had tassels on its trunk and earrings."

"No, it didn't!" said Jade, with a laugh that even got Jon to raise a smile behind his steering wheel.

And another time, when they couldn't go out because of the bad weather, she stood at the window and said wistfully.

"I bet it never rained when we were old-fashioned children."

"It jolly well did," Beck said. "It used to save up the rain for a whole year, and chuck it down all at once. It rained for more than a month without stopping."

Jade turned to her.

"You said it was very hot and sunny," she said.

"It was," Beck replied. "Then suddenly, the sky would split open and the water would fall. It was called a monsoon."

"A monsoon," repeated Jade, still a bit suspicious.

"Yes," said Beck, "you'd be soaked to the skin instantly."

Jade turned back to the window, to what now looked like a polite excuse for an English shower. She was thinking hard.

"When it was hot," she said, "was there air conditioning?" She knew about air conditioning because her mum, Sharon, had just moved into a new office at work and was very proud of it.

Jade was proud too; her chin was held high. Beck saw it, and felt something stir the dusty heat inside her.

"Oh yes," she said, "there was air conditioning at your house. Do you know how it worked? A man sat on the veranda, all day and all night, pulling a string attached to the fan on your ceiling."

"He didn't," said Jade.

"He did," said Beck.

"Not all day and all night," said Jade, her voice fading.

"All day and all night," said Beck, firmly, "for almost no money at all. And do you know why? Because your family had swanned into the country and got into a flap. You needed servants for everything. Fan you? We even had to wipe your ar…"

Jonathon had come into the room suddenly, with a tray of drinks and biscuits.

Jade sat down with her orange squash. In an instant she became as engrossed in the Walt Disney film Alfie was watching as she had been in Beck's tale. But Beck stood with the cup shaking in its saucer till the tea was cold, shocked at how close to the surface her anger was, how easily she'd unleashed it.

The warrior within her was no mere memory; he was still alive.


Jade stayed with her mum for two weeks after that, and Beck managed to calm herself down a bit. She told the nursery school she needed a break from the colouring table, and went on playground duty instead.

The first pictures of spring were painting themselves; buds in the trees, on the common. Crocuses lined the paths across the grass with the colours of saffron, paprika and aubergine: and Beck ran out of frozen curry, and made herself promise on the war memorial not to buy any more.

Then Jade came back on a Saturday morning, with her constant companions, the Barbie dolls, dressed in crinolines and their hair done in ringlets. She'd spent the fortnight in a world where the Ayah watched for tigers while she played in a jungle garden, overgrown with geraniums and wild roses; making mud pies and potions for the servants.

The little girl's imagination was all fired up, and wasn't to be extinguished without a fight. Beck's own spark had started it, and now her conviction in the characters was rekindled.

What harm could story-telling do, when she was so sure it was true? It would be okay to carry on with the tales.

But Jade was no longer content just to sit and listen; she'd looked at the pictures, she'd heard the words, now she was ready to get up and act the entire thing out.

She barely took her nightie off the whole weekend, as it was the only long dress she owned; and when Jonathon managed to get her in the bath, she turned the shower attachment on full blast and shouted, "Monsoon coming!"

All Sunday morning, Beck had to pretend to be on parade while Jade went by in her horse-drawn carriage with a wave at Papa, who was giving the native soldiers their marching orders.

All afternoon Jade hammered away at a makeshift pianoforte, while Beck fanned her with a copy of *The Times* that she really wanted to sit and read.

It was her own fault; she'd set herself up completely, but that didn't stop the resentment creeping back in. After tea, she sent Jade and Alfie upstairs to play, and finally got to look at some current affairs.

"What are they doing up there?" asked Jonathon, over the top of the sports section.

"Barbie dolls, I think," Beck muttered.

"Barbie Dhal," Jonathon said, bitterly. "This Indian thing is taking over our lives."

"I know," Beck replied.

Okay, so it was educational; and the kids would have a head start in colonialism, if such a thing were still studied at school. But it was worrying to find Alf's Action Man's face painted brown, and an army of blonde dolls bossing him around, when she went upstairs to see how they were getting on.

"Jade," Beck couldn't help asking, as she brushed her hair at bedtime, "do you know what mutiny means?"

The minute the word was out of her mouth, Beck regretted it. Not because of the effect it had on Jonathon's daughter; Jade had learned enough new words and meanings for one day. She jumped into bed with a giant yawn.

"No," she said, "goodnight."

Beck regretted it because the word mutiny was at the end of a string of words tangled up in her mouth; she'd just given it a single tug and the whole lot was unravelling like a length of very dismal bunting.

She stood on the dark landing, outside the rooms where the children had fallen asleep so quick, and felt sick. She could never tell them the end of the story she'd started. Its conclusion was so grim that even Jonathon, a grown man and a doctor, would have to be spared the details of suffering. Beck must eat the end of her tale.

She clapped her hands over her mouth to hold in the sick, the bilious flags of the narrative, the black bunting of events which followed the mutiny; and realized why she had always had a sore throat.

One thing was sure, if she wasn't allowed to say what happened, the nursery school teachers would have to let her back on the colouring table.


In the quiet room, Beck wept. The story inside her was so big, so messy that no amount of clean white paper could mop it up, if it should start to spill out.

The pictures filled her head. How could she scale them down to a drawing?

It had seemed so easy before; the right pencil had thrown itself into her hand and known what to do without a command, as if the image was already on the page, just waiting to be traced.

But now Beck had sat for two hours twiddling a brown crayon, and the paper was still blank. All around her little girls and boys were painting apple trees and snakes as if the whole of creation were starting afresh, but Beck was denied its creative juice.

She cleared her dry throat, and heard a huge cry, from outside the quiet room; there was an uproar in the nursery school. Beck told the colouring children to carry on, and went to the door. She opened it to find one of the teachers coming to find her.

"It's Alfred," the teacher said. "He's attacked a child."

It wasn't just a game, it was serious; an assault on somebody he never usually played with. Beck could have kicked herself when she saw who it was.

Her son had hurt an Asian girl, the only Asian girl in the school, the only child in the whole place whose face wasn't white.

"He said," the teacher whispered to Beck accusingly, "that his father is in charge of all the black people."

"His father is dead," Beck muttered back; no excuse, but no word of a lie.

"You'd better come to the Head's office," said the teacher. "She's phoning Rupinder's parents."

Beck looked at Alf who was confused and cross, in the naughty corner, though it wasn't his fault, it was hers. Then she slowly followed the teacher from the classroom, thinking fast about how to explain his racist attack.

"The Singhs are on their way," the Head said, as soon as the office door was opened. "What on earth has got into Alf?"

"Well," Beck managed a rueful laugh, "at the weekend I told him all about the... er, British in India. You know, in colonial times. We had some... um, distant relatives there."

"That would explain 'Papa'," the teacher laughed too.

"Oh no, is that what he said?" asked Beck. She'd hardly been aware that Alf was listening to most of her stories. He must have been watching TV at the same time.

"Your ability to bring history to life is admirable," said the Head, "but I hope you'll be able to explain it to Rupinder's parents when they get here."

In the backwater of Southsea, there wasn't the cultural mix of a city. Most of the people who lived there were the colour of the shingle on the beach, pale stone or tan tones, they were washed by the tides and all looked similar; though, like the pebbles, no two were exactly the same.

And though her mind's eye had been focused on darker-skinned faces, Beck hadn't seen an Indian in the flesh since her accident. It was a shock to meet the Singhs; she found herself staring at a reflection of her soul, when the Head ushered them into her office. The room was getting crowded, but she left a space for Beck to say something; sorry, perhaps.

"Don't worry," said Mrs Singh. "We know what children are like, and we know adults who are worse."

Beck winced. Her white skin was so thin, she'd only have to scratch it to show them what colour she was underneath.

"Rupinder isn't badly hurt," the Head said, "just grazes on her hands and knees where she fell."

Mr Singh met Rebecca's eye.

"It seems that Mrs Salmon told her son about their ancestors in British India, and he took it rather too…" the Head faltered, looking to Beck for backup, but none came.

"He got a bit caught up in the…" the Head tried again, and still Beck didn't fill in any missing words.

"So, come and see Rupinder." The Head led the parents out of the office, with a disappointed look at Beck.

Mrs Singh left with a sad half-smile for her. It said the worse part is being a mother, and that's the same for both of us. The father's look was more painful, and before he tore it away from her, he said something in Hindi to Beck.

*"bh ai, kis duniya me ho? kya soc rahe ho?"*

Well, in what world are you? What are you thinking?

She understood it! It was a foreign language, but Beck finally felt able to speak.

These were the words she been looking for ever since she'd woken up from a story, struggling to put names to faces and translate the tense from present to past.

But she couldn't reply to the Singhs in their native tongue. Only with her eyes, she said:

*"hindustan ke bare me soc raha tha."*

I was thinking about India.

*

"Don't tell Jonathon," Alfie said, on the way home.

"Don't bet on it," Beck replied. She hadn't decided yet whether or not to tell Jon about Alf's racist attack. If her son had done any other bad thing, she might have kept mum; but this one was bigger than she could handle on her own.

Alf had never had a father figure, but he'd seen them on TV. He looked scared all evening; glancing between Beck and Jonathon, and back to the screen, missing bits of the programme he was watching.

In the end, she thought the threat of a big booming voice was probably more effective than the liberal talking to Jonathon would actually give the boy, so she didn't tell him. Better to save the booming voice in case Alf ever did anything worse.

Meanwhile she bit the bullet and said to Alfie;

"No one is in charge of the black people. Remember that, or they might start being in charge of you."

Biting bullets was how the mutiny had begun. That was what Beck had been trying to draw before all the trouble started at nursery. She sat in her smoking chair after everyone had gone to bed that night, and watched the pictures in her mind.

The native soldiers had new guns, better ones; powder and shot came in one neat packet, no more fiddling with their balls. Only problem was, the cartridges were greased with beef fat, and the Hindus had to bite the ends off.

Now Beck had grown used to knowing things that she didn't know before her accident, like how guns worked; and was fascinated by the details that would once have had her yawning. But it still came as a surprise to find her mouth full of the taste of gunpowder, when she didn't even know what gunpowder tasted of. And all she spat out was the smoke.

Once she'd stopped telling Jonathon about the big things, like Alf attacking Rupinder at nursery school, or why the Indian mutiny had started, Beck found herself less able to tell him the little things too; like how much she loved him.

Soon it was just small talk; the kids didn't eat their tea, there was nothing on TV, the hyacinth bulbs they'd planted in the garden were all coming up white.

"But the white ones smell the nicest," said Jonathon.

143

He seemed happy enough. His job at the hospital was absorbing, the journey home straightforward. When he got there, it was a relief not to be a divorced man in an empty house.

With Beck, he had found a body. It was one who had already died, but she'd stopped mentioning that. She'd stopped saying much at all. Her throat was sore again.

Not just slightly sore, this time, it was very sore; but Beck never thought of going to see the doctor anymore. The doctor lived with her now and saw her every day. He didn't seem to notice anything wrong; like how pale she was or how flushed sometimes, or how she drank glasses of water, gallons of milk, and grimaced after every gulp.

Then one day, she happened to sigh deeply when he was sitting next to her on the sofa, and he turned and sniffed the air with a look of professional concern.

"That's an infection," he said. "Rebecca, open your mouth."

Doctor Comfort peered into her chasm of putrefaction.

"Tonsillitis," he said. "Quite acute. It must be painful. Why didn't you say?"

"Ah…" Beck began.

"Because of the crying wolf?" he asked her kindly.

Beck started to howl.

He patted her on the shoulder, left her on the sofa, looked for his bag and found antibiotics. Beck still cried.

"Take one straight away," Jonathon ordered. "Oh, darling, you should have said."

He made her a drink and made her go to bed.

That's why he's such a good doctor, thought Beck as he felt her head. He loves it when people are ill.

"Listen," Jon said, as he left the room, "I'll sleep in the spare bed tonight. Give you some space."

Then he turned off the light.

First they'd stopped talking, and now they weren't sleeping together. Beck lay alone in the darkness and listened to the sound of Jonathon removing Barbie Dolls in crinolines, shawls and sunbonnets from the bed in the spare room where Jade slept at weekends.

In the darkness she could see him wearing the same clothes; he was scurrying away from her in a long pink dress. Beck blinked, but the memory was indelible now; it couldn't be wiped from her mind's eye.

All the English people started sleeping together. After the fuss about the bullets they fashioned a crude defense, and hurried behind its low mud walls.

Beck heard the single bed creaking as Jonathon climbed into it, and pictured his feet sticking out beneath Jade's short pink quilt. He didn't need to suffer the discomfort; surely the doctor knew that a case of tonsillitis didn't require quarantine, even if he hadn't worked out that a sore throat caused by not talking could by cured by communication.

Jon slept in the spare room the next night too. Just a cuddle would have made Beck feel better; but instead she felt like a rebel soldier whose lady had fled from his contagion.

Lying awake long into the night, she read *The Joy of Sex* and wished it were the *Kama Sutra*. When she finally went to sleep, her legs were wide open. All the next day she kept her mouth closed; only opening it to throw pills in like exploding shot, and spit out grape pips.

But when the weekend came, and brought Jade to stay, Jonathon rejoined Beck in the double bed. He lay so close that she was forced to remain in the present with him, to remember that only her antibodies were fighting now; and the war between them was all in the past.

Doctor Comfort was looking forward to a peaceful future. That weekend was Easter.

"We're going to church," he said, on the Sunday morning.

"What?" said Beck and the children in surprise. They thought Easter was a celebration of chocolate, and had been planning to spend the day scoffing eggs.

"New life," Jonathon said, "that's what it's about. We of all people should be grateful for that."

He sent the children upstairs to brush their teeth, and smiled at a bemused Beck.

"What?" she said.

Jon pointed to where the Christmas tree had been standing a mere four months beforehand.

"You were lying there, effectively dead. By a miracle you came back to life. My beloved has risen again, and where can I go to give thanks for that, if not to church?"

He spread his arms wide in a questioning shrug, and Beck walked into them, into a hug. They stood together until the children came back downstairs, and felt their closeness; for Jonathon it was a union of body and soul, but Beck knew her heart still wasn't in it.

They sat together in church, holding hands beneath the same wooden cross, with Christ, the nails and the blood all carved out of a single tree; and Jonathon was secure in monotheistic awe, but Beck saw many gods with blue faces, elephant noses and hundreds of arms.

Under the crucifix they were dancing, wreathed in gay paper flowers and weeping tears of milk; under the Christian hymns they were chanting, alternative words and music that set up such a counterpoint in Beck's head she couldn't sing along.

Jonathon became more composed as the service drew to a close. His hand felt cool in Beck's hot one. If he hadn't led her down the aisle as the organist stumbled to the end of the final hymn, she might never have found her way out of the church. She'd lost her sense of direction, and didn't know east from west.

Feeling disorientated she stood in the graveyard, watching as Alfie and Jade chased each other around the graves. Cold stone crosses and weeping angels; that's what death meant here.

But with another religion, they would be dancing. The Hindus had a different idea; the endless circle of life and death, the certainty of rebirth.

It's just another country, only separated by sea; but in India everybody believes in reincarnation, even the kids.

"They were good, weren't they?" Jonathon said to her, but she didn't respond, so he raised his voice and spoke to the children. "You were very good," he said. "Would you like to go to church more often?"

"No," said Alf.

"Not really," said Jade.

"It smells funny," said Alf.

"And the seat made my bottom hurt," said Jade.

"Never mind your base functions," said Jonathon, "what did you make of the Easter story?"

"There wasn't a story," said Alf, indignantly.

"It was just talk," agreed Jade.

Back at home, Beck lay on the sofa and listened to Jonathon moving a boulder from the mouth of a tomb with his tale of resurrection.

"Christ came back to life, which was a bit like what happened to Rebecca," he said, "but without any medical intervention."

If he believes that, she thought to herself, why doesn't he believe my story; it's just as probable, and a lot more practical. Beck closed her eyes and wondered why the official line had got so rigid.

There it was again – look at that! The moment she closed her eyes, she saw it. Mutiny. The soldiers would not be paid unless they took off their uniforms and went unarmed to get it; went begging in native clothes for what they had already earned. Most of the men wouldn't stoop, and decided instead to conquer.

But warrior Beck wound on a proud turban, pinned it with a jewel and a feather, and went into the compound like a peacock to show how much more handsome she was than the plain white ladies. It was lighter than a helmet, and made him feel taller.

He wasn't interested in the money; only in one sovereign head amidst the hundreds of nameless faces all jiggling and jangling together in the hot pocket of their entrenchment.

The place was already starting to smell; a peculiarly British mix of panic and pompous brutality; like a bulldog crossed with chickens. What use would money be, when everyone was behaving like animals?

In the living room, Jon went on unwrapping Easter eggs from silver paper; not letting the children take a bite until they'd understood the symbolic meaning of the chocolate ovoid.

And in the place of the dead, Beck was getting what she wanted too.

She saw a woman behind bars, trying to keep her little brother and sister on the veranda of their prison, in the captivity of the country they had captured.

Beck could see it with her eyes closed, more permanently than if she'd painted it on paper, for that could be torn into pieces or screwed into a ball. She saw the woman and children engaged in a genteel tug-of-war on the veranda.

And when she opened her eyes, as if she'd been asleep on the sofa though actually she was more awake than most, Beck could see it still; but now it was Jonathon, with Jade and Alfie tugging on each hand, drawing him towards the door, dragging him outside.

"We want to go to the park," they cried; and he was bending like a willowy maiden, a slender thing, to their whim.

Beck started to get up.

"It's alright, you stay there and snooze," Jon said to her over his shoulder, as the children pulled him out of his usual shape. "They've been listening to my sermons all afternoon, and a breath of fresh air won't hurt them."

"Don't be so sure," Beck's throat opened with a battle roar, but luckily he'd already closed the front door.

The next day, Jonathon came home from the hospital saying that there was going to be a Doctor's Ball in June.

"A really fancy do," he said. "Bow-ties and ball gowns, you know. I think we should go."

Beck thought the hospital doctors always wore bow-ties, just for going to work; and there was no way she would ever wear a ball gown. But she was glad that her strange and unladylike behaviour hadn't put Jonathon off going out with her as a couple, so she simply replied that they might not be able to get a babysitter for that night.

Then she thought no more about it until she found him getting a dress suit out of a dusty trunk that had been lying still unpacked on the bedroom floor.

"Smells a bit musty," he said, heaving it onto a coat hanger. "I'll give it an airing. Decided what you're wearing yet?"

"Well, no," Beck faltered. "I didn't think we'd be able to get a babysitter."

"Leave that to me," he said, hanging the black ghost of his past on the wardrobe door.

Beck watched it, motionless.

"When did you last have that on?" she whispered.

"Why, does it look too small?" Jonathon gasped, shoving his reflection into the mirror next to it. "I've got to start jogging again. I haven't been once this year, and we're nearly halfway through."

He sucked his stomach in, and Beck shuddered.

"Stop it, you look fine," she said. "I just wondered when was the last time you…" She was struggling not to read too much into a couple of pieces of posh cloth that Jon had worn before they met.

"Oh, some glittering evening," Jonathon said, still posing in the mirror, "a gala event. A glamorous blonde on my arm…"

"Sharon?" gulped Beck.

"Of course, darling," said Jonathon. "Actually it was a tarts and vicars party. I made a dog collar out of paper. Sharon went as herself."

He left the room abruptly then, leaving Beck to contemplate her own reflection and the empty suit swinging next to it. The trousers did look a bit tight. If Jonathon couldn't get them zipped up they would have to give the Doctor's Ball a miss.

Beck got off the bed and went downstairs to cook his favourite pasta dish for dinner, with double creamy sauce.

But before she got a chance to find out if he could pull the trousers all the way up, Jonathon dropped a bombshell. The following Saturday morning he came back from collecting his daughter, and bounced into the kitchen where Beck was still washing up breakfast things.

"Sharon will have them both," he said.

"What?" Beck frowned.

"She'll keep Jade that weekend and have Alfie too," he said. "So we can go to the ball."

Beck dropped the spoon she was washing.

"No way," she said. "Your ex-wife is not looking after my son."

Jonathon looked surprised.

"Well she wasn't a very good wife, but there's nothing wrong with her as a mother," he said mildly.

"She's not having Alf," Beck spat again, her reaction instant and seemingly irrational.

"Why not?" said Jonathon.

Beck spluttered, up to her elbows in soapy water.

"Because I don't know her, and I'm not leaving Alf with someone I don't know," she said.

"He'll be fine," Jon replied.

She'd found the spoon again and pointed it at him.

"Look," she said, "if I want a babysitter, I'll find one. I don't need Sharon to take care of my son."

"But you told me you couldn't get anyone for that night."

"I never asked anyone!"

"Why not?" Jonathon bellowed in confusion.

The children, who had come into the kitchen to see what all the shouting was about, turned around and went straight back out again.

"Because I don't want to go!" The truth was out too. In her fear at the thought of Jon's Ex looking after Alfie, Beck just let it slip.

There was a long pause while it fell. Jonathon waited till it hit the bottom; Beck didn't want to go to the Doctor's Ball.

"Why not?" he asked.

There were so many reasons, she hardly knew where to start.

"Well, firstly," she faltered, "I don't want to go back to the hospital."

"It's not at the hospital," Jonathon said, "it's at the Queen's Hotel. There's a big ballroom with chandeliers, and you can see the promenade lit up through the picture windows. Honestly, it's really plush!" He added a flourish in the manner of the architect of Southsea's longest standing and grandest hotel. It had as much glass as a conservatory, as many turrets as a castle; and the Queen it was named for was not Elizabeth but Victoria.

All the more reason, Beck thought, to stay away. If ever she were going to feel like a fish out of native water, forced to wear an unfamiliar dress, it would be there; at that final outpost of Jonathon's empire.

But he was so excited about it.

"There'll be oceans of champagne," he said, "and though the evening will start sedately it will probably end with everybody stripping off and skinny dipping. Oh please, Rebecca, I really want to go!"

What could she say? Her soul was the ruler of her heart, but neither of them was rock hard. She looked down at her hands in the washing-up water, bubbles ringing her wrists like strings of pearls or chains of slavery. Beck was softening.

"Alfie, with Sharon?" she whispered.

"He'll be fine," Jonathon said again. "It's only for one night, and it's bound to have happened, sooner or later. He and Jade are getting on so well."

This was not to be denied. Beck sighed.

"You can come too," he said. "We'll go over in the afternoon, and you can check it out; meet Sharon, see where Alf will sleep, etc. And then," Jonathon removed Beck's hands from the washing-up bowl, shook the water off them, and wrapped them round his neck, "you shall go to the ball, Cinderella!"

He swung her from the sink.

"Sharon will keep him for as long as we want on the Sunday," he said, "so we can be completely pumpkin-like till tea-time."

Jonathon was now leading her around the kitchen in a most indecorous ball dance.

"Fairy godmother, really!" Beck giggled; but seriously, she did have one wish. If only she hadn't woken up from her coma with more memories than a woman in love needs, how happy she would be.

The Doctor's Ball was three weeks away, to the day.

Jonathon must have tried to zip his suit trousers up, surreptitiously, for he stopped eating puddings and started jogging along the seafront every evening instead.

Alf often went too, but for him it was a sprint.

"That boy," Jonathon said to Beck one night, "has an unhealthy interest in things naval. He's obsessed with enemy submarines."

"I thought he'd got over that," Beck replied.

"It's not so bad for my health though," Jonathon said, "running all the way to Eastney, to see the Mulberry harbour."

Moored off the furthest end of the prom was a famous floating quay used in the Second World War. Alf was fascinated by its history, and how it had been towed to France for the D-Day landings.

"Strange child," Beck shook her head. "I'm sure I don't know where he gets it from."

"Infiltration," Jonathon said. "We saw a fishing boat, and he swore it was full of spies."

While Alf watched the skyline, Jade was eyeing hem-lines; in her element, she was helping Beck chose a ball gown for June.

The last time Beck had worn anything long, apart from her face, or flouncy, apart from her attitude, was on her wedding day; and she'd never worn anything frilly outside of her underwear. But now she was being urged by Jade to find the longest, flounciest, frilliest garment possible.

When Beck was shopping for wedding dresses she'd only had herself to think about; a young woman, who could have worn anything, from ivory to cream, meringue to mini-skirt. But now there was this other character to please, the ancient dark-skinned warrior prince; and though Beck couldn't exactly see him when she looked at herself in the mirror, she could certainly sense him looking at her.

And he looked ridiculous in everything she tried on. She was squeezing him into the shapes and colours of the thing he most abhorred. Most of the other white women in the communal changing room were only worrying about their cellulite.

So, although Jade was in raptures about every dress Beck put on, and Jonathon was always at the ready with his credit card, two Saturday shopping trips came and went without Beck buying a stitch to wear.

The excitement of the ball distracted Jade from Beck's story, and she didn't ask for another installment of the serial that led to a killing. At the shops Beck bought books for the children's bedtime, hoping that they'd never wonder what happened next; for she could not tell them what befell the old-fashioned boy and girl she'd drawn so realistically and brought to life.

Even Alf's enemy submarines didn't seem to threaten to his well-being so much as the next episode of Beck's saga, with thousands of rebel soldiers poised to attack. But although she'd promised herself that she would not speak of it again, Beck couldn't help thinking about it.

She felt like a coiled spring, a cobra, a sabre; something that wouldn't fit into a frock, and could only do damage to the Doctor's Ball at the Queen's Hotel.

Beck hired her dress from a shop called Tat and Taffeta, with only two days to go. It was old, and black; and although she actually looked rather beautiful in it, she was long past caring.


They had to go to Sharon's first, early in the afternoon, on the day of the ball.

Though Jonathon had never said much about his ex-wife's looks, Beck knew that Sharon would be blonde. Every other detail she'd envisaged was wrong; instead of the sharp face there was a soft, round one, instead of the hard eyes lined with black there was a baby-blue pair. Instead of the surly demeanor, the door was opened with a sunny smile.

It served Beck right, for judging the woman on her name alone; but Sharon was dyed blonde, and a shade or two peroxide whiter even than Beck's prejudice had allowed for.

Beck's own hair was in curlers. She had not wanted to go so unglamorously to meet Jon's ex, and had told him too.

"But Rebecca," he replied, "how you face the past is not as important as how you face the future. It doesn't matter what you look like to Sharon, but it would be nice if you impressed the pants off my work colleagues."

So Beck was spending the day in rollers, in order to coast through the evening, when she would be promoting herself as Dr Comfort's new partner.

It fitted her plan of trying to forget the past altogether; though the way she'd wrapped a scarf around her head made it look decidedly like she was wearing a turban.

"Oooh," giggled Sharon, when they were introduced.

Then Jade appeared in the hallway behind her, in shorts.

"Alfie, come and see my climbing frame," she cried.

Alf dropped his camouflage hold-all at the foot of the stairs, and ran after Jade without a word of hello to her mother.

"Alfie loves to climb," Beck muttered apologetically to Sharon, who didn't seem to have taken the least offence.

"It's a big one," she was saying. "My... Les made it out of odd bits of scaffolding."

Les was Sharon's new husband, though she obviously wasn't ready to call him that in front of Jonathon. Beck completely missed this little slip that could have fed her fears for weeks; she was horrified at the prospect of Alf on scaffolding.

"Can I see it?" she asked.

"Of course," said Sharon, "come in the garden."

It was one of those cloudy June days, the typically disappointing backdrop to English weddings, barbecues and balls. Beck looked up at Alf, crouching atop a grey construction, against a grey sky.

"Mum, this is magic!" he said.

He was level with the first floor windows, though it was a very small house; a two-bedroomed terrace so tiny he could see into several of the neighbours bedrooms too.

But Alf wasn't that kind of inward looking. Arms outstretched he was soaring into the sullen clouds.

"Mum, I'm a spitfire," he screamed in delight.

Beck's gaze plummeted through the fuselage of the climbing frame to see where Alf was going to crash land.

At the bottom, on a bed of soft grass, was a thick mattress, perfectly positioned to catch falling children. Beck caught herself then, thinking that people who live in terraced houses don't love their kids. How much more could she misjudge the likes of Sharon?

"I must have got my superiority complex from the Indian prince," she thought, "because I only live in a semi. He was the one who had a fort."

It was true; Beck had always felt that she was better than other people, without ever having cause to. Perhaps her past life at the top of the caste system had this effect.

She grasped a piece of scaffolding near the bottom of the frame and gave it a shake.

"Great," she said to Sharon. "I shouldn't think you'll get Alf off till bedtime."

"Do you want to see where he's going to sleep?" Jonathon said, as if Beck were some sort of health and safety inspector.

Embarrassed by his tone, she laughed and shrugged, and pointed at the old mattress on the grass.

"He can sleep on that if he likes," she said, and gave Sharon a wink.

This was going a bit too far. Now Sharon thought Beck was taking the piss.

"We have got a proper bed for him, you know," she said. "A put-u-up in Jade's room. Les borrowed it from his mum."

"It's really, really nice of you," Beck gushed, trying so desperately to be sincere now that it was all she could do to stop herself adding, "I don't even want to go to the bloody ball."

"Come on then," Jonathon took Beck's arm to escort her from the garden. "Bye kids. See you tomorrow!"

"Have a good time," said Jade, swinging upside down from the flying fortress.

Alf just made the sound of bombs dropping.

"Bye, you little Fokker," Beck said weakly, and gave him a wave.

"Where's Les today then?" Jonathon asked Sharon as she led them to the front door.

"In the pub," she said, "he'll be back in a minute."

"Give him my regards," said Jonathon. "Perhaps we'll catch him tomorrow."

"Oh, he'll probably be in the pub tomorrow too," said Sharon.

Again, Beck was missing crucial nuances in the conversation between her partner and his Ex. Her own reluctance to meet Sharon now seemed so rude, she was thinking how to end on a politer note.

"Thank you for having him," she burst out.

Sharon was still talking about Les, so she looked a bit confused.

"He's got pyjamas, toothbrush and toothpaste and his enemy submarine in the bag," Beck continued. "Normally, he's asleep by half past seven, but he tends to get up at the crack of dawn. Oh, and he's allergic to taramasalata."

"Well don't worry, we're not having that," said Sharon. "I don't even know what it is. He'll get fish fingers and chips for tea, here."

"Oh, that's his favourite," said Beck, and blushed as pink as the silly fish dip.

Sharon had shut the front door before she could say a better goodbye.

"She didn't like me," Beck wailed as they walked up the narrow street to the car, and her voice rebounded from the pebble-dash walls like grazed knuckles.

"I didn't know you wanted her to," said Jonathon.

They went to the ball in the car, but they should have gone in a horse-drawn carriage.

All the way there, Beck felt like she was being dragged backwards by something with hooves. She could hear the hollow sound of coconut-shells, as they walked across the forecourt and up the stone steps of the Queen's Hotel; and she was sure it wasn't just the clippety-clop of her high-heeled shoes.

It continued as they crossed the marble foyer and up the stairs to the ball-room. Only when they paused at the top to marvel at themselves in a gilt-edged mirror did the tip-tapping stop.

Jonathon and Beck made a handsome couple; one slim and distinguished in a dress suit, face underlined by a velvet bow-tie; one tall and strong in black taffeta, bare shouldered and full skirted, with corkscrew ringlets in long brown hair.

Which was which? Beck wasn't sure, as she raised her hand, who would respond in the mirror, the man or the woman. It was a dizzy moment at the top of the stairs, not knowing whether to adjust her dress or dress suit.

"You look lovely." In the looking glass, the male figure's lips moved.

"That's you," Beck murmured in reply.

"Oh look," Jonathon turned from their clear reflection to the crystal refraction of the ballroom. "There's Doctor Simpkins! Crikey, he's got a whole case of champers. Come on, quick! This is a medical emergency!"

He grabbed Beck by the hand and she rustled softly after him, to stand listening to the men talk about work, and simpering at their silent wives.

At least, that was how it started. Doctor Simpkins really had acquired twelve bottles of champagne, and there were twelve members of their immediate party.

The talk wasn't about work for long, and the wives didn't stay silent. By the time they sat down for dinner, the men in white coats were stained.

At the point of asparagus spears, one of the doctors admitted that he'd killed someone, by accident. Over the rack of lamb, another confessed he'd killed a patient on purpose. And at the moment of Death by Chocolate cake, the most senior consultant amongst them came clean and said he'd flunked medical school and forged his qualifications. He wasn't even a real doctor.

Their partners, the tight-mouthed ladies, tipped whisky in the coffee and told the inside story on gynaecologists, and the confidential details of receptionists.

The whole meal was so saturated with alcohol, that everyone went soggy over the cheese and crackers. They were crumbling like the Cheshire and blue as the Stilton. Some of them ended up in tears, but Beck and Jon were crying with laughter.

The seating protocol had split them up, but they raised their glasses to each other across the collapsing table. Ever since Beck's coma things had been so hush-hush between them; but hearing about other people's scandalous lives made them feel they had nothing to hide.

Maybe they weren't drinking as fast as the others, or maybe their time was going slower; but Beck and Jonathon were the only ones still sober enough to stand up at the end of the meal, and dance on an even keel.

It should have been a reel. The Queen's ballroom was so Victorian that Beck wouldn't have been surprised to find people lining up for a quadrille. Instead, it was just couples shuffling slowly in circles; the sort of dance nineteenth century lovers were dying to do, and were getting ever closer to. Once they'd invented the waltz, with its close body contact, no one bothered so much with choreography any more.

Beck and Jonathon took a turn around the dance floor, and were gradually joined by their dining companions, who had picked themselves up from under the table, and patched up their differences.

Doctor and Mrs Simpkins were dancing nearby. The middle-aged lady kept catching Beck's eye over her husband's shoulder; and when they sat down again she quickly engaged Beck in conversation. Mrs Simpkins' chandelier earrings were swinging.

"Oh, don't you feel like you've been here before?" she asked, breathlessly.

"Pardon?" said Beck, picking up a glass.

"The historical ambience," panted Mrs Simpkins. "I believe in reincarnation, don't you?"

Beck choked on her drink.

"I think I lived in Victorian times," the lady continued. "The swish of a long skirt feels so familiar."

"What are you on about?" her husband asked rudely.

"Reincarnation, dear," she said. "You wouldn't understand."

"Wouldn't understand, my arse," Doctor Simpkins said, turning drunkenly to Jonathon. "Previous lives? I'll tell you who doesn't understand what. Women don't understand science." He thumped his fist on the table for emphasis.

"But one of the key principles of physics is that matter never dies," said Beck.

The doctor looked at her in surprise.

"So?" he said.

"It just turns into energy."

"And?" He still didn't get her point.

"Back into matter again."

He picked up the empty whisky bottle on the table, and turned it upside down with a sigh.

"So you've proved that women can remember their O-level notes," he said.

"No, I've proved that there's a scientific formula for reincarnation," said Rebecca. "Flesh is matter, spirit is energy." She pinched his arm. "Doctor Simpkins, you are never going to die."

He pulled his flesh away, quickly picking up all the other bottles and looking in them for a drop of spirit.

Then, without another word to Beck, the doctor started doing what empty vessels do best; he made a lot of noise. He lined ten green bottles up on the table and started tapping out a tune on them with cutlery.

One of the other boys found a jug of water. It was full, and pure as the truth of the words Beck had spoken; but they were no more going to drink it than they had listened to what she said. They poured it into the bottles, until they could play a scale with a spoon, and chords with knives and forks.

But Jonathon drank the water that was left, and looked thoughtfully at Beck across the clear glass.

As he had predicted, the evening ended in the sea. The blind drunk led each other into the waves, and while the salt water didn't exactly wash their sins away, it erased most of their memories.

The next day no one would remember who was a murderer and who was a manslaughterer; and even the senior consultant who wasn't really a doctor at all didn't get struck off, though his dining companions of that night never seemed to treat him with quite the same respect again.

Jonathon and Beck, strolling home along the prom at two o'clock in the morning, recalled more than most.

"Who told you that stuff about matter and energy?" he asked her.

"My O-level science teacher," she said, more concerned now about salt stains on the hem of her hired black taffeta.

"Yes, but who told you it was a formula for reincarnation?" he said.

"Nobody told me. It's obvious," she replied. "If energy never dies, it must be endlessly reborn."

"But how do you know that spirit equals energy?"

"Having seen you on the sofa on a Saturday afternoon," said Beck, "I can't be sure. But I've never seen anything more solidly made of matter than your body."

He looked at her, and she saw the same expression on his face as earlier; it was the opening of an enquiry. A crack had appeared in his disbelief.

"But it's so watertight a theory," he muttered.

"What can I say? God is unfillable."

Beck turned back to the sea-stained material of her skirt, with its hemline as long as the promenade, trying to see where the watermark was under the fairy lights.

So, she'd come home from the ball with an invitation. Beck was going to have another go at proving it to Jonathon; the pair of them were playing lead parts in a story, and this life was not the first installment.

It would be just like the siege, all over again. And again, she besieged him with illustrations; but this time she didn't do her artwork at nursery school. It wouldn't have been appropriate to use crayons and coloured pencils for what came next.

She needed India ink, for stomach wounds and severed limbs; charcoal for the smog and the smears. Beck found a craft shop in Southsea that could supply her with the roughest textured paper ever made. But no matter how graphic were her scenes of war, Jonathon still didn't seem to appreciate the details.

She screwed them into balls, and threw them like bullets at him, into his smug encampment on the sofa; then went back to the kitchen table to try again for the ultimate hit. She smoked while she worked. It fuelled the fight.

Rebecca didn't have a period that month; there was too much testosterone in her body.

She didn't sleep with Jonathon either. He had retreated to the spare room again, but it seemed like the right move to Beck too, so she hadn't asked him why. Surely he was meant to be unattainable, and she had to try and reach him through a lot of smoke and shouting. That's what their relationship was all about.

Every time she finished a picture, though, she posted it under his bedroom door and waited for the sound of a bombshell dropping that would mean he'd got it; he'd finally remembered what was what, and who was who in their history.

She felt that moment getting ever closer.

"Mum," Alf burst into the kitchen.

"Mmm?"

"Mum, stop drawing!" Alf shouted. "Thunderbird One has gunned down Thunderbird Two. No, Thunderbird One has gunned down Thunderbird Three. No, Thunderbird Three has gunned down Thunderbird Two."

"Okay," said Beck.

She really did feel okay about him being so into aerial warfare, until he made paper airplanes out of her pictures.

"Alf!" she shouted, finding them on the floor, all creased wings and bent noses after a battle. And she really did shout; he'd never had it so loud.

"Alfred Salmon, you little piece of shit," she screamed. It wasn't the words so much as the tone that terrified him.

He burst into tears, and didn't stop crying till bedtime. Then Beck went back to the kitchen table and drew until Jonathon came looking for his dinner.

"Aren't you shocked?" she asked, handing him a piece of sandpaper.

The picture was grainy, all gunpowder and ashes. He glanced at the rough drawing, then back at her face. She was big eyed as the Indian men, seeing the mess their dirty bullets had made.

For a moment Jonathon was silent; the same silence as the prisoners found alive in the entrenchment; making a white space, like a page no black words could touch.

Then he turned the paper over, and looked on the blank side.

"It's certainly shocking," he said. "But it's got nothing to do with me."

That did it. That night she did it; the one she'd been saving for the last straw, the picture that would break Jonathon's resistance to his background.

She had to stand up and draw it. The image was too uncomfortable to do sitting down; a starving woman could not be depicted at the kitchen table.

As she worked, Beck referred back to the original picture she'd done of Jonathon, the nineteenth century Barbie doll with long blonde hair; grown a bit yellow on the top shelf in the living room, and already curling with age.

She held the images side by side, a 'before and after' advertisement, to show the effects of the siege. The curves of the first contrasted with the razor sharp shoulder blades and cheekbones of the second. The hair had turned black with grease, and brick dust from the shelter that had fallen around her ears.

Drawing in the smoke filled room, Beck was so choked with feelings about the girl, that she hardly gave a thought to how Jonathon would feel when he saw her.

Even if he didn't yet identify with the character, he was familiar enough with her rosebud-lipped, robust-hipped appearance to find her sadly changed. But the new look was unisex, so he might finally see through that off-putting femininity to the simple human soul, his own, that lay beneath.

This is what Beck hoped would happen when, at three in the morning, she opened the door to the spare bedroom and put on the light.

"What's up?" Jonathon, the doctor, thought he was on call. "Is someone ill?"

"Sort of," Beck said. "You'd better see these."

He looked at the clock before he looked at her pictures; three AM, two sheets of paper. As well as the portrait of the bombed-out Barbie, Beck had done one with the little girl who looked like Jade clinging to her big sister; both of them hungry, both looking at the warrior prince as if they wouldn't eat him if he'd been made of chocolate.

Naked under the pink quilt, Jonathon looked at Beck in much the same way.

"You could have waited till the morning," he muttered.

"Is that all you've got to say?"

Jonathon lay down again. The pictures fluttered to the floor, landing half under the bed. Beck wasn't having that; she'd spent half the night on them, half the night perfecting that superior sneer from her memory, only to have him turn his nose up at her again.

She picked the papers up and shoved them in his face.

"Look at the state of you," she said. "Aren't you going to surrender?"

"It's not me," he turned his back on her, and snuggled under the covers of the single bed.

"She's starving too. Your little girl…"

Jonathon snapped. He was out of bed in one movement, ushering Beck to the door of the spare room with an angry hiss.

"Don't even say her name in that sentence. It constitutes abuse!"

Beck gasped.

"But you can't mean… I would never actually…"

Naked and snake-like he whispered her onto the landing, but when his arm rose it was not to strike her. Jonathon was handing her back the pictures.

"This is some sort of pornography, Rebecca," he said, "and unless you burn it, Jade won't be coming to stay here again."

Beck gasped another disbelieving laugh.

"But…" she said.

Jonathon closed the bedroom door quietly, but his threat slammed to. Beck backed away, still not believing what she'd heard him say.

Pornography? Jade not coming to stay?

She stumbled into her own room, fell on the bed and looked at her pictures again. She didn't turn the light on, but she could see them in the dark.

On the dark landing, though, she hadn't noticed the little boy standing in his Action Man pyjamas. Alfie put himself back to bed; and Beck fell asleep on top of her covers, with her clothes on, thinking a despicable thought.

"I'll photocopy them! Then I'll burn the originals, if that's what he wants."

When she woke up again, only an hour later, she knew that she wanted Jonathon, pink and present under his quilt, more than she wanted to keep the black and white etchings of his past.

She tiptoed back into the spare room, sat on the edge of the narrow bed and said:

"Let's do it."

Jonathon had only just got back to sleep. He returned to consciousness with the helpless rage of a budgerigar who'd been caught and caged again just as it was making for the open skies.

"What?" he said.

"Let's do it now," Beck said. "Let's burn the pictures."

Jonathon's mind clung numbly to its perch.

"Oh God," he groaned. "Can you not wait till morning?"

"We should burn them while it's still dark," Beck said. "In the garden. Come on."

"Oh God," Jonathon groaned again. "Can't you do it by yourself?"

"No," Beck shook her head. "I drew them by myself. I'm burning them for us."

Modern though the man of medicine was, he knew an old-fashioned sacrifice when he saw it, even at four o'clock in the morning. Alfie was a bit confused, though, when he looked out of the bedroom window to see what all the noise was about.

His Mum and Jon were dancing in their dressing-gowns around a small bonfire. Bright orange against the black lawn, it mocked the subtlety of the yellow and grey dawn. Alf watched the grown-ups' antics until the sky became light enough to see that their dressing-gowns weren't done up properly; then he went back to bed again, shutting his eyes tight against the loose behaviour of the night.

He couldn't shut out the sounds when they came upstairs and both got into Mummy's bed; even though he put his head under the pillow and pretended that bombs were dropping on top of him.

But by the morning, everything was back to normal. Mum had burned the pornography, and Jade could come to stay.


The grey dawn had turned into a rainy day; warm and thundery, a real headache. It was the first weekend of the school holidays.

Jonathon had driven off to get his daughter; Alf was waiting at the window, watching out for them. Beck lay on the sofa and watched him, clinging to the net curtains.

"You've grown," she said. "You come up to the next row of holes now."

His fingers were stretching a new place in the lacy pattern out of shape.

"Alfie," Beck said, "it's your birthday soon. What would you like to do?"

He didn't reply. He was making a strange whistling sound.

"Alf," she said again.

He stopped his noise, but then the phone rang; it was for Jonathon, someone whose name Beck had to remember, and it made her forget what she'd been asking her son.

"One of these days I'll get round to washing those nets," she said instead.

When Jonathon and Jade arrived they had decided to go swimming.

"Not in the sea!" Beck said.

"In the swimming pool," said Jonathon.

"Paradise," said Jade.

"Can I come too?" asked Alfie.

"Of course you can, you always do," Jonathon replied, in surprise. Alfred never usually asked.

Another funny thing happened on the way to the swimming pool. Alf didn't want to walk with Beck, didn't want to hold hands or talk to her. Today both the children went with Jonathon, hanging on either side of him with Beck strung out behind.

She tried not to mind and marched on under the rumbling sky, but her footsteps echoed; echoed the march they'd all been on before. And though she'd burnt the pictures, the story was marching on, down the road to the river.

The siege was over, and they'd gone to the water's edge; the resilient threesome, with the warrior one, supposedly taking them to safety. This was a different road now, and these were thoughts she'd sworn not to think. Beck was trying hard to keep the anger out of her head and her heart; but she couldn't keep it out of her hands. She was holding it there, solid as the shape of a sword or a gun, pointed at Jonathon's back as he walked in front of her with the children.

She thought she had purged herself of that old black and bronze fury, and the jewel-flashing rage; but her grip on them was firmer than ever. She could see them, really see the weapons held at arms length; more clearly than the plastic bag of swimming things that swung from her shoulder. Rebecca was still holding a gun and a sword.

She changed clumsily into her bikini, leaving little nicks in her thin white skin as if she'd been shaving black hair off. Luckily Jade and Alfie didn't ask her to help them change; Jonathon did it, quickly and efficiently, and the three of them ran into the water while Beck was still trying to fit all her stuff into a locker.

The sword wouldn't bend, the gun wouldn't budge, she couldn't get them inside. The insubstantial plastic bag, towel and clothes went in with no force whatsoever, and the locker door closed with a final bang; but Beck's pair of weapons remained outside. She had to take them into Paradise with her.

Beck found a seat by the poolside and sat down stiffly. Before long, Jonathon appeared.

"Aren't you going to swim?" he asked, sitting down beside her.

She thought of the damage she would do in the water with a sword, and her eyes filled with tears.

"It was all a trick," she said.

"What was?" he frowned.

"Bringing you down to the river," she said. "There was no safe passage. It was a trick."

"What are you talking about?"

"The boats," said Beck. "You were promised boats, remember? But as soon as you were all on board we set fire to them. Their roofs were thatched, and burning straw fell into your hair. You threw the children overboard."

Jonathon went white. Even the grey curls on his chest seemed to get a shade lighter in that instant. He got up and walked away.

Beck saw him plunge back into the water, amidst the summer-holiday children and their long-suffering parents. She dithered for a minute, wondering whether to lay her gun and sword down on the table; but no, she couldn't leave such dangerous weapons unattended. Beck jumped in at the deep end, with the sword over her shoulder, the gun in her hand, and spare ammunition between her teeth.

It gave her a horrible smile. Jonathon saw her coming, through the swathes of sink-or-swimmers, long before she found him hiding in the shallows. He hadn't been able to find Jade and Alf, and hoped that they were in the queue for the water chutes, up a slippery staircase. He could no longer assume that Beck meant them no harm; and he couldn't even see her gun, only the grimace she'd fixed around the bullets.

Beck had to spit them out before she could speak.

"I came in after you," she said. "But in all the confusion I couldn't see you. The water was black from the burning, and red from the bloodshed."

Jonathon shrank from the voice she raised above the swimming pool people screaming. Then over her shoulder he saw Jade and Alfie slide down the chutes and land in the splash pool nearby. He guarded his expression so it wouldn't give them away. Beck didn't turn around.

"In the water nearly everyone was dead," she went on. "A few red bubbles were still rising to the surface, a lot of long hair and petticoats floating. Sun hats; but none of them were yours."

"Because I wasn't there," said Jonathon. But he didn't say it very loudly.

Beck had him backing away; the fake waves were lapping the tiled shore at his feet. He was almost on dry land.

"You were in the reed beds that lined the river bank," Beck pressed him further. "I slashed a path straight to you; smelling where you sat in fear. You'd shat yourself!"

"I had not!" Jonathon raised his hand and slapped Beck, a ringing slap that silenced everyone around them for a moment.

She'd had it coming to her for a long time, but those who tutted him disapprovingly never knew that. Neither did they notice that Jonathon didn't hit Beck like a man hits a woman; he smacked her like a woman smacks a man.

Beck noticed though. Her grin was triumphant.

"She's not very well." That's what Jonathon told Alf when he asked where Mummy had gone. "I sent her home to lie down." The doctor sat by the edge of the pool, fingering his invisible stethoscope as firmly as Beck had clutched her sword.

He could hear his own heart beating. He was having palpitations; but when they got home, Beck hadn't been lying down at all. She'd been drawing at the kitchen table.

"Oh Mum!" said Alfie, miserably surveying the pencils and paper where there should have been fish fingers, chips and peas. "We're hungry."

Rebecca just laughed.

Jonathon made sandwiches with shaking hands. He got crisps and chocolate biscuits and fizzy drinks; naughty things for the children who were being punished for no good reason. He loaded their plates guiltily as they watched TV, then went back into the kitchen to face Beck.

"Recognise this?" She confronted him with her latest drawing.

He didn't look at it.

"I recognise the behaviour of someone who is mentally ill," he said, in a professional tone. "This can not go on. You really need help."

"Please," she said, "just look at the picture."

He forced his eyes to stick with hers, to stay on their shiny surface, not slip into the unreflective world of pen and paper.

"I thought we'd burned the pictures," he said.

"Yes, but I'm on fire too, and I can still see them," said Beck, thrusting the picture at him again. "Please, just say you recognise this house. Then we'll both know I'm not mad."

"Art is not the antidote to insanity," said Jonathon, turning away. "It took me seven years to train to be a doctor, and not so much as a doodle. It's all about writing prescriptions; pictures don't come into it."

Beck sat back down at the table.

"Then I will never be cured," she said, tearing a clean sheet, a hopeless paper bandage, from her sketch pad, and starting to draw again.

Alf came from the living room with an empty plate. He looked at her uncertainly.

"Mum," he whispered, "when it's my birthday can I have the party at McDonald's?"


All his friends were there, but it was a pretty soulless affair; even when Beck absent-mindedly told Sam's mother Maisie that she didn't eat beef because she'd been a Hindu in a previous life.

Maisie had tactfully forgotten how, only a year ago, the two of them had criticised these ready-made parties, for their polystyrene cartons and lack of parental creativity. She did, however, remember as if it were yesterday Beck's dishy doctor coming, when Beck had collapsed on the sofa.

"Ooh, he was gorgeous," Maisie said, with one eye on her son, "I couldn't believe it when you said he'd asked you out. Sam don't squirt that Coke!"

"It was unbelievable," Beck replied quietly.

"I suppose it must be nearly your first anniversary," said Maisie. "Really, I'm going to stick that straw up his nose myself if he doesn't stop it. Sam!"

She lunged at her son, but Beck took a step backwards. Only a year, and he'd got so grey. The day she first saw Doctor Comfort in his surgery, his hair was brown.

"I'll look after Alfie, if you want to go out for the night," said Maisie, coming back with a bent straw, "to celebrate."

"Thanks." Beck spoke from far away. He'd got so grey. She'd done that to him; not his divorce, but his new relationship, the one that was supposed to rejuvenate. All the more reason to believe that theirs was an old, old story; this past year merely the tip of a prehistoric iceberg in which the pair of them were frozen, turning each other from grey to white.

"Oh Sam!" shouted Maisie, as suddenly there were ice cubes scattered all over the table.

She flew at the spillage, flapping paper napkins; but one of the restaurant staff was there in an instant, half clown, half corporate clone, with postmodern platitudes.

"No problem," he said. "Just get up and move to another table."

The boys cheered.

"This is a brilliant party, Mum," said Alfie as he pushed past her.

Beck smiled a tiny ray of sunshine. He hadn't said anything as nice as that last year.


"It's our anniversary on Saturday," Beck said to Jonathon when she got home.

He looked at her suspiciously.

"In which life?" he said.

"This one, silly," she giggled, glad to be able to say something uncomplicated for once. "It was the first time we went out together. Remember? A Chinese meal, and that seventies disco."

"Yes," said Jonathon in relief. "Now this is the sort of event I do remember; one that actually happened."

They sat at the same table they'd sat at the year before. It was quieter in the Chinese restaurant this time, and Jonathon and Beck had been doing too much shouting to talk normally. They hadn't faced each other at dinner since the Doctor's Ball.

"You were fantastic that night," said Jonathon. "No, sorry, wrong word. You were factual. It was evidence you gave; the only scientific evidence I've ever heard for reincarnation."

"Thank you," said Beck.

"But since then, you've really gone downhill."

She blushed, and looked down at the tablecloth. That was pink too. So were the serviettes, and the menu's shiny cover.

"When you were talking scientifically I could listen to you," Jon went on, "but when you turn it into art, I can't look."

The pictures had kept coming, even though she'd said she wouldn't do any more. All week, Beck had been painting a house, from inside and outside, from floor to ceilings; and though she hadn't rammed them down Jonathon's throat, he found them on the kitchen table when he got up for breakfast every morning.

Rebecca was getting sicker. Jon could tell by how ill her pictures made him feel. The house was a bungalow, built around a courtyard, bare but for one big tree. Shady verandas lined the open space that always seemed to be smoky; and glass doors gave way to the dim interior. Jonathon could have seen through them, but he didn't look too closely, didn't want to know what was happening inside the house.

It was enough to smell the stench that seemed to come off Beck's pictures; a choleric odour, opium and curry paste that meant Jonathon hadn't managed to stomach any breakfast for days.

So he was really looking forward to the Chinese meal, its blend of spices more beneficial than anything Beck could stir up with her paintbrush. The taste spectrum from lemongrass to star anise cleansed his palate. And when his plate was clean he looked up at Beck and smiled.

"Fancy a dance?" he asked her, without bitterness.

"Really?" she said. She hadn't expected him to prolong the evening beyond dinner. But then, she couldn't see him wanting to hurry home either.

A year ago, they could have gone anywhere together, on their first date; tonight they would be awkward together anywhere. Now they didn't seem to know each other so well.

She heard him suppress nearly everything he wanted to say; but that had been happening a lot lately. Indoors, only the odd comment escaped him.

"It feels a bit crowded in here," he said mildly, one night in the bedroom.

"Try sharing it with so many women that there's not enough room for everyone to lie down at once," Beck had replied.

"I think the toilet needs cleaning," he said on another occasion.

"At least you've got one," Beck said. "Imagine being cooped up with a hundred shitting females and just one bucket between you."

The woman's house was his prison. That was the size of their relationship. Her four walls constrained his person, the glassy walls through which watched her jailer gaze. But Jonathon didn't want Beck to look at him like a squatting creature from the dim interior. He wanted to get out and strut his funky stuff.

"Look," Jon pointed, Travolta style, through the restaurant window and across the street; "the seventies disco is still going strong."

When they got inside, it was as if they were still there from last time. The year between had worn away like the velvet pile on the nightclub's plump banquettes.

The alcohol also helped. Jonathon was back at the bar every twenty minutes, refreshing their glasses of red and gold, which glowed in the lights from the dance floor.

They stayed on the edge for ages, waiting for the time warp to work on them; waiting till they felt as tall as the platform heels, as light-headed as the Afro hairstyles of the other dancers. They didn't talk much, but smiled and nodded at each other, feeling the same music thumping in their chests as if they were of one heart, pumping the same love.

And then, when they were so full of the stuff it had to be strutted, Jonathon held out his hand to Beck and escorted her onto the dance floor.

As a new song started he struck a pose, one finger pointing skyward, to indicate his hopes that the second year of their relationship would be better than the first; no more electric shock, no more near-death horror. Now, as the song said, they would be concentrating on Staying Alive!

Drunk as he was, and with the dance floor spinning around the axis of his pointed finger, it took a few bars of music for Jonathon to focus on the posture his partner had got into.

Beck was trying to keep her balance, in the dark and blood red light, with bodies reeling around her; women thin as sticks with short hair, men who were wearing women's underwear, all dancing in the house of whores.

She put out her sword to steady herself. Her what? Her sword; the one she'd stolen from the sheath of history; snatched from a dream she would never have seen if it wasn't for the flashing Christmas tree lights.

It was an on and off sword. She couldn't always feel it, but it had never left her fingers, and now she could see it again in the disco strobe.

She was the only one who had such a weapon, the only man in the house of hysterical women. That's why they couldn't see it, even Jonathon. He didn't know what she was doing when she crouched low, in a warrior pose, and raised her sword above her head, ready to smite those white ladies.

Jonathon thought she was still dancing. As she squatted low and prepared to spring, he thought she was still dancing. As she rocked back on her heels and pointed her toes, he was dancing too. Even when she moved away from him in the crowd, slashing circles with her arms and kicking out with her legs, he still thought they'd end the dance together with a bow and a curtsey.

It was only when Beck leapt on some girl with a yell he could hear over the music and held the complete stranger in a stranglehold that Jonathon realised the truth. This wasn't dance, it was drama; it wasn't a mime, Beck meant it.

Still locked on the first girl, Beck was reaching for a second; bringing their heads together in a cymbal crash. They crumpled in a glittery heap.

Before Jonathon could reach her in the crush, Beck had jumped on the back of a big bloke in a flowery bodice and embroidered bloomers, and was cutting him down to size.

His friends were trying to pull her away but she kept them at bay, with angled kicks and sharp elbows as if every part of her body were a sword and no one could touch her.

Her tongue's lash was the worse.

"Your white skin shows the dirt," she shouted.

The music had stopped. Everyone could hear what she said. Jonathon cringed at her Indian accent, and tried to interrupt before she could speak again. But the bouncers got to Beck before he could, men so big and burly they wouldn't have been afraid even if they could have seen her as she saw herself; a highly-trained fighter.

They happened to be Scottish, these bouncers; two brothers, with brawny forearms. Their own accents, as they peeled Beck easily from her third victim, were just like the Highland soldiers who came to stop the original massacre. Though they were neatly dressed in black and white, she saw them as Tartan clad warriors with wild red hair and raw whisky breath. And though they came too late to save the original ladies, they got to Rebecca in the nick of time.

"What is she on?" one said, as she writhed in his arms.

"She's on her way out of here," the other replied, clearing a path off the dance floor.

"Wait! She's with me," Jonathon rushed after them. Everyone turned to stare at him accusingly. "I'm a doctor," he added, as if that would explain both her behaviour and his being with her.

"Should have stayed at the loony bin disco tonight, Jim," said the first bouncer, ushering the pair of them into the foyer where red paint was peeling from the walls and signs of other scuffles showed around the nightclub's doors. "Want us to call an ambulance to take you back?"

"No, it's fine thanks," said Jonathon, taking hold of Beck's arm firmly. "She's not as bad as she looks."

"Well, we don't want to see her in here again, anyhow," said the second Scot, and that was the end of it. He took up his position, impassive against the door post and watched the pair of them stagger off down the street.

"He's not a fucking doctor," he said, as Jonathon steered Beck drunkenly round a corner and out of sight.


But Jonathon Comfort was now going to behave more like a doctor than ever before; more like a doctor than a lover to Rebecca, though he would do it out of love for her.

From his office at the hospital he phoned his colleague Doctor Lacey; the GP Beck had tormented with an imaginary tumour, but hadn't been to see once with her symptoms of a genuine mental illness.

It was Monday morning, but Jon's throat was still sore from Saturday Night's fever; his head was still pounding from the hangover, or was that his heart?

"She attacked three disco dancers," he said. "If it were anyone else I would definitely recommend sectioning."

"And you think it all stems from the electric shock," Doctor Lacey's voice buzzed over the line. "She didn't have any psychotic tendencies before?"

"No, she was just a normal neurotic," replied Jonathon. Of that he was quite sure.

But he wasn't telling Beck's story straight; he wasn't telling it all. He never said anything about how she came out of her coma convinced that she had died; lived and died, a previous life in a distant land and a death that still seemed so close.

He didn't mention the details with which Beck had described this life to him; everything from the trousers she wore to the troubles she saw, drawn with extraordinary precision, page after page. He omitted to say how she suddenly seemed to know things about a culture that had been foreign before; how she'd filled their freezer with curry and referred to the drizzling English rain as a monsoon; how she couldn't get in a car without talking about riding elephants, or watch a gun battle on TV without discussing the relative merits of the flintlock pistol.

No, he didn't tell the doctor the whole story, and he didn't show her any of the pictures, though he'd kept most of them and could use them to cross-reference the points in Rebecca's story; before, during and after what she referred to, so familiarly, as 'the siege'.

There was something else Jonathon didn't tell Doctor Lacey. Something he hadn't even told Beck. She'd been talking in her sleep, in a language he didn't know, but which he suspected was Hindi.

All this added up to absolutely no evidence that Beck was mad, and plenty of proof that the story she was telling was true. True, but strange: so strange, in fact, that if Doctor Comfort had told his colleague the truth she'd probably have thought that he was mad too.

So Jonathon let Beck do all the talking when Doctor Lacey came to see her that evening.

"I hear you had a fight in a nightclub," the Doctor said.

"A fight in the night, yes," Beck raved. "But it's over now; and there's no one for you to save, Doctor. They're all dead." She didn't realise it was her Doctor Lacey had come to see. She was looking right through the professional suit and briefcase, at a place too hot to wear such clothes, a scene too heavy to carry such baggage.

"We stripped them off," Beck said, "we stripped the bodies naked; and thin brown boys picked the precious metal off bone-white fingers." She shuddered. "Then we threw the bodies down a well. There were so many of them, we couldn't fit them all in. I had to chop some up, cut the arms off," Beck's own limbs slashed the air as she spoke, "squeeze them in longways. Rest in pieces. Sorry, you've come too late, Doctor. They're all dead."

Doctor Lacey gulped, and took the cup of tea Jonathon offered her.

"Actually there was one old lady still breathing," Beck went on, "and two little girls who screamed at the mouth of the well for their mothers. We threw them down it too. They weren't dead. But they are now." She looked the doctor in the eye. "We threw more bodies in on top."

Doctor Lacey spat out her mouthful of tea.

"I know, it's disgusting," said Beck. "But they were only women, white women at that. He'll tell you," she nodded at Jonathon. "He was one of them; the worst of the lot, pale flesh pinched in the middle and spilling out on top. Yellow hair. Go on," Beck said to Jonathon, "tell the doctor what I did to you."

But Jonathon didn't. He didn't say the words, and he didn't show the pictures. Kneeling on the carpet, he scrubbed at a tea-stain in the shape of India.

In his silence, the other doctor opened her briefcase and got out the paperwork for sectioning a patient. The decision was made and the forms were signed and Rebecca Salmon was required to undergo hospitalisation on the grounds of her mental health.


"I don't believe it," she said, as Jonathon swung her suitcase down from the top of the wardrobe and laid it on the bed. "Mental hospital?"

"Shall I help you pack?" he replied, smiling as brightly as if he'd promised her a holiday in the sun. He pulled open her top drawer, and Beck was so confused, she took out her bikini.

Jonathon looked at the skimpy garment.

"Er, I don't think you'll be needing that," he said, and saw Beck's bottom lip wobble. "But you can take it if you like."

"I can't believe it. Mental hospital?" Beck said again, and sat down on the bed, looking as deflated as the empty case beside her.

"Well, it's not exactly," Jon said. "It's the mental wing of your normal hospital. Mandelson Ward One." He unzipped the suitcase and found that it wasn't quite as empty as it seemed.

"Oh look," he said, taking out some souvenirs from Beck's last stay there; the plastic name tag that was attached to her wrist in Intensive Care and a Get Well Soon card from Maisie. He showed them to her. "See, it's just that you didn't get well as soon as we'd hoped. Sure, you're physically fit; but psychologically you need more treatment…"

He was all doctor; she could detect nothing of her former lover in his bedside manner. Sinking back on the pillows she shut her eyes, and started to cry.

"What about Alfie?"

"I'll look after him," Jonathon replied. "I've sorted it with a social worker." Never mind social worker; this man was a saint!

"But listen," he was saying, "it could only be a couple of days; just till you prove that you're of sound mind. All you have to do is stop waving your imaginary sword around. Stop getting so historical all the time…"

She opened her eyes. "Well, I can stay at home and do that. I don't have to go to hospital."

"Yes you do, they're expecting you now," Doctor Comfort insisted. "The forms have been signed and countersigned, and the healing process is in motion. If you don't go willingly now, you'll have to go under police escort."

"No," she stared at him. "That's ridiculous. You can't possibly bring the police into it."

"The police are always bringing people in," said Jonathon. "I see them every day at work. Darling, it's no big deal; please just come in with me, and stay for a quiet chat with a psychiatrist. The food isn't bad. Think of it as a… as a…" He faltered under her gaze.

"No," she said. "I'm not mad. You know I'm not."

Jonathon buried his head in his hands.

"You are driving me mad," he said, in a muffled tone, "that's all I know."

It was true; she had driven him to despair, and he wanted the police to come and take her away. He could no longer reason with her, and he had lost his own reasoning. It would take the long arm of the law to reach out and rescue him from the well of their relationship.

Wearily he went downstairs and dialled 999.

*

The police came wearily too. They knew what they had to do; they'd done it so many times before. Sectioning mad people; it was boring, in a bizarre kind of way. In an everyday sort of way, they dreaded it.

Two male police officers turned up; but the boys in blue weren't really the right men for the job.

For Beck, they needed to be brigadier-generals. Men with iron ramrods in the backs of their jackets; and, in front, rows of medals like five-shilling pieces. They needed faces of deeply lined brown leather, framed with mutton chop beards or walrus mustaches, white as their hair. Colonial grandfathers, they should have been; men who could order an execution.

"I told you," she said to Jonathon, as she was led out to the police car. "Don't you remember? They caught me. A big battalion came and caught little me. They strung me up, they hung me; but not until I'd licked the floor clean, and picked up the children's clothes, don't you remember?"

Jonathon didn't reply. He didn't have to argue any more; the law was on his side. He sat in silence in the police car. Beck, sitting next to him in the back as if it were a taxi, couldn't stop talking.

"What will you tell Alfie?" she asked.

Jonathon didn't reply.

"He's going to hate me for not saying goodbye," she said. "Will you collect him from nursery? There's hardly any food in the fridge, I was supposed to go shopping. Sugar Puffs, there isn't even any cereal for breakfast. And bread; you've got to get bread."

"Okay, okay," muttered Jonathon. "Now shut up."

Maybe he was worried that she didn't sound mad enough, that the police would get suspicious about why he was sending her inside; especially when they realised that the doctor was living at the same address.

But the two officers in front didn't seem interested in undercover detective work. It was just small talk as they drove to the hospital; 'See *The Bill* last night, mate?' Over and out.

There were no sirens, no flashing lights, no screeching of tyres as the police car pulled up at the hospital. Nothing to say that a dangerous lunatic was entering its grim incarceration. Beck just got out of the car and walked inside.

She wasn't exactly wearing a straitjacket, but Jonathon was holding her very tightly by the arm. He steered her though the hospital foyer, past the lifts that would have taken them up to Intensive Care, where she had lain blameless in the days after her electric shock, before she became guilty again of the sins for which she was now being committed.

Beck thought longingly of the tubes and wires, the dripping and bleeping of Intensive Care. If only she could get back to the baby-like state she had been in then, the coma without words. If only her past-life secrets had stayed in its silence. Now she was heading for a ward where she would have to tell the story again and again.

She was not gibbering, not foaming at the mouth; but people coming the other way along the long corridor to Mandelson Wing could see exactly where she was going.

"Come on," Jonathon muttered, as Beck dragged her feet on the screaming lino. "Come on!"

"Why don't you just strap me to a trolley," she snapped.

Jonathon looked mortified. "We're nearly there now," he said.

But Beck was trying to slow down the passage of time. She put out a hand to steady herself on the hospital wall that seemed less real than the world she had lived in since her accident. It was a chalky green she could have dusted away with a flick of her wrist and coloured again more vibrantly with crayon.

"If only reality could be rubbed out too," she said.

A whoosh of white coat overtook them in the dark corridor, whistling cheerily.

"Everything all right?" it asked as it went past, not stopping to wait for an answer.

"Doctor Young," Jonathon said to the white back.

It turned and came right back.

"Doctor Comfort," the man replied with a nod. Then he looked at Beck. "Ah yes," he said.

"Rebecca, this is the consultant psychiatrist," Jonathon said. "He's going to make you better."

He pushed her forwards, as if she was supposed to curtsey like Ophelia in her mad scene. But Beck hung back.

"I shouldn't be here," she said. "It's all a big mistake."

"That's for me to decide," replied Doctor Young.

"He's an expert," Jonathon said.

"What, an expert on me?" Beck asked rudely.

"Ha ha ha," Doctor Young replied. "Yes, please come inside."

He swerved violently to the right and disappeared through a pair of swing doors.

"This is it," said Jonathon. "Mandelson Wing."

The doors swung back and hit him in the face.

"Ha ha ha," said Beck. Then she ran away; back down the slippery, squeaky corridor, past the row of lifts that could have taken her back in time, and into the hospital's crowded foyer. Here she made the fatal mistake of looking behind her to see if the psychiatric staff were giving chase. Doctor Young was nowhere in sight, but while her head was turned she tripped over an old man in a wheelchair.

Beck fell to the floor, and took too long to recover; for when she finally stood up again she found a hand on her shoulder.

"Hello," said Doctor Young, "you appear to have hurt yourself. I have a bed where you can rest while I assess your injuries."

Doctor Comfort appeared too, and took Beck by surprise; sweeping her up in his arms and carrying her back through the foyer while the crowds parted as if they were in the last scene of a romantic movie. There should have been a love song – lifting us up where we belong – as Jonathon manfully conveyed Beck towards the mental ward.


He threw her on the bed and collapsed in a chair panting.

"It's not too bad, is it?" he asked.

"Not too bad for bedlam," said Beck. "But the people tied to their head-boards are probably on a lunch break."

"Nonsense," said Jonathon. "This room is semi-private. Four patients at most, though you seem to have it to yourself at the moment."

Later, though, Beck thought, there'd be faces gurning at her from the walls.

"And oh, look at the view!" Jon went on.

Beck looked out of the window.

"Wow. Some stubbly bushes," she said. "I expect that's where they keep the mad axe-men."

He just tutted at her.

"Jonathon," said Beck. "You can't leave me here. It's crazy."

He looked at his watch.

"I've got to get Alfie from school," he said. "Come on, you know it makes sense."

She burst into tears.

"Don't talk to me about sense," she sobbed. "You wouldn't know sense if it seduced you with the lights on. Why would we be having such a dark time together if our problems hadn't started in a previous life?"

"Bye," said Jonathon decisively, and stood up to go.

"No," Beck shouted, "please don't go. I'm sorry, okay. I'm sorry I killed you, and I'm sorry I was so horrible to you when you were alive. I don't know why I took such a dislike, but the instant I saw you my blood was boiling."

"See you," Jonathon was backing firmly towards the door.

"Take me with you!"

"Rebecca, for God's sake calm down," Jonathon said. "You could walk out of here tomorrow. You've just got to prove to them that you're not mad. You've got to stop telling that story."

"No," Beck said, "I've got to prove that my story is true." She rocked backwards and forwards on the bed. "Then you'll know I'm not mad. Then you'll get me out of here."

Jonathon pointed a steadying finger at her.

"When you leave," he said, "it'll be by yourself. And you'll be taking the straight way out, down that long corridor."


There was a television on a ledge above Beck's bed, and it was turned on. A studio discussion was taking place with a cacophony of voices arguing like the characters in a mad person's head; but Beck didn't look at it.

She watched the door through which Jonathon had disappeared, until a lady in a pink nylon overall popped into view.

"Cup of tea, love?" she shouted.

Beck jumped. "Do what?"

"A cup of tea," the lady said again. She came into the room, thick white china rattling in her hand.

"Who are you?" Beck asked.

"Freud," the woman replied.

"What?" Beck laughed.

"Freud," said the tea lady. "Short for Freuda."

Beck laughed again and shook her head in disbelief.

"I don't get it," she said.

"You know," the lady spelled it out for her. "F.R.I.E.D.A."

"Oh, Frieda!" laughed Beck. "It's your accent. I thought you said Freuda."

"I did." She plonked the cup and saucer on Beck's bedside table with a crash.

"Where are you from?" Beck asked.

"London, love," Freud said, "East End. Not any more though. It's changed too much."

"East is always east, though," said Beck.

"Yeah," Freud straightened the cup in its saucer, and gave Beck a sideways look. She could handle the nutters. "There you go, love," she said, and started to leave the room.

"Wait!" cried Beck. "What am I supposed to do now?"

"Drink it," the tea lady replied.

Beck didn't mean that. She knew what to do with a cup of tea; but she didn't know what to do with herself, left alone on Mandelson Ward One. It was too quiet to be called M1 for short.

Luckily a nurse came in, before she'd got to the bottom of the cup.

"Pop your nightie on and get into bed," the nurse said. "Doctor Young will be making his rounds in a minute."

"He can see me with my clothes on," Beck said.

The nurse looked surprised.

"Yes, but…" she began.

"He doesn't need to see my body," Beck said.

"Yes, but…" the nurse began again, then she broke off and looked nervously at the door, "it's usual to… Oh no, he's coming."

Doctor Young burst onto the ward, whistling loudly. He glanced at the empty beds then headed for Beck's.

"Where's Val and Tina?" he asked the nurse.

"Out in the community," the nurse replied. "They'll be back at tablet time."

"So who have we here?" he said.

The nurse looked for the name at the foot of Beck's bed; but Dr Young was looking at her face instead.

179

"Ah yes," he said.

"Rebecca Salmon," the nurse read.

"So," the psychiatric consultant sat down in a comfy chair, "are you a Becky?"

"No. I'm a Beck," she said.

"How long have you been a Beck?" he asked, and stretched his legs.

"I can't remember." She curled up on the narrow bed.

"That's what they call a river in Yorkshire," he said, "a beck. Do you see yourself as a river, at all?"

She shook her head.

"A stream?" he asked.

"No," she answered, barely opening her mouth an inch.

"What then?" he said. "What body of water best describes you? Blue Lagoon? The rapids? A muddy puddle?"

She shrugged.

"I'm just a part of the sea," she said. "But you can't see which part, because I look the same as all the rest."

"You are a bit different," he said. "Most Rebeccas end up as Becky. Who started calling you Beck? Your Mum and Dad?"

She snorted.

"No," she said.

"What do your parents call you?" he asked.

"They don't call me anything. They call me from beyond the grave," she said. "They're dead."

"I see." Doctor Young spoke sympathetically. "When did they die?"

"The day before my wedding," Beck said.

"Both together?" he asked. "How?"

"Airplane crash."

"How sad for you," the consultant psychiatrist said.

"Worse things happen at sea," Beck replied.

"Nevertheless," he looked at her critically, "that's one of the things we must talk about later. What I want to do now is get to the bottom of this Beck. Who first called you it?"

"My husband," she said.

"Ah. And where is he now?"

"He's dead too."

Beck almost felt sorry for the doctor as he reached for a deeper sympathetic response, like a handkerchief from an awkward pocket.

"Good grief," he said. "You must be no stranger to it."

"We are on talking terms," she said.

"Have you had a lot of counselling?" he asked.

She nodded modestly. It wouldn't do to boast about how much counselling she'd really had.

"And it's helped you with the loss of everyone you loved?"

"Yeah," Beck said slowly. "I'm okay."

Doctor Young's smile started to look unnatural as he frowned inside. This woman didn't seem to be mad. What was she doing here?

"You've dealt with all those deaths," he checked.

"Well," Beck said, "they weren't serious, were they."

"What?"

"They didn't really die."

"Oh?"

"There's no such thing."

"I see," the psychiatrist said eagerly. Now she was speaking his language. The woman was barking.

"So what happens then? Do we live forever?" he asked.

"We have done so far."

"Yes but," Dr Young leaned forward in his chair, "we weren't born at the beginning of time."

"Have you ever delivered a baby?" Beck asked him.

"Often," he answered.

"Don't you think that if they really were 'new born' they would die of shock?"

"They do gasp," said the doctor, "but that's just the first breath…"

"When my son was born," Beck interrupted, "he looked me in the eye. He held my gaze for ages. How did he even know where to look, if he'd never seen a face before?"

"It's the light," said the psychiatrist. "The eyes are bright."

"Maybe," she said. "Anyway, that's how my name got shortened, if you really must know. My husband called us alphabet, Alf and Beck."

Alf came to see her, when visiting time was almost over. He hurried into the ward, holding hands with Jonathon and looking worried; but he didn't say much, just stared at Beck. It was late in the evening, but her eyes were still bright.

"He got upset," Jonathon hissed. "Wouldn't go to bed until he saw you."

Beck patted her hospital blanket.

"Hop up here," she said to Alfie. "This bed is on wheels, but I haven't been anywhere on it yet. Where shall we go?"

"You should come home," he said.

"I know. What did you do at school today?"

"I made up a story," he said.

"Oh! What was it about?" she asked. War; it would be about war. They were always about war.

"It was about a boy," he said.

"And what happened to him?" asked Beck.

"He lived in a horrible place," said Alf. "Lost Angeles."

"*Lost* Angeles?" asked Beck.

"Yeah," he said with a drawl.

The angels were missing, in Alf's world. He fell asleep beside his mum on the narrow bed, and Jonathon picked him up and carried him out of the mental ward.

She fell asleep feeling sadder than she'd done in her whole life and probably the one before.

"I've got to get out of Mandelson Wing," she said to herself as she nodded off. "Please, let me find a way." Her thoughts became a prayer. "Please, God, let me find a way to prove that my story is true."

By the middle of the next morning, her thoughts had become a cacophony to rival the studio discussion blaring from the TV above her bed. Beck needed to listen to some music, to hush the voices in her head; and there was a set of headphones dangling above her. She grabbed them like an oxygen mask in an airplane emergency, and clasped them to her ears.

The hospital radio played popular and classical music so mixed up that a commercial station could never survive it. Beck caught the tail end of 'Delilah', then the DJ cheerfully announced that they hoped it would clear up soon.

Meanwhile, he said, Mr so-and-so, in for a heart by-pass operation, requested some Beethoven to help him get better.

It started as the sighing of violins, the gentle groaning of strings that grew more taut until the heroine of the piece, the piano, began to play. Then the accompaniment held its breath, plucking gasps of delight at the tone, at the sweetness of the tune.

But its song was so mournful that soon the strings wept where the piano touched them. Black keys were minor cracks that stopped the music's skin from healing; though white notes bandaged themselves around the broken chords. And seeping through the twin cups of Beck's headset, the eternal thing nursed open the way to her soul.

Rebecca had gone rigid in the bed. She was having a seizure. Nurses rushed in. Nurses rushed out to get doctors. Doctors got heart-starting apparatus.

But Beck's heart hadn't stopped. Not this time. Actually, it did stop but not for very long. It missed one beat; just long enough for her to remember another scene from her dim and distant past as if it were happening now.

Jonathon was sitting at the piano, in a roomful of nineteenth century ladies. He was playing the Beethoven Concerto. Other ladies and a gentleman accompanied him on violins and cello and the brilliant Indian sun lit them through cracks in the walls.

It shines on his profile and makes a halo of her hair. His lips are moving as she plays and it looks like she is speaking his music, singing the right hand and the left hand at the same time.

Why couldn't Beck see what a great woman Jonathon was until it was too late? He was playing the second movement of Beethoven's *Piano Concerto Number Five* better than the guy on the radio.

But he dropped everything, when the hospital phoned to tell him about Beck's turn for the worse. Jonathon stopped what he was doing and came at once. Rebecca opened her eyes and saw him bending over the bed.

"How are you feeling?" he mouthed gently.

She took off the headset.

"I'm fine now," she said. "Just a bit bored."

Jonathon looked surprised.

"Shall I bring you some magazines?" he asked.

"That would be nice." Beck's tone was completely normal. "And would you see if they've got a CD I'm after."

"Sure," said Jonathon. "What is it?"

Beck wrote the name down. She didn't say any more.


"I had to go into town," Jonathon said when he came back at tea-time. "That music you wanted is rather obscure."

Beck smiled at him with a mouthful of cold stew, but still didn't speak. It was crucial to her plan that she remained in control of the emotions that usually spewed out of her like the hospital food could have. She swallowed everything on the plate.

A squeak of trolley wheels announced the arrival of Freud, who peered in pink nylon from behind a wobbling stack of crockery.

"All finished?" she said.

"Yes thank you," said Beck.

"Cup of tea?" asked the tea-lady as she cleared Beck's plates away.

"Please," said Beck. "Tell me, Frieda, is anyone using the CD player in the day room at present?"

"I don't think so, duck," she shook her head, but poured the tea with a steady hand.

"Then shall we adjourn?" Beck asked Jonathon. "And listen to my new CD."


The day room was not well named. It had no windows and so could equally be called a room of the night. The faint smell of fag smoke spoke to the sickly yellow flowers which sprawled over the armchairs and spread to the walls. The carpet was worn from the meaningless pacing of mental patients.

It was to this place that Jonathon and Beck repaired for the evening; he was quietly confused, but she was silent with excitement. In her hand she held the silver disk; the evidence of their former existence that Jonathon had gone out and bought that afternoon.

Within a few revolutions, she was convinced, he would finally believe that her story was true. She didn't have to say another word. With her trigger finger she pressed the play button, and watched Jonathon's face as the first notes filled the room.

He was staring at the brown carpet. His expression didn't change; maybe the frown lines softened a little, but that was all.

"Wait till the piano starts," Beck said to herself. "Then it'll hit him."

It didn't. More like a hug, the melody squeezed a sigh out of him and left his shoulders slightly more relaxed. He sat back in the armchair and smiled at Beck.

"This is nice," he said.

She had to bite her lip to stop from screaming: "Nice? NICE?" The tune started at the top and descended at once; each note lower than the one before, spiralling carefully. It wasn't nice, it was like walking downstairs.

Why was he not taken to that hot drawing room, where the smell of incense mingled with the ladies perfume; and the tables, chairs and even the pianoforte, stood with their legs in bowls of waters to prevent them from being eaten by ants.

It was like going downstairs, to a different room in the same house. Surely, the music could be heard through walls made of bamboo, fanned by the *tatti* screens that cooled the air. There was not even a door; but there had to be a key.

When the movement finished, Beck played it again; still watching Jonathon's face for a sign that he was starting to remember. A muscle twitched in his cheek. Was that the tickle of a golden ringlet? He rubbed his tummy. Was that the ache of tightly laced stays? As the music came to a crescendo he cracked his knuckles in the way old pianists do.

Was his body remembering what his mind could not? Beck played the track a third time. Now Jonathon sat in the armchair with his eyes closed, and as the piano began its blissful torture again a single tear slid from under each lid.

"That was nice," he said, when it had finished. He opened his eyes, but they were so bleary he didn't see Beck staring at him beseechingly.

"Have you ever heard it before?" she asked.

"No, I don't think so." Jonathon picked up the CD case and started reading the cover.

Now Beck's eyes were filled with tears. What if each note, each nuance was recorded in his bones but not in his brain? How many times would he have to listen before the memory would dawn like consciousness returning in the morning.

"Do you want to take it home with you?" she asked him.

"Me?"

"It might be nice to listen to as you're falling asleep tonight."

"But… it's yours."

He was acting like she'd never shared anything with him before. She tutted and pressed the eject button. As the disk slid from the machine she saw herself in the silver mirror of its surface; and knew she never had.


Jonathon went home, and Beck went back to bed in Mandelson Ward One. It was tablet time, and the other occupants had returned. They were twins, in their late forties; identical down to the pinafore dresses which smelled of urine, and the hairy moles on their chins.

Val and Tina were the sort of people Beck had seen on the street by day and wondered where they spent the night. Now she was sharing M1 with them.

"What's your name?" one of them asked her.

"Beck," she said, and looked from one to the other. "What's yours?"

"We're Valentina," they whispered proudly, as if it was only individually that they were smelly middle-aged vagrants, and together they were a goddess of romance.

"What do they give you the pills for?" asked Beck.

"For keeping quiet," Val and Tina said.

When the nurse came in to administer the medication, Beck kept her mouth shut too. She didn't want any, much as she missed doing drugs in the evenings.

"Do you want a sleeping tablet?" the nurse said, coming towards her bed.

Beck shook her head. She was waiting for the morning.


When Jonathon came she couldn't contain herself a moment longer. She pounced on him as soon as he arrived, carrying a paper, and bag of what could have been croissants.

"Did you listen to the music in bed last night?" she asked.

"I did, as it happens," he said.

"And?" she demanded.

"I fell asleep."

186

Jonathon sat down in the comfy chair beside Beck's bed and opened the newspaper.

"Do you want the women's bit?" he asked her, as a smaller section fell out into his lap.

Being in a mental hospital, Beck went mad. She tried to stuff the paper into his mouth, screaming "Remember! REMEMBER? You used to play that music, you bastard. I've heard you playing Beethoven's *Concerto No. 5* with my own ears. I've sat on my own arse and listened to you doing the slow movement."

"No," gagged Jonathon.

Nurses and doctors came to help, as Beck attacked Jon with the morning's news. They took him away and sedated her.

She was lying quietly on her bed when Freud rattled in with the tea trolley.

"What was all that about then?" Freud said.

"What?" Beck murmured, slowly turning her head.

"That hoo-hah."

"Oh, that," said Beck. "Hello Frieda."

"Come on, spit it out," said the tea-lady, pouring Beck a cup.

"Well," Beck shrugged, "it's silly really. Ever since I was in a coma from getting an electric shock I've had memories of a past life, and Jonathon was in it too until I killed him, which I feel really bad about, but he doesn't believe me."

"Doesn't believe you feel bad?" said Freud.

"Doesn't believe I killed him," said Beck. "Doesn't believe we were alive. I've told him everything about it, the place, the people, I've done pictures of it, acted it all out; but he won't even countenance it."

"Blimey," said Freud.

"Yes," said Beck. "So finally, I played a CD of the song he used to play, because I thought it might jog his memory if he heard it over and over again, but he just fell asleep; hence the hoo-hah."

The cup Freud was passing Beck wobbled in its saucer.

"Where did this life happen then?" she asked.

"India." Beck downed the tea in one.

"It's a big country," said Freud, taking the cup back abruptly to refill it. "You want to try narrowing it down a bit."

She gave Beck a second cup of tea.

"When did this life happen?" she said.

"Nineteenth century," Beck slurped.

"That was a long hundred years," Freud said. "You want to try tightening it up a bit."

And she stood there for ages, listening as Beck told the smallest details of the biggest story. She stood until the tea for M 2, 3 and 4 was cold.

As she hurried away she said to Beck, "There are stories in my family what sounds like yours. Way back, our men was East India Dock workers. I've heard tell of that hoo-hah, and it's got to be in the history books."

"You're right," Beck shouted after Freud, as she rushed her trolley out of the ward, "but how am I going to find a book like that in here?"

"Don't worry, I'll go to the library," is what she thought Freud replied, rattling noisily out of the door.

"So, what was all that about then?" asked Doctor Young.

Beck had been summoned to his office. It was at the heart of Mandelson Wing, at a busy corridor intersection between the four wards. The reception desk rustled and buzzed nearby, and mad people were milling all around.

She had insisted on getting dressed for the excursion, though the nurse seemed to think it would be fine to go wandering around the neighbourhood in her nightie and dressing-gown, as if Beck were mad too.

Breezing into Young's office in a silver polo-neck, Bermuda shorts and knee-high boots she felt normal.

"It was nothing," she said.

"You attacked Doctor Comfort," the psychiatrist replied.

"Yes, but… it was nothing."

She was standing with her hands on her hips in front of him. Doctor Young gestured for Beck to sit down.

"It didn't look like nothing to me," he said.

"You don't know how much there is," she answered emphatically. "On the scale of things I've done to Doctor Comfort, it hardly registered."

"You frequently abuse him?"

"Yes," said Beck, "in so many ways."

Doctor Young looked like he was going to say one thing then stopped and said another.

"And how do you feel about that?" he asked her.

"Awful, of course," she said.

"So why don't you stop?"

"Because," Beck sighed, "I've got to persuade him that I'm right."

Young nodded. She was a sadist, he decided.

"Tell me," he said, "have you always been like this, or does it date from the electric shock?"

"I've always been like this, but I didn't know it until the electric shock."

He looked at her carefully, still standing in her tall leather boots.

"What happened the first time you tried to... correct Doctor Comfort?"

"He didn't like it."

"How long before you tried again?"

Beck thought.

"The next day," she said.

"What method did you use?"

"A very sharp pencil."

Beck sat down now. The psychiatrist seemed to understand her. His pen was making copious notes.

"And anything else?" he asked.

"Everything," she boasted. "Chalk, crayon, felt-tip."

He raised an eyebrow.

"Nothing sharper?"

"Oh, I see what you mean," she said. "Well, I had my own dagger and sword, and I could borrow a bayonet."

He put down his pen.

"Be serious. Jonathon's never had that sort of injury," the Doctor said.

"Except for the loss of his head." Now she could see Doctor Young didn't believe her. Drat. "It grew back," she said, trying to get him on her side again.

"Let us go back too," he replied. "Tell me about your relationship with your husband."

"What do you want to know?" Beck asked.

"Did you dominate him sexually?"

Beck laughed.

"I was eighteen when we met, all lopsided shoulder pads and a frizzy perm. I didn't do anything sexually."

"You must have developed?" Young said.

"Yes, I developed. Then he died," Beck snapped.

"Sorry," said the psychiatrist. "How did that happen?"

"A car crash."

"Strange. I thought you said your parents died in a car crash. Was it the same one?"

"No, they died in an airplane crash. It was the day before my wedding, and they were on their way from Pompeii."

"But that's a ruined city," said Young, suspiciously.

"Well, that's what they were into. There was nothing they liked better than wandering around a fallen civilization."

The doctor didn't look convinced.

"All their holidays were archeological," Beck said. "They'd been to Machu Pichu the year before and Ephesus before that; but they always came back to Pompey."

"Until the day before your wedding. Didn't you postpone it?" he said.

"No," Beck was surprised.

"Why not?"

"Because I didn't think they were dead. I just thought they were late," she said. "Look, I didn't kill them, and I didn't kill my husband."

"My dear girl, I'm not suggesting you did," said the psychiatrist. "I simply want to, shall we say, dig up the reasons for you being here today."

He'd already crossed out sadist. Now Doctor Young took the lid off his pen again.

"You want to persuade Jonathon that you're 'right'," he said. "But have you ever been wrong?"

"Of course," said Beck. "I'm wrong all the time."

"Oh?"

"It was wrong to do what I did in the past, and it's wrong to be remembering it now. There has to be some kind of punishment. I need to make amends…"

Doctor Young started to doodle thoughtfully, with large letters in an illuminated manuscript that she could read from the movement of his hand. In the knotty message of veins he was writing an M, and an A, maybe for masochist.

"So," he said, "how would you like to be punished?"

"A neck for a neck," replied Beck. "But Jonathon will have to admit that I'm right, before he can admit that I'm wrong."

"How can you be right and wrong?" the doctor said.

She stood up.

"Doctor Young, how many of me can you see?"

"One," he said.

"And no matter what I say to you, how many of me will you see?"

"Only one," he said.

She spread her arms, part casual, part crucified; then let them fall.

"No argument could persuade you to see otherwise?" she asked.

The psychiatrist shook his head.

"Then I will always look mad to you," she said.

Doctor Young threw his notepad on the desk.

"I don't get it," he said. "What do you mean?"

"If you can only see one of me," Beck repeated clearly, "I will look mad to you. Because there isn't only one of me. There's two."

"Aha," the psychiatrist could hardly contain his delight. A diagnosis, a palpable diagnosis! He snatched up his pad again and wrote confidently 'multiple personality schizophrenic'. Then he underlined it twice.

Beck sailed out of his office and collapsed in the corridor. She had to be pushed back to her room in a wheelchair.


Somebody new had arrived on the ward while Beck was away. A lady sat cross-legged on the fourth bed, dealing a pack of cards into the diamond shape between her knees. She had her head down, long brown hair concealing her face completely.

Beck didn't feel like introducing herself. She lay on her side, looking out of the window as night fell on the scrubby bushes outside. But the darker it got outside, the brighter the inside of the room became, reflected in the glass till she could see every detail of the ward and the woman behind her.

The nurse came in and offered Beck a sleeping pill again. This time she took it. She wanted to be dead.

Her slumber was deep and seemingly dreamless; but when she woke up next morning there was a word on her lips that hadn't been there before and must have come from somewhere.

"Kunpah," Beck murmured, before she was fully awake; "Kunpah," she said, rubbing her eyes. Then she sat up and said it again. "Kunpah? What on earth is that?"

She was still blinking at the question when Freud came in with the early tea. She saw to Val and Tina first then came slowly over to Beck, looking shifty. With her back to the twins, Freud dropped a pile of books on Beck's bed; and Beck shouted aloud with relief:

"My story is in print!"

"Shut up," hissed Freud. "You'll get me sacked." She poured an elaborate cup of tea for Beck with more clattering of saucer than usual, and whispered: "I'm not supposed to give literature to the patients. Only magazines."

In a cloud of steam from her urn, the tea lady rattled her trolley quickly through the double doors.

Beck looked at the books on her bed. There was no need to read the words on the covers; they leapt off the title page like an ambush, a surprise attack though they'd laid in waiting for ages.

THE INDIAN MUTINY it said, and THE MASSACRES OF 1857.

The covers had pictures of men fighting, in red uniforms and white *dhottis*, pith helmets and turbans. They were fighting with guns and swords, on horses and elephants; while in the chaos, children were slain and women swooned in dramatic Victorian attitudes.

This was it. This was Beck's war, the one she was still fighting. But as she turned to the first page, a new chapter began.


Freud came back at lunchtime, with a dish the hospital cook called curry.

"Any luck?" she asked.

Beck barely looked up from the books.

"This is it," she said. "This is my war."

"Oh good," said Freud. "Pudding?"

"No," Beck replied, "I've got to show these to Jonathon."

"He won't be back, love," Freud doled out a slab of suet anyway. "Not after you attacked him. Hospital policy."

She poured on the custard, with an attack of horrible coughing. Beck was still reading and only saw it out of the corner of her eye, but she could have sworn that the tea-lady spat something pus-coloured into her vat.

Across the ward, Val and Tina gave a shout.

"There's the poxy cat!"

Now Beck looked up in surprise. Outside the window, a moggy had jumped onto the weathered ledge.

"I haven't seen it for ages," said one of the twins.

"Oh look, it's got a mouse," said the other.

The end of a tail was whisked into the cat's mouth just as the cook was wiping the trail of spittle off her chin.

"This place is so unhygienic," said Beck.

"You can't talk," said Frieda, "sitting there in your petticoat."

"It's not my petticoat," said Beck, "it's my…"

But at this moment Doctor Young appeared on his afternoon ward round. He went straight past Val and Tina, past the mysterious fourth patient, to where Beck sat in front of a bowl of custard with a thick skin.

"Aren't you hungry?" he asked, sitting down uninvited in Beck's comfy chair.

She shook her head.

"I'd just like to finish the chat we had yesterday," he said. "You left my office rather abruptly, and I wondered what you meant by there being two of you; because we have some rather good drugs for that sort of thing."

Beck looked up to see the twins stiffening, across the room. She sighed and closed her book on the massacres of 1857, but left her finger in the place to remember where she was.

"Drugs?" she asked the doctor.

"Yes," he nodded. "Val and Tina will tell you. They work wonders on those unwanted voices in your head."

"The voices in my head," Beck said, "are as real as you. I can nearly prove it…" and she began to flick through the pages of the book again. "If I could only pinpoint where… Meerut, that's when it all began, then it spread to Delhi, but I wasn't there. Downstream, I was further downstream…"

"I think I'm going to get you a sedative." Doctor Young reached for the button to call the nurses.

"You can sedate me into a coma, but that won't stop it, that was what started it," Beck said.

"You need to relax."

"I've been relaxed. That was the problem. Now I need to be uptight and finding the facts," she gabbled. "They're all in this book, I'm sure of it. This is the evidence to prove my story is true."

The consultant psychiatrist didn't look at the book Beck was waving, right under his nose. He just looked at her face, and sometimes over her shoulder to see if the nurse was coming yet.

"I need Jonathon," she said. "I need his scientific brain. He'd be able to work out where the Ganges goes."

Val and Tina were laughing.

"What about you two?" Beck turned to them in desperation. "Do you believe in reincarnation?"

"They don't even know what it means," the doctor said, in an unprofessional aside.

Beck stood up and shouted at the twins slowly:

"Have you been here before?"

She spoke as if they were foreigners asking for directions on the tube. Doctor Young didn't notice her tone; he was hearing the fourth patient, in the bed next to Beck's, speak for the first time since she'd been admitted to M1. Fanning out her pack of playing cards in front of her pretty face, she said:

"I believe in fortune telling."

"I see," said the psychiatrist, quietly.

Beck was still shouting at the twins: "Have you been here before?"

"They're always going to be here," Young said, "but you don't have to be, Beck. You're a bright girl. You've just let this master/servant stuff get out of hand."

"I'm not into S and M," she shouted. "Unless it's slavery and mutiny!"

"I rest my case," said the psychiatrist. "So please, lie down."

"Do you believe in fortune telling?" the fourth patient asked him.

"I could probably be persuaded," he said.

"What?" Rebecca was outraged, and jumped off her bed. "You'd give more credence to a pack of cards than a pile of history books." She snatched the deck from the mystery woman, and spread them out in front of him. "Let me say what I can see."

"Somebody cross her palm with silver," the new lady said sarcastically.

"She don't want silver," said Freud, clearing Beck's untouched custard away, "just a hospital meal she can eat."

Beck stared at the cards and the pattern they lay in, on the bed next to the book about 1857. One of clubs, five of diamonds, four of hearts and seven of spades. 1547.

The cards gave more than the date, though. Their message was about a big

194

fight, more money than love, a lot of burying to do. In another language they told of a curse, made in anger which seeped into tree roots and was sap in the wood which made this pack of cards. The truth was tree-ringed in everything; but Beck didn't see it and neither did Dr Young. He just saw a raggle-taggle nightdress rising around her Gypsy thighs as she sat cross-legged on the bed, and smelt the musk that rose.

His own rising answered it. Clutching his trouser pocket he muttered, "Er, I've just been paged. Urgently." Then he left his patients to their own devices and rushed from the room.

What madness would have reigned in Young's absence from Mandelson Ward One, if Freud were not still there. She settled Val and Tina down in their twin beds, and restored the pack of cards to the one who played Patience.

Then she picked up the pile of books and gave them back to Beck, who read on as if her life story depended on it.


She'd nearly reached the last chapter by tea-time, when Freud came back.

"Cheese, ham or fish paste sandwiches?" the tea lady asked.

"There's no Kunpah," Beck said, slamming the book shut in frustration. "I was so sure I'd find it."

"Your man is outside," said Freud.

"Here?" Beck flushed, and her eyes didn't seem so red. "Really?"

"He's insisting that the nurses let him in to see you, hospital policy or no. And he's got your little boy."

"Then I'll have a selection of sandwiches," Beck said happily. "Jonathon will persuade them to let him stay for tea. He's a doctor."

But it was as a dad that Jonathon came, and brought a sad little boy to see his mum, because all the explaining had only made Alf feel more confused. The grown-ups hardly spoke, but Alf lay next to Beck watching television, and went with her to the machine for crisps and Coke, and eventually fell asleep feeling much better.

Beck must have dozed off too, but when she awoke the clock in the ward said three in the morning and her son was still beside her. She turned to Dr Comfort, but saw that he was lost, in the books he'd found on her bedside table. Jonathon was reading THE INDIAN MUTINY OF 1857.

As if it were her diary, he was reading, while she was dreaming. Beck watched for a while, waiting for him to look up from the pages, but he never did; and the next thing she knew she was waking up again at seven o'clock.

"Where did you get these books?" Jonathon asked her, as soon as her eyes were open.

"Freud, the tea lady, brought them for me."

"Who?"

A familiar rattle in the distance made Beck smile as she explained.

"I told her my story and she'd heard it before. Her grandfather and great grandfather worked in the East India Docks, and some of their tales were still alive in the family. Her dad is ninety, but she asked him about a native rebellion. Then she got the books out of the library."

"So you've never read anything like them before?" Jonathon said.

"No." Beck turned to see Freud appear with the morning trolley.

"Didn't you do history at school?" Jonathon asked.

"Of course I did," Beck replied, "but it was just, you know, the six wives of Henry the Eighth. Hello!"

She greeted Freud triumphantly, but the tea lady was so intimidated by Beck's doctor in the comfy chair that she served her brew in silence. Alf woke up as Beck shifted to take the cup, and Freud muttered something about getting him an orange juice, before she rushed away red-faced in her steam.

Val and Tina too hurried off to the bathroom; with their outsize vanity cases full of beauty products which only seemed to work on the inside.

"So, tell me," Jonathon said, pointing his finger at the picture of the mutiny on the cover of her book, "which one is you?"

It took Beck a moment to realise what he meant. The words didn't sink in at first, though she had been waiting to hear them for months. As if it were a proposal she was longing for, and the only phrase her ears would accept was 'will you marry me'; Jonathon had just said 'are we getting wed, or what?' and Beck didn't reply.

"Which one is me?" she echoed him numbly.

"Which one was you," he said.

She stared at his finger pointing at the illustrated men fighting.

"You believe it?"

"Oh my God, Beck," Jonathon shouted, "If you haven't read this book before, then I'd be mad not to believe your story. If you didn't know this history existed, you couldn't have made it up. The whole thing started with the bullets, exactly like you said."

"Yeah?" said Beck.

"Smeared with fat the soldiers couldn't touch. It started small as bullets and ended in an enormous slaughter."

"You believe it?" Beck said.

Jonathon slapped the hardback cover, laminated by the library.

"It's all here," he said. "Your every detail is verified."

Then he pounded the book again as if it could be a Bible; and shook the fight between black and white. Finally, Jonathon had found an acceptable face for her facts, an accurate illustration for her argument. Shame it wasn't one of the hundreds of pictures Beck had drawn herself.

"So," he said, "which one were you?"

Now that he believed her, she had to be honest with him. Finally, Jonathon was admitting that the massacre had really happened, and that Beck had really been there. Now she had to tell him the truth.

She reached out and took the book from him. He tensed for a moment, then let it go, but his eyes stayed on the cover.

Beck spread her hand slowly over the shiny hardback till all the characters were obscured.

"To be perfectly honest," she said, "I can't pinpoint the actual person yet, or locate the exact place name. Obviously it's the right era and the right area, but I can't quite find the right man."

"Oh," said Jonathon.

"The details of his story are so specific," Beck said; "the sand trenches, the thatched boats on fire, the river of blood; the house full of women, the well full of bodies. A book like this should include such unforgettable images."

She opened the cover to see an old map of the Raj inside, with scenes of atrocity marked in italics.

"I'm sure it was a place called Kunpah," she said, "on the river, downstream from Delhi." Dreamily Beck traced a finger along the line of the Ganges.

"Let me see," Jonathon snatched the book, "I'll find it."

He started to scour the map, muttering 'Kunpah, Kunpah'; so matter-of-factly it could be a motorway exit. When Freud drove back onto M1 with the bacon and egg trolley Beck gave her a kiss.

"Thanks!" she whispered.

The carton of orange juice with a straw she gave to Alf in bed, as if he were a big baby with a bottle. But Beck had lost track of time since she'd been in Mandelson wing. It was Monday the first of September and Alf was starting school.

Doctor Comfort grabbed the sleepy boy and carried him like a new satchel over his shoulder. He ran out of the ward, but came straight back for something he'd forgotten. Jon grabbed the library books from the bedside table.

"If," he said to Beck, "I find Kunpah; you could be home by tea-time."

Home by tea-time! She could have sung it to a music-hall tune. She could have danced down the corridors in her nightie, fitting in with the other mental patients as tightly as she liked. For Rebecca Salmon was certifiably not insane; and she would be home by tea-time.

Morning coffee, lunchtime, afternoon tea; Freud came and went, came and went with her eternal trolley.

"Doctor Comfort's taking his time," she said.

"I knew it. He can't find Kunpah," said Beck. She stared out of the window. In the hospital garden it was getting dark, and she was getting worried.

The lights were on in the ward when she finally saw him coming through the double doors, with double the number of books he'd left with this morning.

"Did you find it?" she asked as soon as he reached her bed.

"Kunpah does not appear on any maps of the Raj," Jonathon said.

"Oh shit!" said Beck.

"Because they didn't spell it like that," Jonathon said. "Kunpah was the insignificant village where Indians lived before the British built their garrison on top; a town they called Cawnpore."

"What?" said Beck.

Jonathon gave a horsey laugh.

"It's the English accent," he said; "'haw haw haw, we're going to Cawnpore'. The place was exactly like you remembered; all sweaty crinolines and curry soup. We built our empire on bonnets and bullets, and were surprised to get shot in the head."

"Cawnpore?" said Beck.

"Yes." Jonathon tossed a book from the top of his pile onto her bed. "That's how the British pronounced Kunpah. I followed a trail of footnotes through these books till I found a tome of its own."

THE CAWNPORE MASSACRE, the title said. Rebecca had found her way home.

She flicked through the pages, but none of the words seemed to matter now. She didn't need to read them because Jonathon had.

She stopped flicking at the pictures. The photographs were sepia tinted but the faces were all black or white, and some of them were familiar. Here in the pages of a history book were people Beck actually knew.

Commanders and Maharajas, commissioners and deposed princes alike posed stiffly for the camera; the alibis for her past-life, captured on a light sensitive plate.

Bang, it went, as each image hit the silver salts, and each of the great leaders blinked and missed himself captured for posterity. Bang went the primitive camera; Bang went the explosive chemicals it used; and every photographed face Beck saw was dead.

Through the pin-hole of time, Beck eyed them now, and no longer needed to rebel. It was over, the battle, the war; they were all dead and she didn't have a cause to fight for.

As she slammed the book shut the ward doors were slung open. The consultant psychiatrist was on his rounds; a misleading term, he was making in a straight line for Beck again.

"Uh oh," said Beck. Their last consultation had not ended happily. "Please let him set me free. Jonathon, say something to persuade him."

"Good evening, sir," Jon began.

"Heavens, Doctor Comfort, how formal," Young said.

"It is a matter of some seriousness," Jonathon said. "Doctor Young, I have reason to believe…"

He faltered, and stopped. Beck nudged him.

"Believe," she prompted.

"It's not Rebecca who's mad, it's us," Jonathon finished in a rush.

"You? And I?" The psychiatrist was surprised.

"And the rest of the Western world, sir," said Jonathon. "There's no evidence that we only live once, and every indication that we are born again; yet we persist in measuring sanity with a one inch stick."

"Be more explicit," Beck whispered.

"I have proof," said Jonathon, "proof beyond my wildest imaginings, that everything Beck said has been the truth."

Young looked from him to her, incredulously.

"You mean, she's right?" he said.

"She's right," said Jon.

"So, you've persuaded him," the psychiatrist said to Beck. "You win. What are you going to do now?"

"I'm not sure. What do you suggest?"

He took off his glasses and looked at her more closely.

"If it's sex games you're after," he said, "try something less dangerous. Seek and find a way to fight without hurting anybody."

"Er," Beck blushed on her own behalf and Jonathon's, "we're not actually into…"

"Well, if it's world domination you want," Young interrupted her, "same thing applies. Do it nicely."

"Cup of tea?" Freud arrived backwards through the swing doors, pink nylon posterior first. "Go on. Could be yer last one."

She looked like a cockney char-lady, but seen in the right light, her job had a mythical quality. She might have been the gloomy daughter of an ancient Greek king, doomed to spend eternity pouring the contents of her urn into a bottomless pit.

Beck had certainly had her fill, but she let Frieda spill another cupful into the hole of patients.

"Cheers!" she said, raising the universal china tea-cup. And when Beck tipped it down her throat, it tasted the same as all the others she'd drunk; but now that she was free to leave she realised how horrible the hospital tea was.

She was free to leave. Doctor Comfort swung her bags off the bed, and the consultant psychiatrist snatched her notes from the rack and signed them with an air of finality.

"So, I'm definitely not mad, then?" Beck said.

"Put it this way," said Doctor Young, "Either you are or I am; and I'm the one staying here."

Val and Tina didn't look up from their tea as Beck left. She'd been in their world too briefly to make a space that needed the word goodbye. And the psychiatrist was already deep in consultation with the pretty patient in the next bed.

"Didn't you see her flamenco dancing?" she was asking him. "Never mind, I can show you mine."

As Beck walked out of Mandelson wing, she did feel better. She went the way Jonathon had said, back down the long straight corridor, on her own two legs; without the warrior who kicked and struggled so much on the way in.

Who would have imagined the psychiatric ward could have healed her. Yet who could have dreamed the doctors there would be Freud and Jung.

Driving south from the hospital on the hill Jonathon was euphoric. He opened the sunroof and let out a whoop.

Beck looked up and saw the first stars coming out.

"Take me home," she told him.

"I thought you were just being horrible when you called it a whore house; but its name really was the Bibighar, which means the same thing!" he said, and gave her a beautiful grin.

Beck looked out of the window as they entered the city surrounded by sea. The land was so flat that continental ferries moored in the docks could be easily mistaken for the tower blocks on Portsmouth's horizon, with their rows of little lights starting to appear in the dusk.

Beck felt like a passenger returning from overseas, though her voyage was an out-of-body one. Without physically leaving the port, she'd been on a journey of such spiritual range that its starting point now seemed strange.

But as Jonathon drove her back to her front door, she was ready to re-enter.

"What do you want to do when we get in?" he asked excitedly.

"Have a nice hot bath," she said.

It was nice to wash all the blood off. Beck soaked in the tub until the water was red from her memories and she was clean. She got out and left the stains in, then she pulled out the plug. As the blood-streaked water drained away she heard the doorbell ringing in the hall downstairs.

It was Maisie bringing her son back. Beck heard the exchange; Alfie's high voice, Jonathon's low voice, and Maisie's laughing. The lounge door banged as the boy ran to turn the television on, and other voices joined the conversation.

Beck watched the water spiralling down the plug-hole until it was all gone. Downstairs, the programme Alf was watching finished too; she heard the theme tune to *Dr Who*. Still Maisie was talking to Jonathon in the hallway and Beck stood looking at herself in the mirror, naked.

It was a long bathroom mirror and she looked in it for a long time. She looked until she finally felt like the person standing there; a woman, white with blue veins, and a period starting again.

Then the front door shut and the visitor left and Beck put a dressing-gown on. Down below she heard Jonathon go into the lounge and say 'Mum's home', then Alfie was running up the stairs shouting 'Mum! You're home!'

She bathed him too. She rinsed the bath thoroughly and ran him a fresh one, but so soon after her symbolic immersion, it couldn't help but feel like his baptism back into their life together.

"What story do you want?" she asked him, when she had hugged him into his pyjamas and into bed.

"No story," he said.

"What then," she asked him, "the truth?"

It was a silly joke for a five-year-old.

"No," he tutted, and looked at the ceiling. Right above his head was a mobile of airplanes from World War Two.

"I just want you to stay here, Mummy," Alf whined. "You always go to hospital."

"I've been twice," Beck said firmly. "Once for my body and once for my soul. I shan't need to go again."

He grunted sleepily, eyes starting to glaze over as they gazed at the airplanes in his night sky.

"And I promise," she said, "that it is not possible for me to leave you. The way we are together is not with our bodies, but our souls."

His eyes closed slowly, and for a moment his face was at peace; then as sleep dropped he took cover, under the covers, as if from a bomb. But Beck thought the war was over.

"Everything will be alright now," she whispered to her son.

Jonathon woke her up in the middle of the night.

"Listen," he whispered. "I've had the most amazing dream."

His breath was heavy with the scent of the night, his face inches from hers on the pillow.

"I was in the Bibighar," Jonathon said, "and the massacre was over. The bodies were gone; buried in the well in the garden. There were a few quiet moments before the soldiers arrived."

Beck nodded. She knew the scene Jonathon was describing intimately.

"I was looking around," he went on, "at blood trickling down the walls, soaking into the matting on the floor. I saw a few artefacts lying there; tiny shoes and lace collars, pages torn from the Bible. I picked one up and read it."

Jonathon's sleepy eyes were suddenly shining. Beck thought it was tears.

"You'll never guess the verse that was written there," he whispered.

Beck, just woken up, couldn't think of a single line from the Bible. But Jonathon had been going to church a lot; not just on Sundays, but in the week too. He was discovering all sorts of obscure passages.

"What?" Beck shrugged in the pillows.

"Blessed are those who have not seen and have believed," Jonathon said. "I'm sorry Rebecca, I should have believed you. I should have believed you from the beginning."


She was a bit bleary-eyed as she walked Alf to school on Monday morning.

It was his second Monday in the Infants, and Alfred Salmon already knew where to go, who to sit with, what to say when the teacher called his name; but it was Beck's first time as a new mum.

"Here?" she said, at the gate. "Do I just leave you here?" It seemed too big an entrance for such a small boy to go through alone.

"Yes," said Alfie, "and don't try to kiss me. Look, here's Sam."

The boy ran into school hand in hand with his best friend and Beck was left standing next to Maisie in the crowd of early-morning mothers, all unbrushed hair and badly matched outfits.

"Hello," said Beck. "How are you?"

Maisie looked exhausted. She took Beck's arm.

"I'm glad to see you back," she said. "Fancy a cup of tea?"

They went round the corner, to a new age café that Maisie liked. Beck had never been there before.

The crockery was patterned with suns, moons and stars, and the table cloths were covered in astrological predictions. Around the walls was a border of angels, in white and gold.

Wind chimes announced each new arrival through the heavenly door. Several mums from the school run had got there before them, and Beck also recognised a young man in sandals, who she'd seen in the shopping centre on Saturdays, playing a didgeridoo outside Boots.

Everyone was quiet, reading from a pile of holistic magazines, or listening to the background music of aolian harps. Customers at the new age café didn't have to take their shoes off, but Beck went on tip-toe as Maisie led her to a table by the window.

The watery autumn sun shone through stick-on stained glass and made mystic splashes of colour where they sat.

"They're pagan symbols," Maisie whispered.

"What do they stand for?"

"I don't know," said Maisie, "but I don't think it's McDonald's."

Beck giggled, and hid her face in the menu, laughing even harder when she saw the choice it offered.

Tea and coffee were found under Nectar of the Gods; soft drinks were listed as the Elixir of Life. The homemade cakes and biscuits had names that made them sound highly beneficial, and not at all fattening. Both women were tempted by the Buns of Adonis.

Maisie gave their order to a waitress in a brilliant apron that made Beck blink and wish for Freud in her washed-out overall, serving with all the sterile imagination of hospital food.

"I hear you're much better now," Maisie said, as they waited for the buns to arrive.

"Mmm," Beck nodded. She wasn't sure how much Maisie knew about her illness; whether she realised it had been mental this time. "Thanks for having Alf while I was inhospitable," she said, "I hope he wasn't any trouble."

"No," said Maisie, "no more so than my own." She didn't know that Beck had been on Mandelson wing, but even if she did, it wouldn't have ruffled her feathers. Maisie had a new concern.

"Phew," she said, and blew her fringe off her forehead with an important puff. "I'll tell you why I'm so worn out, Becky. I've been promoted."

"Oh?" said Beck.

"I don't work at the nursery any more," Maisie shook her head vigorously. "I've moved up to the big school, with Samuel."

She was only a voluntary classroom assistant, but the way she said it made it sound like she was acting deputy head.

"It's much more challenging," she said.

Two cups of tea arrived, and the Buns of Adonis. Maisie barely glanced at the cream filled cleavage, she was so busy boasting.

"It's four times a week and I hear all the big children read."

"Ooh," Beck tried to appear impressed.

"And I'm allowed to go in the staff room," Maisie went on, then she suddenly seemed to hear herself. "Sorry," she laughed, "the power has gone to my head."

"That's okay," Beck said.

"Anyway, they always need more volunteers, so you could do it too, if you wanted," Maisie smiled and startled to tackle her bun with a fork.

Was Beck ready for a promotion? The idea of moving up with Alfie was indeed challenging; but her thoughts were stuck in the nursery school, at the colouring table in the quiet room, where the silent child, Jack, still sat. The more Beck thought about it the more she felt that her work there wasn't done yet. Perhaps she could return for one more term, to build up her strength before tackling any bigger children.

She was still thinking about it as she wandered home, but slowly her thoughts turned to smaller and smaller children; babies, in fact. She and Jonathon had one child each; how perfect it would be to have another one between them.

Rebecca had a mysterious smile on her face, as she walked past a wool shop with a display of knitted bonnets and bootees, and went into a supermarket to buy something for Jonathon's dinner.

"Steak!" he said in surprise.

"And a nice bottle of red wine,"

"I thought you didn't eat cows," Jon was still at the door with his coat on, smiling in disbelief.

"I'm having lamb," Beck said.

"That's even worse Mum," Alf shouted. He swung his legs violently under the kitchen table.

"And Alfie is having burgers," Beck said. "God only knows what kind of animal made those."

After the family feast of meat, Jonathon and Alf watched a football match while Beck washed up. The washing-up turned to wiping down; she cleaned every surface in the kitchen, while in the lounge the game went into extra time.

She spent it shining the pine; then opened the cupboard under the sink and found something to pour down the plughole. Beck was getting the place spotless.

The match went to penalties and she went in to see it; the only part of the game she saw the point of. Jonathon's team won, and he was jubilant.

Beck might not appreciate the finer details of football, but she knew that being on the winning side made a man's testosterone levels soar, and she really appreciated that.

It was bedtime for Alfie. They roared football songs, while he was in the bath and she was cleaning the loo. Alf changed the lyrics and made them all about poo.

Then Beck watched him fall asleep, still laughing, till he looked up at the mobile of old planes, and his face changed as he slipped away. It drained suddenly, and the childish expression went down the twin plugholes of his eyes.

Beck cleaned till Jonathon went to bed too; tired of watching her crawl round the skirting boards with a damp sponge.

She came to a stop in the corner of the kitchen, and climbed into her armchair. It had been two weeks since she'd sat there, and had the pleasure of its caress. Grubby red velvet surrounded her, its hold soft and firm, and she squeezed it back, her hand finding the hole deep in its lining. With sure fingers she reached inside for a small box covered in gold silk.

Call her Pandora, but Beck opened the box for knowledge; and inside she found a paradox, a black substance that always made things look brighter.

She took out the other ingredients necessary for her sub-religious ritual of rolling joints, and balanced them on the arms of the armchair. This was the order of her daily practice.

Sticking Rizla together; skins, she called them, as if it she were making a body; laying them in a pattern, her particular creation. Everyone she'd known who smoked had their own style.

Splitting open a cigarette with a lick along its seam; popping off the filter and pulling the whole package apart with an audible sigh of relief.

Tipping the tobacco into a more spacious fold of paper. With fingertips she prepared it, like a farmer ploughing furrows for precious seeds. And into the nicotine soil she crumbled the pollen, the flowers, the leaves, the stalks and the oil of a miraculous plant; seeds and all, everything but its roots which stayed connected to the earth.

Rolling it up, neat and tight, white like the original fag, but significantly longer. She would start to feel real excitement as she put a twist in one end and turned it upright to put a roach in the other.

Tearing little pieces of cardboard, an inch square or so, first from the cigarette packet, then from anything else to hand as the demand increased; takeaway food menus, junk mail; the house she lived in as a student lost whole phone book covers to the creeping inches of card. They were rolled up individually and slipped into joints, never to join up their letters again, or piece together the printed words.

The archeologists of the future would have a field day, Beck thought, with the roaches. She fixed hers in carefully, with a bandage of cigarette paper torn in a triangle.

It had healing properties. She held it for a minute in one hand, while reaching for the matches with another; and like a goddess with many arms she put away the bits and pieces of her modern homeopathic process and prepared to smoke the product.

She closed the box, her spiritual aid; the first thing she'd rescue if the house were on fire and the children and Jonathon were out. Then, binning the skeleton of the original cigarette, Beck put the one she'd rolled in her mouth, and struck a match to light it.

It was an act of self-communion, an auto-baptism. She could have done it once in a lifetime, or once a month, but Beck was there every week. Skinning up, she called it, as if her body needed another layer; a protective haze on the outside.

When she held a match to it, though, the lights went on inside her; illuminating her head, so she could see what she was thinking. Surprising thoughts. Having a joint was always the same; it was different every time.

Tonight, it was like opening up a dusty attic full of old baby things, a place she hadn't been for years. There was a cot, covered in cobwebs, and the outline of a pram.

Beck coughed. Smoking might have been bad for her body but it went through her mind like a cleansing fire; and all the inner furniture came up in bright colours. Everything squeaked, or rattled, and was decorated with ducks or rabbits.

Wandering through the room of baby-walkers, bottles and bathtubs, Beck found that its contents were still functional, and still fun.

When Fred died she thought she wouldn't have any more children. No, more than that; she hadn't thought about children at all. Life was too precarious; and her toddling Alfred could have been a doddering old man for all the confidence she had in his survival.

The reproductive part of Rebecca shut down. The attic of baby things was boarded up. Until tonight, when it was fumigated by the smoke of her joint; and Beck felt able to conceive.

She went upstairs to bed with Jonathon, but first she cleaned her teeth.


It didn't happen that night. Jon was already asleep by the time Beck slipped between the sheets. She cuddled up close to his warm and snoring form, grateful for his breath that curled the hair upon her cheeks. She was happy, for now, to lie there basking in the possibility.

But it didn't happen the next night, or the one after. A new pattern was emerging. Though Jonathon was full of energy during the day, his enthusiasm was for a different part of their relationship.

From seven o'clock in the morning, he probed; it was gentle, but it persisted through breakfast till he got in his car and went to work. And when he came home again at tea-time, he was probing still. The whole evening was taken up with his enquiry.

With endless questions about the past, and requests for every detail of their previous lives, Jonathon tried to squeeze the whole story out of her again; but Beck had finished with it. She was ready for the future.

She answered him, in fairness, the best she could; but it was a half-hearted attempt to re-live the experience. She'd lived it two too many times already.

When each evening came to a close, though, it was the end of another gripping installment for Jonathon, and he went to bed exhausted.

"He's as knackered as the Victorian lady," thought Beck, as she looked at him lying there. "I won't be getting a shag tonight."

She resigned herself to the fact that he would have to work through the whole thing before he'd want to sleep with her again. Right now, he saw her as an Indian man; a rebel soldier, a threat to his life.

It was going to take a long time for him to fancy her.


Beck threw herself into her work. She went back to nursery school. They offered her the quiet room; but Beck didn't think she could handle the colouring table.

In her current state, she could just picture the pink and purple phalluses and fallopian tubes she would do; a long paisley prayer for the unborn child. Pages of womb shapes she'd have to take home, the unmistakable question mark of an embryo curling around the exclamation marks of sperm. Microscopically, millions of times, she'd repeat the pattern; perhaps until she actually had a baby.

Beck knew herself. She could be a bit obsessive about painting. Under the circumstances it might be better to get out into the playground, for some exercise in the fresh air.

But she soon found that the outdoor children weren't quite like the indoor ones; there was much more shouting involved. Beck preferred to see their imaginations develop on paper, rather than on tarmac, on three wheels, on each other.

The hurly burly of the playground was too much like her mind could be, too boisterous. Beck preferred her mental state to be like the quiet room; peaceful and contemplative. Therefore, she concluded, the best thing would be to spend as much time as possible at the colouring table, with the little boy who never said a word.

Beck was also really taken with the sexual paisley idea, and thought it would be okay to do it, so long as she didn't tell a soul. She would sit on it like a hen on her eggs. No one would know how broody she was.

*

A stomach growing round with child was certainly the last thing on Jonathon's mind. He was solely concerned with the slim figure of his former life.

"Tell me again how small her waist was," he would say to Beck excitedly; and for the hundredth time she would show him its slender circumference with the circle of her hands.

"Are you sure you can't remember what her name was?" Jonathon urged repeatedly. "Come on, it can't be that difficult. What do you call a nineteenth century English woman?"

Beck stared at him as if he was telling a joke she didn't get.

"I know," he cried. "Victoria! We'll call her Victoria."

"I suppose it's as good a name as any," Beck shrugged, "for the lady who's ruling our lives."

Jonathon guffawed.

"Oh, I bet she never laughed like this," he said with glee.

"No, I never heard her laugh like that," Beck agreed.

But after that, it was all she heard. If she asked Jonathon what he wanted to drink, he replied; did Victoria prefer tea or coffee? Or would she rather have something stronger?

If she asked Jonathon whether he needed anything ironed for the morning, he replied; did Victoria favour plain or striped shirts? And how did she feel about spotty ties?

It was getting ridiculous. As they sat watching the news one evening Jonathon shook his head.

"I can't even begin to imagine what Victoria would have made of that!" he tutted.

Beck hadn't been paying attention, didn't know what passing crisis he was referring to; but one thing was clear.

Jonathon had another woman. She had come between them, and there was nothing Rebecca could do.

She had introduced her to him, and encouraged them to become closer. Now he was completely besotted, and there was nothing Beck could say.

After all, she had until recently been seeing another man herself. Dark and handsome, he had dominated her life. Now she had split from him and was back with Jonathon, side by side on the sofa; but no matter how close they were sitting their relationship was very open.

It was going to take a long time for them to make a baby.


Beck threw herself into her work. At the back of a cupboard in the quiet room she found a roll of plain paper. Scrolling it out across the colouring table she started her new project; a meditation on patience, in pink and purple paisley.

First she sharpened the fleshy pencils to fine points. The marks she made must be microscopic, and only visible out of the sun; a semen spill across the sky, like the Milky Way.

Her art was so secret it had to be rolled up at the end of every session and put back in the dark cupboard. Only Jack, the deaf and dumb boy who always sat next to her, saw what she was doing.

Beck found a second scroll of white paper for him, and watched in amazement as he slowly filled it with colour. Darker than her pale splashes, and bolder in design his grew; with giant leaves and stones showing granite faces.

While Beck's skin-tone images of ovulation and ejaculation spread across the page, Jack was doing evolution; weaving the greens into a canopy, with gold highlights in places where the sun found a finger-hold, and the shadows of animals hiding in the trees.

Jack's scroll was a natural history to complement Beck's human biology. His unrolled at the same pace as hers, until Beck increased her sessions at nursery school from two mornings a week to four.

It was better than spending the time at home; Doctor Comfort's joy was turning into rage, and Beck was in the firing line.

The novelty of his Victorian ladyship, and the voyage of self-discovery that followed, had led Jonathon to a place that was hotter than India.

When he first found out that Beck's story was true, he had been so excited. As well as pumping her for every detail she could remember, he plundered the library for all the books ever written about the mutiny of 1857.

Then he immersed himself in the plot and characters, rehearsed the dialogue, and realised the scenarios. But just when it seemed Jonathon was fitting the part perfectly, it started to feel too tight.

The constraints of the corset, the confinement of the siege, the final captivity in the Bibighar were getting to him.

"Why don't you go out?" Beck asked, one Saturday, when Jonathon was standing at the window, dripping with sweat.

"And spoil a lifetime of conditioning?" he shouted.

It was louder than the children's television and Alfie stared at Jonathon in shock.

"Shhh," Beck soothed. She understood Jonathon's anger, but she couldn't turn it off. They would just have to wait for it to burn out naturally.

It was the start of half term and Jade was coming to stay for a week. There would be no letting off steam in the spare room for Jonathon.

He tossed and turned furiously in bed beside Beck, until she slipped out and tip-toed downstairs, to give him space for a sleep.

Seven nights went by with Beck smoking in the kitchen till the small hours. Several packs of cigarettes were sacrificed to the fire she lit to keep her spirits up on the long and lonely vigil. She kept the window open, and burned joss sticks to clear the air; but they only made it smell more reminiscent of that awful Indian summer, over a hundred years ago.

"Yuk, Mum!" said Alfie, when he came down each morning; but Jonathon never seemed to notice the smell. Not in the kitchen, nor on Beck's breath. He just wasn't getting close enough.

She didn't think he'd even noticed her climbing out of bed each night, but finally, on the Sunday before school started again, Jonathon followed her downstairs.

"What the hell is going on in here?" he said, bursting into the kitchen as the clock was striking twelve.

Beck hardly dared to breathe, holding a lungful of smoke; but Jonathon got a whiff of what she was doing.

"It's criminal, Rebecca," he shouted.

She knew he didn't approve of drug-taking, but was still surprised by the violence of his reaction. Beck opened her mouth to answer, but nothing but smoke came out.

"Look at you," Jonathon continued. "Still sitting under the mulsuri tree!"

"What's a mulsuri tree?" Beck asked.

"Look in the book," Jon said, pointing at the one about the Cawnpore Massacre which he was keeping on the kitchen table and slowly committing to memory. "There was a tree in the courtyard of the House of Women, remember, a mulsuri tree; and you sat under it, every day, smoking that stinking hookah."

He stood with his hands on his hips and gave Beck the bollocking that Victoria should have given her Indian prince.

"You just sat there smoking and watching me suffer," he went on. "Impotent, that's what you are."

It was an interesting choice of words, and this time Beck didn't need to look anything up in a book. Impotent was how she felt. The warrior under the mulsuri tree, watching the untouchable woman he wanted, and Beck who wanted a baby with the man who wouldn't touch her; both knew exactly what impotent meant.

Jonathon came to the end of his tirade.

"You're just a big lump of dope," he said.

Beck stubbed out her joint in the ashtray.

She followed him back to bed, but he turned his back on her and went straight to sleep. Still, Beck tried to console herself, there were probably lots of men out there who'd love a girlfriend that was just a big lump of dope. Shame Jonathon was the only one for her.

She met Maisie at the school gates next morning, the first Monday after half term. Maisie was looking worse than usual, with hair everywhere and a jumper that clashed with her skirt.

"How are you?" Beck asked her.

"Bit stressed," Maisie said. "Fancy a cuppa?"

Beck had been dying to go to the new age teashop again. Her first visit had had a lasting effect; but now she was feeling in need of revival.

Their children ran into school as the bell rung, and the mums walked round the corner to a place where wind chimes were ringing. As they opened the door, the long thin sound of a digeridoo drew them in, and the waitress smiled at them as they sat down.

Beck watched Maisie trying to flatten her hair.

"What's up then?" she asked.

"Oh, you know," Maisie said, "the kids. And everything." She brushed her fringe out of her eyes, and met Beck's gaze. "How's Jonathon?" she said.

"Fine," Beck said quickly. "How's...?" Maisie's husband was a faceless character whose name Beck could never remember.

"Don. Fine," Maisie replied, just as quick.

Perhaps if they were drinking something stronger than tea, they might talk about their men; but this was a teashop and they chose cakes.

"There's an item on the menu," said Maisie, "that is so big you have to share it between two. Will you try it with me? I've fancied it for ages, but I'm always on my own."

"What is it?" said Beck.

"Sconehenge."

They found it on the menu, marked as a site of special importance with a warning about its size.

"It's a monument," said Maisie, "made of scones."

"But what does it taste like?" asked Beck.

"I don't know," said Maisie. "Apparently there's jam and cream involved."

"Well, what are we waiting for?" said Beck, and summoned the waitress.

When the waitress came, she seemed to have a miraculous memory for faces. She knew Maisie and Beck had been there before. In truth, the waitress was the sort of person who remembered clothes; she had never forgotten Maisie's patterned jumper.

And Beck remembered her purple tie-dyed apron; so they were all square.

When she heard their order, the waitress nodded like a superior nun at a couple of novices.

"Have you had it before?" she whispered.

"No," Maisie replied. "Can you tell us what to expect?"

The waitress shook her head.

"The ring of scones will reveal its secrets to you," she said, as she made mysterious markings on her pad. "And what will you be drinking?"

It was tea, of course, nothing more; so the two women still avoided talking about their men trouble in any depth. Maisie said her husband was decorating the hall. It was a surface conversation; wallpaper, paintscraper, all superficial stuff.

"He said he'd finish it by Saturday," Maisie added, "But it's been so long I don't even like the colour any more."

"What is it?"

"'First Sunrise'."

The waitress reappeared suddenly with their order. She had moved silently in her billowing robes and they were startled. She put a plate on the table and uttered reverently, "When the key scone is aligned with your forks, then you will be enlightened."

Maisie and Beck excavated the henge of crumbling cake greedily, gobbling everything they unearthed. Beck had expected the scones to be rock-hard; but the chunks she dug from the jam and cream cement melted in her mouth, leaving raisins to chew over.

As she and Maisie dismantled the scone circle, their conversation became more philosophical.

"If he were a doctor, like your Jonathon," said Maisie, "I'm sure my Don would be more…" She licked cream from her lips. "I'm sure he'd have finished the wallpapering by now. It's embarrassing, living with everything stripped bare. I need a façade, especially in the entrance hall. Every time I open the front door I feel so exposed."

"Oh dear," said Beck.

"And if he were a doctor, like your Jonathon," said Maisie, "I'm sure my Don would have more sense of decorum."

"Mmm," Beck nodded. Jon certainly had decorum; but if he were more like Don he might press her up against the paperless walls to make babies. She could just see them having sex on a decorating table that was permanently erected, yes, right there in the entrance hall; bare skin tickled by brushes of stiffening glue. But she didn't tell Maisie that.

Even in the middle of Sconehenge Beck couldn't reveal all her secrets.

They finished together, at the altar scone; forks slowing so that neither would take the last morsel of cake. They left a large crumb, as a sacrifice, and a large tip for the cook; though they felt heavier, rather than enlightened, as they stood up to go.

"I'm just popping to the loo," said Maisie.

While she waited, Beck looked at a noticeboard by the door. It was covered with cards advertising the bizarre practices of new age people:

Use Shiatsu and JuJitsu to Relax You, they said,
You'll Unwind when you have Realigned your Mind,
Get Feng Shui and Fairies or 2000 Hail Marys
With protein and starch foods combined
Try Crystal Reading or Automatic Writing
Chant the whole Mantra Alphabet

From Aroma to Yoga, through Vishnu and Wu Shu
And win a Free Trip to Tibet
Use Aura Photography or Tantra Pornography
There'll be a Second Coming yet.

Beck skimmed the list of threats and promises pinned to the board; some handwritten, some professionally printed with logos of rainbows or bodies tied in knots, and complicated Celtic borders. Then one card leapt out at her, and actually seemed to mean something.

*Past-Life Therapy.*

Beck read it again.

Past-Life Therapy.

It said it again.

A therapist for problems with previous incarnations. What kind of crazy person would that be?

By the time Maisie came back from the toilet, Beck was writing their name and number on a napkin.

She didn't even wait to get home before phoning. She used her mobile as she walked along the road, pressing the keys with haste.

D.P. Horobin? Man or woman? There was no reply. The past-life therapist was out.

Beck held on till the early evening, when Jonathon and Alfie went out; not for a jog, Jonathon had given that up when he became a Victorian lady, but for a sunset stroll by the sea.

Towards the Eastney end of the promenade was a beautiful rose garden. It was built in what had once been a fort, but flowers now grew over the high stone walls; so Beck had been surprised to hear Alf say, one June day when she'd taken him there as a toddler; 'Where are all the sailors?'

"What do you mean?" she'd laughed at his sweet little face. "This is a flower garden."

"But it used to be full of sailors," he said.

As they left, she'd noticed a plaque on the wall; strange how she'd never seen it before. It was in memory of The Cockleshell Heroes; a secret unit of Royal Marines in canoes. This site had been their training base in 1942.

Now was the wrong time of year for roses, but Alf still dragged Jonathon into the garden every evening on their walk.

As soon as they had gone out, Beck phoned D.P. Horobin again. This time, the past-life therapist was in.

"Er, hello," said Beck nervously. "I saw your card in the tea shop and wondered if I could make an appointment to see you."

"When would you like to come?"

"As soon as possible, really." Beck's voice sounded strange. She was holding her breath.

"Tomorrow?"

"Oh, yes, fantastic, thanks!" The breath gushed out, and Beck wrote D.P. Horobin's address on the napkin.

"See you at eleven o'clock then." The phone went dead.

Beck put her end down more slowly, the voice of the reincarnation counsellor ringing in her ears. She still wasn't sure if it was male or female.

Beck was late for her appointment the next day. The time by her watch, as she knocked on D.P.Horobin's door, was eleven minutes past the hour. All the clocks inside the house said eleven eleven too.

"Come in," said D. P. opening the door.

For a moment, for a long moment, Beck still wasn't sure if this was a man or woman. So unremarkable was the face, that its features spoke neither of the strength of a male nor the softness of a female; the hairdo too was unisex.

Beck stepped into the hallway, but had to know who she was speaking to, before she could go any further.

"Er, I don't know what to call you," she said.

"Doris."

Just about, by dint of the name, D was a she. She led Beck into a small sitting room, where there were a few more feminine touches; dried flowers in the fireplace and a display of knick-knacks on the mantelpiece above. Beck's sense of disorientation was subsiding as she sat down in an armchair.

"Been here before?" asked Doris.

Beck was about to shake her head, when she caught the meaningful gleam in the therapist's eye.

"I think so," she replied cautiously.

"Of course you have," Doris' tone was matter of fact. She shifted forward on the sofa, and fixed Beck with her look. "Now, let me explain what's going to happen. I am a trained hypnotist…"

"You don't need to hypnotise me," Beck burst out. "I can remember it already."

"Oh," Doris was surprised. "How come?"

So Beck told her the whole warrior plot, from the coma to the full stop.

"I got over it," she finished, "but having finally persuaded Jonathon to believe me, he got stuck in the story. I don't know how to get him to move on."

"Yes," Doris nodded, "you see, it's because he hasn't actually remembered any of this life himself. He's heard it all second-hand from you, or read it in a library book. The point of past-life therapy is that a person has to live the moment again, really live it; but they only need to do it once. Only once, then the sting goes out of the tale forever."

Beck sighed. "I've been selfish," she said, "forcing Jonathon to listen to it over and over again. But I couldn't forget it till he had forgiven me. Now I'm free and he's floating like a ghost between two lives."

"Mmm," Doris agreed. "That's a problem."

"So what can I do?" Beck pleaded.

"Let me hypnotise you."

"But I remember it all already!" Beck felt they were going round in circles. "It's Jonathon who needs therapy, not me."

Doris waited till Beck had stopped huffing and puffing, and the air was very still.

"You don't know the whole story," she said. "The troubles that you and your partner are sharing in this lifetime stem from what happened in the last one. But the troubles in that life stem from the one before."

"The one before?" echoed Beck. She'd never even thought of that.

"And the one before."

Beck was overwhelmed. "How many lives have we had?"

"How long is history?" Doris said. "You and Jonathon are soul twins."

"What does that mean?"

"Two halves of the same whole, trying to be one again."

Beck just stared now. She couldn't speak.

"Incarnating together time after time, in the attempt to get your relationship right," Doris went on gently. "Half the time, one of you spoils it; half the time the other one blows your chance of being a happy whole. But you've had it before, and you know you can have it again; blissful union."

"Me and Jonathon?" Beck whispered with tears in her eyes.

"You and him," Doris nodded. "Look, have a cup of tea, then think about going into a trance. I'll put the kettle on." She stood up, but kept talking. "Don't worry. Even if you split up, you'll never separate. But you can't go on feeling guilty, and he can't continue to be the victim; find out what started it if you want a future together."

Beck watched the woman speak, already slipping into her spell. The face, even now she'd put a sex to it, still looked so ambiguous. Doris was neither black nor white, but somewhere in between. Her hair was neither straight nor curly, her lips neither thick nor thin.

It was as if Doris, who knew how fleeting the physical form was, had a body that defied any image. Her looks were perfect for a past-life therapist.

"Forget the tea," said Beck. "Just hypnotise me."


Beck was feeling sleepy. She was lying on a river bank in the warm sun, listening to the sound of the water talking; an endless narrative of long words that flowed over her. On and on went the voice of the water; she listened without sinking, and heard what it said.

Beck was feeling sleepy, but she got up and walked where the river directed her to. The flowers that marked its edge nodded peacefully.

She found the tree where the hypnotherapist told her it would be. Straight and tall, it was an old one. And sure enough, there was a door in its trunk. The handle was twisted honeysuckle rope. Beck turned it, the bark creaked apart, and she stepped inside.

Inside was an elevator. She was in a lift. Now the voice that guided her rang as the floors moved beneath her.

"We will not be stopping at your life in India," it said, from the tannoy on a wall of deep red carpet. "Instead, when the doors open, you will step into the life you had before. You will arrive as it is about to end." The voice paused. "Okay?"

Beck nodded peacefully. Soothing elevator music was playing, and it did seem to be okay. She was already a safe distance away from herself.

"Ten, nine, eight," the countdown had started, in little green lights over the door; "seven, six, five," it said. "When I get to one you will arrive. Four, three, two."

Beck saw the lift doors opening, heard the pneumatic hiss of a portal in her subconscious, which was parting to reveal a different world.

"Step out," said the hypnotherapist.

Beck did as she was told.

D.P. Horobin spoke again.

"Where are you?"

Beck was lying in a bush, in the middle of a wood. She was buried but she wasn't dead yet.

There were leaves beneath her, leaves beside her and leaves above her. Thorns were sticking into her skin, but they didn't prick as much as her heart; bleeding red, she was, into the green undergrowth, feeding blood into the dark wood and growing pale.

"If you can't see where you are," said the voice, "look down at your feet."

Beck's feet weren't down, they were up; tangled in the bush in front of her face.

"Are you wearing shoes?" Doris asked. "Or are your feet bare? Are they dirty or clean?"

Bare, of course. Bare, and blue with cold. Only horses wear shoes, Beck felt like saying.

"Where are you?" Doris asked again. "Have you found your feet?"

Beck still didn't reply. She was busy getting out of the bush, and retracing her steps, back through the woods, out into the open countryside, along the rutted lanes that went through nameless villages. She followed her footsteps all the way back to the muddy field by the manor house, which was the closest she came to home.

"Now have a look around you," said Doris.

Beck had already seen the nag-nibbled grass, trimming a spinney of ash and elder, and the imposing chimney pots through the trees. She had seen the ring of tents around a campfire, with flame-licked patterns painted on, and flickering door flaps.

"Perhaps you will see someone who was important to you in this lifetime," the therapist said slowly, but Beck had already spotted her father. He was coming quickly across the field in an embroidered waistcoat and a worn leather apron full of something he'd poached from the stream or rustled from under the landowner's nose.

He squatted down next to an old lady with a grey pony-tail, and Beck could see him showing her what he'd got. Even from the copse at the edge of their camp, she could hear them cackle.

But she still didn't speak, and the hypnotherapist had to keep fishing.

"Or," Doris said, "you might meet someone who will become significant in your next life."

There was a bugle call behind her. It couldn't be clearer than that. Beck turned to see red through the trees; the streak of a fox, the sleek of the huntsmen's red jackets. At the front of the pack was Jonathon, dashing as the young Lord of the Manor. He was riding to hounds as if he'd never met a woman worth chasing.

He had gone in a flash, but left a lasting image. Like a hoof print on the path through the woods his impression was. Beck felt downtrodden just to look at him.

"What happened between you?" The voice of Doris came from the dust he'd kicked up.

Their love was so fast; it only took one meeting for them to fall, one glimpse through the trees to fell them. It was a carry on, like they'd been having a long affair. But how could they have met before, with him so high in the saddle of a horse, and her picking fungus from the forest floor?

"Forget breeding," he said. "I'll make you a lady."

She was already a lady, a Gypsy lady, as highly desirable as any of noble English stock. But she had desires too and they had not yet been met by any of the Romany men who had come to woo her.

"What's your name?" asked D. P. Horobin.

It was Rosa.

"Rosamund?" said Jonathon.

"Don't call me mud," the Gypsy held her chin high, "just because I'm made of the earth."

"No, Mund. Rosamund means rose of the world." The young man blushed. He really liked her. It was a bulge-in-the-breeches attraction.

"What's happening now?" the hypnotherapist murmured.

They were standing on a mound, and all around them the Gypsy fiddlers made music like war. Posh young Jonathon proposed to barefoot Beck and made another enemy; the fire.

Her heart had been a hot potato that none of the Gyspy men could hold, not even her Daddy could handle it. She had never found her equal.

Now here was one whose heart was a white stallion, whose soul was clean sheets; whose company would lift the red taint off her life. She lusted after his purity.

But she couldn't have him. If Rosa agreed to marry the Lord of the Manor, her family would call her dirty. No one would ever talk to her again, and no one would ever touch her.

It was an easy decision for the girl to make, but the young man took it hard. When he'd gone the Gypsies fell asleep by the fire, drunk on the night's ritual, but Rosa stayed awake until the fire died.

"What are you thinking?" The voice of Doris Horobin hissed from its embers.

Who says I can't have him, though? What does my father know about cleanliness? He's never given me anything white in my life.

That's what Rosa thought as she sat under the stars, with Dadus snoring on the ground beside her. If he could have replied he would have said; my seed. That white is your life. But he just snored, and the hypnotherapist asked the next question:

"What are you going to do about it?"

Run. She must have been drunk, but the girl got up and ran. Out of the ring of fire and blood, of men's bodies and bender tents, she went without anyone watching her go.

Only the moon saw, as Rosa stopped to piss in a ditch.

"Do you want to keep going?" it said.

She could still go back. Dawn wouldn't wake the Gypsies from their grassy sleep. There was time to follow the course of the shallow stream back to its source and see if there was a bed for her at the big house.

Rosa was a brazen lady; what though the doorknob was cold steel and the servants' manner was cool. She went in anyway. They sat her in the kitchen where a fire burned between four walls and ceiling. Not outdoors, she didn't know when the night she ran away became the next day.

Rosa was a beautiful lady, but her clothes were not warm enough. The cook gave her a shawl, which she was eternally grateful for, but it was too late. By the time the Lord of the Manor invited her upstairs, she was shivering all over and her throat was too sore to speak.

Rosa was a bold lady, but she'd caught a cold and couldn't catch her man. His father, bullish in a red tasselled nightcap, would need a lot of persuasion but Rosa had lost her power. A gnarled walking stick showed her the way out of his house. She wasn't allowed to see Jonathon, but just before she left he appeared to her through the banisters. As the young lord squirmed an apology she had never seen anyone look so small, and she'd known a lot of low-life.

"I will marry you," he said, "one day, when I'm free."

What was the promise worth to Rosa? She'd traded her health for it; a feverish flower made its way back to the Gypsy's field. And she'd traded her hearth; for when she got there, her family and friends were gone.

In her panic, she ran the perimeter; trying to find something familiar, something to follow. All she saw was a pile of horse dung with a kind face.

"Come on," it said, "let's go."

By rivers and over bridges, through villages and into the woods she followed the path of the gaily-turning cartwheels that were carrying her kinsfolk out of her reach.

The year was 1547, and there was no way of travelling faster. She walked until she ran out of steam. Rosa didn't give up; she simply fell over and didn't get up.

The girl was lost in the trees, but if anyone had looked they would have spotted her, red as a berry in the green sedge. Specks of blood were on the leaves, but neither the hunter nor the poacher was looking there. Both the young Lord and her old Dad thought they'd lost her already.

And that is how Rosa was buried but not dead. It had to be a natural grave; she didn't fit in anywhere else. Not quite right in a gypsy caravan, but all wrong for the manor house.

She died with nothing but the promise Jonathon made her. He'd marry her when he was free. For the price of a life, it was too cheap.

"It's time to come back now," said the hypnotherapist. Deep in the woods, Doris pointed out the tree with a button to call the lift. Beck pressed it with her mind. Before the doors closed she looked back at the lonely body she was leaving behind.

Birdsong turned into soft elevator music as Beck rose through the levels of consciousness. With a final ching, the doors opened and so did her eyes.

D.P. Horobin was back in her living room. The colours seemed wrong at first, as if the place were a television picture that needed adjusting. Beck blinked a few times.

Reality seemed flat, but she was full of relief. The body in the woods had been saved from anonymity; the grave was no longer unmarked. The part of Beck that had been buried there was back to tell the tale.

She smiled gratefully at Doris.

"How did you get on?" the therapist said.

"Didn't I say?" Beck was surprised.

"Not a word."

"Didn't I weep inconsolably or curse in strange tongues?" Beck asked.

"You were completely silent," Doris said. "So did you get anywhere?"

"Yes!" Beck replied.

"Lived and died?"

Beck nodded, bursting to start her new story.

"And do you feel better now?" Doris asked.

"Much, but…" Beck began.

Doris stopped her. She held up a hand.

"Don't tell me," she said. "You don't need to tell me."

"But…"

"Listen," the past-life therapist said. "Learn from your previous mistake. You know a deep secret. Now keep it that way."

"But Jonathon was part of it," said Beck. "Surely he has the right to…"

"What was his name?" interrupted Doris.

"Er, I don't know. Lord something," said Beck. "He was…"

"And what was your name?"

Beck couldn't remember.

"It's on the tip of my tongue," she said.

"And that's where it should stay," said Doris. "It's not what we say but what we do that counts. Words don't last from lifetime to lifetime, they don't survive the change of tense. All languages translate into the same thing; action."

"So let me say what Jonathon *did* to me."

"No," said the therapist. "You have to let it go, or else it will go on and on: 'you broke my heart, I'll break yours'."

"But…"

"Stop the cycle of bickering," D.P. Horobin said. "Otherwise you'll die again with your souls still behaving like children."

*

Beck went home on the bus. She sat upstairs, at the front, feeling that she could see in a new direction. Her vision was so shiny and exciting.

But what was the point of having a story that no one wanted to hear. Even the therapist, who Beck had paid to tell her problems to, refused to listen. It seemed like a wasted life.

Beck collected her son from school, and took him shopping for new shoes. Her own feet still felt bare.

The woman before them in the queue was stressed out; she shouted at her kids who were running all over the shop in their socks.

Beck wished she could say something to help her: like, your life will be over in a minute. Don't take the part you're playing too seriously.

Instead she found herself paying for the dearest pair of trainers in the shop without a word. The money she handed over seemed to flutter from her hand like leaves from a tree. Only an evergreen could hold on to it; and Beck knew she was seasonal.

Alf was so happy with the flashing lights in his soles he was good all the way home. At bedtime, Beck read him two chapters of a wizard school story they'd bought in Smiths next door to the shoe shop.

His eyes were closing as she closed the book and turned off the bedside light. Then, thinking that the parental role was over for another day, she stood up to leave the room.

One of the World War Two airplanes hanging from the ceiling spun violently. Alf awoke with a cry.

"What's up?" said Beck.

"It's too dark in here," Alf gasped. "It's too dark."

"But it's always like this," Beck said. The landing light was coming through the gap under the door. Besides he'd never complained about it before.

"No, it's too dark. Open the curtains," Alf wailed.

"What?" said Beck. She could hardly understand what he was saying, his voice was so choked.

"Open the curtains," he cried again.

"Don't be silly, we always close the curtains at night time," Beck tried to calm him down, but Alf was now sitting up in bed.

"Please, Mum. Open the curtains," he kept saying. "Open them, please. You know I would do it for you."

She opened them, as wide as they would go, and the sky outside was full of stars. It reminded her of the astrological art she was doing at nursery school, the heavenly map of her desire for another child. Alf closed his eyes against the twinkling, but Beck sat and watched him for a long time after he'd fallen asleep.

Who was this funny boy, she wondered; and how would he feel about a brother or sister, one that was equally his and Jade's?

The new addition would forge a biological link, where the bond had only been friendly before, Beck thought; and surely biological is best, for a soap-powder sparkling happy family. Snow white; star bright.


It was nearly Christmas again, a year since Beck's accident.

The colder it got outside, the more she wanted Jonathon to melt. At home, she was warm towards him, but his mood remained frozen.

He still talked about the Victorians all the time, and read everything he could find about the Raj. He still acted like a victim. But now his rage had a blade; he was using humour to get back at Beck.

It wasn't exactly cutting-edge. If Alf asked her what she'd been doing all day, Jon would say, "Oh, she's just been hanging around." If Beck tried to joke along with him, to keep the atmosphere light for the children, he would say, "Stop it, Rebecca, you're killing me."

And tea-time never went by without him spilling tomato ketchup on the carpet and asking her to lick it up.

Beck was under daily attack, but the children were not suffering. Jade only came at weekends, and Alfie was spending more and more time at Sam's house. Jonathon often volunteered to take him and collect him, even when it was three nights in a row. It always seemed to take him longer than it should to drive round the corner and back again. Once Beck asked why he had been gone for nearly an hour.

"I was talking to Maisie," Jon replied. "We ladies must stick together."

Beck knew what Maisie felt about the handsome doctor, and it wasn't an urge to swap knitting patterns. She wasn't tempted by his recipe for kedgeree, or his tips on keeping white collars stiff when it's sweltering.

But Beck also knew that the bored housewife Jonathon felt like was not Maisie; so she wasn't too worried about the intimate moments they shared in her kitchen. She was more concerned about the amount of time Alf was spending in their house.

"You and Sam are together all day at school," she asked him one tea-time, when he was rushing out again. "What on earth do you do all evening?"

"Oh, I don't play with Sam in the evenings," said Alfie. "I play with his Dad."

Beck and Jonathon shared a look of horror; purely in the present, nothing to do with their past.

"What?" said Beck.

"I play with his Dad," Alf repeated innocently.

Beck's knife fell to the floor.

"What do you play?" she said.

"On his computer," Alf replied. "All about the war."

"You mean a game?" Beck was starting to breathe again.

"No, it's not a game. We look up guns and planes and old soldiers. All real. Not a game." Alf was quite indignant now.

"Okay," Beck sighed with relief. She picked her knife up. Scraped a bit of fried egg off her shoe.

"It's the Internet," said Alf.

"I see," said Beck.

"We sent an e-mail to a veteran," said Alf.

Beck gave up trying to eat. She pushed her plate away, and looked at her son. It was obviously educational. She didn't know any other five-year-olds who had e-mailed a war veteran. But it was weird.

She decided to take him there herself tonight; talk to Maisie's husband, what was his name? Come on, come on, it rhymes with Jon. Don. Find out if he was obsessed with military history too, or whether Alf was just being a pest.


When the front door opened to reveal Beck standing there, Maisie could not conceal her disappointment.

"Where's Jonathon?" she said. The top three buttons of her blouse were undone, and she was wearing a pair of skintight trousers Beck had never seen on the school run.

"At home." Beck's tone was just sharp enough and her look just arch enough to let Maisie know that she could see through her, to the unfinished walls of the hallway.

"Sorry, come in," Maisie was blushing now.

"I've just found out that Alfred has been spending his evenings playing on the computer with your husband," said Beck. "And I don't think it's on." She stepped onto the dustsheet that covered the hall carpet.

Poor Maisie still looked flustered.

"Oh, well, neither do I really," she said.

"Can I just have a quick word with Don?" Beck asked. "Make sure my son isn't outstaying his welcome."

"Don't worry about that," Maisie replied. "He loves it. None of ours show the slightest interest."

She led the way past the lounge where Sam and his bigger brothers were sprawled around watching television, and into a small study. Alfie pushed past Beck at the door.

"Hi, Mr Mahon," he said, bounding to the desk.

"Hello Alf," Don said. He was the sort of man whose glasses reflected whatever he was looking at so you could never see his eyes. Both circular sur-faces were completely taken up with his computer screen; it was impossible to tell what he was thinking, but his voice was full of excitement.

"Captain Waring has responded to our e-mail," he said. "He's answered all your questions. There are some fascinating details about how they drove a line of lorries into the sea to make a pier."

"Let's have a look," said Alf, and grabbed the mouse.

His Mum watched from the door as the text scrolled down, and saw that the terms coming up were as enthralling for the man as they were for the boy he was reading to. Blah blah… the Allied pocket, Don was saying; blah blah… the little ships.

Beck glanced at Maisie. There seemed no need to speak to her husband now. He was obviously not being harassed by Alf. They were equally captivat-ed by the account of improvised landing jetties for a war at sea.

"I'll come back in an hour," whispered Beck.

"No, stay and have a cup of tea," said Maisie.

But Beck made her excuses and left. She didn't want to sit in Maisie's kitchen staring at the inches of cleavage that were meant for Jonathon to see.

She went home to see Jonathon instead.

He was watching a documentary about sacred cows, and didn't speak until it was over, when he grudgingly asked Beck how she had got on.

"Have you ever tried the Internet?" she said in reply. "Anything you want to know will be answered in an instant. And you can meet everyone who has asked the same questions as you, no matter where in the world they are."

"Hmm." Jonathon looked thoughtful.

"Anyway, they're doing Second World War stuff. In the sort of detail only a few old soldiers can still remember."

"And Don's into it too?" Jonathon asked. "Alf's not just being a nuisance?"

"They're allied forces," Beck said.

Nevertheless she didn't leave it too late to go and collect him. It was way before eight o'clock that she took the car keys from the mantelpiece.

Jonathon was watching a programme about Bombay taxi drivers, but he jumped up when he heard the rattle of the keys.

"I'll go," he said.

"It's okay, you stay there," Beck replied.

"No," he flicked the TV switch, "I'm off."

"Jonathon!" Beck protested as he straightened up and snatched the car keys from her hand. "I want to go."

"Well so do I," he replied. He hurried to the door.

"Can't we both go?" she asked.

"Wouldn't you rather have a bath?"

After the front door slammed she stood in the living room, in the shocked silence you get when a television is turned off too quickly. Jonathon never missed a programme about India. He'd even videotaped an Open University course about the Caste System. Maybe the attraction of Maisie was greater than Beck thought.

She didn't have a bath. Favouring the relaxing powers of smoke over water, she would rather have a spliff. Beck sat in her tatty red armchair by the kitchen window, blowing the pungent fumes out into the quiet night air. Physical tension went with them, but her mind remained fixed on the object of stress; Maisie's cleavage, straining in a bra that might as well have been whalebone, pale as a Victorian lady's.

Jonathon was going to love it.

Beck smoked two joints and he still didn't come back. It was nearly nine, long past Alfie's bedtime. She stood in his bedroom window with the lights off, waiting for their car to come round the corner.

When it did, she felt angry. Not at Jonathon; she was supposed to have forgiven him. She took it out on Alfie. Her hot air stirred the mobiles on his ceiling, sending the spitfire into a spin.

"It's over, you know," she said, as she tucked him crossly into bed. "The war was over a long, long time ago."

"Then how come I still remember it, Mum?" he said.


Just when Beck had finally won her soul's war, her son had restarted a fight of his own. She was not his enemy, but he was against her. So Beck only phoned D.P. Horobin again because she didn't know who else to turn to for help.

Alf was showing all the signs of a past life, and probably a horrible death, in the Second World War; and Jonathon, still cross about the way Beck had treated him in their previous incarnation, now seemed to be having an affair with her best friend.

Jon had been staying all evening at Maisie's house, not just dropping Alf off there and picking him up later; and though he claimed to have been on the computer, even bringing home print-outs about the Cawnpore Massacre from the World Wide Web, Beck was starting to worry.

Maisie avoided her at the school gates in the morning, and went to the new age tea shop with another mum instead. Beck would have to go back there, though, to get D. P. Horobin's phone number off the noticeboard.

She had thrown the original serviette away after her last visit, convinced that she wouldn't need the services of a past-life therapist again. Beck screwed up the purple paper napkin embossed with silver runes, and threw it in her kitchen bin.

Her plan was to wait for Jonathon to forgive her naturally, not force him to by telling him how badly he behaved when she was a Gypsy and he was a Lord. She was determined not to let that rubbish spill over into this lifetime, though there was enough of it to fill a couple of carrier bags besides the bin.

Beck held on until it was a week before Christmas, and Jonathon's spirit was no closer to goodwill than it had been the week before.

"Can't you take Alf round there and come straight home again?" she asked him, as he was shrugging himself into a black overcoat in the hall.

"I'll probably stay," Jonathon said.

"But we need to get ready for Christmas," said Beck. "It's nearly here and we haven't done anything yet."

Jonathon opened the front door, to a blast of cold air.

"We should write a list of presents for the kids," she added desperately. "Please come back."

"I could," he said, "but I want to use the computer."

"Why don't you get your own?"

"What?"

"Why don't you get your own computer."

Seven words got him back on her side. Six little words and a big one did what all the dialogue, and the pages of pictures hadn't been able to.

"Why don't we get one for Alfie," he said.

Suddenly they stood in a new formation on the doorstep; both in the same team.

"Could we?" Beck whispered.

"If he's good," said Jonathon. "We can easily afford it."

"Then would you spend more time at home?"

"Well," he said eventually, "you'll have to wait and see in your stocking for that." Then he called for Alf and ran to the car.

Beck felt slightly more warmth in the air as she closed the front door behind them. She thought Jonathon was starting to thaw. With a small smile she curled up to smoke in the red armchair by the kitchen window, and wrote a long list of things to buy for Christmas.

This year everything would be new; she'd throw away the tatty old tinsel and the angel whose sellotape showed at the top of the tree, but at the top of the list would be a computer for Alfie, if he was good.


Beck found out exactly how good Alf had been, at school the next day. The sign on the gates reminded her; it was parents' evening.

Jonathon dropped her back there after tea. Alf was very quiet behind them.

"Why don't you two go late night shopping," she said. "Start getting things in for Christmas."

There was no response.

"Wrapping paper? Turkey and tinfoil?" she said to Jonathon as she took her seat belt off.

"Actually, I promised to…" he paused, but Beck saw what was coming, "…to go and pick up some e-mails."

She got out of the car without another word, slammed the door shut and started shouting on the pavement as they drove away.

"It's e-mail, not e-mails! You never used to say the Royal Mails, so why pluralise it now!"

Other parents at the gate looked at her strangely; but Beck had been good at grammar when she was at school and still felt strongly about its correct use. She sighed, and joined the shuffling procession to the teachers' desks.

Alfie's teacher was called Ms English, and Beck was looking forward to a well informed chat with her. There was a long queue, though, and while they waited each parent sat at their own child's desk, looking through their exercise books.

Beck was used to sitting on small chairs from her work at nursery school, but she could see other parents dotted around the room who weren't so comfortable with the position. They were mostly mums, but one or two dads had come too; and there were low giggles as the lanky forms folded themselves into thirds like pieces of their children's maths work.

Beck was laughing too as she started leafing through some of Alf's sums; but the smile soon left her face. His books were covered in graffiti, mindless and violent; with scribbled spitfires, bombs dropping and rows and rows of crudely drawn soldiers' graves.

Beck was a single parent. Who else should her son take after but herself; where else could he live but in the past, and what else would he do with his time but maudlin doodles?

Really she should have been surprised if Alf was different from her; but Beck was shocked at their similarity. He was a war artist too. She felt her face go red as she looked further into his body of work, right up to the barbed wire drawn between the staples at its centrefold.

Then the teacher called her name from the front of the class. Beck hurriedly stuffed the books back into the box on his desk, and as she stood up Sam's dad came and sat down in the seat next to Alfie's.

He gave Beck a shy smile.

"Where's Maisie?" she whispered.

"Wanted to stay at home tonight," Don said.

"What?" Beck was incredulous. Sam's mum was missing parent's evening and his dad had come instead? Something was very wrong here. Maisie and Jonathon were alone in the house.

"Mrs Salmon," the teacher said again, and this time it wasn't a question.

Beck was shaking as she approached the desk.

"I'm worried about Alfred," Ms English said. "His work is awful, but he's actually quite bright. Did you have a good look at his books?"

"Er, yes," Beck stuttered, and started trying to explain away his obsession with war.

"Oh, that's not what concerns me," said the teacher briskly. "They all do that, especially the boys; if it's not guns and gas masks it's car crashes or volcanoes erupting. No, I'm not averse to the little testosterone splashes in the margins; it's his complete lack of scholastic achievement that worries me."

Beck looked blank.

"Did you not see?" the teacher said impatiently.

Beck shook her head.

"I've been teaching him for a whole term now," Ms English said, "and I can honestly say he hasn't learnt a thing."

Beck could hardly take it in. She looked over her shoulder at the desk Alf shared with Sam, where Don was now sitting in place of Maisie.

"What's he like at home?" Ms English asked.

Beck shrugged.

"Never there," she said.

The teacher frowned so deeply her glasses started to slide down her nose. She was coming to all the wrong conclusions about Alfred's mum, who was doing nothing to put her right.

"Where does he go?" she asked suspiciously.

"Sam's," Beck said. "To surf the Internet."

"I see!" The teacher pushed her glasses up again. "As I thought, he's a bright boy; he just needs to apply himself to the boring details of literacy and numeracy. Now, how do you suggest we tempt him back to the basics?"

"Don't worry," said Beck, and stood up, scraping her chair dangerously on the classroom floor. "I'll teach him."

*

She came down on Alfie like a ton of bricks. He didn't know what hit him. One minute he was sitting in Sam's front room, listening to the banter of older brothers he didn't entirely understand; the next minute there was a big banging on the front door.

"Okay, okay, I'm coming," said Sam's mum, and hurried out of the study where she'd been on the computer with Jonathon.

Alf's mum was behind the door, and the minute it opened he heard her roar:

"Where is he?"

Alf hid behind the sofa, but Maisie showed Beck into the study.

"Here he is," she said, shakily.

There was a short pause before Beck replied:

"Not him. Where's my son?"

Beck had never played the heavy parent with Alfie. She had always trodden lightly on him, even when she told him off. She had always respected his person.

But tonight she grabbed him roughly, hauled him to his feet, smacked his face and dragged him out of the house by his ear.

"Help! Jonathon!" the boy yelped.

"Shut up," Beck said. "Get in the car."

She threw him onto the back seat, and slammed the door shut.

"What's up?" asked Jonathon.

"Just drive," Beck replied.

Maisie stood on the doorstep as they pulled away. Beck stared angrily at her. Sam and his brothers were watching from the front window, framed in a triangle of light they'd made from pulling the curtains back.

The living room looked warm and cosy; but in their view, Alf would never be cool again.

"Mum! Did you have to?" he said.

"Did I have to?" she shouted. "Did you have to do something at school?"


The next day was the last day of term. On the way, Beck made Alf promise to try harder.

"Or you will not be allowed out to play," she said. "There will be no Sam's, there will be no Santa, unless you do sums and spelling every morning of the holiday, even on Christmas day."

There would be no presents, said Beck, if Alf didn't catch up with the schoolwork past. Chains on the big gates rattled bleakly as she said goodbye to him, without a kiss for the pale little face that puckered up at her in disbelief. Alf had never seen his mum looking so strict. Surely by tea-time she would be her soft self again.

It was hard walking into the new age café. Beck did not want to bump into Maisie, but it was impossible to look through the stick-on stained glass window to see if she was inside first.

The wind chimes rang loudly as Beck closed the door behind her, and a CD of pre-Christian carol singing accompanied her to a table. Opening the menu, she hid her face in it; looking over the top at the other customers, who were all eating winter solstice cake.

Luckily there was no sign of Maisie, sitting among the astrological table-cloths, flicking through the new age magazines. She must be at school listening to children read. Beck relaxed and picked up one of the beneficial publications, full of articles about primal screams and lucid dreams.

Then she saw an advertisement for educational software; Maths and English computer programmes for five-year-olds. This resolved some of the tension within her; now she could buy Alf a Christmas present and still punish him for not working hard enough.

Perhaps he'd do better, learning cyber lessons from a virtual teacher. Beck had explained to Jonathon what Ms English told her at parents evening, last night after Alf had gone to bed. Jonathon just laughed it off.

"Rebecca, he's only five," he said. "That woman is far too hard on them. Maisie says she's a tartar."

"Maisie says she's a tartar," Beck mocked his prim tone. Did the two of them talk like Victorians too, now; with Maisie in her whalebone wonderbra, and Jonathon drinking tea with his little finger cocked.

The waitress brought Beck a piece of the Pagan Christmas cake. There was a Green Man instead of a snowman on top, and the Santa was made of wicker. Underneath the icing, it was not so much a fruit cake as a vegetable one, mainly carrot.

"Where's your friend today?" the waitress asked.

"Having an affair with my husband," Beck replied.

The waitress blushed till her face was tie-dyed purple as her apron. It was only after she'd rushed back behind the counter that Beck remembered Jonathon wasn't actually her husband.

He had proposed to her, but that was lifetimes ago, when she was a sexy young Gypsy and he was the heir to a country seat. Lifetimes she'd been waiting, and they still weren't married.

It was like a saga, a long story following one family for several generations; only Beck's was the saga of one soul and several incarnations. From a rebel soldier to a single mother, she kept coming back; and every time, she met her match. In every place, from battlefield to playground, she found her soulmate. They were born to be together, but they always seemed to end up killing each other.

Beck finished her tea and stood up to look on the notice board for the phone number of the past-life therapist. It was exactly where she had found it before, next to cards advertising practices that made it look positively old-fashioned.

She wrote down the number on a napkin and took it home in her pocket. But Beck really hadn't wanted to contact D.P. Horobin again. She was just fingering the buttons on her mobile phone, when Doris answered.

"I'm desperate," Beck said. "Please, please can I see you?"

"How about tomorrow?" the hypnotherapist asked.

Beck was squeezing the serviette in a sweaty hand.

"Yes, yes," she gasped.

"Same time, same place?"

"Yes," Beck said in relief, and dropped the serviette with its ink running. Now, perhaps, she would get somewhere.


What Beck had forgotten was that tomorrow was the start of Alfie's school holiday, and he would have to go to past-life therapy too.

Still feeling cross with him, she packed a bag of schoolbooks and didn't explain when he asked where they were off to.

"You're just going to sit and do sums," she said. The look of horror on his face made her add; "Don't worry. It's only for an hour."

"Can't I go to Sam's instead?" he said.

"No. I told you. You're sticking with me until your schoolwork has improved by a hundred percent."

Alf was so horrified that Beck had to ease off a bit.

"Anyway, we're going on the bus," she said.

They sat on the top deck and Alf was in much higher spirits by the time they got off in North End. Beck had a job to find the house again, though.

In this part of the city they all seemed to look the same. The land was still as flat, but further from the sea there seemed to be more certainty that the buildings would stay put.

In Southsea they had a haphazard look, all different, as if no one had ever built more than one house at a time in case it sunk back into the shingly morass.

In the Salmon's street no two houses were the same; a grand facade towered over the squat cottage next door, as Georgian rubbed shoulders with Victorian. In gaps left by the bombs of the Second World War a few small modern houses had been inserted. Above, the rooftops sloped at sharply contrasting angles; some of the Gothic detail was genuine but most of the Stucco was stuck on.

So Beck had a bit of trouble finding D.P. Horobin's house, it fitted in so seamlessly with the rest of the street. As they walked up and down the avenue lined with laburnum trees and houses clad in the off-white tiles of a public toilet, Alf solicited her for information.

"Who lives here?" he said.

"None of your business," she answered. "You're just going to do your work."

"Are you a spy?"

"I'll be watching you. If you finish a whole page of sums we'll have lunch in a café."

She was late for her appointment again. Her watch said eleven eleven as she knocked on the door; and the green lights on the VCR read the same when Doris showed them into her living room.

"Right, you sit there," Beck said to her son briskly. Small though the lounge was, there was a large floor cushion in the window, next to a low table. Alf settled into the nook and started to get his books out of the bag.

"Sorry," said Beck to the therapist. "I forgot it was the school holiday."

"That's okay," Doris looked past her, and gave Alf a smile. "He'll be fine."

Beck turned to look at him too and realised that he was about to ask D.P. if she was a man or a woman. She stepped between them, and bent to open Alf's maths book.

"Now, you just get on with your work," she said, "and remember, if you manage a whole page we'll have lunch in a café."

Alf looked hungrily at his sums.

Beck sat down on the sofa.

"Relaxed?" said the therapist.

Beck shook her head.

"Have you told your partner about the other life you shared?"

"No," said Beck. "I've been trying to show him how old our love is, but he's found someone new."

Doris glanced at Beck's son.

"We'd better not talk about this now," she said. "The best thing would be for me to hypnotise you again. Are you ready?"

"I suppose so," Beck said, but she wasn't really sure how another hypnosis was going to help.

The therapist seemed to speak louder than before as she led Beck to the tree with a door. She lingered longer by the river, describing the way it flowed in more detail. She waited by the bank for Beck's thoughts to catch up, and seemed to keep looking back as the footpath led her into the trees.

Beck was feeling sleepy, moving slowly. A sunny day buzzed like the sound of bees in her ears. She would have swatted it away, but her hand was too heavy with honey to lift.

At D.P. Horobin's command, Beck saw the elevator doors opening; but she could not walk inside. Her feet were still, though Doris's voice went on.

"Going down," she said. "Down, down, gently down. When the doors open again, you will step into a previous life; a time and place most significant to the state you are in now. You will not be afraid, though the sights you see may be terrifying. Guardian angels will be watching over you."

She didn't say that last time, thought Beck; and opened her eyes a crack to look at D.P. just as the elevator doors were supposed to be opening.

To her surprise, the therapist was looking straight past Beck at Alfie. Beck turned to see him too, crouching on the floor cushion, shaking all over. Alf let out a scream.

Instinctively, Beck jumped off the sofa, but Doris held up a hand to stop her.

"What's happening?" she said calmly to Alfred.

"Bombs," he replied. "Bombs falling everybloodywhere."

"Are you hurt?" the therapist said.

He shook his head.

"Not yet. Christ, that was close. It got some other poor bastard."

"Where are you?" Doris asked.

"On the beach. There are thousands of us. Miles of men dug into the sand, and queues that stretch right into the sea."

"What are you waiting for?"

"Boats to take us home," said Alf. "We're stuck at the seaside on a summer's day, with bombs falling like rain."

Alf stopped and shuddered.

"A hit?" asked Doris.

"Not me," said Alf. "But we're all me's, aren't we? We're all wearing the same uniform, and we all look the same with our brains blown out. The others are facing it better than me; they're either pissed or praying."

"Why aren't you?" said Doris.

"Can't take my eyes off the sea," said Alf. "If the boats don't get us out of here we're all gonners. The streets of the town are blocked with burnt trucks and tangled trolley wires. The houses are blitzed and their cellars are full of sol-diers drinking champagne, with the command nowhere to be seen."

Alf's eyes were closed as he spoke, and his tone was disbelieving.

"On the beach, men are playing ball games, swimming and sunbathing in their shorts. A chap sits in a deckchair with a drink and a book; but the Hun are coming. Their tanks are rolling over the burnt trucks and trolley wires, tak-ing drunken Tommies prisoner at cellar steps in every street; getting ever closer to the beach, where soldiers sing hymns together, standing in circles on the sand."

Alf screwed his eyes up tighter and his tone was desperate.

"I lose my life on that beach, which isn't to say that I die. I just imagine it a million times; being shot at, blown up, or drowned at a moment's notice; and going naked into my death."

He stopped.

"What?" said Doris.

"They're coming," he said. "A fleet of little ships on the horizon. Only been waiting three days. And here's a naval officer, at last, to tell us what to do." He sat up straighter on his cushion. "Can't embark at the harbour, easy target for Luftwaffe; though the sky is so black, it's a wonder they can see us." Alf coughed, from the smoke, but then it turned into laughter.

"What?" said Doris.

"An Isle of Wight ferry," said Alf. "I'm going home on an Isle of Wight ferry!"

Doris laughed too.

"It's true," said Alf. "It can't come in close enough, so we're evacuated by the spoonful in dinghies and lifeboats. It takes hours, with the sandy shallows full of collisions, and propellers breaking on boats already sunk. But I even see a man going to and fro in a canoe."

"A canoe? Where did that come from?" said Doris, then Beck saw her clap a hand to her mouth, cross with herself. But Alf didn't seem to mind the interruption.

"They came to save us," he said. "Fishing boats and pleasure cruisers; trawlers and dredgers and even a brown-sailed Thames barge make up the fleet. The sea is kind to the little ships; and all the weathered sailors say they've never seen it so calm as we sail across the English channel, with S-boats below us, and Stukkas above…Thank God for that!" His face broke into a chalky smile. "The white cliffs of Dover."

"You made it!" Doris was smiling too.

"Not quite," said Alf. "Few hundred yards out, a yacht next to us hits a mine. Men all around me hurt by debris. Right in my face a bloke loses his features to a flying cleat. We pull survivors out of the water, though there's no standing room on deck. A chap is lifted out of the briny only to find his legs have stayed beneath. He bleeds all over us and is dead before we reach port."

"But you survive?" Doris asked quietly.

"Part of me does," Alf said, and left a long pause. "But there was a lot more war fought after Dunkirk."

"What did you do when it was all over?" said Doris.

Alf shook his head.

"I went home to my wife," he said, "but I was no more use to her than a gas mask with a hole in. After many years, we had a daughter."

"Ah," said Doris, "that's nice."

Alf started to cry.

"What's happening now?" the past-life therapist asked.

Alf's shoulders shook. Beck took a step closer.

"Oh," Alf sobbed, "Mummy. I never did get off that beach."

Beck held him. His five-year-old body was the size of a bucket which would have to be dipped many times in the ocean of grief before the water started to subside.

Alf kept coming up full from the depths; and he cried it all out. As his sobbing died away, Doris Horobin talked him back to her small room, so that when Alf opened his eyes on the featureless lounge, recognition was already there.

It was lighter. Everything was lighter; the windows and the walls; the weight of Alf's body, the weight of Beck's heart.

"How about a nice cup of tea?" said Doris.

Beck nodded gratefully.

"And Alfred?" said the therapist. "I think I've got some orange squash?"

Alf grimaced.

"I'll have tea too, please," he said.

Beck had never known him turn down the offer of something with E numbers. She looked at him in surprise.

"On that boat," he said, "in the middle of all that bloody chaos, someone still managed to brew up a bucketful of tea and pass it round. That's British spirit."

They didn't linger long over their cuppas. Beck and Doris were both in shock, and Alf thought he was only staying an hour anyway. He packed his books into Beck's bag.

"I didn't do much maths," he said casually.

"That's okay," answered Beck.

"Can we still have lunch in a café?"

D.P. Horobin was showing them to the door. She put a hand on Beck's shoulder.

"Please phone me tomorrow," she said. Her eyes were full of importance.

Beck's mind was racing with things to discuss, too, but she walked slowly down the road with Alf, and waited ages for a bus. North End was thronged with Christmas shoppers, and the number 23 crawled back to Southsea through the traffic.

They didn't get off at their usual stop. By some unspoken agreement, Alf and Beck sat tight in their seats; and stayed there until the bus stopped at the harbour. Then they could see the Isle of Wight ferry.

They stood on the quay and watched as the car ferry sailed past them and out into the Solent.

"Of course, it wasn't exactly the same one," said Alf; but even so neither of them took their eyes off the unprepossessing vessel till it reached land on the other side. And they stood there so long that they saw the ferry start to sail back again; with only a few lorries at this time of year, none of the coaches and caravans of the summer season.

The little ship grew larger and larger as it came across the water again, and when it was nearly back in port Beck spoke.

"Do you want to go?" she said.

"I suppose so," said Alf, and turned away from the sea wall.

"No, I mean, do you want to go on the ferry?"


Alf was five again, dancing the dance, chanting the chant; like any excited child about to embark on a boat.

Beck bought the tickets with Jonathon's money; plastic for wiping off sea spray and kid spit. Alf snatched them out of her hand.

"I want to give the tickets to the man!" he shouted.

While the cars drove into the oily belly of the ferry, foot passengers walked a gangplank. Crossing the water, which slapped at the ship's hull fifteen feet below, Alf went quiet again.

As soon as they were on board the ship, Beck knew that they were close to Dunkirk. She steered Alf towards the canteen on the top deck, and sat him at a table by the salt smeared window.

"What would you like to eat?" she asked.

"A sandwich."

"What?" He hadn't said chips.

"A bully beef sandwich."

"Oh. And what about a drink?"

"Tea."

"Again?" He hadn't said Coke.

"Yes, that'd be great," said Alf.

Beck left him staring through rainy glass at the grey sea, and went to stand in a short queue.

She didn't feel like eating much. She was too upset. Her little boy had been violated by history. He'd seen men dismembered, and now he remembered them.

Beck shuffled forward a place in the queue. She supposed it was no worse than what children saw on television these days. It was nothing that Sam hadn't seen, but Alf had been there. How could she get his youth back?

The canteen didn't do bully beef. This wasn't the nineteen forties. Beck had to choose between Chinese chicken or smoked ham, and she didn't think Alf could handle the Chinese.

"They only had ham," she said, when she got back to him.

"Ham, eh?" he said. "Fancy!"

How could she get him to stop talking like an old man?

"Here's your tea." It sloshed into the saucer as the ferry rode a wave. Beck sat down with a bump. She was only having two shortbread fingers.

"That won't fill you up," said Alf.

The boat lurched again. Beck started to feel sick.

"Why don't you have a proper meal?"

"I couldn't," she said.

"What do you mean, couldn't?" Alf inquired crossly. "Don't be ridiculous. We're not on rations."

He started to chew his sandwiches ferociously. They were gone as fast as the first snack for fifty years. Beck's finicky little fingers took longer. When Alf had finished he wiped the ferry window with his serviette, and looked out again. Half way across the Solent in the middle of winter, and all they could see was grey.

Beck opened her bag.

"Look," she said. "Let's get on with a bit of maths."

She put the books on the table.

"No," said Alf.

"Come on," she repeated. "You need to do some sums."

Beck took the top off a pen with a pop.

"No."

"Just do as you're told," she said.

"Why should I?"

"Because I said so."

"You can't make me."

"I can," Beck insisted. "I'm your mother."

"Not all the time," Alf shouted. "You're not always my mother."

Beck was silent.

"You can't tell me what to do any more," Alf went on. "I've been bigger than you. I've been a man, Mum!"

Beck gave him a shell-shocked nod. She knew what he meant. She had been a man too.


They got home very late from the Isle of Wight. Jonathon met them in the hallway, with his hands on his hips.

"Who the hell is D.P. Horobin?" he demanded.

"What?" said Beck.

"Who?" said Jonathon, holding up the napkin from the new age tea shop.

"Oh," said Beck. "Well, um," she fished around for an answer. "He, I mean, she," an image of Doris floated into her mind, "is... is..." What was she going to say?

Alf took over.

"A past-life therapist," he said, pushing gently past Jonathon and going to put the TV on.

It was better coming from a child. Jonathon took it more kindly. He laughed and looked at Beck.

"What will you think of next?" he said.

Well," she sighed with relief, "you can imagine my curiosity when I saw the number on the noticeboard at the café."

He looked at the crumpled serviette again.

"I suppose so. But what were you doing till nine o'clock at night?"

"We've been to the Isle of Wight."

"Oh," said Jonathon, jealously. He never had. "What's it like?"

"It's... it's..." Again Beck was searching for words. "Actually, we didn't get off the boat; but we could see the shore, and it looked like England. Beautiful Blighty, fixed in time." Beck was searching his face; Jonathon still seemed jealous. "Doris didn't go," she reassured him, "just me and Alfie. It was his field trip."

"Okay, but school is over now," said Jonathon. "Jade gets here tomorrow. We've got to make it Christmas. Come on."

He took Beck by the hand, and led her into the lounge.

They stayed up till midnight making paper chains. Licking and sticking together the shiny colours until they could string them round the room, festooned in rings from the ceiling. Beck was longing for a smoke, but she didn't want to inflame this new, mellower Jonathon; so they ended up going to bed together.

With arms linked like the paper loops they lay; and although they didn't have sex, they came closer than they had for a long time.

Jonathon seemed to have forgiven her for killing him in their last life; and she had forgiven him for killing her the life before. So long as neither of them did it again, their relationship would be fine.

They had a lot of catching up to do, but by tea-time on Christmas Eve everything was ready. Jade and Alfie had decorated their tree. There was a new angel on top, one who didn't need sellotape to stay up. All the tinsel and trinkets were immaculate, and the children were spraying snow over the silver and green.

"Hang on," said Jonathon, appearing with a box. "There's one more thing. This is for Beck."

He handed over the package. She unwrapped it, smiled, and sat down weakly on the sofa to watch as Jonathon and the kids unravelled a sort of magic vine to wind around the Christmas tree.

It was a year ago, almost to the minute, that Alf had asked for them. Flashing lights.

"It's not fair," he'd said. "I bet Jade's got them on her tree."

Now they shared a tree and everything was sparkly.

"Turn them on, Dad, turn them on!" Both children were shouting.

Jonathon looked at Beck.

"Are you ready?" he said.

She had tears in her eyes, but she nodded. With the lights in his hands, there'd be no bang, no smell of burning, no ambulance siren; no life-support machine bleeping when he put the plug in the socket.

Jonathon just hoped they were going to work. They were the most expensive flashing lights in the shop. He flicked a switch and the tree was bedecked in electric jewellery. Topaz, rubies, sapphires and emeralds shone from its prickly branches.

Alf started to dance ecstatically in front of it. As the plastic colours played in sequence across his face, Beck saw that he didn't remember what had happened this time last year. Funny little mind, which knew stories from a war half a century old, but had forgotten the bang when the lights were switched on.

She was glad that Christmas Eve would not always be the anniversary of her accident. Jonathon gave her a glass of fizzy wine to celebrate. Later, when Alf and Jade had hung up their stockings and gone to bed, they had a couple more glasses; and tried to work out the exact sequence of lights flashing on the tree.

"Green, then blue, green, then blue," said Jonathon.

"Red ones, all of them, yellow ones, all of them," added Beck.

"Yellow, then red, then green, then blue," Jonathon said.

"All of them, white, all of them, white," Beck chanted the last part, but her heart wasn't quite there. It was leaning towards her red chair; in the corner of the kitchen, by the radiator, by the window.

Beck was dying for a smoke; it was Christmas Eve, for Christ's sake. But she couldn't go and sit in her special place; it would have broken up the party between her and Jonathon.

They filled the stockings, and wrapped up some bigger gifts. Their children's faces would light up the morning.

Then they went to bed together. In the darkness they remembered they were one. Jonathon got back on top of their relationship and Beck was happy again.

She didn't have a father, but she had Father Christmas. He came in the night and brought a computer, that would fix all her family problems. No more evenings spent at Maisie's house for Alf or Jonathon. Doctor Comfort could stay at home with Beck, and help to make a new baby.

That was her New Years resolution.


Despite plenty of warning, Beck and Jonathon had left their plans for the Millennium to the last minute. Without a party to go to on New Years Eve, they looked a bit worried.

"This is a once in a lifetime event," Jonathon said. "We can't just watch it on the telly."

Beck agreed. They got the children out of bed at half-past eleven and put coats on over their pyjamas. Then they left the house and headed south.

There was a sparkle coming from the sea front; champagne spray, and cigarette phosphorescence.

All along the prom, people were thronging; high on the rocks by the castle, and in the windless dip by the bandstand; from the neon lit arcades of South Parade Pier to the dark expanse at Eastney. All along the walls at Old Portsmouth, the weathered defences of the harbour, people had come to cheer and sing and welcome the New Year as if it were a ship coming in.

It was the royal yacht of the night, with a Janus-faced figurehead. They couldn't make out its features yet; though as midnight chimed across the water, the Isle Of Wight was lit up with fireworks.

Their urban skyline was hung with flashing lights, too. For that crack in time, as the clocks struck twelve, Southsea had a turban of jewels; topaz, rubies, sapphires and emeralds. The true colours of the Christmas tree.

Beck held Alf tightly, because fireworks had frightened him in the past. But tonight the banging didn't bother him.


As their evenings were going so much better, Beck had to do all her smoking during the day, while Jonathon was at work.

It was a terrible thing, but the red velvet armchair sat in the corner of her kitchen from breakfast time till tea, inviting her to sit down. And every time she did, her hand slipped into the hole in its seam, where the stuff for skinning up was kept.

Her afternoons became long lazy meditations on baby names and whether she could bear to try breast-feeding again.

It had been painful feeding Alf, and there was often blood mixed with his milk. Even suckling had been a source of conflict for that child; but he seemed to have got over his war now. Beck was delighted to note that the bomber mobile above his bed had been shot down, some time on the night of the new Millennium.

Alf was commanding a new respect from Beck. Of course, he had always been the hero of her world; the son that shone out of her. But now she saw him as a hero in his own right, someone who stood on his own two feet before she taught him how to walk.

"You're not always my Mum," he had said.

And for some reason, he started to call her Renee. He didn't pronounce it the French way, though when she asked him what it meant he said 'reborn'.


She sent him back to his teacher, on the first day of term, with a little note to say how hard he had been working on his sums and how proud she was of him.

'I'm sure you will see an improvement in his number skills,' the message said.

Alf came home at half-past three with a gold star pinned to his grey jumper, like a medal; but his achievement was not in maths, it was in English.

"I wrote a story," he said, rooting in his satchel to show Beck. "Miss photocopied it."

There were a lot of spelling mistakes, but he handed her the piece of paper proudly, and went off to watch children's television.

Beck sat at the kitchen table and read:

Once upon a time there was an old man who had been in a war, and never got the sound of bombs dropping out of his ears.

For many years afterwards, his wife longed for a baby, but the thought of making one scared him as much as the fighting.

When his wife had nearly given up hope, they had a daughter. The old man did not look at her. He had seen too much, so he kept the house in the dark.

But he could still hear her crying, so he turned the radio up loud. As the baby got bigger she started to talk, and shout and sing. The sound of her frightened him more than men screaming. Her mother was always shushing her.

The girl died of a sore throat when she was four. Just as she was about to die her father walked into her bedroom. It was dark, but outside was a sunny day.

The old man opened the curtains for the first time in many years. In his daughter's last moments she saw the light.


In the dead of winter, Beck couldn't get the smell of white lilac out of her nose.

No matter how many snowballs she rolled, how many joints she smoked, how many curries she cooked; Beck couldn't shake off the summer flowers, or the sadness they made her feel.

It had always clung to her, but now she knew why. She was the little girl who'd died at the age of four. She was Alfie's daughter. It seemed her death had done some good for the old man of war. But if he was her father, who was her mother?

She never knew who her mother was.

Beck had to phone D.P. Horobin again. She'd promised to ring the morning after Alfie's regression, but in the rush up to Christmas she had completely forgotten.

Still, she thought, Doris was sure to have a family, whether by blood or spirit bonded, with whom she'd been enjoying the season.

"I thought you were never going to call," Doris crackled on the line.

"Well, I was trying to bury the past," Beck said, "but people keep getting out of their graves."

"Come tomorrow," said the therapist, as usual.

As Beck hung up, she wondered how Doris kept all her tomorrows free.


Beck had nursery school in the morning, went home to smoke for lunch, then got a bus to North End in the stoned manner she had become accustomed to. Looking out of the window, she played with the perspective of buildings and streets they passed, and the pedestrians waiting at crossing places; not thinking about what would happen when she sat on the couch.

"Do you want me to hypnotise you?" said Doris, as soon as Beck got there.

Beck hadn't thought about it.

"I don't know," she said.

"What's happened?" said Doris, surprised by her defeated tone.

"You know when Alf came back from the war?" said Beck. "He had a daughter, who was me, and she died aged four."

Beck surprised herself too by bursting into tears.

"Are you sad because you died?" said D. P.

"No," sobbed Beck. "I'm sad because I never know who my mother is. Listen to this: the Gypsy me lost her mother when she was born; the Warrior me left his mother when he came of age; I lost my mother the day before my wedding. And now I've found out there was another one; another heart-breaking separation from my Mum."

"Do you want to see her?" Doris said gently.

"Can I?" Beck blew her nose.

"Of course."

Beck went in the lift, again; but whereas it had descended in the past, now it was going up. She felt a popping in her ears as she went higher; and the elevator music got louder.

The therapist's voice was almost drowned out: "doors open... meet your mother... raise hand when you want to come back. Okay?"

Beck nodded, and the lift pinged. She glimpsed an impossibly high number lit up in green, as the doors slid open.

Waiting on the other side was a lady with a sad face. She was looking at the child she longed for, with a desperation that would have kept her alive if it could.

Beck saw the face clearly, marked with lines of grief and guilt and love that gave such a mixed message as she died.

Her eyes moved, to a clearer message; there was a newspaper wrapped around a bunch of white lilac by the bed. She could see the date on it, 1957.

Then it went dark. "Oh no!" she wailed.

"What's the matter?" asked Doris Horobin.

"The curtains are shut," said Beck.

"Well open them."

Beck got off her death bed and moved, a bit woodenly, to the window, where she started rummaging frantically in the folds of curtain like an actress missing her entrance.

"I can't find the opening," she panicked.

"Calm down," said the therapist.

"Ah, here it is," Beck said.

She flung the curtains open. In the face of the sun, she saw the Gypsy's mother, the warrior's mother, and her own dead mother from this life smiling at her. Were they all one? Rebecca passed out.

Afterwards Beck couldn't remember how she got from unconsciousness back to D.P. Horobin's house; but when she came round, she found herself lying in the bath.

The whiteness of this most private room was as sexless as the rest of the house; there was no rose pink potion, and no bristling shaving brush.

"What is it with her?" thought Beck, as she quickly climbed out of the water and started to rub herself dry with a characterless white towel.

D. P. was a conundrum; in everything she stood for, and everything she said. Like: "If you hadn't lost your mother, you'd never have started looking. If you hadn't started looking, you'd never have found yourself."

It was Gypsy wisdom; pearls from the mouth of a toothless old hag: "You can't catch everybody in one lifetime," she said. "You've been lucky enough to meet your husband and your son; but there will always be someone who remains a mystery. So what if your mother is dead? There will always be someone to look after you."

Beck seemed to have heard it all in the voice of the running bath water.

"What is it with you?" she said, bursting fully dressed into a kitchen, which smelled of cabbage and onion.

"In what way?" said Doris.

"Well, have you ever regressed yourself?"

"Oh no," D. P. turned back to the tea. "I can dukker the likes of you, but I don't ever dukker myself."

"So why is everything so... genderless?" Beck struggled not to be rude.

"Look at me," said Doris.

"Yes, but it doesn't mean you can't have a nice house."

"My body is my house," Doris said, "and I'll be moving soon. My next house might be a man's body. Then I'll come back as a woman, and then I'll come back as a man."

The past-life therapist waited for Beck to stop giggling.

"I move home so much it's silly to buy things in pink or blue. I decorate in white," she said strictly. "It's the colour of my soul, not my sex."


Beck wondered what D.P. Horobin would have made of her artwork. It was the colour of sex.

She was at nursery school four mornings a week, on a roll, in the quiet room. She and Jack, the little boy who was deaf, were covering great lengths of lining paper with their own designs.

Jack's were geometric; patterns of triangles mapping a universe, not the stars but the points in between them.

He used colours Beck wouldn't expect a child to choose; blue, green and yellow were out of his range now. It was all black and white, a lot of silver crayon, and when that wore down he used grey. Occasionally, it was tinged with purple, but nothing else; except for the special places where he put a red dot.

Beck was fascinated by his control; it was with a restraint she had rarely seen in adults that he used the red felt-tip pen.

She herself had no such modesty. Her art showed her ovaries; there were fallopian tubes, the womb, the moon; and sperm, sperm everywhere. The wriggling millions flooded her picture with their tiny heads and curved tails, which got into every corner of the page.

The flesh colours, and organic shapes would be screamingly obvious to anyone, she thought. It might take a scientist to see the point of Jack's red felt-tip, but Joe Bloggs could look at Beck's sexual curlicues and realise at once that she was longing for a baby.

Since becoming enlightened as to the real nature of life, Beck's longing for a baby had increased. She'd asked Jonathon if they could have one.

"I'm too old," he said. He was four in 1957 too. "I can't get into nappies again," he said; but it sounded like he could be open to persuasion.

Beck had seen how long the wife of the man who came back from the war waited and waited to have a child. She had somehow inherited the waiting.

Themes from her past lives leaked into the present; and as time went by she forgot what it was like to live without the memories. They were like smells; curry, horse-dung, cough medicine and opium, which came and went in comforting waves. She grew to love the lilac that would suddenly be in her nose though it was February.

But then, at the beginning of spring, something new came up.

She and Jack were sitting in the quiet room, as usual, on the nursery chairs that were so small Beck had to squat as if in prayer. As usual, their parchment scrolls were unrolled on the art table, and both of their heads were bent over the work.

Then Beck raised her hand and rubbed it over her shaved scalp. She felt the bald pate, and the ring of hair that fringed it. Without looking up, she saw that Jack had the same hairdo. They were a pair of monks.

Sitting side by side in a peaceful cloister, spending every day the same way, they were silent except for the sound of pens scratching paper; both bent on some soul purpose.

Without looking up, she saw the cold stone walls, and felt so comfortable. It seemed closer to home than where she was now. To the glory of God; that's what they did it for then. Let none speak, but to praise His name. Let none paint, but to illuminate.

Without looking up, Beck saw it clearly. The black robe, the blinding devotion.

That morning he rose before dawn, prayed, then prayed again. After breakfast, which was more of a meditation than a meal, there was mass; and then he started colouring in.

The first task was getting a shade of paint to match the Almighty's brilliance. Then mixing it to a consistency that would flow like His grace. Thirdly, he must capture the beauty of God's creation in lines on a page.

It was simply the Bible, and they were only copying it. They were not trying to write something novel. Unlike Beck and Jack, whose work expressed their individual longings, the monks both had the same yearning; to see the face of God again.

Beck looked up, and it disappeared. The bright colours and cheerful chaos of nursery school instantly overtook the grey stone walls of the cloister. The scrolls that were unrolling across the art table were just wallpaper again.

But Jack was still there, and still silent.

Beck looked deep into his eyes.

"Do you know?" she asked him.

She saw the answer and it scared her. "Yes," said the boy who couldn't speak. To think that he knew they'd been here before too. The boy who sat next to her, joining the dots; the man illuminating the manuscript; still living in the story, a thousand years later.

In her brother Jacques' eyes Beck saw a world that looked very different to the spinning planet she thought she knew. Nothing as simple as green and blue. This was a metric map of silver, with decimally-placed red dots.

Beck stood up, scraping the chair legs and stumbling on her own legs to the door.

"I've got to get out of here," she said.

Beyond the quiet room was a busy school hall with children everywhere. Beck rushed into the teacher's toilet.

She stood there panting, then pulled her pants down. Collapsing on the seat she let her head sink onto her knees.

"I can't live like this," she said.

But she couldn't sit there forever. A teacher would be trying the door soon. Beck had to stand up and move on.

She tugged the end of the toilet roll, and it unravelled like another bloody scroll. Words appeared in her mind as clear as if they'd been written on the paper: 'Those who say don't know; those who know don't say'.

Beck would have to become one of those; as silent as Jack, as the monks they both used to be. What she knew, she couldn't say.

But she didn't know, and she had always known, exactly how complete her loss of speech would be.


She and Jonathon kept trying for a baby. Slowly a lump began to grow. A lump, not a bump.

She didn't say anything to the doctor, but Beck knew something was wrong.

While Jonathon filled her at one end with the stuff that life is made of, Beck was still pouring smoke down her sore throat. In her body, the forces of good and bad fought; and bad only won because Beck had thought it would from the beginning, and was fighting on its side.

She spent every day of the year 2000 sitting in her red armchair, smoking. A few nights every month making love, hoping.

The swelling was not new life, but death. It started in her throat; and developed so fast that the Millennial autumn was also the autumn of her own life, and the winter would be her last.

If Jonathon had examined her properly, when they'd first met, the cancer would not have spread to her nodes, and bones, and breathing spaces. If he'd asked her to open really wide, the first time she saw him, her throat would not look like the red armchair, with worn patches in its velvet cushions, and a dope hole just like the lesion in its seam, when he looked inside now.

It was a big mistake for a doctor to make, but he wasn't as sorry as he might have been. After the initial shock, the horror of a terminal diagnosis; after the panic of treatment, the clumsy use of chemicals to defy the inevitable; they were sitting side by side on the sofa, one evening, when Jonathon began to laugh.

"It's funny," he said. "Turns out I killed you, this lifetime; turn and turn about."

And though she wasn't supposed to make a sound, Beck laughed too. Not because she thought he was right. Though she wasn't supposed to speak, she said he was wrong.

"You didn't kill me. I killed myself."

She had always been aware of the risks of smoking. It was a slow, sulky suicide.

And though she was going to die, Beck was happier than she'd ever been in her life; because Jonathon agreed that they had both died before. He believed with her in reincarnation. He lived with her in eternity.


On Southsea seafront, a single string of coloured lights strung along the prom did just as well for Christmas as they did for the summer season.

From lamppost to mock-Victorian lamppost they were hung in a permanent celebration of the edge of the land. Reflected in the waves that kissed the shingle, refracted by the drizzly mist which hugged the common; the fairy lights shone.

Jonathon and Beck went walking in December, in the four o'clock twilight which seemed so unfair. Where were the long hot evenings of June?

"This was where we came on our first date. Late at night and the warmth of the sun was still loving the war memorial," said Jonathon. "Do you remember? We were drunk."

Beck nodded. Of course she remembered it. A Chinese restaurant and a seventies disco. They did the same thing a year later. It was in memory of their first date; but she had met him before.

He'd jogged past her, on this stretch of prom, at this time of day, way back in a sunny month. The time when late afternoon meant the promise of evening, instead of the threat of night.

Jonathon was wearing shorts and Beck watched him disappear with a delicious sense of loss that came, in hindsight, from knowing she would see him again.

Now, corduroy trousers and a green wax jacket were concealing his body, and she was under a woolly hat; her hair having fallen out from chemotherapy.

They cut across the common; eyes down to avoid the dogshit on the grass.

A group of new age travellers were trying to camp there and the police had come to stop them. Colourful caravans and panda cars were parked at odds to each other, and people were standing around shouting.

Beck and Jonathon looked up as they went past, and wrapped in their own story, didn't take much notice. But the sight of the Gypsy eviction planted a seed in Jonathon, which turned into a dream. Though he didn't remember it the next morning, he started to plan an occasion for them to re-enact the scene.

It was going to be a wedding, in a stately home. The manor house they'd been to on a family outing long ago could be hired out for civil marriages. Jonathon booked the registrar, a banquet and a band, as a surprise for Beck. He could see her on that grand, sweeping staircase; in an off-the-shoulder wedding dress, with a tattered sort of skirt.

And though they made a pretty sad-looking couple, walking out of season by the sea, their spirits were surprisingly high. The only thing that still made Beck cry was the thought of saying goodbye to her son.


"Alfie," said Beck, before she couldn't speak any more. "I'm going to die soon."

"No, Mummy!" He burst into tears.

"Don't be too sad," she said. "You know we've been together before, and I'm sure we'll be together again. I keep making such a mess of my lives."

"Don't leave me," said Alf.

"I won't," said Beck. "I'll be watching over you, like an angel."

"But I won't be able to see you," he sobbed.

"Look up," said Beck, breaking down. "You'll see my sellotape."

Doctor Comfort was looking after Alf.

"He's going to be fine," he said to Beck. "But he's a funny boy. Why does he call you Renee?"

Rebecca knew, but didn't say.

"I used to know a Renee," Jon suddenly remembered. "She lived next door to my Grandma Ramsey when I was small. We used to play together, but I think she died."

If she hadn't, they might still have been friends. They might have become childhood sweethearts.

Now Jonathon was finally going to marry Beck, but he wasn't fast enough. A week before the wedding and she couldn't say I do. She was back in hospital, on morphine.

It had put her in a funny mood. She'd done some mental arithmetic and worked out that it takes seventeen days to count to one million. She was trying to convey this to Jonathon, in a voice like a solar wind.

"What?" he said.

She didn't bother trying again; but with her scorching breath, told him an even more incredible fact. Renee had intended to grow up with Jonathon, grow old with him; and had hurried to be reborn so she could try again.

"We're meant to be together?" he said, only partly understanding her. "I know, Beck. But oh, my love, how will I know when I see you again?"

"We're not supposed to know. It spoils the game."

This time Jonathon didn't even pretend to understand what she said; but he was glad to see her smiling. Everybody tries to avoid the void; but death is just a door. Rebecca Salmon's last words didn't have a ring of finality to them.

Her throat was eaten and her air was drunk, by the lump she'd got from smoking. She died the day before her wedding was supposed to be. It was the story of her life.

# Ray

The old sun was coming up over the hill, as the man came down. With a ring of fiery hair around a bald crown, and a beard he came; down a road like a chalk scar in the hill's gorse-bushed cheek. Making his way barefoot through the brambles, his steps were part marching, part waltzing; as if he couldn't decide whether to do a war dance or a ball dance.

Down he came in an old white sheet, which flapped in the wind; and a scarf, redder than the berries, tied round his neck. So tightly that the thing he was singing could have been a Gregorian chant or a Gypsy song; a strangled sound, if anyone had been around to hear it.

Down he came to the sea, which twinkled at him like a pair of grey-blue eyes he'd seen long ago in the rain; which winked at him like fairy-lights through a mist. Something he'd never seen.

The old sun lit up a new day, as Ray trudged down the hill, past a hospital. Its buildings were ruins, without the ghost of a white coat, or the echo of a bleeping machine. No accidents, or emergencies; the world was too tired to hurry, too worn out to care.

Ray felt as if he'd been walking forever. He slashed his way through the undergrowth with a stick he used like a sword, but never seemed to find what he was looking for. He'd come from seventeen to a million miles, on a journey of time more than distance.

The traveller stopped where the road stopped, at the water's edge.

Casting his eyes along the cold, crabby shoreline, he saw a rundown jetty.

It was just an old lorry, driven backwards into the sea, and left there long enough for weed to cover it.

Sitting on the jetty was another man, who stood up when he saw Ray, and pointed to the sign beside him.

"Snorkelling trips! See the hidden ruins," he cried.

Ray stepped closer.

"Where are we?"

"This is Portsmud," the man said. Looked like he'd been waiting there long enough for weed to cover him too.

"What happened to it?"

"The tide came in."

There was not another soul in the scene, nothing but a second slightly longer jetty in the distance.

"These are my prices," Vithon said, pointing at his peeling sign. "Ten for a snorkel in shallow waters."

He didn't often do his sales pitch, but was instantly the professional.

"Picture yourself hanging there," he said, "suspended above the Guildhall Square, where you can still see the colossal stone steps; and clearly make out the statue of Queen Victoria, clad in algae with a crown of barnacles."

Vithon's own chiselled features were extremely fine. He smiled with white teeth at the man in a toga, grey as the clouds fast gathering again.

"Or you can pay twenty, for a deeper dive, out at the furthest reaches of the old sea walls." He spoke persuasively, but Ray was shaking his head:

"Ten or twenty is all the same to me. I've got no money," he said.

"Oh," Vithon jumped off his pier and crunched towards the stranger, over the sandy shingle; the shingly sand of this place in time, where boundaries were breaking down, and other forms of payment were possible.

"Well, what else have you got? What would you give to see Portsmud under water?" he said.

Ray's hands disappeared into the folds of his toga, and came out with a small, shiny object.

"How about this?"

"What does that do?"

They were two equally inquisitive souls. Everything they said was a question, and sometimes the questions were answered. But they didn't speak exactly the same language. Vithon's was strangely abbreviated. What he actually said was:

"What does th@ do?"

Ray flicked his thumb, and the thing lit up.

"It's a lighter," he said.

Fire in his hands, fire at his fingertips; the other man reached out for it.

"Gr8!" he said. "That's worth a guided tour."


The water was cold and choppy. Ray gripped the sides of the boat.

"I can't do it," he said.

"Come on," Vithon called from the waves, "it's BUtiful."

Ray slipped into the water, and swallowed the scene beneath, rather than saw it. History spat down his snorkel, and seeped behind his mask. It gave him a salty slap. He held his head under, and the scarf around his neck got wet and seemed to tighten till he could hardly breathe.

What he saw could have been ocean floor; the steps, the regal shapes, not just the work of man. Nature could chisel and chip, it could lay slabs, it could cement. It was the lack of colour on the sea bed that made it impossible to tell whether time, tide or man had painted it there.

Ray struggled back into the boat and tried not to cry with cold as Vithon rowed them back to shore. The second man was tougher-skinned. He was only wearing an old t-shirt and cut-off shorts, but he managed to keep up a running commentary in the rain that had started again.

"Portsmud flooded for good in the year 2197," he said, "when the sea walls finally came down. Many people from North End fled the waves that had long been straining to reclaim their city, but most of those who lived in Southsea drowned in the tragedy."

"Have you got a towel?" Ray asked, as they beached on the slopes of what had once been Portsdown Hill, high above dry land.

"Come into my cab," Vithon replied. "I'll warm you up."

It was lined with fur, and still had electricity. Vithon made Ray a cup of tea. Through a steamy window, the traveller watched another craft landing on the next jetty. One passenger got off, one passenger got on, and the small boat rowed away again.

"What's that?"

"It's the Isle of Wight ferry." Vithon sighed. "Do U wnt 2 go?"

"No," said Ray. "I've always promised myself, when I got to the end of the road I'd stop."

"HwDUKnThsIsTNdOfTRd?" said Vithon. His local accent was strong, but Ray understood him: "How do you know this is the end of the road?"

"Because it disappears into the sea."

Later, they stood there, catching dogfish for dinner; and for a few minutes the sun came out and showed the world what it used to be made of.

Vithon took in the new man, from bush-tangled hair to feet that were dirty and bare.

"What's your name?" he asked.

"Ray."

"Raymond?"

"Don't call me mud," the traveller held his chin high, "just because I'm made of the earth."

"No, Mond. Raymond means king of the world."

Then Vithon blushed and looked back at his fishing line. He focused on the place where the thread went into the water, to infinity.

Ray was looking at the road going back up the hill, the way he'd come, from infinity.

He never knew he was going somewhere until now. He studied the cheek of Vithon, gazing at the sea.

"This must be the end of my journey."


The next day, Vithon took Ray for a deeper dive. He had some basic breathing apparatus and a pair of ancient wetsuits.

"I know they're crude," he apologised, as Ray struggled into the mildewed rubber. "Portsmud's been flooded for fifty years, and this wetsuit was there when it happened!"

It was raining again, and even windier than before. The sea was rocking as they set off.

"Don't worry," said Vithon reassuringly as he rowed, "it's not so bad when you get below." He had slipped into work mode:

"We are now above the Guildhall Square where we snrkld yesterday. If you look to the right, you'll see the tip of the Millennium Tower, built around the year 2000; the only thing still visible above the water. As I row south, we pass over what were 1ce streets and houses, from high rise flats to the QuEn's Hotel."

"Can I see?" said Ray.

"No, it's just rubble and weed," said Vithon. "But fanC goN further? There's something outst&ing!"

It was as far as they could go, at what used to be the edge of the land. Where the sea used to start, they stopped and dived in. With tanks of air strapped to their backs, and pipes stuck in their mouths; they could live in death. They could breathe in the water.

In the disorientating light, Vithon pointed his finger, but Ray saw the monolith first. It stood like a fine underwater salute, dead sailors raised to the vertical, still cocking a snook overseas.

They swam to it, swam round it, like people might have dreamed of flying round it once; then dived down the sides of the war memorial, like it had never dreamed of being stroked. They went to the ear-popping bottom.

And there were the names. Behind a mere hand-swishing of sand, there were row upon row of them carved in stone. Vithon showed him the chiselled figures in amazement, but Ray didn't seem to appreciate the words. He'd never learnt to read and write; though he was always asking questions.

As they left the sunken garden of remembrance, through a crumbling arch-way, Vithon's airpipe caught. He pulled it gently from the crevice, but it tore; bubbles escaped in panic. Vithon was about to panic too.

But Raymond was there. He took his own mouthpiece off, and offered it to the other man. Ray gave Vithon his air. They sat for a while, taking it in turns to breathe at the bottom of the sea; and though it was murky, and their masks were misty, they held eye-contact for the whole time.

"Yes," said Ray, as they came back out of the water at the place where the road went in. "My journey ends here. You must be what I've been looking for."

Sweet; but when Vithon tried to kiss him, Ray raised his hands in a warrior pose.

"SteD on!" Vithon said.

"Sorry," Ray unclenched his fists. "I'm still a bit defensive."

"You've been on Ur own 2 long, that's all," said Vithon.

Now they were together.

The great opposites were finally in union. In was out, up was down, hot and cold co-existed. Hard lived in harmony with soft, and darkness happily shared the floor with light.

Lying in the fur-lined cab, Ray and Vithon had a taste of sugar and spice. The only thing was, they were both men. But now they'd come together, they could never be apart. The world had stopped turning for this.

After a month, Vithon started talking about marriage.

"I never knew what I was waiting here 4," he said. "It must have Bn U."

They were rinsing their wetsuits when he raised the subject. It had been a perfect afternoon, snorkelling through what was once called Victoria Park; but tall weed now waved in the currents where trees used to wave in the breeze.

It was time to reunite the forest and the sea.

"Will you marry me?" Vithon asked Ray.

"Will you marry me?" Ray asked it back again. The eternal question had an answer.


There was only one way to do it properly; they had to go to church.

It took three days to walk from Portsmud to Windchester, and it rained all the way.

The couple hugged the hillside and their conversation kept them dry, but the first night they slept under a hedge, and woke up prickly.

Ray pulled a pair of headphones from his toga, and travelled to an old-time techno beat. Vithon trudged alongside, only hearing the bass line. He was keeping his eyes skinned for the bunny rabbits and blackberries that seemed to be the main meal of their trip.

At twilight on the second day, they stumbled into a crumbling settlement.

"Barratt Homes," Vithon pointed out the signpost to Ray, whose eyes never followed the words.

Across the quaint village square, they met a lady coming out of her cottage.

"L%kn4AB&B?" she asked.


The first finger of dawn was pointing out the dust in her attic bedroom when the travellers rose next morning, and set off again for Windchester.

Ray yawned as they walked through the water meadows. The ancient town was just visible through the mist. Vithon looked at his partner as they marched toward it; with his rumpled hair and crumpled toga, its folds full of nameless lumps and bumps.

"We're probably going to need some money," he said.

"I still haven't got any," Ray shrugged.

"Not what you'd call cash," Vithon wheedled. "But you always seem to have plenty of currency about your person."

"There is one thing." Ray pulled an old mobile phone out of his pocket. They both stopped walking and stood in the drizzle, staring at it dumbly. "Sometimes it does this." He pressed a button and it rang, in a haunting tone; *uh-huh-huh-huh-staying-alive-staying-alive.*

"I know what that is," said Vithon. He rummaged deep in a damp pocket of his travelling pack and pulled out a piece of folded paper.

Slowly, laboriously, with his tongue sticking out between his teeth, Vithon dialled the number that was written on the paper. Ray watched without a word. He'd never realised what the ringing device was for. When the digital sequence was complete Vithon held the phone to his ear.

"Mother?" he said. "Mother!" he smiled. "You've got a new son. I'm just about to get married, Mum. I've met Ray." Vithon paused, then smiled again. "Would you like to speak to him?" He passed the phone to his lover.

Ray had long since held it in his pocket, fingering the keys; but he had never held it to his ears. It seemed so silly now, when the voice of his new mother was there.

He hardly understood what she said to him, but the words didn't matter. Like a baby at the breast, listening for comfort, it was form rather than content that made him feel loved. Maybe the mother didn't even speak the same language, but her tone bought Ray, the endless traveller, home.

Vithon said goodbye to his mum as they rounded a bend in the water meadows, and Windchester came closer in the rain.

"What about your mother?" he asked, as he gave Ray back the phone.

"I don't know," Ray stared at the tiny glowing screen. "I didn't know it could do that. I traded it a long time ago, for something I found in the woods; a leaf of paper with words on, which meant nothing to me because I never learned to read or write. So I swapped it for this bleeping thing, but the bloke didn't tell me I needed a number."

Ray put the phone back into the folds of his toga. "Sometimes I dream of numbers flashing, a big countdown lit up in green," he said, "but I always wake up before it gets to one."

They meandered around another rainy bend on the mead, and then a couple of quiet streets led them quickly to the city centre, where they found themselves in a crowded bazaar. Stalls with colourful awnings flapped, signs swung above.

"But where's the church?" said Vithon, looking around for a spire.

It was meant to be in the middle of society, but he couldn't see it. The couple had to ask a barrow boy where to get married. They chose the one with the most illustrious-looking stall.

At the edges of the market the stalls were shifty affairs; grubby faces peered over piles of cheap gold and diamonds; dirty eyes blinked behind stacks of TV screens, and miles of white cable.

Nearer the middle were more permanent erections, and Ray pointed to one with a big sign of an apple, made in gold.

"Let's ask the fruit and veg man," he said.

They chose the richest one in the market. He rubbed his hands with gusto as they asked.

"Wind blew the spire down, long time ago now. Fall blocked the church entrance, but fear not; there's a back door, and two or three on either side. I'll take you through mine, but…" he paused. "It'll cost U."

"UGTBK," swore Vithon. "I'm not paying."

Church was meant to be free, but Ray who'd ranged more widely in the world knew differently.

"Is this NE good?" he asked the man, in the language he was picking up. And he pulled a shiny compact disc from a fold in his toga.

With a tut that said it wasn't worth a tenth of what he asked for, the stallholder took it out of Ray's hands and threw it on the counter. Then he took off his apron and said;

"Come on then. I'll show you T way to T Lord."

It was a long walk under arching stone, with murals on either side.

Two giant hands reached down from the sky, one full of silver coins, one full of apple seeds. At this point in history Man still had a choice. He held out his hands for the money.

All he got from God was a giant smack, and the coins scattered everywhere. Then man took the seeds and planted them carefully in the earth. But while he was waiting for them to grow again, many of his people starved.

When they got to the end of this avenue, Ray was ready to turn back.

"This is stupid," he said. "He'll never agree to marry us."

"Let's just try," Vithon replied.

They followed their leader out of the cloisters, into the open space of the nave. The outside had come in. Ivy grew up the columns, and pigeons flew in the marble branches of their high canopy.

Beneath Ray's bare feet, grass was growing through the mosaic floor, and moss cushioned the pews. The church was alive and well.

"Couple of customers for you," the greengrocer called.

Near the altar, a man was on his knees, underneath a Christmas tree that seemed to be growing apples. They recognised him by his ring of white hair and black robe.

"Forgive us, Father," said Vithon. "If we can call you Father?"

"They call me Jk," the holy man said, nodding at the stallholder. "How can I help you?"

"We want to get married."

Jk smiled, and stood up.

"It's been a while since I married anyone," he said.

"Can you rmba how 2 do it?" Vithon asked anxiously.

"I'll have to check the book for details," the Vicar said. "Come with me."

He tucked his hands into his robe and headed for the vestry; but there was a loud clang from the altar table where the market trader had been standing.

"What are you doing?"

"Just looking," the stallholder said. "I thought it was a model warship."

"No, no, that's a sacred vessel," said the Vicar, "for communion purposes."

"Sorry." The fruit and veg man picked it up and put it back on the table. Then, with a cheerful wave at Vithon and Ray, he went his way and they went the other, following Jk through the vestry door.

"Is there anyone who actually, er…"

"Comes?" said the Vicar. "Well, it's rather small, but yes; I do have a congregation."

They walked past a rack of cassocks, hung like a choir that had lost its voice; and stained glass windows that were broken and boarded up. One had been replaced. In the background was a Christmas tree, strung with coloured lights, but the central image was a three pin plug, pulled out of its socket.

"What does that mean?" Vithon asked.

"God is the power," the white-haired old man said.

At the other end of the vestry, a spiral staircase led them up to the scriptorium.

"Right, let's have a look at that book." The vicar's breath steamed in the cold stone room.

"I bet it says you can't marry two men," Ray said gloomily.

"The old one does," Jk shrugged, "but I go by the newest testament. Now let me see."

As he lifted a book off the shelf, Ray's mood lifted too.

"What is it all about?" he asked.

"What it is all about," the Vicar replied.

"Can I see?" Ray said.

The colours of calligraphy glowed as the book was opened, and illuminated the room.

"This is the newest testament I've got. It's quite rare. The story starts with the apple."

"Is that the apple we saw on the way in?" said Vithon.

"Certainly," said the Vicar. "The apple of knowledge. When it comes to the crunch, Man can not eat money."

"OIC," said Vithon.

"And this is the one they actually called 'The New Testament', though it's even older, obviously." The Vicar took another book down. "And extremely rare! It was all written by hand."

"Can I touch?" Ray was looking at the book entranced.

"Of course," said Jk.

Amid a fusion of leaves, the story grew in bud and flower, shooting green sentences from the rockery of capital letters. If there ever was a tree of wisdom, this was where it had its roots. This manuscript was the garden where words and pictures bore fruit.

Ray turned a page, but left his hand where it was, where it would have been; writing with liquid gold on vellum, to preserve the glory of creation.

"It's the most beautiful thing I've ever seen," Vithon was reading over his shoulder.

"But what does it mean?" Ray said.

Jk pointed a pale finger at a random passage and began to read aloud:

"*As he went along, he saw a man blind from birth. His disciples asked him, 'Rabbi, who sinned, this man or his parents, that he was born blind?'*

"'*Neither this man nor his parents sinned,' said Jesus, 'but this happened so that the work of God might be displayed in his life.'*"

Vithon burst out laughing.

"What language was th@?" he spluttered.

"The language of ages," the Vicar said, in his own voice. "Ages and pages."

"I understood some of it," Ray said in surprise. "The bit about sin!"

Father Jk looked at him.

"You didn't," he said, "if you think it means you. Listen carefully. You were not born in sin. You did not sin before you were born. You can not sin against another soul." He held his fingers up, one two three, like the plug that was the sign of his faith.

"The only sin is against yourself," he said; "and only so that you can see it."

The illiterate traveller's face was alight with understanding. His own white finger followed the path the Vicar's had taken through the ivy and trellis-work.

"*The work of God might be displayed in his life*," he tried to say.

Now everyone was laughing.

"Come on," the Vicar took the book gently out of Ray's hands, "I've got one more to show you."

He put the New Testament back on the shelf and pointed out a document even more antique.

"The Old Testament," he whispered. "We can't open this one. Its leaves are too delicate, but the story also starts with an apple."

"Is that the 1 that says we can get married?" Vithon asked.

"No, this is the one that says you can't," Jk replied. "But as I told you, it's too old to open. Wait, while I bring us up to date."

It felt like a lifetime as he flicked through the pages of the newest testament, finally marking his place with a red felt-tip pen:

"All you have to do before I can marry you is answer one question."

"Is it difficult?" asked Ray.

"No, it's elementary," said the Vicar. "In the fight between fire and ice, who wins?"

It might have been easy, but Ray and Vithon couldn't do it. They stayed in the ancient study, looking for the answer, till the Priest ran out of time.

"I must prepare for the mass; if not for the masses!" Jk escorted them to the door. "You're welcome to come back when you've worked it out."


"EzE!" said Vithon, as they fell out of church and into the market place.

It was getting dark, and prostitutes were starting to appear; eating the fruit and arguing with the customers.

One of them shouted at Ray and Vithon as they stood on the edge of the crowd:

"Give us a ki$."

"No, no," they shook their heads politely, "we're getting married."

The lady laughed.

"Well, if one of you is going 2 B a bride," she came towards them, trailing a lacy shawl, "you'd better take this."

She held out the webspun garment. Ray took it and turned to Vithon with a smile, as the whore twirled away.

"You look like an 0:-)," said Vithon. "But Y don't you take that old thing off?" He touched the grubby red scarf that Ray always wore.

"I can't," the Gypsy replied. "The knot's too tight. I've never been able to untie it by myself."

"Here, let me help you." With doctor's fingers, Vithon loosened the choker. "Now, you can breathe!"

When the scarf was off and the shawl was on, the two men split up and scoured the post-modern market place for the rest of their kit.

The clothes were cast-offs, like the tatters of civilisation in 2247 but they made the perfect outfits for Vithon and Ray's wedding.

When they met again, after their separate shopping trips, Vithon was resplendent in a white coat and crinoline, complete with a feathered cap. Ray was wearing a jewelled turban on his head, and a dress he'd bartered his mobile phone for.

They gazed at each other in the hazy light of a drink and drugs stall. Then they swapped Ray's CD player for a bottle of champagne. Half-drunk, when it was half drunk, Vithon kneeled down to roll their remaining possessions in Ray's old toga. He tied a knot in the white sheet.

When Vithon stood up again they both knew the answer to the marriage question; and they celebrated with a kiss. A kiss, sealed with champagne, petitioned by a curse; a life-saving kiss, a last-breath kiss. A kiss which only finished so it could start again.

"I like your petticoat," Vithon smiled, in the pause between.

"It's not a petticoat!" said Ray. "If it looks like a petticoat, I'm taking it off!"

And so it was that he went to his wedding in a turban and a bikini. With sandals and knee-high socks he walked a path paved with gravestones, and cobbled with fossil bones.

He followed his forerunners, along a cloister scrawled with words and pictures, between parchment walls of paisley designs, quite dark until the illumination at the end.

The lifestory led them into church, where Jk was waiting at the end of a long aisle. Ray and Vithon walked up it together. They stopped in front of the Vicar, who asked them the marriage question:

"In the fight between fire and ice, who wins?"

"Water."

Ray and Vithon, Rebecca and Jonathon, Raji and Victoria, Rosa and the Viscount finally got it right.

# Acknowledgements

I couldn't have done this without:

Richard Measey; my muse (and CTO).
Heather, June, Janette, Viv, Elaine, Eileen; my dear proof-readers.
Merric Davidson; my Literary champion.
Debbie Hatfield and the team at A&B; first among publishers.
Hazel Naughton, and her smiling camera.
Louise Doughty, and her Gypsy wisdom.
Patricia Wooldridge, and her poetry in the workplace.

I couldn't have done this without:

My children, Tom and Ella Rose; but I could have done it a bit quicker.

*

"There is nothing concealed that will not be disclosed,
or hidden that will not be made known.
What I tell you in the dark, speak in daylight;
what is whispered in your ear, proclaim from the roofs.
Do not be afraid of those who kill the body but cannot kill the soul."
 Matthew 10 26 – 28.

May the whispering in my ear never stop.

# Bibliography

Michael Aston *Monasteries*
Nigel Hunter *How They Lived: A Mediaeval Monk*
Peter Levi *Frontiers of Paradise: A Study of Monks and Monasteries*

\*

Christian Reincarnation
http://www.near-death.com/origen.html
Evidence For Reincarnation in the Bible
http://ourworld.compuserve.com/homepages/mark-mason/ch16ex1.htm
Reincarnation and Christianity
http://www.elevated;fsnet.co.uk/index-page14.html

\*

Barbara Adams *Gypsies and Government Policy in England*
Peter Chrisp *Living in History: A Tudor Kitchen*
Isabel Fonseca *Bury Me Standing*
Angus Fraser *The Gypsies*
Wayne F Hill and Cynthia J Ottchen *Shakespeare's Insults*
Alice Makrell *History of Fashion*
The Patrin Web Journal – Romanichal Word List
http://www.geocities.com/paris/5121/rumney.htm
The Patrin Web Journal – Timeline of Romani History
http://www.geocities.com/paris/5121/timeline.htm
The Patrin Web Journal – Romani Death Rituals and Customs
http://www.geocities.com/paris/5121/death.htm
The Patrin Web Journal – Romani Beliefs
http://www.geocities.com/paris/5121/beliefs.htm

\*

Charles Allen *Plain Tales from the Raj*
Tej K Bhatia *Colloquial Hindi; The Complete Course for Beginners*
Christopher Hibbert *The Indian Mutiny*
Klaus Klostermaier *A Concise Encyclopedia of Hinduism*
Margaret MacMillan *Women of the Raj*
Jane Robinson *Angels of Albion; Women of the Indian Mutiny*
Andrew Ward *Our Bones are Scattered: The Cawnpore Massacres*

\*

Walter Lord *The Miracle of Dunkirk*

\*

Carol Bowman *Children's Past Lives*
Dannion Brinkley *Saved by the Light*
John Diamond *C*